The Adventur
Pirate of

Volume One

by Theoden Humphrey

To Faith,
May ye always on your adventures,
have fine winds and following seas!

T.F.B 2023

Table of Contents

Log #1: Arrival

Captain's Log
Date:
Location:
Conditions:

It cannot be.

I am captain of the *Grace of Ireland*, and the twenty-one men remaining of her crew. I have been master of this ship these past five years, so I know – aye, I know – the log should begin with the day, our location and conditions, heading and speed of the ship. Curse me, but I would record all that if I could be sure –

if I could just *know* –

It cannot be, it cannot!

– if I could only know that I am not mad. That we are not in Hell.

I believe it is the 23rd of June in the year 1678, by the common reckoning. I think we are at anchor in a cove on the eastern shore of the New World. It is the 73rd day since we started our cruise, from Galway Bay in Connacht. The ship is leaking, as it has been since we left Irish waters, but we cannot beach and careen her until the storm that chased us here has passed over. Four men are manning the pumps for now, and the Mate assures me we will survive the storm afloat.

Unless, of course, we are already dead.

I don't know who to pray to. Or who to curse, come to that.

I prayed for our deliverance as my mother taught me: in the language of our land and our people, stretching back through the centuries, through generations of Gaelic kings to the seven Sons of Mil who wrested Erin from the Tuatha De Danann, and the gods and goddesses who birthed them and watched over the people of Danu, and over the Milesians in turn.

But I confess to doubting these gods and goddesses of Ireland. For sure it is that prayers rose up to them in untold thousands, washed clean with tears and sanctified with innocent blood, when the English Devil Cromwell descended on our land like the plagues of Egypt, like all the conquerors and raiders and savages out of the west and the

5

north who have laid waste to Ireland since the dawn of time. And these gods, Dagda and Nuada and Lugh, Danu and Goibniu and the Morrigan – they failed us in our hour of need and let the black-souled English slaughter whole generations, and paint the stones of Ireland red with blood that will never wash away.

The gods of old did not save Ireland. They did not save my mother, Maeve ni Cathan, the daughter of kings, the great-granddaughter of Grainne ni Maille herself, with ancient knowledge writ in her brain and her bones and her blood. They let her be raped by an Englishman on the streets of Drogheda. Raped by a Puritan, by a man of God come to conquer heresy and sin – so those men claimed their purpose to be.

Raped by my father. And nine months after he gave my mother a bastard son, he gave me the name of his own fate, his doom for the sin of his lust, and the even greater sin of allowing my heathen mother to live after he defiled her: Damnation.

My friends call me Nate.

Perhaps I should pray to the God of my father, the God of Abraham and Saint Patrick. The God of Cromwell. But why should he listen to me? Sure and no man has been born so far out of His sight, the get of a corrupted hypocrite and a proud pagan, raised by one to hate the other.

And I think it no help to my pleas that I have earned my name a hundred times in the ten years since I reached manhood, in seeking my vengeance on half of my blood in the name of the other half. Even if my father's sins had not passed on to me, I have a gracious plenty of my own, theft and piracy and plunder and, aye, murder.

No, the Father of Adam will not listen to me, either. I think he may have already sent us to his Hell and barred the gate after us. Certain it is that the living world, the home of His beloved children, could not hold such things as I have seen this day.

Such things . . . –

I must be mad.

I have lived my whole life at sea, fishing with my uncles before I could walk the length of the curragh, rowing their trading galleys past the English blockades, and sometimes through them. I have been to London and seen the greatest ships ever built by the hand of man, three decks and four masts and enough cannon to drown out the thunder itself.

But that *thing* that I saw when we came in sight of the shore! I thought it was a part of the land: the White Cliffs of Dover on the shore of the New World. Until it *moved*. Until it blew *smoke* from its back, like the spume of a whale, and sounded a horn that could have drowned out Gabriel's trumpet, and then it sailed across the bay before us. *Against* the wind. *Against* the tide.

I looked at it through my glass, and I swear to you it held men. Men crawled over it like lice. They waved and they cheered. It was a ship. A ship that could not be.

I *must* be mad.

But if I were, would not those impossible sights continue? If my eyes were deceived, if they had betrayed me then, would I see my hands on this page, the quill in my fingers, the spatters of ink from my pot? All is still, now; nothing in my view is unfamiliar to me. We sit at anchor in a cove, the land around us thick with greenery. Though I do not know the trees, still, they are *trees*. My men look like men, my ship still like the ship I have sailed nearly every day since she was refit three years ago, the ship I have sailed thousands of miles in the past two months, from the seas of Ireland to this distant shore.

Could it be the Isle of the Blessed? Have I followed the path of St. Brendan the Navigator, himself? How can I know? We sailed off the ends of charts a month gone. Perhaps we sailed off the edge of the world, too.

But I think we would not be welcome in Paradise. And if we were, sure my ship would not still leak.

It was a hundred feet high, two hundred. Pure white, shining like the clouds in a summer sky. It would have stretched from one end of the village where my mother raised me to the other, and beyond. It was smoking – there was *fire* on it – fire, the curse of ships, the terror of all sailors. And it sailed through the waves, without sail, without oars.

I looked through my glass and I saw the faces of the men and women aboard. I saw children. They smiled.

I looked at its bow and I saw written there in letters as tall as a man, "GRAND PRINCESS."

It was a ship. A ship the size of a mountain.

We are in Hell.

Log #2: The Trap

Captain's Log
Date: 24th of June, 1678. Dawn.
Location: Unknown
Conditions: Storm, high wind and waves. Anchored in unknown bay.

We are at anchor, riding out the storm that chased us into the shore. The land holds no hints to our position; there is naught in sight but trees. The wind is strong enough to tear off the canvas like whore's smallclothes, were the sails not reefed; the waves lap the rails and surge ever higher. Eight men needed to work the pumps, and I fear they may not suffice.

I was fool enough to mutter somewhat about Hell and our position, in the presence of the men. They are terrified now, hunched below decks like damned souls on Charon's galley, crying out as if they feel the infernal flames already with every lightning flash and thunder clap. O'Flaherty has tried to calm them, but to no avail; I think Burke may be riling them up and laughing behind his hand.

But perhaps it is neither Burke nor my tongue's slip that has put infernal thoughts into the men; after all, they crew a ship for a man named Damnation, and we were pursued across the ocean by the one they call the Devil's Lash. What is a humble sea-dog to think?

I confess that I will abide in Hell, and right merrily, if it means that whoreson Nicholas Hobbes be off my rudder, and never darken my spyglass again.

As this is the first opportunity I have found to write at length, I will lay out the whole tale for this record. We shipped out of Galway, at night, to cruise south and east around Cork and toward Cornwall and Wales, where fat English tubs waddle along the coast, full of English wealth. And if we came across any Irish ships, well, so long as they were not of the same clan and sept as I or the men, then we would participate in the ancient Gaelic tradition of sharing the wealth: some for he at the point of the sword, and more for the one at the hilt.

We had only been eight days at sea, just passing Cruachan and looking toward Clear Island, when we spotted an English carrack with her mainmast down, limping along only with her fore and mizzen, and the canvas on those letting through more wind than it caught. We had a disputation, with Quartermaster O'Flaherty and Bosun's Mate Burke proposing an immediate assault, and Master's Mate O'Gallows and I in favor of sailing by in preference of richer prizes. I contended that the ship, clearly the worse off for a sea battle, would have nothing left to take; the romantic Ian quoth, "'Twould be base to set on an ill and wounded gaffer such as this! Let him limp home and ease into a mug of ale and a chair by the fire!" Indeed, the ship did look much like a toothless maunderer, weatherbeaten and frailed by years and hard use. But O'Flaherty would fain waylay that poor benighted vessel, for any fight had long since been knocked from its decks. "Sure and there may be but little to lay hand to – but what 'tis, 'twill fall into our palms like overripe berries."

Alas, while I had called O'Flaherty and O'Gallows to my poop deck for this discussion, Burke had taken his and the Quartermaster's argument straight to the men, and my brave Irish sea-wolves were eager to see what scraps could be gnawed off the tattered bone. I confess I let myself be swayed by their cries and pleas, perhaps because I knew that my fellow sea-brigands often miss valuable goods, taking only what comes first to hand or what is plainly worth stealing. But not all that glitters is gold, we are taught – and not all that is gold, glitters.

So we attacked. The carrack fired but one culverin, which was overcharged so that the shot flew far beyond the *Grace*, the sound rolling and echoing like thunder. The sound, in truth, did us more harm than the shot, though we knew it not, then. We tacked nearer with great care, for the carrack was upwind of the *Grace* and close enough to land that we needs must keep a weather eye open for shoal water. As we approached, Burke gave a glad shout: "Look! There's naught but a few sorry bastards left!" For indeed, we could see but little activity on her decks: two men back by the tiller, two more attempting to reload the culverin, and but a single man on the lines, for which reason the poor battered ship sailed straight for shore with what wind she could catch on her quarter.

"Just sit back, lads! I'll handle this myself," boasted Burke, that gibbering ape. The men laughed, but even that day, when none of us knew what misery and what tribulations O'Flaherty and his trained monkey had brought down on our heads, I cursed the day our quartermaster forced that blackguard of an Englishman on me as my bosun.

For it was just as Burke was posturing, cutlass and pistol in hand, that an alarum was raised from the lookout above. "Two sails! North-west! Sails ahoy!" Bless that man – 'twas young Balthazar Lynch – for not forgetting his duty and losing himself in the excitement of the coming plunder and my bosun's capering. He saved us that day.

Two sails indeed: they came around the head of Clear Island, where they had lain hidden in wait. The double-powder shot had been a signal that someone had taken the bait: and now the noose was tightening 'round us. Two fine ships, a brig and a galleon, flying British colors; their sails were crisp and white, stretched taut by a good wind that brought them directly across our bow. Their cannons gleamed, and their decks and rigging held dozens, scores, of men.

I lost no time: I roared at the helmsman, McTeigue, to come about, and sent the men up to drop all sails. We had a lead now, being downwind already, and I hoped we could escape in my good speedy ship.

But while I had been watching the approaching enemy, I had, like a fool, forgotten the third ship: the bait ship. As soon as they saw us start our turn, men which had been crouched behind her rail leapt up and lined the bow, some climbing into the rigging, some running out cannons that had been covered with canvas and debris. And as we slowed and turned, our sails flapping, they fired on us. The *Grace* was holed – alas, my lovely lady! But her wound lay above the waterline, thankfully. The yards on both masts were damaged by chain shot, and eight good men went down in a hail of musket-fire. Eleven more were wounded in that volley, and five of them would die in the coming days.

I almost wished that Burke and O'Flaherty had been numbered among the dead, except my mother taught me never to wish death on any man, as it brings the Reaper's attention on the wisher as much as the target. And a moment later, I was glad for their continued health, as both men leapt into action, chivvying and hurrying the men to the lines, to bring the wounded to Vaughn's cabin below, to ready the cannon should we need to fire. With their help, we made the turn and fled south-west – into the horizon and the trackless sea.

They came after us, of course. The bait ship was left behind soon enough: she did not have new sails or a smooth hull hidden behind the rail with the men and cannon. But the brig and the galleon came for us. The galleon had a bow chaser, a basilisk, but by fortune's blessing we were out of range and stayed there.

As it turned, it was the other ship that we grew to fear. The brig carried less armament than the galleon, which let her fly over the waves, nearly as fleet as my *Grace*. And in our damaged, undermanned state, she could match us.

And match us she did.

Log #3: The Chase

Captain's Log
Date: 24th of June, 1678. Noon.
Location: Unknown
Conditions: Anchored and slowly sinking in the storm.
But alone.

Inspection complete, so much as is possible in the storm. Leak worsening, water coming over the rail with every fifth wave. Meal of rotting biscuit and raw fish. Most eager to make landfall, but bloody storm continues.

***

Returning to my narrative…
Thus began the most hellish, gods-cursed time I have known in my eight-and-twenty years. I have known battle, as sailor and as captain; I have been deprived; I have been ill. God's teeth, I'm Irish, born of an English rapist in the time of Devil Cromwell. I have known suffering before.

But sea battles are short, a matter of hours at most, and frequently the fighting itself a mere pocketful of minutes. 'Tis the sailing, the tacking, the wearing, the coming about and bearing into the wind, that swallows the sand in the glass. A hurly-burly ashore is measured in heartbeats and footfalls, and quickish ones at that.

Growing up Irish under English tyranny took longer, but 'twas never all bad. I had my mother's love, and the love of my sept and clan, who forgave me my English blood for the sake of the love they carried for my mother, love which ran hot in their blood and burned deep in their bones. And aye, we went hungry at times, when the English stole our crop or our catch; there was illness, as there ever is; I bore the shame of bowing to English soldiers as they beat and chastised my kin. But there was always revenge to look forward to, with the English. And always – hungry days, sick days, every day –

there was music, and ale, and my mother's laugh, as high and rich as the lark's call. She acted as chieftain, in those days when the English had ripped out our heritage and broken the lines of battle chiefs and Gaelic kings. She would call the sept together whenever food ran short: first she would plan for the next day, when every man would go to the boats to take what we could from the sea, and every woman and girl would find roots and nuts and watercress; anything we could put in our bellies. Then once the plans were set and everyone knew his task, and we all knew that the morrow would bring some sustenance for us – at least enough to keep a space between belly and backbone – then we would sing and dance, and drink, if there were ale or whiskey to be had. Mad Cousin Diarmuid would even share out his mead, though no one else could taste that foul Northman's brew without your tongue curdling up in your mouth, poisoned with sweetness. But we'd drink it, right enough, and we'd forget our hunger and our anger and our despair. And my mother would laugh. Our suffering would ease, at least for a while.

But this Hell that I and my men have lived for the last two months: it never stopped. It never went away. That pox-hollowed, malformed, gods-rotted shite-kettle has sailed after us for *two months*. It never left our sight, in all those days.

The wind was perfect, the seas and skies calm but for an occasional summer squall that refreshed like a good Irish rain, and kindly topped our water barrels for us. The wind never failed, never changed direction; it blew from the north-east as if it were going home after a battle, and we sailed before it as though the gods called us on.

Surely the devil was giving chase.

That first dawn was the worst. We saw the galleon turn away and give up the chase as night fell on the day of the battle; as darkness overtook us, we were sure the brig would fall off, as well. 'Twas a hard night, filled with the stink of powder and smoke and the pall of blood, as Surgeon Vaughn wielded the knives and the saws and the hot irons of his trade. Three men succumbed to their wounds that night, and the rest of us felt every inch of our hurts as the fever of battle drew down and left us cold and empty as the grave. I found that I had taken a splinter to the shoulder-blade, but had not known it in the madness of battle; 'twas a simple wound, sewn up ably by young Lynch, who wields a fine needle. 'Twas the first time I had bled on the decks of the *Grace*, as we have never been boarded, but the stains of my blood were not the only ones on her planks that day. Those who could, slept, but most sat awake, mending sail or splicing line, hoping that busy hands could stop the screams of Vaughn's surgery from reaching our ears. It did not work.

And then morning dawned, and our spirits lifted even as the darkness did. There is no more beautiful sight than the sun rising on a new day that you never expected to see.

I bear witness to this: there is no uglier sight than the sails of your enemy seen in that same dawn's rosy glow.

That whore's bastard did not fall off with darkness, and he hadn't given up in the night. He had followed us, without burning a single lamp, never changing his course. We had slowed some, sure that we were alone; I was glad now that I had not given the order to reef the sails so we could tend to our wounded men and ship. The gods' mercy had stayed my command, and so we sailed through the night, and lived.

He was close enough to fire, had he bow chasers, but he did not; instead he had a figurehead that could be made out clearly in the bright dawn light, even without a spyglass. And that statue put more fear into us than any cannon would have. No cry went up when the sun's rays revealed that ship, a mere three hundred yards away; we all saw it about the same time, the only signal needed a pointed finger and a growing silence that called out louder than any bosun's roar. And as we all looked out on it, our eyes, sad and reddened with smoke and exhaustion, all drew to the figurehead: it was the shape of a beautiful woman, bare-breasted, with her hands raised over her head; on her face was a look of anguish, and across her sides and hips were the marks of a whip, red stripes painted and carved into the wood, where her skin was cruelly torn.

We knew of that figurehead, as every Irish rover did. A few whispered to those whose eyesight was too blurred with age or injury or lack of sleep: "'Tis the Lash! The Devil's Lash!"

Even among the English, there is but one captain cruel enough to adorn his very ship with the marks of his favorite device. The man christened with not one, but two of the Devil's own names: Captain Nicholas Hobbes.

I ask you, how can that be? Did his mother – if he had one, if he was not spawned from a blood pool under a headsman's block – did she never hear the boys down the lane damning each other to Old *Hob* for a bloody nose or a splash into a puddle? Did no carriage driver threaten the wrath of Splitfoot *Nick* on a slug-paced oxcart blocking the road? Did she not think of the man her son would become if she added Nick to the nigh-curst surname she already had fitted out for the bawling babe? Why not just call him Lucifer's Spawn Hobbes and call it a day? If you're bound and determined to do aught you shouldn't, then be sure you do it with a whole heart and not a half-measure, as my mother taught me. Mayhap Fucking Bastard Hobbes would suit the man better, at that.

Any road, it was he: Captain Nicholas Hobbes of the *Sea-Cat*. Better known as the Devil's Lash, when not in polite company – nor in society impolite enough to curse him as he deserves. He is perhaps the most feared and most reviled privateer captain who sails under English colors; certainly he is the most feared and hated on this ship of mine. His tenacity is legendary – and not exaggerated, I assure you – and matched only by his cruelty. It is said that every man aboard was pressed into service by Hobbes himself, and his equally heinous mates Stuart and Sinclair – one the first mate and one the bosun, but the two so alike and both such brutes that no one knows which is which, nor who is who. Sailor's lore is sure only that those two savages are the only ones who would willingly sail on that ship, even when this profession of ours includes the foulest, basest dregs of humanity as can be dredged from under the tables in the stinking hells and poxy brothels in the most benighted ports on this green and glowing Earth.

Well. The sun rose, the ship was spotted and named for what she was, the vessel of Hellspawn. The order was given to lower all sails once more and crowd the canvas, and we pulled away from the *Sea-Cat*. But we did not lose Hobbes. He never fell below the horizon, and no fortunate fog bank arose; of course there was no land to hide us from his sight, or even to make landfall and disperse, leaving our ship but saving our lives. There was nothing but ocean ahead, and the *Sea-Cat* and her whipped lady behind, all that day.

And the next day. And the next.

When I was nine years old, I spent two weeks with my uncle Seamus while my mother traveled to Dublin to bear witness between a family of our clan, the O'Learys of Knocknagroagh, and the

Englishmen who had despoiled their land and robbed them of their meager possessions. Not a day passed after her departure before I got it into my head that I could, and should, use our bull, King Henry (My mother named all our animals after Englishmen. She found them to be fitting appellations.) as my steed as I reenacted the exploits of Finn MacCool. Suffice it to say that King Henry, while he seemed at first amenable to taking on the role, eventually objected strenuously to my direction. He broke the fence of his paddock, shattered the chicken coop, trampled half a dozen of our chickens and my mother's favorite cat, Guinevere. He also broke my leg, which was certainly the least important bit of destruction, as he also broke his own, and Uncle Seamus was finally forced to kill the sad beast. As I was lamed and, at first, unconscious, Uncle Seamus could not thrash me properly for the deed when his blood was still high; and so he determined a course that would cause me far more torment: he declared that my punishment would wait until my mother returned home and learned of what I had done.

Those two weeks, which stretched almost to three as my mother was delayed in Dublin, had been the longest of my life. Trapped indoors by my broken leg, denied any pastime apart from meditation on my crime and my impending doom, by the end I had concocted such torments that I nearly swooned with terror when my mother came into the room, having been informed by Seamus that I had somewhat to tell her. Perhaps she knew that I would have done myself more misery than she could inflict, and so she did not have me go out to the yard and eat the mouldering remains of King Henry's dungheap, nor did she coat me in chicken offal and set her three remaining cats on me, two of the gentler thoughts I had crafted in her absence.

No: she took me to meet my father.

But that is a tale for another day; I lack the strength to set my pen to the deeds of a second English bastard. All I will say is that those three weeks of waiting, imagining what my mother would do to me but always hoping for some miraculous reprieve, were the worst agony I had known.

Until Nicholas Hobbes chased my ship across the breadth of the Atlantic Ocean.

Log #4: The Chase, Part II

Captain's Log
Date: 24th of June, 1678. Evening, or nearly so: twilight hidden by storm clouds.
Location: Unknown
Conditions: Thunder and Lightning. Very very frightening. Wind and waves high, but ebbing.

For two months, Hobbes's ship never left us. We made what repairs we could, but our mainmast yard was damaged beyond repair by chainshot, and we had no way to replace it. Perhaps something could have been found, but McLoughlin, our carpenter, had been killed by a musket-ball, and no one else had any particular skill at woodcraft. We tried to hoist more sails, to lighten our load, to make better use of the wind – but all was for naught. We sailed dark in the night and took unexpected turns in the blackness; but somehow, whenever we tried such tactics, the sun would rise and show sails behind us, sometimes far away, but always visible. And they always gave chase, eventually closing what gap we had opened, never coming close enough to enter battle.

I do not believe I truly slept for those two months. I cannot even be sure it was two months; I missed days in this log, and no man aboard kept his own calendar. Even Vaughn, the surgeon and an educated man, stayed below with his books, as ever; the sailing of the ship means no more to him than the pulling of a plow concerns a field mouse: occasionally he is disturbed by it. The passing of time follows that same path for him, unnoticed and unmourned. Perhaps he has the right of it.

But for two months, the wind never slackened or changed and no storms came; there was enough rain and enough fishing to keep us alive, but we saw no other sails and never lost sight of the *Sea-Cat*. It was enough to drive us all mad, the months of waiting, imagining our fate yet hoping for a reprieve – a reprieve that did not need to be as miraculous as the one I had hoped for as a lad, awaiting my mother's return: all we needed now was for Hobbes to give up the chase. Who were we? One Irish pirate vessel, perhaps with some small repute due our success in the English shipping lanes, but no Henry Morgan, no Francis Drake. Why did he not give up?

Someday I will have Hobbes at my mercy. I will ask him then.

It may have been madness that brought us so close to our doom, at the end. Certain sure, if it was not madness, 'twas folly. I took ill, of course, for no man can stay upright under that strain for that long. When I did, 'twas left to my mate, Ian O'Gallows, to carry out my wishes. But he found himself pressed on two sides by the ship's quartermaster, Sean O'Flaherty, and the bosun, Edmund Burke, a brute of an Englishman allowed aboard my ship only for the sake of O'Flaherty's patronage, and the need to keep peace between myself and the man elected by my crew to be my equal in all things but battle. O'Flaherty chafed under the fact that we were on the eve of battle every hour of two months, and thus my word was law throughout; so when I lay insensate in my cabin, he seized his moment. With Burke at his side, they overruled Ian and commanded the men themselves. Perhaps Ian allowed it to happen, and if so, I cannot fault him; though their course was folly, it was a possibility that called to us all for those months, and may have become inevitable even had I stayed at the helm to the bitter end.

They slowed the ship and prepared for battle.

I regained myself in the night, and staggered out of my cabin to see what had transpired during my incapacity. O'Flaherty had command, with Duffy at the helm; it was a cloudy night, and we were running silent and dark, so that I almost stumbled over them in the darkness as I moved blearily toward the dim light of the hooded lantern standing at O'Flaherty's feet. They greeted me; somewhat warily, I think now, though I saw nothing amiss at the time. O'Flaherty told me how long I had been below – the better part of two days – and our approximate position, though we had sailed off the edge of our charts more than a month ago, and were navigating mostly by legend and hearsay about the length of a cruise from Ireland to the English colonies of the New World, where so many Irishmen suffered in chains after Devil Cromwell came to our shores. They assumed we were somewhere east of the Carolinas, but did not know how far away from the shore – perhaps as much as a thousand miles. They thought we might be close to the island called

Baramundi, or perhaps it was Bermuda – they could not recall the name.

I began to examine what I could discern of the distribution of our sails, and grew alarmed as I realized that sails had been reefed: my ship had been slowed. It was then that the most peculiar sight ever to light my eyes came to pass. I realized that the rigging was growing far easier to discern; that there was, in fact, light in the darkness. It was a blue light, unlike any illumination I had experienced, and as I rubbed my eyes, trying to clear away any lingering phantoms of sleep, I found that the hair on my arms, and on my neck, was standing erect. Then I knew what it was, this light, from many stories told by old sea-dogs around tavern tables: it was the fire of St. Elmo, seen by one mariner in a thousand but boasted of by every man jack who sails the sea.

Imagine my wonder as I observed my ship, every inch of her glowing like a falling star, growing bright enough to see, and then bright enough to read by. It was a sublime beauty, a moment out of time: a waking dream that brought joy to my heart – a heart which had felt no goodness for weeks, a heart which was filled with nothing but a rising dread and falling hopes.

And then imagine my horror as I turned to look at O'Flaherty and Duffy behind me, and saw the same eldritch fire crawling over the sails and lines and rails of the *Sea-Cat*, the scourged lady at her bow almost near enough to spit on. "To arms!" I cried. "To arms, and 'ware boarders! All men on deck!"

O'Flaherty attempted to forestall me, but it was too late. My awaking at the wrong moment, my awareness of the enemy ship at the same moment, thanks to a mysterious wonder of the sea – it had to have been fate, or the caprice of the gods, that saw fit to ruin the plans of O'Flaherty. I do not know if I should regret it.

For the moment my voice was raised, the hatch burst open and the men came boiling out, wide awake, armed to the teeth and ready to kill Englishmen. For indeed, O'Flaherty and Burke had intended to bring our pursuers to the fray, and, hoping surprise would balance their greater numbers, had hidden the men belowdecks until Hobbes's men had grappled and boarded us, thinking our boys foolishly asleep, and thus boarding with false confidence instead of battle-ready wills. Perhaps it would have worked, if the timing had come together properly.

But now it was ruined. For the men rushed above yelling, and the English spotted us and veered off our stern just long enough to fire on us with grape shot and muskets. My men went down like mown hay before the scythe. I fell, as well, wounded in the arm and lightly across my scalp, a minor gash that bled more than it harmed, though it was enough to stun me for a moment as my blood and the blood of my men pooled on the deck of my ship.

Then the blue fire of St. Elmo flared like lightning, turning as white as moonlight and as brilliant as the sun on the waves. There was a clap of thunder, and the deck reeled beneath us. *"Rogue wave!"* rose the cry, and perhaps it was. The light turned a color I have never seen, a lurid brilliance tinged with darkness: as if a rainbow bled its life's blood on our eyes. I heard the screaming of a *ban-sidhe* rise far off and then fly at us at great speed, arriving with a tumult and crash as of a cannonade. The deck bounced once more, the light flashed, and then – all was still. All was silent.

The sun broke the horizon then, and we saw that the ship had turned, and the sun was rising before us, a line of dark storm clouds just above her bright face, like the angry brows of a goddess scorned. The seas were calmed, but for the three-foot chop; no sign of the rogue wave that had tossed us moments before.

And no sign of the Devil's Lash. The cry went up as we realized, and we rushed from rail to rail, like children following a soldier's parade through town. But there was nothing, no ship, no sails in sight. There was a brief cheer, quickly lost in confusion; and then I set men to tasks, seeing to the wounded and the dead, turning the ship about to sail due west and seek landfall and safety from the coming storm. It was not an hour before we spied land ahead, and a matter of half a day before we could make out the trees along the shore. So much for O'Flaherty's navigation. Perhaps it was Duffy's, but he fell in the fusillade, so I will not speak ill of the dead.

Thus came we here. The storm is upon us now, and my strength flags again, my eyes heavy, my hand numb and shaking on the quill. I must rest. Perhaps I will wake in Hell. Perhaps I am there now.

But if I am in Hell, where is the Devil's Lash?

Log #5: The Glass Palace

Captain's Log
Date: 25th of June. Dawn.
Location: At anchor in cove. Still afloat.
Conditions: The sun shines, and hope blooms in those golden rays.

We live. I say again: the fairest sight of all is the sun's rise on a new day, arriving like an unexpected guest who bears good tidings.

The storm broke and fled in the night, though in truth it should have spelled our doom before it did. For our survival this dawn, we must give thanks to the capricious gods, and to my mate and friend, Ian O'Gallows. (A name he bears half for his father, a Scotch gallowglass, a mercenary who came to Ireland to fill his pouch with gold fighting in our wars, and instead found himself filling the pouch of a comely Irish maid, one of such spirited blood and poetic temperament that she loved the man but never bothered to know his name beyond, "Ah, Love!" The other half-measure of the name O'Gallows is the just reward for Ian's meritorious service in a lifelong quest to end on that renowned apparatus, made holy by the blood of so many Irish kings. And the shite of an even greater number of English rogues, as Ian says it true.)

The seas found the hole in the *Grace*'s hull at last. Ian was at the watch and heard a report from the men at the larboard pumps that they could no longer keep pace with the water in the bilge. Ian went below to inspect, and found water pouring in through the wound in our lovely lady's skin. He went to the carpenter's closet, near abandoned since McLoughlin's death on Irish seas, and found a short plank end, a great handful of long nails, and a hammer. He held the plank in place with his feet, his back braced against the deck and muscles straining against the might of the seas, while Roger Desmond nailed the board in place with enough iron to charge a cannon. It was nothing like a proper patch, but it held back the water enough to let the pumps keep us afloat.

Now with the dawn we are at last headed ashore. I will take Lynch and explore on foot to the south, and O'Flaherty and Carter will head north. We seek a strand where we can beach the ship without fear of intrusion. We seek also for civilization, and knowledge of our whereabouts – but always, the ship's health comes first.

***

I have returned. I do not know what is uppermost in my mind, in my heart: the dread I feel, or the wonder. For the nonce, it is perplexity, bewilderment, and confustication. WHERE THE BLOODY HELL ARE WE?

We took the boat to the shore, found a bare patch between trees – and such strange trees! Standing aloft on roots like a cathedral's buttresses, growing right from the sea, with salt crystals visible on their tangled roots. O'Flaherty calls them *mangroves*. He was transported to the Indies where he turned pirate before returning to Ireland, so I take his word on matters of local knowledge now. Though I don't know why: wherever we are, it is not the sugar plantations of the Caribbean. I do not believe O'Flaherty has ever seen these shores any more than I have. Nonetheless, we tied the boat to one of the strange trees and spent some minutes regaining our land legs, learning the uncertainty of the land – which is softer even than a peat bog, though perhaps not quite as odoriferous – and then we were off.

Lynch and I slogged through mangrove bog for a mile or so before the ground came solid to our step. We knew to use the mud to keep off the insects, or we would have lost more blood to them than we ever have to the English. But the stench was most unpleasant, as was the heat, even in the trees' shade.

Not half a mile after the bog turned to good earth and the mangroves made way for proper trees, we came to a wall. I cannot say how that sight heartened me: we were not lost, we were not doomed to wander in the wilderness until my ship sank and we starved for our ignorance. A wall meant men, and with men we had a fighting chance. That's all an Irishman needs.

The wall was six feet high, with broken glass embedded in the top. A fine piece of masonry, too, as good as any cathedral wall I have seen. The surface was covered with a plaster smooth as a shaved and sanded plank, the extent slightly curved but the top straight and level as the horizon. But trees grew within a pace of it, so its defensive value was somewhat less than its craftsmanship. Lynch scurried over it with no more difficulty than he had climbing the rigging, and though my days as a mast-monkey were far behind me, still I had not much more trouble. The woods continued on the other side for a dozen paces, and then cleared. We paused at the edge to take stock.

That's when we saw the house.

House? Fah. 'Tis a palace the likes of which no man has ever laid eyes on, I warrant.

There were brief gardens with plants unknown to me or Lynch; puffed shapes like immense *dent-de-lion* gone to seed, and tall trees with nary a branch on slender trunks but for a crown of great leaves, bright green and serrate, bursting out of the top, many times the height of a man – they might make fine masts, perhaps, though they may be too flexible. Then a terrace of some sort, with a columned portico or promenade – Christ and Dagda, I have not the words for it. I have never seen architecture like it.

It was the size of a vast cathedral, a king's palace: thirty or forty feet high, an hundred feet across – nay, more. It lacked ornament: not a single piece of statuary, no mural nor frieze, not even a curved band of stone. I'd call it a Puritan's proclivities that stripped it bare, knowing that humorless race landed on the New World's shores and live there still, but no: 'twas the edifice itself that served as decoration, that gloried the eye and honored the wizard who built it.

The walls shimmered and shone as we approached cautiously through the gardens. I noticed there were no crops, no edibles, and surmised we must be on the far side from the kitchens. I told Lynch through signs to 'ware guards on the parapets, but we saw not a soul. As we drew closer, the risen sun gleamed from the walls, which had a strange appearance: smoother even than the wall we had crossed, yet rippled, and the sunlight reflected from the surface. I surmised they were solid steel, as I have seen such metal forged so that light ripples on its surface like that of a pond teeming with fish and fragments of wind. This wall curved, as well, and I wondered if the people dwelling here could not lay a straight line.

But then before our eyes, the wall *changed*. What I had taken for ripples of forged steel was in truth a curtain, a curtain than now drew away, moved by no hand. Why did this curtain wall gleam in the sun, you ask?

Because the curtain was inside of a *wall made of glass.*

I could not fathom it, at first. 'Twas Lynch, crouched beside me, whispering, "Glass! 'Tis made of glass!" that set the truth in my 'mazed mind. I know not how to imagine a wall made of glass, without flaw, without blemish, without frame, ten feet high and a hundred feet wide, without saying that it must be magic. This was a sorcerer's palace, I thought then.

And then, within the glass – though the eye did not pause for an instant at its surface, clear as the mountain air – we saw the master of this palace, and I corrected myself: this was the palace of a sorcer*ess*. Her robe – silk, I thought, though I have never seen it on a person, only on a bolt liberated from an English trader; sure it was not the rough-dyed homespun I have seen on most colleens at home – that robe revealed more of her curves than it concealed, and lovely curves they were, indeed. I glanced at Lynch to be sure he was not entranced or inflamed by this first sight of a woman in nigh three months, but he was glancing at me to determine the same, and so we looked back at the marvels before us.

She stood at the window for a moment, staring out at the sun on the water, a delicate half-smile on her face – a face as lovely as the rest of her, a face to bring out the poet in any Irishman – and then she turned and walked across a wide room, a reception hall, perhaps, though I saw no table large enough to seat a proper company of men. There were low couches and chairs, rich carpets; the floors were of some pale stone, and as smooth as the glass wall I saw them through.

The sorceress went to a wall of cabinets, and produced a miracle. She grasped a handle, pulled the cabinet open – and light shone forth from within, brighter than any lantern I have seen! Within the cabinet, and affixed to the inside of the door, there were what appeared to be foodstuffs, though the room was so wide that I could not make out all the details; too, I was dazzled by that light: surely she did not keep a candle burning inside a closed cabinet! But then, no candle ever shone like that.

She removed a bottle of some kind, and a smaller handful. She opened another cabinet, which I could not see into, and then she poured, with her back to us. She turned and we saw she was drinking a golden fluid from a clear glass cup; in her hand she held something that might be fruit, though I did not know its shape. It looked to me like a golden sausage. But I watched her peel it and eat it raw, so a fruit it must have been.

But what can I know of this? Perhaps she devoured the severed finger of a demon before my eyes. Or perhaps it was . . . some other part.

She put down the glass of golden nectar and took up a strange object: only just larger than her hand, slim and long and flat, covered in knobbly protrusions. She waved it at the wall, and then I knew it was her sorceress's wand, for the wall opened, of its own accord, revealing a great mirror in a black frame. She waved the wand again, and the mirror showed images – but not images, for they moved. *They moved!* It was a window of some kind, revealing not the other side of the palace's grounds, but showing other places and people, like a scrying pool or some such wizardry. As Lynch and I watched, it changed a dozen times, revealing a man's face, then three people gathered around a strange object I did not know, then a map with strange names written on it – alas, she waved her wand and the map disappeared before I could discern any useful details; but I will swear the words were in a script I recognized, even if I could not see what words they spelled out. Then it was a woman with a metal rod pressed to her wide open mouth – was she singing? – and then a jeweled pendant, surrounded by words, like the illuminated page of a monk's manuscript. I made out the number 29.99, before the mirror's magic showed two faces – no, it was one face, but shown twice, side-by-side. But perhaps it was not the same face, for the one on the left was older, more blemished than the right side face. Mother and daughter, perhaps?

The sorceress stepped closer to the mirror then, and gazed at it; it was now that she ate her golden sausage-fruit and drank her golden nectar. She dropped the peel – the skin? – and the empty glass onto a wide shelf beside the cabinets full of light, and then took up her wand again and waved it at the wall of glass. And the wall opened.

Two doors, made of glass framed in some strange, smooth white stone, swung wide without a hand to move them. Lynch and I froze, knowing the slightest movement might draw the sorceress's attention to us. I know the lad's fondest wish now was the same as mine: we had seen enough, and now we wanted nothing but her departure, so that we could return to the safety of our ship and our friends. But she did not leave: she came out onto the terrace, no more than thirty feet from where we crouched behind shrubbery. Then she took off her robe.

I will not speak of what I saw then; it would be ungallant. Suffice to say that I am not innocent of women, that I have known the fond caresses of more than a few generous and loving lasses; but never had I hoped to see so much bared flesh outside of a bed. What garment she did wear was little more than paint on her skin; certainly it hid no more from our sight than it did from the gods'.

She walked across the terrace, away from us – I can close my eyes and see every single step, so closely did I observe her every swaying, undulating movement – and then dove into a pond that we had not noticed hitherto. She swam – better than any man I have ever seen, and more than a few fish, as well – across and back, across and back, a score of times. Then she emerged once more, taking up a small blanket to dry herself, an operation I observed just as carefully, especially when she bent to rub the blanket down her smooth leg – but I blush to continue.

She went inside, closing the glass doors, this time by hand. She disappeared through a doorway, granting Lynch's and my wish of minutes before – though I confess my wish had become somewhat different by that point.

When we spoke, when we had recovered our wits enough to whisper, Lynch asked, "Is she a temptress demon, Captain? A succubus?"

I shook my head, but not because I knew him to be wrong. "She may be. Though I think this land too fair to be infernal. Look you." I pointed to the ocean, visible to our left; before the glass palace was the perfect cove, ideal for our purposes. A wide, flat expanse of white sand that we could draw the ship upon, a spit of land dense with trees and shrubs to hide us from the view of passing ships, should such exist in this strange place (We have seen none). Stout trees to anchor lines for drawing the *Grace* out of the water, and lashing her safe against the tide's caprices. And overlooking all, this glass palace, with a pond of clear water to drink and magical cabinets full of food, howsoever strange.

"Hell would not have such perfection laid before us," I told Lynch. "Not without a legion of demons, armed and belligerent, to keep us from it."

No, I had realized, as we watched the beautiful sorceress emerge from her magical, impossible palace, where we were and what we were seeing. "She is no devil," I told Lynch. "She is a Faerie Queen.

"We are Underhill, in the Land of the Fae."

Log #6: Observations and Discoveries

Captain's Log
Date: 25th of June. Noon.
Location: At anchor in cove, but not for much longer.
Conditions: Sun's heat nigh overwhelming. But is it a human sun?

I sat with Lynch and looked at nothing, in all directions. I looked at the beach, the cove, the trees; I looked at the glass palace, the magical objects inside. I looked and saw no living soul, anywhere about, but for the boy next to me.

I knew then that we must seize this palace, wresting it from the grip of its sorceress-succubus-queen. But how? My mind sailed back through a hundred stories of Faerie-Land, the tales that accompany any Irish boy on the path to manhood; none told of any man conquering a Faerie keep. I knew clever ways to escape their clutches, involving wagers and games of chance or skill; but never had I heard of a man taking possession of a Faerie home.

But what choice had we? We must have shelter, and fresh food, and the *Grace* must have that beach. Perhaps O'Flaherty will find a place better suited, but if not, we have no time to creep along the coast in search of a more accommodating anchorage. So be it: we will treat this as a ship to be grappled and boarded, her captain's disposition and the secrets of her hold unknown to us; cause for caution, but not cowardice.

First, then: information. Lynch and I consulted and then split to walk the perimeter of the palace; Lynch took the landward side, as the lad cannot swim, and I went out to the strand and the sea. I gave him my pistols and powder, and cautioned him to run from all ills; he assured me he would. Good lad, that Balthazar Lynch. I watched him go, as quiet as a church mouse in his deck-rough bare feet – quiet even though he was slung about with enough killing implements to board a ship by himself – and then I started on my path. I do not hesitate to admit that I crawled on my belly away from that domicile: the last thing I wished was to draw the Faerie Queen's attention.

I made it safe to the deeper brush, and then I rose to a crouch and made my way rapidly out along the strand. It was an easy enough trek, the underbrush thin, only clumps of tall grass and more of those puff-ball shrubs, with trees spreading their canopy overhead. I slowed as I neared the end of the strand, as I could readily imagine a watchtower out here; there could not be a better place to ensure early warning of attack or storm, or from whence to signal passing ships. But there was none. Perhaps they do not need this in Faerie-Land. I determined I would place men here, should our design succeed. I looked back to the north, but could not make out the *Grace*, hidden by a curve of the shore and treetops taller than her masts. I was gladdened by this, for we do not seek attention.

Then into the water and across the cove. I kept my stroke small, so that only my head would be visible from shore, and the burning sun, still not far above the horizon, would prevent any vigorous scrutiny. The water, ah! It was as warm as any bath, and a clear blue that I had never seen, not even in the purest mountain stream of my Ireland, though I have heard as much from transported men such as my quartermaster. Still, one always expects exaggeration in a seaman's tales, so this confirmation was a surprise. A most welcome one, after three months aboard ship without bathing.

It was a matter of minutes to cross the cove, through the gentle chop, and under the calls of seabirds; with every breath, this Faerie-Land seemed more of a paradise. I knew of the temptatious nature of the dwellers Underhill, however, and I hardened my soul against the beauties and comforts around me. We will not stay here; not against our will, nor with it. Men do not belong in this place. We will take what we need, and we will depart for familiar shores. I swear it.

I emerged, dripping, and moved slowly up the south'ards beach, crawling like a serpent until I was hidden once more from the palace's sight by shrubbery. I made my way along, observing all I could of that Fae place; though what I saw, I could not understand.

When I had gone an hundred paces inland, I heard a rustle nearby and tensed for confrontation, but 'twas only Lynch. We withdrew somewhat from the glass palace – there was another wall, identical to the first, blocking the south'ards approach; we crouched close, though we did not look at each other as we spoke, but kept an eye both to the palace and to the wall, alert for sentries walking its length.

Lynch confirmed my own strange findings. This palace appeared to hold no guards at all, not a single man-at-arms; not even a maidservant had we seen. There were no guardroom, no watchtowers anywhere; Lynch had described a pleasant path leading right to the door, without moat or gate to bar the way! Stranger still: we found no garden, no livestock, no fishing smack or nets, not even a well or a rubbish heap or a privy – though Lynch confessed he had seen many objects and structures he could not surely identify.

Perhaps the Faerie Queen does not need guards. And perhaps she does not need servants beyond her own magic. Does she not need to eat? Do the Faerie Lands not produce food as we know it, grown from earth and water and sunlight? Too, would she not wish for a retinue, for companions to while away the lonely hours? If this sorceress's existence be naught but solitude, silence broken only by the crash of waves, then all the beauty of this place comes to nothing. I will take my bonny ship and my salty lads, with thanks.

Lynch led me back the way he had come, so I could see some of these strangenesses myself. He showed me the door, with its welcoming path; there was a large shed, perhaps a barn, connected to the palace by another path – stones set in the even ground, bordered with a strip of tiny pebbles – but still, there were no animal sounds nor smells, and I saw neither fodder nor dung.

We were moving around to the far side of the barn-shed when the palace door opened and we held still, moving only enough to observe clearly. The sorceress herself emerged, now dressed in clothing only slightly less strange than before: a thin skirt that met no standard of decency I have known; it covered less than a slip or nightdress, and her coat ended mere inches below her waist. Her shoes were like slippers, but her heels were raised on spikes; she wore a strange mask that covered only her eyes with a strip of dark, hard material, stone or metal, I could not say, but she could apparently see through it, somehow. She walked to the barn-shed, carrying a cloth bag of some kind behind her shoulder, the bag as wide as her shoulders and hanging behind nearly to her knees, flat and flexible as a cloak; in her other hand she held a case with a handle on top. She raised the hand that held the case – was it leather? Perhaps hardened, to hold the boxy shape? Or leather-clad wood? – and pointed at the barn-shed; there arose a rumbling noise from the far side, as of a small herd of cattle moving within; but no cattle emerged.

I heard a bird's chirp from inside the barn, and then sounds like heavy doors opening and closing. The sorceress returned to her palace and swiftly emerged again with two more boxes, even larger and heavier than the first two; so massy she must drag them along the ground, though quick and smooth as if she were carrying only milkpails or a posy of daisies. Surely any wooden chest of that size would be far too heavy for a woman to carry – but she is Fae. Who can say what is heavy to her, or what strange otherworldish material makes up the substance of her possessions? And they could not be wood nor leather, not of any animal I have known: both of the boxes were a pink so bright it hurt the eyes to see.

This time she set down her burden, closed the door of her palace and locked it with a key too small to see – or perhaps it was but the touch of her elfin hand – and then dragged her chests to the barn again. More heavy doors closing, and then from within we heard a rumble like the growling of some great slavering beast: we readied our weapons, sure she was setting loose a pack of Faerie hounds, or perhaps bears, wolves, lions.

I do not know what came out of that barn. It was shaped something like a wagon, and the sorceress sat within it, only her head and shoulders above the raised sides, and she was blocked on one side by a pane of glass affixed to the wagon. But the wagon was bright red, and it shone and gleamed in the sun; it had wheels, but the wheels had no spokes. There was a metal grill on the side facing us as it moved out of the barn, with two round protuberances that could have been eyes, but I saw no signs of life in that thing.

And the greatest mystery of all: if it was a wagon, there were no beasts drawing it. It moved of its own accord, though I do not doubt it was guided by the sorceress's Fae will.

She drew away from the barn, paused, and I heard the same rumbling and clattering from the far side of the barn as the sorceress had caused with the wafture of her hand; perhaps it was a door closing as magically as the glass door of her palace had opened to the sea? Then the wagon she rode in rumbled and growled, and then moved away and out of our sight, blocked by the barn-shed we crouched beside. And we were left alone, beside the unguarded palace of a Faerie Queen.

We waited, still as calm water, for a hundred breaths. Then, when nothing else moved, we thought her gone, for now. I set Lynch by the door to keep watch for her return, after first leading me back to the north wall, closer to the *Grace*; I gave him the strictest instructions not to go inside, not to leave the shelter of the trees, but just to watch. Then I scaled the wall, again with the help of a close-growing tree and with no more difficulty than before, and then made my way back to my ship. I cannot describe the warm rush of joy I felt in my breast upon setting my foot once more on the *Grace*'s deck; this ship is my home in these strange waters, as well as my steed for traversing them, and I do love her so.

I reported only our current status to O'Gallows, gave him orders to keep watch for O'Flaherty's return, and then retired to my cabin to set this down in my log. I am starting to believe this document is an important one: perhaps when we return to Ireland, I will carry the records of the only trip men made Underhill and back again since the days of yore.

We will make it back again. This I swear.

***

The glass has turned twice since I returned to the *Grace*, and O'Flaherty and Carter are now here, as well. I do not know what to make of their report, but I set it down here, while they refresh themselves and ready the men for the assault.

The first words out of O'Flaherty's mouth once my cabin door had closed behind him were: "'Tis paradise, Nate! This be the pirate's dream, sure it is!"

"Aye," I said. "But such is the way of this place: to seem like every glorious wonder a man ever clapped eyes on. But it is a trap, sure as you stand there before me."

He frowned and then his brows raised with surprise. "Ye know where we are? Did ye find a landmark, or a guide?"

"We are Underhill," I told him then, "in Faerie-Land." I had said nothing to the men of my discoveries, nor to Ian; I wanted O'Flaherty's opinion and any further evidence he could provide, so I could prove my sanity when I told the crew. And though I like the man not at all and trust him but little more, I cannot fault the mind hidden behind that unpleasant face. Though I wish to the gods that he would not call me Nate, but I know of no politic way to stop him.

That face frowned again – 'twas the ugliest sight I had seen yet on this day of wonders, and it made me smile to place its scarred, filthy lumpen grotesquerie beside my memory of the Faerie Queen's ethereal loveliness in my mind's eye – and O'Flaherty sat himself on my sea chest. "What did ye find?" he asked. "Where is Lynch?"

Though it rankled to have to report first, as it rankled to have him make so familiar in my cabin, I reminded myself that he and I are of equal rank, according to our ship's Articles, signed by every man aboard, and by me. So I told him of the cove and its beach, and of the palace of magical wonders, and especially its beauteous mistress. I confess I waxed somewhat poetic in describing her, since I was looking at his hairy, warty brow as I did so, which afforded me some amusement; though I kept that hidden, of course.

But when I had finished, O'Flaherty shook his head. "I do not think we are in the land of the Fair Folk," he said to me. "The one we found was far from fair." And he pulled from inside his shirt the three objects that rest on the shelf before my eyes as I write this. As I stare at them now, I must agree with him: the Fae would not have such things. This is the stuff of men.

But then what did I see at that glass palace?

Was it not real? Were my eyes deceived?

I know not.

O'Flaherty and Carter had trekked north, their experience identical to mine and Lynch's, but lasting somewhat longer in the swampy act; their slog through mangrove and mud and biting insect was closer to two hours than one. But finally, the trees thinned for them as well, and they saw – the pirate's paradise, as O'Flaherty said.

"Ships," he told me. "Ships and boats of every size, from dinghies and wherries to craft as large as the *Grace*, and greater still, curse me for a liar else. There must have been a thousand of them, tied to piers and docks and quays. And not a single cannon among 'em."

I scoffed at this, of course, but he assured me: he and Carter had explored carefully. He had even managed to creep up and peer into one of the smaller boats, and there was not a single piece aboard. Not a firing port, not a barrel of powder, not a cannonball stack, as far as the eye could see.

"'Twas a fishing fleet, then. Was it not?" I asked him.

He scowled and nodded. "Aye, there were fisherman's boats, right enough. I saw poles and lines, and a few nets. Some were pleasure boats, as the fine bloody folk use for boating on the Thames or the bloody Shannon, and a few were little more than small boys' coracles. But Nate, there were masted ships like I've never seen before – and some even larger, without masts or sails at all, stab my liver! Perhaps they be galleys, as the heathen Moors row, but I saw no oars, nor ports nor benches. And I looked, smite my eyes if I didn't."

I nodded. "Aye – they are Faerie craft, no doubt, and moved by the Fair People's magic, just like that wagon I saw that spirited away the Sorceress."

O'Flaherty paused to consider. "Aye," he said finally. "Perhaps." He pushed the three objects into my hands. "But I think no Faerie magic made these."

He had a bottle, a wine bottle with paper somehow glued to it. "Boone's Farm Strawberry Hill," it proclaimed. I took off the top, after a few moments tugging at it before I found it had to be twisted off – and what glass blower could thread his work so a cap could be screwed on? – and sniffed. That smell was enough to convince me O'Flaherty had reason in what he said, though the glass palace in my memory still held sway over my thoughts. Perhaps a taste of the dregs left in the bottle would have convinced me entirely, but I couldn't stand to put my tongue to the test. There was also some tobacco, tiny cigars wrapped in paper and enclosed in a paper box marked "CAMEL." I broke one up into my pipe and lit it; it tasted strange, but still allowed me a sweet smoke, and at my urging, O'Flaherty joined me.

Then we looked at the third object.

I don't know how to describe it. It was made of paper, but bound like a book or a pamphlet, with tiny slivers of bent metal, and it lacked a cover of leather or wood or cloth; and the paper was unlike any I have ever seen: it was slick, and it shone under the light. The paper was covered with images far more than words, and such images! If they were portraits, then the greatest artists of history are mere children flinging paint around like morning porridge by the spoonful compared to the genius who painted that; but for the size, and the object in my hand, I would have thought I looked on living flesh.

Lots of living flesh. *Every inch* of living flesh, in fact.

I have known men who owned portraits of women. I have known many men who carried locks of hair, or small swatches of cloth, to remind them of a woman's scent, the softness of her skin. Of course I have known boys who drew or carved the shape of a woman in secret, as a canvas to paint the dreams of love upon.

But *this*.

They were nude. Bare as any babe, but no childish shapes were these! Breasts of every sort, legs and arses and . . . and . . . EVERYTHING! Pages and pages of – EVERYTHING! I know not who this "Bare Bitches" is, whose name adorned every page and must thus be the artist behind these images (nor do I know why he bears a dog's name), but I long to meet and talk with him. If he owns a brothel, with such ravishing beauty there, so much smooth and willing flesh, then I know where my men will spend every coin we plunder, and every one they can beg and borrow, too.

O'Flaherty had found these things, the bottle, the tobacco, the wondrous pamphlet, on a man he had discovered unconscious under a tree by the shipyard. "Sure and he was drowned in that wine, for you could smell it from ten paces away – though it might have been swallowed up in the stench of the man himself, damn my nose." Somewhat familiar with the look and behavior of a drunkard, O'Flaherty and Carter had not hesitated in searching the snoring man's filthy garments for booty or information. I asked if they had found any coin, and O'Flaherty said no, but the shifting of his gaze when he said it told me otherwise. I said nothing then, but kept it in mind: should our conflict ever come to a head, this would be the knife hidden in my sleeve. O'Flaherty had signed the Articles, too – had in fact introduced the idea to the men, along with the existence of his position and the insistence on every man voting on each decision affecting the ship and crew, all ideas garnered from his time cruising in the Indies – and the penalty for holding back loot from the company was as clear as the water on these shores.

But information was the most vital booty that O'Flaherty brought back. Now we know that the coast to the north is no good to us, being nothing but swamp to the edge of the shipyard that, though it might give us rich pickings in future, offers no safe haven for the wounded

Grace and her exhausted, depleted crew. And now we know that, though none of us can possibly say where we are, nor what manner of people live on these shores – nor can I explain the magical place that Lynch and I saw, nor give a name to the woman who ruled it, be she human sorceress or Faerie Queen – still we are in a world of men. Men who drink, and smoke, and lust. O'Flaherty has shown that to my satisfaction.

Perhaps I should not dread a face-to-face encounter with that sorceress, after all. She did eat and drink like a woman; perhaps she is no more than she seems. I am sure to have the chance to find out, once we have taken her palace for our own.

O'Gallows will remain. It should be me, while he and O'Flaherty lead the assault, but I am needed to lead the way to the glass palace and Lynch. To make Ian's task easier, I will take both O'Flaherty and Burke with me, along with Hugh Moran, Donal Carter, Owen McTeigue, Shane MacManus, Seamus O'Finnegan, Robert Sweeney, and Ceallachan Ó Duibhdabhoireann, known to us as Kelly. I am hopeful that Kelly will discover his warrior's might. He lost an eye to a splinter when the Lash's men fired on us, and hasn't been the same man since.

That leaves Ian, Surgeon Vaughn, and Abram O'Grady, the cook, along with Francis Murphy, Liam Finlay, Arthur Gallagher, Michael Rearden, Raymond Fitzpatrick, Roger Desmond, Padraig Doyle, and Lochlan O'Neill, called Salty. 'Tis enough to move the *Grace* down the shore to the cove, though not if there are any trials or terribulations. But our first assault is likely to be enough, I judge, if the glass palace holds no dangerous secrets that could bar our way – or spill our blood. If there be complications, then some of us will surely escape to carry word and warning; together with the *Grace*'s cannon, they should carry the day. And if none of us come out of the palace alive – if I do not come out of there alive – then I find I care not what comes of the rest of them here with my ship. Ian says we should simply bring the *Grace* with all hands aboard, for a frontal assault on the beach; I hope it will not be necessary to risk the ship in any but the uttermost need.

And so with sharpened swords and axes, charged locks, loaded rifles and pistols, we will fill the ship's boat with men. We determined to row down the coastline to the strand, rather than slog through the mangroves; though we will land on the near side of the wall rather than the palace side; I do not wish to creep with ten sea-legged tars through that thin underbrush, all within sight of the palace. For myself and two of the lads I brought aboard from my own village – Moran and McTeigue, both kin, McTeigue my own mother's brother's son – I know we have hunted 'cross heath and over moor, through forest and stream and bog, and sure we could move without any more sound than an Irish deer in a spring meadow, once we stiffened our knees on land once more. But the others? Burke could not be silent if he were three days dead, and I doubt rotting in his grave would improve his smell, either, which would reveal his presence and ours as readily as the clanking of his damned manacles. Perhaps I should not bring him along. But that mad bastard of an Englishman is the bloodiest savage I have ever seen in a fight, and we do not know what we may face. Perhaps the very stones will rise up. Maybe the grounds are sown with dragon's teeth, as Jason and his Argonauts faced, soldiers springing from the earth itself. We will have need of Burke and his swinging chains. And should he take a mortal hurt in the fight, well.

I will wish ill on no man. I do hope to take the palace without shot fired or blood spilled.

We go now. Gods be with their beloved Gaelic rogues.

***

O, blessed be the angels of Ireland that look over their proud, bonny sons, even in this other world! Christ and Dagda, blessed St. Brendan and St. Patrick, too: why can you not draw back that curtain of fear that lays over all struggles of blood and iron, that terror that has put more men in the ground than any plague, any famine, any tyrant in the annals of history? Is bravery not enough? Strength, celerity, skill with arms? Must we overcome the *madness* of fear, as well?

Ah, I know very well whence came the cause of this hurly-burly I have just waded through: 'tis just that my men are not soldiers. They are pirates. And pirates fight with boiling blood and roaring curses, the hack and slash of the cutlass and the blast of the thrice-charged blunderbuss; we do not know the discipline of Cromwell's New Model Army, and would spit on it if given the chance. But I would never wish to be faced with the sight of my men charging at me with red eyes and shining swords: 'tis a braw sight, to be sure, even from amongst 'em. But 'tis a mad sight, as well. Gods damn me, what a brou-ha-ha that was.

We rowed through the calm, placid water, like one of O'Flaherty's bloody fine folk in a pleasure craft on the Thames. We came to the strand, we landed and found the wall; I crossed, leaving the men ready at a word to swarm over and bring wrack and ruin along. I found Lynch, waiting, soaked in sweat but with his powder dry and his hand steady: he had my pistols drawn and primed, both aimed at the palace's glass walls, where we first saw the sorceress queen. He saw me come, signaled with a tip of one barrel before he leveled his aim once more. I made my way to him, thanked him for his alertness, and asked for his report.

"The palace, Captain," he said, then cleared his dry throat with a soft rumble. "The Palace is not empty."

Log #7: Assault on the Palace of Glass

Captain's Log
Date: 26th of June, 1678
Location: Careened on beach at Glass Palace Cove
Conditions: Safe at last. In need of repairs.

Though I intend this log to serve as something of a sailor's tale, a written record of our fantastic voyage, I must first and foremost keep the records of this ship. Thus: we have taken the Glass Palace, with a minimum of casualties but with more chaos than might be wished; the *Grace of Ireland* is drawn up on the beach before us, securely lashed, and is being scraped and cleaned. We must find the means to repair the hole in her, and the weakened planks and joins, and then she will be seaworthy once more. Until then, we have food and water, a clear view of the approach of enemies, by land or by sea. We are secure.

I did not foresee this outcome when I crouched in the shrubbery by Lynch, and heard his report that the palace was no longer devoid of inhabitants. I paused long enough to offer a brief string of my most pungent curses, a supplication to the gods of Ireland and a tribute to the patron deities of buccaneers. Then I took one pistol from Lynch, matched his aim, and pressed for details.

"'Tis a woman – only one, Captain. But I don't know if she will call out the guards, or what horrible things may come at her beck if she be an enchantress. She came in another of those growling beasts, which now waits at rest to landward."

I clapped him on the shoulder. The men can never see their captain unsure or indecisive; it saps their courage when they need it most. "Come. The time for watching is done."

We moved quickly back over the wall to where the men waited, and then I laid out my battle plan, with Lynch's help describing the terrain and the targets. When all knew their bidden tasks, Lynch led us back over the wall, and at a creep through the shrubbery until we could spy the beast-wagon Lynch had seen the woman arriving in. It was a dingy green, long and low to the ground, and looked not unlike a great serpent; I feared it may prove as deadly and insidious, as well.

O'Flaherty's eyes widened when he saw it, but he nodded, his jaw firm, when I whispered, "Ye will be ready, aye?"

"Aye," he whispered back, and directed his men to their stations and tasks. I nodded and left, with Lynch, McTeigue, and Kelly following.

We crouched in the shrubbery, as close as we could come to the seaward door – the incredible glass portal through which we had first seen the Faerie Queen. The curtains, which I had mistaken for rippled metal, were closed once more, which suited our purposes admirably. I took a second pistol from Kelly, whose main task involved only his boarding-axe and the strength of his great bear-like frame, half a head taller than I and twice as wide, with arms and legs like tree trunks. With only one eye, as well, the man would not be performing any feats of marksmanship, which were better left to Lynch, McTeigue, and I, the three men aboard most likely to hit any chosen target howsoever small. I pointed at the place we would strike, and then we waited.

It was not long, no more than half a minute, before we heard a roar from O'Flaherty, followed by the crash and thunder of muskets as the lads fired a broadside at their target. We were out and running, swift and silent as foxes, our eyes racing over the palace windows and walls, seeking any spying eye in hopes we could put a ball in it before the alarm was raised on this side. But anyone's attention could not but be drawn to landward, as the first roar of the guns was followed by a bellow not far quieter, as Burke led a charge from the bushes. We heard the crash of his chains against metal, and the shattering of glass; a strange bugling sound arose, and was followed by the discharge of more flintlocks.

On the seaward side, we made it to the terrace and paused to wait for Kelly. The great brute was still half in his cups from the whiskey that O'Grady feeds him with his morning biscuit (Aye, I know of it, though they believe themselves surreptitious. A captain knows his crew and his ship, else he doesn't live long enough to learn. Kelly's wound festered, for all Vaughn could do, and the pain of it near drove him mad. Too, O'Grady became cook when he traded his man's leg for one of wood, and threw in his hearing, as well, when the cannon he was manning held a spark and detonated the charge even as it was rammed home – while O'Grady's face was laid alongside it so he could examine the carriage, which was cracked. The cannon fired, the carriage failed; O'Grady became deaf and lame, and a cook instead of a gunner's mate – a life of biscuit and porridge, of darkness in the galley rather than glory on the cannons, and of pity rather than honor. He knows that Kelly fears the same loss, that our best fighter will be reduced for the loss of an eye, and his shadow will shrink under him; and so there is whiskey in his water-mug. A clever man might note that I have allowed this to continue. He might see, as well, who I chose to lead the charge.). Though Kelly could move as softly as Lynch, McTeigue, and I, he was not as fleet of foot, and so as we three drew to a halt on the terrace, he was still in the open. I looked back and saw his eye wildly spinning in its socket, and sweat streaming down his face, his mouth open in a grimace of anguish. He was terrified of what he saw, of the palace, the beast-wagon, the glass wall he ran toward, all of it impossible – and yet his captain asked him to throw himself directly into it. His gaze fell on mine for the briefest instant, and then he snapped his teeth together and roared through them like a snarling bull. He quickened his steps and lowered his shoulder, obviously intending, with all the cleverness of a man on the edge of panic – and of a drunk with something to prove – to burst bodily through the glass, rather than hack through the door's latch, as I had ordered. I barely had time to call his name before he was on the terrace and past me, his face turned away and eye tight shut as he threw his formidable weight into his bull rush, a man-shaped avalanche thrown at a mere pane of glass.

All that mass of man hit the Faerie glass: and *bounced*. His head flew into the portal with a thrum like a hawser when a sail snaps tight in high wind, and he flew back onto the terrace as fast as he had run across it, unconscious and limp. The three of us stood dumbfounded, looking as one from Kelly, to the glass door, back to Kelly. Back to the door.

The bloody thing wasn't even cracked.

"Sod this," McTeigue snarled, and aimed one of his pistols at the center of the door. A good man, he paused long enough to flicker his eyes at me; I nodded – we had already raised too much hullabaloo, and we must get inside immediately – and he fired.

The glass cracked, at least. But it did not shatter. Rather the lead ball did, and the shards stuck in the glass pane like flies caught in a spider's web.

Bloody enchanted faeries and their bloody enchanted glass.

I could still hear the hurly-burly from O'Flaherty's men, and so hope was not lost for my plan. I dropped my own pistols and swept up the axe from where Kelly had dropped it. My strongest swing, straight at the point where McTeigue's ball had cracked it, was enough to craze the glass from edge to edge; a second swing, thus heartened by apparent success, finally shattered it entire. A blast of cool air washed over me, and I shivered. Only with wonder that the palace could be cool inside while the sun burned down so fiercely: surely no more than that. I retrieved my pistols, and led the way in, ignoring Lynch as he muttered, "If the cursed *glass* be that strong, what will it take to shatter the guards?"

As we stepped through into the cool shade of the palace's interior – which smelled of fruit and flowers and exotic spices – I saw a head vanish behind a closing door. "Owen!" I shouted, pointing McTeigue at the door; he nodded and raced to it, bursting the latch with his shoulder – fortunately with more success than Kelly had found with the enchanted glass – and was gone in pursuit. Lynch and I swept our eyes around the room, saw no hazard, and leapt through the doorway into the next chamber, the which we had never clapped eyes on before. It was a dining-hall, and a well-appointed one at first glance. But we sought guards, not crockery and wall-hangings, and we moved on. A swinging door led to a dimly lit hallway – though to be sure, the entire palace was brighter than any Irish house I had stepped into; 'twas dim now in the main because of the bright sunlight dazzling our eyes but moments before – the air growing ever cooler as we moved deeper into the palace. I feared we might encounter true winter at its heart, walls rimed white, snow drifting from the ceiling; and I tried to quell the racing of my heart at the thought.

The hallway widened, opening into what I thought a greeting-room of some sort – though my knowledge of palatial architecture is somewhat limited. Light shone down through great windows set in the ceiling, thirty feet above us; a broad staircase led up and the walls beyond opened up into rooms, one on either side. Straight ahead was a door that looked like the portal we had seen the Faerie Queen emerge from with her pink traveling boxes: our goal. "'Ware guards!" I shouted to Lynch, who dropped to one knee and spun to cover my back, while I raced to the door to let in our fellows. I grasped the handle and pulled, but it would not open; I took a moment to calm myself, and then examined the latches, of which there were several, though no bar. I turned one lock and detached a thin chain – but it was not until I *turned the handle* that the door opened. I shook my head. "We're not in Ireland any more," I muttered as I threw the door wide and stepped out to see what had befallen my men.

As I live and breathe, I swear I do not know what I saw then. Mayhap it was an artifice, a mechanical of some sort, broken and shattered to pieces by axe and cutlass and swinging chain. Mayhap it was a dragon lying slain before me, pierced by many holes from musket and pistol, its dark blood oozing out and soaking the ground beneath it; a stench like whale oil and turpentine filled the air. But I do know that whatever it was, it was now quite properly destroyed: shattered glass and bits of metal were scattered far and wide, and five full-grown men were jumping up and down on top of it and yelling curses and assorted maritime foulnesses while my bosun and quartermaster looked on like proud parents at a Mayday dance.

I will not say which of the two was the mother. Nor decide if the feminine title is the greater insult, or rather the implication that the other would marry such a hideous brute.

It did not matter. The time for noisy distraction was over. Clearly nothing had emerged from the barn-shed, and no unexpected patrol had charged down the road. Now we had to secure the palace. A roar of "AVAST!" was enough to halt the hornpipe of destruction being pounded out atop the wagon-beast's carcass, and a curt wave of my hand brought the men rushing in, though I plucked MacManus by the sleeve and told him off to keep a watch on the road that led up to the palace door. To the others I called, "Spread out and search for enemies! No plunder yet! Lynch, Moran, Burke – upstairs." I was relieved to hear Burke murmur a most respectful "Aye, Captain," as he came through the door past me, and he took the lead up the stairs, flanked and covered by Lynch's pistols and Moran's blunderbuss. The man becomes calm and tractable only after he is allowed to destroy something utterly – then and only then is he a model subordinate.

"Christ in Heaven," O'Flaherty murmured as he came in and surveyed the interior of the palace. "No wonder you thought this was Faerie-Land." He reached out and touched a mirror on the wall, the smoothest and finest I had ever seen, and with a silver frame that would pay for a month's supply for the *Grace* and her crew even without the perfect glass it surrounded. "Who lives in such wealth but a royal?" he asked.

"We do," I replied. I gestured outside at the pitiful wreckage he and the men had left. "'Tis surely dead now, but did it live?"

He shrugged and shook his head. "I know not. When we fired the first volley, it hissed at us, and seemed to lower one shoulder, as a bull will when it turns to charge. We didn't have the time to determine what it meant: Burke ran to it and had its eyes with his chains, in one fell crossing-stroke." He turned to look out at the remains. He frowned. "We fired again, and it let out a trumpeting – did ye hear it?"

I nodded. "Aye. That was the beast?"

"Aye, but it lasted only a moment. Perhaps 'twas its death cry, or perhaps it called for help. I know not." He shook his head again, a man with a memory he would throw aside if he could. "I know it made my blood run cold, and the men's, as well. If Burke hadn't charged, and lived, I think we all might have broken and run. But courage prevailed, even if a mad thrashing was all we had thought for in our bewildered heads. Sure and it made a grand noise when the boys were atop it, though. Did it serve? Ye seem unblooded; were ye undetected?"

"Aye, all well." I looked back inside; my men were gathering back in the hallway, weapons lowered, all looking mystified and befuddled. "There's nobody here, Captain," Carter called out, and Sweeney grunted agreement. Burke appeared at the top of the stairs. "Not a bloody damn soul," he growled.

"Well, and there is *one*," McTeigue called out as he came from the shadowed end of the hall. He had a woman by one arm, his pistol in the other hand; he cast her down at our feet. She fell to her knees with a cry, and then crouched there, shivering and weeping, her eyes huge as she looked around at us. She wore a drab grey-blue dress with a white apron; her skirt was too short for decency, though quite a bit longer than what the Faerie Queen had flaunted about in. She was youngish, with dark hair and eyes, and brown skin, though not so brown as a Moor or an African. Perhaps she was a Turk? Of course, if she were Fae, how could a man know what her coloring signified?

McTeigue reached into his sash and withdrew a small object, which he held out to me. "She was praying into this," he said. "I did not know the tongue – perhaps Italian or Spanish, from the sound of it. She held it thus," and he pressed the object to his cheek, near his ear. Then he gave it to me.

It was a small plaque, rectangular and flat, the size of my palm. It was made of some strange material, not as hard as metal or fired pottery, warmer to the touch than stone. Perhaps bone? But it was black. It lacked grain, and so was not wood – unless perhaps it was lacquered in some way. On one side a piece of glass was inset, with a tiny picture painted on it – or under it? there were words and numbers that made no sense to me, though I knew the script.

"She was praying into it?" I asked.

McTeigue nodded. "She was kneeling in a closet, speaking fast and low, rocking back and forth. Looked like praying to me."

I looked at the glass plaque. "Have any of you heard of a heathen god called – Verizon?"

Log #8: Counterattack

"Have any of you heard of a heathen god called – Verizon?"

All shook their heads. I stepped close to the shivering woman. "Do you understand me? Do you speak English?" *Do you even speak the tongue of Man,* I wanted to ask, but I could not tell: was this in truth Faerie-Land? She was plain to look at, no great beauty in her face and form, and if the only magic she could summon to defend herself was prayer to a piece of glass the size of my palm, then this could not be the land under the hill, which was as O'Flaherty's objects had implied. But then, how could this palace be explained? This wealth, lying about unguarded but by a single terrified woman? What were those beastly machines outside? The magic mirror-wall that showed lands that were not those without these walls? The cabinet of light?

She nodded in answer to my question, but said, "*See,*" which made no sense to me. Perhaps she was simple, or deranged. I held the plaque out to her. "What is this? Who is Verizon?"

She looked at the plaque, then at me, her brows furrowed in confusion. "Tell Eff-oh know," she said slowly, and then ran a string of words together, not a one of which I understood. Her tone was pleading, terrified; whatever she was, whatever she was saying, she was surely no threat to us.

I ignored her as she kept babbling, and turned to McTeigue. "Go check on Kelly. Try to secure the door we came through. Stand guard there, the two of you." Then to O'Flaherty: "Leave me three others to guard, and take the rest back to the *Grace.* Sail her to the cove, and we'll beach her and careen." He nodded, told off Lynch, Burke, and MacManus to remain, and led the others out the landward door and over the north wall.

I crouched down by the still-gobbling woman. "Stop," I said, and when she did not, I grabbed her shoulders and shook her. I hoped she was not hysterical; I did not want to strike her. She stopped her babbling and met my gaze, though she shivered and shook and worried her lip with her teeth. Speaking slowly and clearly, I said, "Be there anyone else here?"

After a moment she shook her head. She started babbling again, but another shake made her stop. "Are there guards? Soldiers? *Any* men?" She frowned, seeming not to understand, but then she shook her head again. "*No* men? No guards?"

"No," she said. "No pole lease."

I frowned, and looked to Lynch and Burke, who now stood close by. "No palace?" I asked them. "Is that what she said?" They shrugged.

This was profiting us nothing. We needed to secure our position. I held the plaque out to the woman, and she reached up her hand for it; then I dropped it and stamped my heel down. It shattered most satisfactorily, and she flinched away. I grabbed her chin and turned her to face me. "Verizon cannot hear you now," I told her. I straightened and turned to Burke. "Watch her. Don't hurt her – she may be a hostage for us, if there are troops about." He nodded, and rattled his chains menacingly at her; she shrank back from his grotesque leer, but did not move away or try to escape him.

I turned to Lynch. "Go up top. Try to reach the roof, or a parapet. See what you can see from –"

I was interrupted. *"Captain!"* called MacManus, still guarding the landward door. I beckoned Lynch to follow, and strode to where MacManus crouched by the open portal, a loaded musket in his hands. He was peering out with one eye, all else concealed behind the doorframe. "Aye?" I asked.

"We have guests," he said, and nodded outdoors. I moved to the other side of the doorway and looked out, but I could hear it now; a single glance showed me what my ears had already discerned.

Another beast-wagon, this one white, came roaring up the path, raising a cloud of dust as it growled and snarled. The things were common here as ponies, it seemed. It came to a halt with a shrill screech as soon as it spied the corpse of its fellow. The sides of the wagon opened, and two men stepped out.

"Ready arms," I told my men, and we three took aim.

Then a second beast, a black one, came growling down the road and stopped by the first; four men emerged from this one – all armed.

I tapped Lynch on the shoulder where he crouched beneath me beside the doorway. "Get McTeigue. Tell Burke to bring the woman up here, under control." Lynch nodded and scampered off.

"See any powder?" I asked MacManus.

He nodded, but did not lower his aim. "Aye, the one in the blue head-scarf has a pistol." He blinked. "I *think* 'tis a pistol, any road."

"Him first, aye?"

"Aye aye, Captain," he confirmed, and cocked back the flintlock.

The men gathered around the wreckage of the green wagon-beast, looking furious but bewildered. They spoke rapidly and loudly, gesturing to the house, the carcass, and each other; they spoke the same tongue as the woman. All were of the same race, it seemed: the same skin and hair and eyes. The one with the blue scarf carried a strange but unmistakable pistol; the others had but knives and bludgeons. We had a clear advantage, then, though we were outnumbered.

Just then Lynch and McTeigue scurried up behind. Lynch took a position under a window to MacManus's right, and readied his pistols; I was glad to see his hands were steady despite his youth.

"Kelly is recovered. He will hold the sea-side," McTeigue told me, and relief spread through me. This might have been a threat to us: the man with the pistol could hold us here – I had to assume he had other pistols, perhaps strapped to the beast in something like saddle-scabbards – while the others crept in the back and engaged us hand to hand; but I would pit Kelly against all the rest, even if he hadn't had an axe and a cutlass and a narrow doorway to stand in. With those, I knew the only way into the house was through the four of us here.

Or perhaps to shatter one of the many wide windows and reach our unguarded flank. Gods, this was the barest, most vulnerable keep I have ever struck. I knew that we must handle this here, face to face: we could not bear a siege.

"Ready with the hostage, Captain," I heard Burke growl. I turned and saw that he had his chains wrapped around her, one pinioning her elbows to her sides, the other about her throat. One pull of his arms would snap her neck – and the look in her eyes showed that she knew it.

"All right," I said. "Stand her in the doorway, Burke. Stay behind her lest they fire. MacManus – if that pistol comes up, the man goes down. Lynch, Owen, stand ready if they charge." All of them nodded and grunted assent, and prepared themselves. I called out, "Drop your arms!" and nodded to Burke. He shoved the woman out into the doorway, pulling back on the chain about her throat just as she called out "Juan!"

"Flora!" came the answering cry, and then more in that foreign tongue – Spanish, I thought now, if I had heard their names aright. That made sense if we were in the Indies, but then nothing else made sense with that. I glanced around the edge of the open portal and saw that all held still, that one of the two from the first wagon held back the other, who pulled toward Burke and the woman, his manner showing the desperation of either a brother or a lover.

The man with the pistol raised it and snarled, "You motherf–" A shot boomed, a puff of black smoke from MacManus's flintlock, and the man flew back, his pistol falling to the ground – fortunately not discharging when it fell – with his life's blood as it poured from the hole in his chest. MacManus swung the musket around and handed it to Lynch, who gave over one of his ready pistols without missing a step; he had spent a full year as a powder monkey, hauling charge and shot for the big guns, and reloading muskets and pistols for the men, and though he had proven himself capable of standing on the firing line, still old habits live long and grip hard, especially in the heat of battle. In moments the flintlock was leaning against the wall ready to MacManus's hand, and Lynch was back under the window with his second pistol ready, a naked dagger in his left hand.

The effect of MacManus's marksmanship was most salutary: all the men dropped their weapons and raised their hands – all but the first two, who still struggled together, one to reach the woman, the other to keep him alive instead, as McTeigue and I planted our aim on his breast.

"If you want to live, stand still!" I shouted.

"Let her go, you son of a bitch!" the man in front shouted in response. His address to me clearly showed his failure to comprehend his circumstances.

I took up a more cheerful tone while I explained to him. "Ye have little room to stand on demands, boyo. Perhaps ye should do as I say, and hope to earn some of my goodwill." I noted the rearguard were beginning to sidle back to their dragon-wagon. I did not want them raising an alarm, returning with more men – especially not once the *Grace* was beached and vulnerable. "Shane," I murmured to MacManus, "did ye learn how to kill those metal beasts?"

He blinked. "Anything what takes punishment like that'll no' work so very well afters," he muttered back. "But the feet are soft."

"And the eyes," Burke growled from the doorway where he still held the woman immobile, between himself and the men outside.

"Aye, and the eyes – the round bits in front," MacManus whispered.

"Kill it, then – the one in the rear, the black one. All on my mark." I took aim. "Left foot is mine."

"Right foot," called Lynch, easing one eye up over the sill.

"Left eye," said McTeigue.

"Let her *go*, you bastards! FLORA!"

"Fire."

Four shots barked as one, and the front of the black wagon-beast exploded with a crash of glass and a harsh sibilance; a thin plume of vapor spurted from the foot where my ball struck home, and a thicker spurt of steam from the middle of the metal grate where the beast's nose should be, which must have been MacManus's target. Lynch cursed; he had missed. The rest of us chuckled and tossed our guns to him to reload.

Once again, our gunnery was effective. The three in back stopped creeping away, and the two before stopped struggling and were still. The white beast-wagon did nothing at all; perhaps after all, they did not live.

"Down on your knees, my fine lads – don't believe we're out of shot in here. Or that you will fare any better than yon metal beast – for rest assured, the next pull of the trigger will spill your guts on the ground. You're of no use to us, dead or alive, so all's the same, to my way of thinking. Dead's quieter."

McTeigue made a thoughtful noise and then said loudly, "Aye, but messier. They'll bleed all over the stonework, if we shoot them now." I glanced over at my cousin, and he winked. I had to hold back a laugh.

"Aye, 'tis a fair point," I said. "You gentle souls – take five slow steps back. Any of you who does not move will cost this sweet lass a finger – but move too quick, and it will be her neck."

They stepped back smart enough, but stopped at five steps.

"Lynch – go bring Kelly up here, and take his station." The youth scurried away on my whisper. I tapped McTeigue, and we stepped out to flank Burke, pistols aimed at the foremost two. MacManus, his iron reloaded by the nimble fingers of Lynch, could bring down all of the other three in mere moments.

But whatever else these asses were, whether human or Fae, colonists or slaves or Spaniards, they were not fighting men. They charged into unknown danger like daft fools, and then surrendered as quick as chastised children confronted by an irate sire.

I looked at the lead fool, the angriest one. "On your knees, there, lad. Or my bosun will snap her neck." I clapped Burke on the shoulder, and he grinned his hideous grin.

The fool frowned, but he went to his knees. Docile as a lamb, they were: all the other four knelt as well. I noticed they could not take their eyes off of their dead companion; had they never seen a man shot before?

"Captain," Kelly rumbled from behind me.

"Kelly – find something to bind them with."

"Aye."

"Owen – go gather their arms. Bring me that *pistola*."

McTeigue stepped out cautiously, swinging well wide of the choleric one so the man would not be tempted to try for McTeigue's pistol. He took the strange pistol from the ground beside the dead man's hand, and tucked it into his sash. He gathered up the knives and clubs the others had dropped, stepping back from them quickly with his arms awkwardly full; but not a one of them moved. As he returned to me, Kelly emerged, tearing strips of cloth off of what might be a curtain, or a bedsheet, perhaps.

"Start with him," I said, gesturing with my barrel before I stuck the pistol into my sash and took the strange weapon McTeigue brought me. "Don't be gentle."

At the word, Kelly stomped on the angry fool's ankle, twisted back and under him, and there was a crunch. Then Kelly's great hamfist clouted the fool on the side of his neck, and he collapsed like a sack of grain.

"Juan!" the woman called out tearfully, and Burke pulled the chain taut around her throat, stopping any other syllables short of her lips. Kelly ignored her, as well as the other front man, the one who had held the angry Juan back from his fool's charge, and who now cursed Kelly from the sole of his feet to the crown of his head and back to his ancestors. Kelly rolled the stunned Juan onto his belly, pinioned his arms and lashed him securely. Then he stepped to the cursing one and waited for the man's breath to run out. Then he called out to me, "Gentle or no?"

"'Tis his choice," I replied. Kelly curled his paw into a fist under the fool's nose, and rumbled in a voice like thunder, "Smell ye that, aye? If ye think it smells bad now, just think of the stench after I reach into your belly and tear out your liver and lights to bait me hooks with."

The fool's dark skin faded pale, and he quieted, his eyes locked on Kelly's huge, scarred – and surely odoriferous – fist. He placed his hands behind his back, wrists crossed, and hung his head.

"Aye, and that's well," Kelly rumbled. "I prefer gentle, I do."

"'Tis not what your last whore said!" called McTeigue, in great good humor now that the battle was done, and won. MacManus and Burke guffawed at this.

Kelly was unperturbed. "So ye had occasion to speak to your sister, then?" he asked, and then all of us laughed, McTeigue as well.

The other three chose gentle as well, and before long we had all of them inside, seated with their backs to the wall. Juan had awakened, but his anger was mollified when I had Burke remove his chains from the throat of the maid Flora, and had her trussed and seated by Juan's side. He still was not cheerful, as Kelly had seemingly cracked his ankle, but he answered my questions fair enough, and in English, without my having to threaten the lass more than twice.

I learned all I could from him, and had just ordered Kelly and Burke to lay them out in one of the chambers and lock them in, when a cry from Lynch at the seaward door brought light and joy fully into my heart.

"Captain!" he called. "Sails ahoy! 'Tis the *Grace*, Captain! She comes!"

I sent McTeigue out to join MacManus watching to landward, and then Lynch and I stepped out onto the terrace to welcome our ship and our companions. As it has seemed to me since I first beheld her, I cannot conceive a more beautiful sight than my *Grace*.

I still do not know where we are. But for now: we are safe.

Log #9: Information. And More Questions.

Captain's Log
Date: 26th of June
Location: Coast of Florida, America, near Miyammy (20 mi. south)
Conditions: Landbound until repairs completed. The *Grace* cannot sail.

The condition of the ship is more dire than I had heretofore suspected. O'Gallows momentarily patched the hole and saved the ship, but he could not have fixed the loosened planks around it. They near sprang off the ship with the barest tug. I do think that, had that storm lasted one hour more, my sweet ship would be at the bottom even now.

The scraping proceeds apace, and we are cleaning out the water barrels and refilling them. The palace's supplies are meager, at best; we will empty the larder within a day or two. We must find a source of food and good timber for our repairs. If our information may be trusted, then all that we need may be within reach: but I think that unlikely.

'Tis now the morning after the battle, such as it was. I did essay my sextant after dawn, and marked a reading of 25 Degrees North, but I do not know if the sun and horizon are the same to which I am used, and therefore are my measurements suspect. I have no chart to mark our position on, in any case, and thus cannot guess at our longitude. All of our information must be suspect until we have a source of knowledge which we can trust. I am not familiar with this feeling: in Ireland, in Irish seas, I am the fountainhead of knowledge, or my men are; long familiarity grants us all the surety we need. Of course we know where we are: we recognize that spit of land over there, and the stars overhead, or the shape of the winds and currents. One does not need to question what one knows of home: the mere fact that it is *home* is proof. This is a feeling, most joyful, that I did not recognize until it was lost to me.

Last night, after we careened the *Grace* and made her fast, we celebrated our survival: we emptied the whiskey stores aboard and found a few good bottles in the Palace. One called *Tequila* was most popular. O'Flaherty and I sampled the wine selection, finding it more than adequate to our needs.

It was a grand celebration. For all the men we lost, still our musicians survived, they being my cousin Liam Finlay, and Arthur Gallagher and Roger Desmond, playing the flute, fiddle, and drums. They played many a fine air – "Roger the Cavalier," "Sail On, Sail on, Sailor Laddie," "The Roving Exile," and "Willie was a Wanton Wag" among them. They trilled everything from country jigs and reels, to the melancholy songs of the hills of Ireland. Many eyes were damp at that: we all long for home, and the drunker we got, the more we longed and the easier we wept. But Ian O'Gallows, our shanty-man, leapt up as the night grew most engloomed, and sang us a rousing hornpipe, while Kelly and Lynch danced, to much laughter and loud roars of approval. Somehow the great brute's feet proved near as quick as the slender boy's, and at the finish, Kelly made a step of his hands, which Lynch leapt off from, and Kelly tossed him a full man's height above his own into the air. Lynch turned two full flips and landed on his feet with a royal flourish, to great approbation. I cannot think when those two have found time to practice the move, but sure it was well polished before this night, when Kelly was already too far gone in the whiskey to have planned anything beyond putting down his feet and then picking them up again – and indeed, when the dance was done, even that sequence proved troubling for the man, who stumbled and fell back into his seat by the fire. Ah, but Lynch's eyes were sparkling with joy as he bowed for our cheers and cries; he'll be a right champion with the ladies, if we find any worth the wooing.

Vaughn had examined our few injuries: Kelly's head, which he declared as rock-hard as ever and his brains no more addled than before; O'Finnegan had a cut on his cheek near his eye from a shard of glass or metal from the wagon-beast; the prisoner, Juan, had a broken ankle which Vaughn set and bound for him. After seeing to those, Vaughn explored and examined every inch of the palace, busily scribbling away in his notebook as he went. I must remember to ask him to share his notes for this recollection of our voyage; I think the man's observations would be most useful.

The prisoner, though forthcoming, has not been entirely helpful. As often as not, my questions confused him. I know not if the cause is his shabby command of the English tongue, or if he is an imbecile. Perhaps both.

I began by asking who he was and why he had come. The Palace maid, Flora, was indeed his sister; the man who had arrived in the same wagon-beast as he, who had held the headstrong Juan back and thus saved his life, was their younger brother, Ignacio; the family name was Lopez. The other four men – three, now – were friends of theirs from what he called the Neighborhood, which I took to be the name of his village. He became rather strident, insisting that we faced future vicissitudes owing to the death of the man in the blue head-scarf, shot by MacManus; he said that the Latin lions would come looking for "payback." This was his word for "vengeance," it seemed, or perhaps "justice." I know not if he speaks of a military unit, perhaps picked troops, or of some other group of men; he was not clear on the point, merely referring repeatedly to Latin lions. He said these seven bravos came to the Palace because Maid Flora called them, on her telleffono, which I could not make sense of though I render it here as he did say it. She must have some means of signaling which we had not seen, and they did not wish to reveal; I ensured that we have a close watch kept for further attempted incursions, by lions or men, and resolved to discuss it with Vaughn and Ian.

I asked Juan Lopez where we were, and he responded with "Matheson Preserve," though he could not tell me who Matheson is or was, nor what was preserved or preserving. He said we were about twenty miles south of a place called Miyammy, a city, but when I asked for the latitude, he was flustered. I asked if he and his companions were Spaniards, and he answered affirmatively, but only after a longish and suspicious pause. Then he added "We're Dominican." I presumed that to mean they adhere to a certain church; certainly a Popish one, if they are Spaniards. When I asked what country this Miyammy owed allegiance to, he said, "America." But when I said, "The British Colonies?" as simple confirmation, he became more confused. Finally he asked if I referred to Bermuda, or the British Virgin Islands (At which name some of my men in range of hearing grew quite intrigued); he said these two locales were far away, that one would have to "fly" there.

I inquired as to the local strength of the Royal Navy or the Armada, hoping to ascertain whether England or Spain held greater sway in these contested waters; his only response was a shrug and a shake of his head. Then Ignacio, his brother, volunteered the intelligence that there was a naval base by Fort Lauderdale, to the north, but he knew nothing of royal ships near Miyammy. I asked if there were marines, or other troops nearby, but they were puzzled once more. Then one of the others stated that there was a National Guards barracks in Miyammy; I took that to mean we were within a day's ride of a military troop. We must therefore repair the *Grace* and leave here soon. As soon as it is manageable.

As to the repairs, I pressed the prisoners for information regarding the location of supplies, both foodstuffs and good seasoned timber, as well as a carpenter we might hire. Strangely, they did not know of a local carpenter, though when I asked if they were recent arrivals, they claimed to have lived here for all of their lives, but for Flora, who had recently come from "the D.R." But one of the others spoke up, saying we could find timber at a place called Home Dee-Poe; he said they would have a carpenter there, or at least someone with some expertise. I presume there are many carpenters in this Miyammy, but that is apparently where the troops are, as well, and thus is to be avoided. I pressed for detailed instructions on how we could find this Home Dee-Poe, and also a store which held foodstuffs, which they insisted on referring to as Piggly Wiggly. I presume the locals hereabouts raise hogs as their favored livestock. Perhaps they wallow in the swamps to escape the sun's heat.

Today we will divide once more. I will send O'Gallows, Carter, and Sweeney to this Piggly Wiggly; they will carry some of the valuables from the Glass Palace to trade for foodstuffs. Moran is organizing a battery on the strand guarding the cove, and we have fortified the landward entrance of the Palace. I will send O'Flaherty, Burke, and eight more to this Home Dee-Poe (Perhaps it is Homme de Poe? Are there Frenchmen in this place?), where they will have to find a carpenter and hire his services without giving away our nature or current vulnerable position, convince him to return with them, and bring whatever supplies he will need to fix our ship. I will remain here and consult with Vaughn; I can no longer put off the satisfaction of my curiosity. I must know where we are, and how we came to be here.

Log #10: A Magic Window and Food from the Pig

Captain's Log
Date: 27th of June
Location: Glass Palace
Conditions: Ominous

I can no longer trust O'Flaherty.

I have never warmed to the man; though he saved the lives of my men, including my cousin Hugh, since he came aboard the *Grace* he has ever seemed knotted with subterfuge. His introduction of the position of Quartermaster, a Caribbean invention with no place on a good Irish ship, and his near-instantaneous assumption of that position, were close enough to mutiny to have him strung to the yardarm and shot in the belly on many another ship. But I always knew that his intentions toward the ship and crew were only for their benefit, and his decisions, while often counter to my own conceits and predilections, and sometimes deserving of the name *Rash*, still they were ever reasonable.

Until now. Now I can only name him a fool and pray he hasn't doomed us.

But I must needs tell all.

I must not fail to record Vaughn's discovery. His investigative methods may deserve to be called foolish and rash as well as O'Flaherty does; I remain unconvinced that he had sufficient reason to go prodding about the magical implements of the Palace and its absent mistress, and as my orders expressly forbade any interaction with any unrecognizable object, Vaughn might be called mutinous as well. But there is nothing of ambition in that man – not for anything but knowledge, any road. If Vaughn crept up behind me on my poop deck and shot me in the back, I know he would have intended it as a scientific experiment: studying the trajectory of the ball, perhaps, or observing the natural reactions of a pirate captain upon being shot in the back. His goal would only be publication in his Royal Society, the approbation of Christopher Wren and Robert Hooke; he would offer me a share of that same recognition as recompense as I lay dying. All he thinks of is science and curiosity and discovery; his presence on this ship owes much to that singularity of purpose, and how it has blinded him to practical considerations in his past. But that is another tale.

This tale begins three turns of the glass after my two expeditions had set off: O'Gallows to the north seeking food, O'Flaherty south-west after lumber and carpenter. I was examining Moran's gun emplacement – a nice piece of work, that; I gain more confidence in my cousin's ability and foresight with each task I set him, and of course his loyalty has ever been beyond question – when Lynch came running along the strand, calling out for me with an excitement that bordered on hysteria. I saw at once that though there was some fear in his eyes and in the shivering of his youthful voice, wonder glowed in his smile, and so I ordered him to stop and take deep breaths until I was finished with Moran. Though I did hurry then, to compliment Moran on his work, and order more powder and shot carried out to his emplacement, and I did run back to the Palace with Lynch cleaving to my heels all the way.

As I came into the Palace, I was greeted with a fanfare, a flourish of trumpets fit for a king: as flattering as it was mysterious, if I may say. From whence did it come? We have no horns, nor men who know their playing. As I was about to call out to Vaughn for an explanation, my sight adjusted to the dim interior after the bright sunlight without, and I saw the surgeon, and behind him the reason for Lynch's wonder.

The magic window was alight.

In it I saw an image of madness: it appeared to be grown men running around in their underclothes, which were as brightly colored as any noblewoman's ball gown, chasing after a child's ball, which they kicked, and hit with their foreheads and threw themselves on the ground after. The image kept changing so rapidly that I fast grew dizzy and had to look away, just as I heard a tremendous cheer as if the king had just stepped onto the field, perhaps himself wearing bright red smallclothes and kicking a ball.

I turned to Vaughn, who was rapt. "Vaughn," I said, but he did not respond. "Vaughn," I repeated louder. Nothing. With a crewman I should have struck him or shouted my loudest in his very ear – but my surgeon was a fellow ship's officer, and more gentleman than all the rest of us. I placed my hand on his arm and said, "Llewellyn?" Then he turned to me.

He nodded slowly. "Yes, Captain."

"How?" I asked, gesturing at the window, which now showed horses splashing through a mountain stream. He held up the flat, knobbed wand which I had seen in the hands of the sorceress. I grew somewhat irate. "My orders were clear: nothing mysterious is to be –"

Vaughn cut me off with an impatient gesture. I swallowed my words. If O'Flaherty's insubordination and foolishness have been good at all, sure they have taught me patience and forbearance.

The Welshman held out the wand, and I saw there were perhaps three dozen knobbly protrusions, pearly gray, projecting from the black wand. As I looked close, I saw that there were words written on the wand beside each protrusion, in white – words and numbers. Vaughn pointed to one knobbly bit at one extreme of the wand: On/Off, it said.

"I pressed that one. None other. Observe." He pointed the wand at the window and mashed his finger on the protrusion.

The window went dark.

He pressed it again, and the window returned; now it showed a group of people eating something fried in oil, and laughing as they ate.

"It was too clearly labeled to do anything other than what it did. *Quod erat demonstrandum.*"

"You don't know that, Llewellyn. It could have brought a trap On, or raised an alarm. It could have turned off the very sun, for all you knew."

He looked at me for a moment. "But it did not."

As I began to speak again, the fanfare played once more, shattering my thoughts. I turned back to the window. The letters "BBC News" unfurled across the face of the glass, along with a strange sketch or perhaps a carving, a frieze or bas-relief of what might have been the world, but – then it was gone, and a man was telling me, "Welcome back." He continued on before I could respond, and though he seemed to speak directly to me, his words descended rapidly into madness, nonsense. But as I turned to Vaughn for any clarification his sharp mind might offer me, he pointed wordlessly back to the window.

Over the man's shoulder was a map, which after a moment I recognized: it was Ireland, and England there below it. It was home. What was the man saying? Something about Euro – perhaps Europa? Receding, or recessing, and austerity. And – was that "pounds?" British pounds?

Was he speaking of treasure? Perhaps a prophecy?

I opened my mouth to ask Vaughn's opinion; when there was the snap of a flintlock, the crash of a pistol charge from behind us. The magic window coughed and spat fire, bright white like falling stars flashing across its face and out through the hole that appeared in the middle of it: a hole the size and shape of a pistol ball. The window went black and dead, small plumes of smoke floating up from its broken face.

Vaughn and I turned slowly to the door, from whence the shot had come.

O'Grady lowered his arm, his hand shaking. His eyes bulging from his reddened face, his teeth set in his lower lip, the corners of his mouth flecked with foam: he looked like a madman. I thought, *Perhaps madness is why he fired a pistol at his captain's back.*

It was apparent that he intended no more than the destruction of the magic window, and so the pistol which had leapt into my hand went back into my sash. I stepped slow and calm to O'Grady; his eyes flicked back and forth between myself and the magic window he had shot. As I reached out and took the pistol from him, slipping it from his fingers without the slightest resistance, his attention focused on me. He shook his head, slowly.

"It is evil, Captain. *Evil.* 'Tis Satan's work, I'm sure. I'm sure! It must be! I be a good, God-fearin' man, Captain, and I cannot abide it. 'Thou shalt not suffer a witch to live –'"

I cut him off with a blow to his ear, followed by a ringing slap to the other cheek. I will not listen to hypocrites quoting from their holy book, citing scripture to their purpose. I will not hear that statement again, whether it is my father speaking of my mother, or one of my pirates speaking of this fey place. Never again.

O'Grady looked daggers at me for the insult to his honor, but a moment of my own stare wilted him like water poured over stiff canvas. I held my stare while his sank down past my chest, past my belt, down to the ground under my feet. I reached out and tapped him in the chest with his pistol's barrel, so he would look at my face, and know what I said – the man reads lips. Then I spoke slowly, but quietly, as he could not hear me in any case. "Firing a gun behind your captain's back may be seen as mutiny, Abram. I could have you hung for it." I paused, but he said nothing – and so perhaps saved his miserable life, as I was not much in the mood for argument. "Perhaps I should have you hung."

He shook his head slowly, his face pale but his jaw set. "It's the Devil's work, sir. You said it yourself when we arrived here, I know you did. We are in Hell, sir." His eyes came back up to mine, and they were fierce once more. "It is a test, sir. A test. We must not use what is placed before us. We must not surrender to the illusions of the Tempter! Knowledge was what he offered Adam and Eve, sir! I – " He faltered and his eyes dropped. "I would not have you fall, Captain." He snorted a weak laugh. "You're a good man, sir, despite your name."

I shook my head. He wasn't mad, it was the world that had gone mad around him, around us all. He was a good Catholic – which was counter to my own thoughts, my own beliefs, but I could not tell him to give up his God and his Church merely because my own faith followed a different path. How could I know that he wasn't right, and I the damned fool? He thought he was protecting me.

But I couldn't let him go without chastisement, or the next man to pull a trigger behind me would not be aiming over my shoulder. I raised his head again with a gesture. "Ten strokes," I told him, and his jaw clenched. "I'll lay them on you," I said, and he relaxed and nodded.

We did it there, to save him the shame of being watched. Vaughn left the room in search of other, less obviously infernal, sources of information. O'Grady took down his shirt, after I retrieved a tarred end of rope, and I gave him ten solid lashes below his shoulderblades. I only drew blood with the last two, and only because no lashing is finished without blood. Then I clapped him on the shoulder, and brought him out to McTeigue, who was supervising the scraping of the *Grace's* keel. McTeigue nodded at my order without blinking it, handed O'Grady a chisel and told him off to a section of barnacled planking. I returned to the great room and awaited the next arrival.

But would it be good news, or another step into madness? How long could we stay here before we all lost our senses?

Fortunately for my nerves, the next return was one of gladness, not madness: we heard a shouted hail from the landward side, and I raced to the front portal to stand beside the men on watch, all of us peering toward the road. O'Gallows came up the path, roaring a hearty greeting, which we returned, gladly. He was flanked by Carter and Sweeney; all three were sweated and red with heat and exertion, but they were hale and grinning for all that – and sweat washes off far easier than does blood, especially one's own.

Each of them was towing a sort of metal cage on wheels, about the size of a deep wheelbarrow, perhaps a one-man handcart as are used to bring vegetables to market. And their carts were piled high with sacks and bags and boxes. Despite their red brows – and some trouble with the carts, which seemed poorly wheeled and stiff-axled – they raced up to the Palace with whoops and shouts of triumph and glad tidings.

They had brought us food. And such food as we had never seen: the largest, most succulent fruits, of the tree, the vine, and the earth; flour as white and fine as any that ever graced a king's larder; sacks full of potatoes as large as a man's fist, some as large as two fists – or one of Kelly's – and meat, cut and red and dripping blood, that brought hunger roaring up from our throats, and had me roaring for O'Grady to drop his chisel and return to his proper station over the cookfires. He had built a galley on the terrace by the waterpool: he had a half-dozen small cookfires set in rings of stones he had gathered from the beach and the gardens, and over each was suspended one of the fine, shining pots he had found in the Palace's kitchen. Our own great black cookpot, O'Grady's favored cooking utensil, was set atop another of the Palace's devices, though this one was not so unfamiliar: it was a firebox, a low metal frame which could be dragged from one space to another. It was made to hold charcoal or wood in a central space surrounded by a wide metal shelf for setting pots on or warming one's feet, and thus one could have a fire in a place that wasn't built for it, as a wooden floor or even the deck of a ship – though an open flame as this was would be sheer folly aboard. The night before, as the men had held their revels around a bonfire on the beach, as proper pirates should, O'Flaherty and I had joined

O'Grady at the firebox, commandeering two of the strange Palace chairs – they seemed to be made of metal frames, with woven cloth strips forming the back and seat, but were far too light and more comfortable than any chair my posterior has experienced heretofore – and warming our feet and our wine mugs on the metal shelf. It made for a fine, if a quiet, celebration.

And speaking of celebration, there was one conspicuous absence from the bounty which O'Gallows had retrieved. "Had they no spirits?" I asked him, once the lack had been noted and bewailed by the men as they unloaded the carts under O'Grady's direction.

Ian shook his head. "No, they had shelves of the stuff, wine and ale and whiskey, shelves a full five paces long and an arm deep – stacked three high. 'Twas enough for a full voyage and a happy crew the whole way. But the proprietor was most adamant that we were not to have any – not a drop." He scratched his head, then his beard; then he looked at his fingernails, his hands; then ran his palms over his vest front and his trews.

"What is it, man? Were ye hurt – are you checking for wounds?" I queried.

He shook his head again, frowning. "No. Tell me, Nate – do I seem over-filthy to you? Do I look the beggar?"

I stepped back and looked him over from bow to stern. "Well, I'll say I've seen you cleaner than now, and closer-shaven. But I've seen ye a damn sight dirtier, too – and even then your rig is far too quality to be a beggar's. Perhaps I'd mistake ye for a highwayman who stole the clothes, but you and the togs strike me as having been in the same dirt at the same time." I looked him in the eye. "Why do ye ask?"

He hawked and spat, and accepted with grateful thanks a mug of clean water that Lynch handed him. After he'd drained the cool draught, he told me of their quest.

"We found the Piggly Wiggly easily enough – yon Dominicans gave a true bearing, and might have earned a small reward, aye?" I nodded, and he went on. "Once we made it to the town and the right street, we should have had trouble missing it: 'tis a building the size of a fort, or a good large meeting hall or church, painted white with a sign as tall as a man, shouting out 'PIGGLY WIGGLY' in bright red letters." I started a laugh, and Ian grinned. "Aye, Nate – and not a pig in sight, not live nor dead." He shrugged.

"We garnered many a stare on our way through town, though it were still early enough for the townsfolk to be about their breakfasts and suchlike, rather than out on the streets. I have not seen streets like those before: every one paved with hard stone, but not a cobble to be seen; it makes no sense at all. And the wagon-beasts – everywhere! All colors, all sizes, some honking like geese, some blowing foul-smelling smoke out their arses. I swear I heard music coming from a few, but it was never a song nor an instrument I could recognize, and I didn't want to draw too much attention by staring and asking foolish questions, as Vaughn would.

"But there were signs naming the streets at every corner, and so we found our way, sure enough. I left Sweeney outside with the arms, so they'd know we meant no harm – I didn't see a single sword nor flintlock on the way through town, not one, though aye, there were few people on the streets for the number of houses and structures. Carter and I went into the Pig – 'twas unguarded and unlocked – and we were hailed, right friendly, as we stood there with our jaws on the floor.   Nate – " he grabbed my arm, his eyes wide – "I swear to Christ and our two damned fathers that you've never seen nor heard of so much food in one place. What we have here isn't a hundredth of it, not one tenth of one hundredth. That place could fill the holds of a dozen ships the size of the *Grace*, and still host a royal procession.

"Any road, we were greeted, as I said, and I asked to see the proprietor – called him the manager, the lad did who spoke to me. And he brought the man out, a wee bespectacled merchant with a fat belly and a bald head, just as you'd expect in a store with enough food for an army. He asked what he could do for us, and I showed him the jewels we had from the Palace, here – two fine rings with gemstones and a gold chain, ye recall, worth a hundred pieces of eight, easy. I offered to trade for meat and fruit, wheat and beans, salt, and rum, of course. I mentioned rum since that's what O'Flaherty says they drink in these Caribbees, aye?

"But when I said that last, he looked up at me sharpish – he had been shaking his head slow, his face right befuddled. He looks me up and down, as you just did when I asked you to. And then he says – he had a strange accent, one I've never heard, a bit English but flatter and harder – he says, 'I know what it's like to be down on my luck. Did you steal these?' Well, I looked properly offended, told him they were family heirlooms, meant to be worn by my sister at her wedding, but we'd just lost the lass to a fever and we were going to try our luck with a trading voyage, and needed supply. He weighed and measured me like a prize sheep at market, and then he nods and says, 'I should send you to a pawn shop, but they'd cheat you worse than I ever could, and who knows where you'd spend cash money?'"

"What's a pawn shop?" I interrupted him.

Ian shrugged. "I did not ask. So then he looked the gold over, and he says, 'So does a thousand sound right for these?'"

I am sure my mouth dropped open. "A thousand pieces of eight, did he mean? Or copper pennies?"

Ian pointed at the piles of food. "Nate, there's a hundredweight of that flour there. Have you ever seen finer? What would that cost, back home? My own mother would trade me for the bread that stuff will make, even in O'Grady's hands. And the fruits? Here – eat this!"

One bite of the apple he handed me then, and I forgot that there were no spirits in the pile. Well, almost. "So why did ye not get the grog?"

Ian shrugged again. "The man refused when I asked. Said he'd see me fed, but would not put me in the gutter. 'Tis why I asked if I look overmuch like a beggar. I thought it better at the time to keep my mouth shut and bring back the food. We can find liquor elsewhere – or we can go back to the Piggly Wiggly and be more impolite when we ask."

I clapped him on the shoulder. "Ye did right, man, as ever. I always know I can trust ye." I sighed then, and looked toward the road. "If only I could say the same for every man of the *Grace*."

And as if I had wished it so, that was the moment O'Flaherty returned, bringing danger back with him, clutched tight in his fool's hands. By the gods, if he'd been lads with me back in Ireland, not only would he have cheered me on through my ride on King Henry, but he would have demanded the next go, and called for my uncle to come watch. The stupid bastard.

What am I to do with him? What am I to do with what he brought back from Home Dee-Poe?

I wish Ian had gotten rum. I need a drink.

Log #11: Der Tale of Der Waffenmeister

Ye Olde Tale Of Ye Man Who Wouldeth Be A Pyrate Kyng
by ~~Elliot Schluchzer~~ Waffenmeister

When I woke up on that fateful morning, alone and lonesome in my lonely bed, I thought it would be a day like any other.

I was wrong.

Entirely and completely wrong.

Wrong.

But wait! Gentle Reader, let me begin at the beginning. A good place to start, one may perhaps presume, peradventure.

Fuck, this is hard. Fuck it: I should just, whatever, say it. What happened.

So I woke up like twenty minutes late or something. I was up late playing Dead Space 2. Oh, not the campaign; I already won that – are you kidding me? What are you, a retard? I beat that shit like three times the first day it was released. Finished on Hard Core. Might have been the first one in Florida, I don't know, it's being looked into. But they released new multiplayer maps for Xbox like three weeks ago, and I figure I might write a guide, sell to whoever publishes those, the Dummies or whatever. I guarantee my shit would be better than anyone else they got working on it. I keep my shit locked down *tight*, you know?

Oh right – my name's Elliot Schluchzer. Waffenmeister is my handle. It means "Warlord." You've seen it if you're on XBox Live, all over the leaderboards. Especially CoD. Or on WoW. I'm getting into live action now, the Society for Creative Anachronism, but I just started that like two years ago, so I'm not as known. But I will be: I'm getting into building shit, armor, barding, shields. Maybe siege weapons, if I can find designs good enough for what I'd want to do. I'm good with wood, since that's my job in the mundane world. I work at Home Depot, mostly in the lumber section. I'm on the table saw a lot. I don't really like talking to the customers, especially the OJs (Old Jews – Miami's fuckin filled to the *brim* with them.), but I like cutting their wood to the size and shape they want. I'm a craftsman, you know? A carpenter, like. At least, maybe a journeyman carpenter. I still work at Home Depot, after all. But I'll get out of it. I'll start making furniture or something, maybe carve stuff. Shit I can sell at Ren Faires and pirate festivals. Those guys make *bank* doing that. Plus there's, like, *acres* of chicks at those things, and they all want to be either princesses or saucy tavern wenches, so they either want to get rescued or ravished, or both. I may not look like Prince Charming, but if I got the doubloons, right? I mean, Donald Trump looks like a fuckin gargoyle with a bad toupee, but that dude marries models. And who knows what he's got going on the side.

Anyway, I woke up late, so I had to hurry to get to work. That's okay, it just means I skipped the shower this morning. Back in the day they only showered like, once a year, so whatever. I still had time to take a dump and eat breakfast, though I had to eat those shitty generic PopTarts my mom keeps buying, so it was like I was just pushing shit out to make room to put shit in.

Heh. That's pretty good. Garbage in, garbage out, right? I learned that in my programming class at Miami Dade Community College. I finished almost two semesters there before I dropped out, what, four years ago? Five? Well, in real life it's, shit in, shit out. Then again, donuts in, or Taco Bell in, or fuckin pulled-pork Cuban sandwich in, it's all shit out. So what does it all matter, anyway?

So I make it to work, and only two minutes late, which wasn't my fault at all, but only because my fuckin Subaru wouldn't start. My dad said he was going to take it and get it checked out this last weekend, but did he? Nooooo. Too busy going to Temple and mowing the fuckin lawn. I swear, I gotta do every fuckin thing myself. Isn't it enough that I work full, well, almost full-time? I buy my own stuff, never ask for money. I even kick down for groceries sometimes, when Mom doesn't buy enough Pringles or Dew or something. Or frozen pizzas – she always buys the wrong kind. It's all about the Tombstone, baby. I mean, really, I'm their child, they're supposed to pay for me. If they couldn't afford me, they shouldn't have had me. Besides, I'm their only kid, so without me, the family name would die out. They should be grateful to me. Not that I'm looking to have kids any time soon. And dude, not like Schluchzer is a name that needs to live on. The only cool thing about it is it means, like, "sob" in German. So I figure, nobody would take the name "Sob" because they cry a lot, right? You'd take the name if you MADE people fuckin cry. So I think we're descended from, like, torturers or Nazis or something. Which is badass. Even if we are Jewish.

So yeah, I got to work like two minutes late, three minutes tops. Maybe five. If I had a supervisor who knew what he was doing, it wouldn't even be a problem. See, a guy who knows what he's doing knows the most important thing is this: you gotta keep the Man off your back. The key to keeping the Man off your back is knowing when you're being watched, and when you can just chill out. So at Home Depot, like, there's a store manager, a guy who wears a suit and stays in the office upstairs. He's in charge of the floor supervisors, and he's on the phone all day kissing Corporate ass. So if that guy – in my store it's a Cubano named Randy Martinez, if you can believe it – if Big Randy *knew what he was doing,* he'd just keep feeding Corporate a line of bullshit, and then, because Corporate never actually comes to the store, he'd run the store however he wanted, because he knows he's not being watched. Then, most important, he could let all his employees do whatever they wanted. You should always keep your employees happy. Happy employees work harder, and get shit done faster, so they have more time to just relax after. Then the customers are happy, because the employees are happy, and everything's perfect. That would be best. It would be so primo if the whole store was just laid back like that. But see, even if it couldn't all be that sweet – even if Randy is a giant fuckin tool, which he is – then the floor supervisors could do the same thing, only smaller. Because Randy never really comes out on the floor, and when he does, he just wants to know that every customer has been asked if he needs help. So when he comes down from upstairs, which he does, like, once a month or something, he walks around and asks every customer he sees, "Are you being helped? Did someone in an orange apron come by and offer to help you with that?" Okay, so the floor supervisors get reamed – reamed by Randy, hah – if the customers aren't being helped, yeah. But a floor supervisor *who knew what he was doing* could handle it, instead of just reaming all of us regular employees out after Randy gets done with them. They'd find a way to distract Randy, or maybe find out in advance when he was going to come down, so we could, like, blitzkrieg the whole store, run down all the aisles asking if anyone needs help. Something, you know, to handle it, just to take the pressure off, keep the Man off our backs, so all us regular people can relax a little bit, and not have to spend all fuckin day walking around in this ass-hot warehouse asking "Do you need any help? Do you need any help?"

Fuck, they want us to help a lot.

So here's my idea, and I know I'm off topic, but whatever, this is my story, shut the fuck up, okay. You put like an employee mini-lounge – make a permanent display of lounge chairs or something – right by the front doors, and just ask every customer right when he comes in if they want any help. And if they say no, just be all, "Okay, well you know where to find us if you have any questions." Then they can shop without being hassled by the Orange Apron squad, and all the employees can hang out. Then if Randy comes down from his throne atop Isengard (Not that Randy's badass enough to be Saruman the White. But maybe he could pull off Wormtongue.) and roams the store, asking people if they've been offered help, they all have to say yes. Then we could just relax and play XBox, or something. Then this job would be sweet. If we had a boss *who knew what he was doing*.

But we have Randy. And Mr. Zuckow.

"You're late, Elliot. Again."

And I want to bust out a bo staff and hit him like 35 times in 3 seconds, and then stand over his writhing, crying busted-ass body and be all, "The name's Waffenmeister, you corporate scum." But I guess if I could do that, I wouldn't be fuckin working here, would I?

"Sorry, Mr. Zuckow." That's what I say instead.

"Go hit your locker and sweep the section. Then set up the Makita table saw and the scroll saw. You're giving the demo today, remember. Ten o'clock."

Fuuuuuuuuck. "Okay."

See, even if what happened hadn't happened, I was still wrong when I woke up and thought this would be a regular Monday. Because it's not: it's a Demo Day. Fuck my fuckin life.

We do a demo every day, here at Home Depot. Take some of the big, shiny tools out front, and from ten til noon, we have to build shit. Or fix shit. Or turn shit on and off. Or assemble shit. Or take shit apart. And the whole time, the sun's just beating down on you like

Mjolnir, the hammer of Thor. And when you work in lumber, like I do, whenever it's your turn you have to do woodworking shit, of course, and so you're sucking sawdust and getting splinters the whole fuckin time. Then, when it's over, you gotta clean shit up. I mean, what the fuck.

But the worst part? It's the OJs.

Don't get me wrong, I'm fully not anti-Semitic. Fuck, I *am* Jewish. My dad's an OJ, so's my granddad and my uncle Peter. I'm down with the old Jews.

But those guys love to talk. They live for it. And they want to save money by doing their own home repairs, but they don't know shit about shit. So they ask questions. A neverending stream of questions, question after question after question. "Where do you get that?" "What does that button do?" "Can I get that in pine?" "If I use one of these, can I do the same thing as that?" "How much did you say that is? Oy! What about with a senior discount?" And all you can do with all these questions is smile, and answer every. Single. One. Because when you're out front doing a demo, every boss in the place is right up your ass, and you better fuckin smile and you better fuckin talk to all the customers, and you better fuckin help em all. Unbelievable.

So all right, this sucks. It's my turn to do demo day. I spend an hour or so sweeping, and then I start hauling out the saws, and the lumber. I bring out an extra big pile of lumber, so I'll have plenty to work on and won't have to go back in for more. I paste on my happy smile, and at 10:00, maybe a minute or two late, I start sawing. I know I'll have to stop the saws and talk to the OJs, but maybe I can, what is it, minimize that shit: the more I saw, the less I'll have to talk. Maybe I'll get lucky and there'll be a big sale on bagels or something, and they won't come by today. I can hope, right? Maybe I'll get lucky. For once.

But that's not what happens.

What happens is the craziest fucking thing that could ever happen to me.

What happens is my whole life changes, in less than a minute.

So I'm sawing, right? I got this OJ in front of me, and he's trying to ask me a question but I just keep sawing, and smiling, and trying to pretend I can't hear him. And then I hear something else. I hear shouting. Loud shouting, not like somebody-got-in-a-fender-bender shouting, but like asteroids-are-falling-from-the-sky-and-blowing-shit-up shouting, the kind of sheer, total volume that goth kids pay bank to hear in concert and all the rest of us avoid at all costs. So I stop sawing, and I turn around to look where the sound's coming from.

Charging from around the corner, where the Garden Center guys have their tree-and-shrub display, come like ten guys. At first, I think it might be the SCA pulling a joke raid or something, but it only takes maybe two seconds for me to realize: this is not the SCA, and this is not a joke. These guys are nothing like my medieval-reenactment brothers.

These guys are fucking scary.

They're filthy, blackened with soot and dirt and old bloodstains from head to foot. They are – *disfigured* is the only word for it: I see fingers missing, eyes missing, parts of noses and whole ears missing. Jesus, that one guy in front, spinning black chains around like some crazy-ass kung fu movie, is missing both his *thumbs*. And they got scars everywhere, livid red-brown scars, raised ridges and deep trenches in their skin, like they've never even seen Neosporin and a Bandaid, let alone a doctor. And they are armed, with cutlasses and battle axes and old flintlock pistols, and I've seen replica weapons, I spend a lot of my time with replica weapons, and just by looking at these, I can tell: these are the real fuckin things. And their eyes are wild and crazy, and they are screaming louder than I've ever heard a person scream.

And they're all coming right at me.

I barely have time to back away and say, "No – please!" in a shaky voice when one of them vaults over my table saw and plows into me, putting the haft of his two-handed axe right into my chest, throwing me back five feet into my pile of lumber. That crazy fucker with the chains swings one down into my table saw, and the blade snaps right out of its housing and goes flying like some giant shuriken, and I'd yell *Watch out!* but I think I've had every breath I've ever taken in my life knocked out of me, and I won't be saying anything for quite a while. Chain Guy keeps spinning the other chain in a circle by his left side, and he snarls at the OJ – I mean actually *snarls* at him, growling like a fuckin dog – and the OJ doesn't even say a word, he just turns and runs off into the parking lot.

Then this other one, this older one with a gray-streaked beard and the most seriously broken nose I've ever seen, he starts barking orders, telling the others to grab as much of my lumber pile as they can carry, starting with the widest planks. And he comes up to me and bends down and smiles at me with brown teeth and he says, "I'd be obliged for the favor of your services, good squire."

Then somebody puts a bag over my head, and they tie my wrists together. They make me stand up and run, with my hands holding onto somebody's belt, and somebody else shoving a gun barrel in my back and telling me to stop, and duck, and go faster – or they'd kill me.

And I am so scared. So very scared.

We run, and duck, and hide, and run some more, and it seems like it takes hours, but who knows how long it takes time to pass when you've got a bag over your head, and you've already pissed yourself, and you know that these guys are terrorists, fuckin Islamic jihadists – though that sounded like an Irish accent, maybe, but whatever, that's like some ex-IRA guy who's now a mercenary or some shit – and as soon as you get where you're going, they're going to sit you in a chair and cut your fuckin head off and put it on YouTube.

What I'm saying is, you can't estimate time or distance when you know you're about to die.

And then, after forever of running and my legs are killing me and my hands are throbbing and burning from the circulation being cut off (and all I can think is "Ligature marks. CSI will find ligature marks on my wrists.") and I feel like so much sweat has poured out of my head inside this bag that now it must be blood I feel running down my face and neck, and this bag stinks and I can't breathe and my lungs are collapsing, and ah, God, *they're going to cut my head off* – they slow down. I hear some shouting back and forth, and then everything goes quiet, except for me whooping for air and trying to get enough breath to beg for my life. Then they yank the bag off.

The sunlight hurts, at first, but we're inside a house or something, so it isn't too bad, and I can breathe. When my eyes adjust and I can blink some of the blood-sweat out of my eyes, I see that I am standing in front of an honest-to-God, no-shit, Jack Sparrow pirate, everything from the tri-corner hat to the sash with the sword and the flintlock pistols in it to the turned-down leather boots. He's looking at me, and he looks pissed. Pissed on a scale I don't even want to think about, like not like Mr. Zuckow's going to yell at me, but more like Captain Jack is actually going to take out those guns and shoot someone in the face; like this guy's temper already goes to 11, but right now he's on 30.

He points at me, looks at Gray-Beard, and he says, "What, in the name of Satan and all the saints he's burning, have ye *done*, O'Flaherty?"

Log #12: O'Flaherty's Comeuppance

"What, in the name of Satan and all the saints he's burning, have ye done, O'Flaherty?"

That's what I asked the man, and a right fair question it was. But the man was standing on his pride – or perhaps believed that I was – and he objected to the manner of my speech. Perhaps he had expected laurels on his brow, huzzahs shouted for his triumph. Bah!

…But perhaps I should have spoken him more gently.

His chest swelled and jaw clenched as his brow lowered in anger. "Ye had best not speak so to me, Cap'n. We're not aboard ship, and this is no' battle. I be your equal –"

I cut him off with an impolite gesture. "Ah, belay that quartermaster shite, ye bilge-brained mongrel. We have no time for it. Think you this is not battle? We are in the greatest danger of our lives, every second. And you have made it worse, you daft idiot!" Perhaps I regained some of my wits, then, for I hesitated for a moment and then looked around at all the men hearing this. I had not meant to shame O'Flaherty with such a public comeuppance. I beckoned him towards the staircase, and the room above, which I had claimed as my quarters.

But he refused. "Nay, *Cap'n*," he spat. "Let all the men hear what ye have to say, and respond as they have a mind to, aye. If this be a proper pirate ship, and we be of the Brotherhood, then all the men aboard have the right." He stepped closer and asked quietly, "Or do they not, *Captain?*" Again he spat out my title like a bit of underdone potato.

I recognized this speech. It was this philosophy, what O'Flaherty claimed was the Pirate's Code, which gave him equal standing on what had been my ship. Before his coming aboard, the men had all been loyal to me as their captain, as knights to their liege lord, as warriors to their clan chief, as it has ever been on Irish ships. O'Flaherty was behind the conceit that the men should *choose* their leaders, that they should vote, that every man's voice should be equal;

and that the men should choose not only their captain, but also their Quartermaster, equal in authority to the captain in all things but battle. Truth be told, I allowed it because others of my men – Donal Carter, Shane MacManus, Padraig Doyle, my own cousin and gunner's mate Hugh Moran, and some that did not live to reach these strange shores, Ian Duffy who was my steersman, Albert Donovan and his brother Tiernan, and Colin Murphy, gods rest their souls – all of them fine sailors and brave warriors – they took his words to heart. Had I not granted O'Flaherty what he sought and let the men vote for their captain and quartermaster, let them write and sign Articles governing our ship and crew, I feared those men would leave the ship, and the heart of my crew would go with them, before the voyage even began. But I did allow it, and they did stay – thankfully choosing me unanimously as captain, which vote having gone otherwise would have occasioned a very different and much less civil conversation about my ship and the owning of her. We had a fine voyage after that day, even with O'Flaherty as Quartermaster and his Code ruling our ship – our ship that had been *my* ship. And several other fine cruises since then; until now, of course. O'Flaherty's Code did make the men feel stronger, more as though they chose this life, this ship, and myself as their captain. Men should know that they choose their own destiny, and I could not but approve of that, and the great fondness the men gained for my fair *Grace*, since all felt some ownership of her.

But here is the truth: the *Grace of Ireland* is *my* ship. I commissioned her, I gave her specifics to Master Spaulding, the shipbuilder in Cork; I paid for her with the legacy my family granted me on my twenty-first birthday, with the money I had saved serving on other men's vessels, leading trade voyages for my mother and our clan, sailing on raids against the British, the Welsh, even the Spanish and the French and the Moors of Algiers. When even that was not enough, I paid with shares in the *Grace's* future plunder, on which I made good for two years before the accounts were closed. I captained her on her maiden voyage, when I and my crew – without O'Flaherty and that apish bastard Burke – cruised through the Irish Sea and lightened half a dozen English vessels before we escaped the King's ships and returned home, safe and sound. I was the sole commander for four years after that, too, and a grand time it was, aye; until O'Flaherty and Burke came aboard with their tales of the Caribbean and the Brotherhood of the Coast, three years ago. It had been near two years since O'Flaherty had convinced us to adopt Articles and cast ballots for the ship's captain and quartermaster.

It was time I took back command of my ship. Past time.

So I agreed to O'Flaherty's demands, and gathered all the men into a circle on the beach before the *Grace*. As they found places to stand or sit in the sand, I saw that they had brought O'Flaherty's prisoner with them; I ordered that he be allowed to stay and listen, as this concerned him near as much as it did the rest of us. I wanted him to see what manner of men had taken him captive, and into whose hands he should trust his keeping.

As soon as O'Flaherty, who had been a-whispering with Burke, joined me in the center of the circle, I asked him, "Who is the captain of this ship?" and I pointed at the *Grace*.

"You are," he said. "But –"

I did not give him the opportunity to but his buts; I stepped to where Ian O'Gallows stood, his thumbs in his belt by his weapons. "Who is the captain of that ship?" I asked him loudly.

"You are, Captain Kane, sir," he responded sharply, without the breath of hesitation that O'Flaherty had taken. Ian's eyes roved over the men as he said, "You are captain of the ship and her crew – you and no other man, sir." This last he directed at O'Flaherty.

Though warmed by his loyalty, I did not give him the gratitude he deserved, but stepped to the man beside Ian in the circle: it was Robert Sweeney, one of the younger men aboard, and one much in awe of O'Flaherty's tales and in fear of Burke's chains – though a good and loyal man, for all that. He hesitated a moment, and cleared his throat when I put the question to him, though I believe his hesitation to be due to nervousness rather than mutinous thoughts. He said, "You are, sir." He cast his eyes down after he said it.

They all responded with those words, as indeed they should. Even Burke, though he stared at me for better than a minute, and sneered when he named me captain of my own vessel. But Burke's insubordinate nature is no surprise; I was more concerned by the number of other men who hesitated before answering. Some even glanced at O'Flaherty before they gave their response. But give it they all did, all naming me; after Burke's belabored answer, I stepped smartly back to where O'Flaherty stood with arms crossed and lips pressed tight together with ire. Still I did not allow him time to speak. "There ye have it. *I* am the captain – I and no other."

He nodded. "Aye-aye, and aye once more, Nate. But if I were to ask them all who be the Quartermaster of this ship, what then?"

I softened my tone then. I needed O'Flaherty, and Burke, and all the hesitant men. I could not drive them away from me, not now, not here. But when we return to Ireland, and I can find a good, loyal, Irish crew . . . I will not forget who hesitated in answering my question. Even my cousin Hugh, damn him. "They would say you, Sean," I answered O'Flaherty. "And they'd be right to do so."

I turned and addressed the men. "None of us knows where we are. The Dominicans called it Florida, and Miyammy, and America, but all I know is that it is not our beloved Ireland. We are far off the edge of the charts, lads.

"Ye all know, as I do, that the greatest danger we face on a voyage is not the British, and not famine, nor plague, nor even fire in the hold. The greatest danger is losing our way." I paused then, and a few of the older men nodded. I continued. "If we cannot find our way home, then nothing else has consequence: not our courage, nor our strength, nor the weight of plunder in our holds and our pockets. If we have water, and food, and a fair wind and clear skies – but we do not know where we are nor where we are heading – we have nothing. For the water will run out, and the food; and the clear skies will turn to black storms; and all of these things may be repaired. But without a location and a destination, we will do nothing but wander. What good then the wealth in our purses?" I looked at O'Flaherty. "What good then the code we follow, or the title we claim?"

I turned back to the men. "Now, I've been caught in a fog that the sun did not dry up. Of course I have: I'm Irish." They all laughed at that; no Irish sailor is innocent of fog. "I was caught in one on the *Gaelic Tiger*, under Silas McNulty, that lasted better than seven days before the wind rose and blew it away. Seven days, becalmed in a gray world without sky, without horizon, without land in sight." McTeigue, who had been with me on that voyage, added his voice and memory to mine – as did Donal Carter, I was glad to see, for all that his hesitancy had been second only to Burke's before he named me captain but moments ago. I went on. "We had no idea how long it would last, no idea how close we may have been to rocks, or to British ships, or to a storm that would put us on the bottom. We had no idea if we were sailing closer to home, or farther away. It seemed the very air had no breath to sustain us, after a while. Every morning, we'd wake and hope to see the sea and sky and sun – and every morning it was naught but more gray. That was the most frightened I've ever been at sea, I don't mind telling you lads.

"Until this voyage. Until this day, right now." I paused, to let them think on my words. In the usual course of events, I would never admit to my men that I felt any fear, or that I had the least doubt as to our course, our destination, or the wisdom of our actions. But this day was not in the usual course of events. We were off the map in more ways than one, and they knew it. If I said aught else, I'd lose them, too. "We are lost, and badly lost. We do not know our way home, and what's worse, we do not know how to find our way home. In Irish seas, the compass, or even one glimpse of the sky, could tell us which direction was East, and we could sail to Europe and then from wherever we struck, we could find our way home. But if we sail East now, what will we strike? Is the compass even true, now? Are we even on the seas of the Earth we know? What dangers lie out there – only the British, the French, the Spanish, the Dutch? The Devil's Lash? Or something more? Be there dragons and demons, Scylla and Charybdis?

"We are in the gravest peril we have ever faced, right now, and every minute until we can point the bow of our ship – *our* ship – toward home. Graver even than when we had the *Sea-Cat* hard on our stern."

I rounded on O'Flaherty once more. "Do ye recall, Sean, whose counsel led us into Hobbes's trap? Who led to the deaths of thirteen men, the wounding of three more?" I watched him redden, but he held his tongue. I did not. "Aye, and whose plan was it to put the Devil's Lash right atop us, and killed another sixteen of our brothers?" I hurried past that, as I did not want O'Flaherty reminding them who had ruined that attempted ambush with an unfortunate cry of alarm. "We seem to be in or near the Caribbean, Sean – ye have named the flora and the fauna, and the sands and seas match your tales of the Indies. Do ye know, then, where we are? Can ye lead us to safety?"

A moment's fierce glare, and then O'Flaherty dropped his gaze to the sand at my feet.

I stepped to him, clasped his shoulder warmly. "Ye be a fine quartermaster, Sean, and the only man I'd want as my second in command." I felt sure my friend and mate – and true choice for second – Ian O'Gallows would know and forgive this lie. "But you have not been plotting the best course. Not on this voyage." I pointed at the bewildered man kneeling beside Burke, the one whose help we needed desperately, and whom they had taken hostage and scared witless. "Not this day. Ye should not be in command." I stepped even closer, my nose a mere handspan from his. "And *you are not.* We are still in battle, even now, even here: we fight for our very lives. We fight our own ignorance, and our own rash impulses, like the thrashings of a drowning man, which just make him sink all the faster. If we make one wrong step, we will all of us die. That is battle. And so long as we are in battle, your own Code, and our ship's Articles, signed by every man here and many who have fallen, say that I am in command – I and no other." My grip on his shoulder turned hard. "Until we are home, you will do what I say, and only what I say. Until we reach Ireland." I put my other hand on the grip of the pistol in my sash. I whispered, "And if ye say anything right now other than 'Aye, Captain,' I'll spill your heart's blood on this ground." I clapped him on the shoulder, stepped back, and waited, hand on my pistol.

"Aye, Captain," O'Flaherty said loudly. Then he whispered, for my ears alone, "Until Ireland."

I nodded, and smiled wide. "Until Ireland."

"UNTIL IRELAND!" Ian roared, and the men all yelled with him. But I saw Carter, and Burke, and Hugh Moran casting glances, one to the other and back. I admit I longed for home, then, with every scrap of me. As if there is not enough to beware, I must needs watch my own men?

There is no greater gift, no more valuable possession, than loyalty.

I dispersed the men back to their tasks and stations then. I was irked to see Burke, Carter, Moran, and O'Flaherty gather and mutter together. But I must convince them, for I cannot control them – they are free men. I will be sure to speak of O'Flaherty's several mistakes in Carter's hearing, and wax poetic on the ties of family near my cousin Hugh.

I may have to watch for a chance to put a blade in Burke. Naught else will sway him.

But speaking of O'Flaherty's mistakes: now I must deal with his latest.

Log #13: Conversations with a Carpenter

Captain's Log
Date: 27th of June, 1678
Location: Glass Palace
Conditions: Situation improving, but morale flags

I stood before the man O'Flaherty had so basely stolen away. I did wonder if my quartermaster had not, in fact, taken a journeyman, or even an apprentice, rather than the master carpenter; he seemed very young, the skin of his face and hands smooth and unlined but for a youth's blemishes, of the which he wore several. He was certainly fat enough to be wealthy, which might have brought O'Flaherty's gimlet eye 'pon him; Sean has ever had an itch to stab at men of wealth and quality wheresoever he finds them. He was certainly as terrified as any man I've ever seen, wide-eyed and sheened with sweat.

Damn your liver, Sean. How could I win this youth over now, to gain his willing assistance? I confess that for a moment I was tempted simply to follow O'Flaherty's lead and compel the man with the strength of arms; but I will not put my ship's fate into the hands of a fearful and desperate man. How can you trust the work of men you have pressed into service? We should have to drag him along with us, to compel any further repairs due to his slipshod work – or even sabotage – with an unending chain of threats against his life and well-being. I would not take this man from his home merely because I could not think of a better way to get what I need. I find I have no taste for stealing men away from their homes.

At least the first step to winning the man's favor was obvious. I whistled up McTeigue and ordered him to cut the man's bonds at once, and fetch him a bottle of wine, if any were left. I held Owen for another moment, and whispered further orders in his ear: my cousin was to stay out of easy sight, but keep a close watch in case the man slipped away from me. I did not wish to compel his service, but I could not have him raising the alarm, perhaps bringing a militia or a troop of King's men down on us.

I made use of the minutes whilst McTeigue sought out refreshment to tender to the man the most humble and genteel apology I could compose. I pride myself on my apologies; they have kept many a colleen from drumming a beat 'pon my pate with cookware, as Irish lasses are wont to do when they discover themselves members of a plurality, rather than the sole monarch of an Irishman's heart. Ah, now, they say it takes a village to raise a child; I fail to see why a man cannot be so raised, as well. Parts of him, at least.

My final flourishes and *bon mots* flowered the air as McTeigue returned with a bottle of clear golden wine; I swallowed a long draught to show there was no poison, and then handed it to my erstwhile guest. He took it with a shaking hand and took a sip, grimacing at the taste. I had found several of the Glass Palace's vintages too sweet, as well, but this one was quite nice; perhaps he had a foul taste in his mouth before. McTeigue shrugged and removed himself from sight. I sat and invited the man to do the same, the which he did following a moment of wary staring.

"I am Damnation Kane, captain of the ship *Grace of Ireland.*" I held out my hand to him, and after a pause – which is often occasioned by the first mention of my name – he met it with his own somewhat clammier hand. "Elliott Shluxer," he told me then (I can but guess at the spelling of it, never having encountered the name before). "Where do ye hail from, Sir Shluxer?" I queried. "We live in The Hammocks," he said (again, I am unsure of the writing of the name), taking a pull of his wine; its taste, like so many others, was improved with repeated applications. "And you are a carpenter, in truth?" I tried to keep my tone simple and friendly-like, but if his answer here were in the negative, he would shortly find himself clapped with a hand-full of Dominicans, and O'Flaherty would be walking home to Ireland.

After a moment, punctuated by several eyeblinks and the forming of a new sheen of sweat, the man said, "I guess, yeah. I mean, I work with wood."

Well at least O'Flaherty didn't attack a pig farmer.

"It is my fondest wish, Master Shluxer, that my compatriots' overzealous introductions of your good self to our humble band will not destroy the chance that we might work together, you and I, and both be enriched by the experience." Aye: *many* a colleen. They may

81

be won by the line of one's jaw, the turn of a calf, white teeth and a roguish smile – but they are kept by the tongue.

This man, for all that he lacked a grown man's creased brow, or a working man's physique, or, apparently, the brains of a schoolboy, still he was no colleen. "You guys are fucking nuts," was his response to my sally.

I informed the man – politely, despite his tone, for I was determined to take no offense from his words, my own men having offered offense enough for all – that I was unfamiliar with this particular colloquialism. "You're nuts, you're all fucking crackpots. A bunch of crazy fucking lunatics," he expanded.

"Ah," I exclaimed, grasping his meaning, "you mean we are madmen." I laughed at this. "Such was never in doubt, good squire. Nonetheless, I have sailed with many and many a madman afore this, and I have found that their gold spends as well as that of a man in full control of his senses." I took a doubloon from my purse, then, and let him see its golden shine. "Sometimes," I went on, and here I added a second bit of shine to my palm, "sometimes it even spends *twice* as well." I grasped his wrist, turned up his palm, and placed my two most persuasive arguments therein with a gentle clinking.

Shluxer put down his wine bottle and looked at the coins. "Holy fuck," he said, an oath I had never heard – and considering the scruples of most saints, including Our Lord and Savior, it was an oath I found rather puzzling. "Are these real?"

"Indeed they are, stout yeoman. And Spanish weight, not Irish, I assure you. For 'twas a Spaniard we liberated them from, along with many of their brethren formerly trapped in Spanish pockets."

He looked up at me then, his mouth unfortunately hanging agape: unfortunate, for his physiognomy did not vouch to me proof of his competence and intelligence, nor even his comprehension of my words. "You're giving me these?" he asked.

I resolved to speak slower, and perhaps a bit louder: I could discern the dirt in his ears from where I sat; perhaps his hearing was blocked by effluvia. Or perhaps it was his thoughts that got in the way of understanding. "I am giving you those, and I will give you more if you will agree to work with me." I accompanied these words with a brief pantomime of sawing and hammering, so my meaning would be clear, it was to be hoped. I gave my belt pouch a jingle, as well.

Shluxer wiped at his brow, and then pressed his hands into his eyes, like a man waking from an unlikely dream into an even more improbable reality. "I don't fucking believe this," he muttered. He stared at the coins once more, turning them to glance at the visage of King Phillip IV minted on one side. Then he took another pull at the wine bottle, and met my gaze at last. "What exactly do you want me to do?" he asked me.

I clapped him on the shoulder – perhaps a trifle too vigorously, as he lost his balance and needed to be uprighted, though he had certainly suffered a shock from O'Flaherty's treatment which might explain his weakness – and rose to show him the task at hand. I guided him to the *Grace*, offered an introduction to my good friend Ian – who explained the provenance of his surname, a tale which generally wins a laugh, but garnered us merely a stupefied gaze and more doubts as to our guest's mental capacity – and showed him the hole in the *Grace's* hull, and the missing yardarm on the mainmast. He gazed into the hole for some minutes, looking as well at the stack of finished planks the men had placed nearby, the only intelligent acquisition they had made, as my present companion apparently possessed less wit than that same pile of wood.

To wit: "You want me to help you fix the hole," he said then.

I nodded, slowly. "And replace the yardarm on the mainmast, and help make her water-tight and sea-worthy. Aye."

"And you'll pay me for it."

Another slow, exaggerated nod. "At twice your going rate. Aye."

He held up the doubloons. "In gold, like this."

I shrugged. "Perhaps some silver. We generally have a fair motley of coins about us, considering their variegated sources." He blinked, and I sighed. "Yes. We will pay in gold."

"That's why you kidnapped me?"

I winced. I took a breath, ready to explain the political realities of O'Flaherty's rank despite his incompetence and rash judgment, but Ian stepped in then, smooth as cream.

"Of course we will offer you *wergild* for that offense against your honor, along with the apology you have already received from our generous captain." This last part came with a glance my way, which met a nod; but Ian could be confident that I would have apologized, first because he knew me for a gentleman of breeding, and second because he has frequently been apologizing to his own colleen even as

I mollify mine. "Or perhaps you would rather have a boon, if there is some service we might offer," Ian finished.

It was then that I first spied the crafty look come into the eyes of Elliott Shluxer. How much would have been easier for me, had I only paid more attention then! I should have known that such apparent imbecility was sure to be joined with a low, animal cunning, and the savage, wanton greed of a starving dog.

"A boon? Like a favor?" Something akin to a smile curved his lips. "What kind of a favor are we talking about here?"

Ian looked my way, unwilling to speak further in my stead. I smiled at the carpenter and raised my open palms. "We have a fine ship and a good crew, once we can set sail once more. We would be honored to transport yourself, or whatever goods you wished, to the destination of your choice. Even back to England, or Spain or France, perhaps." Ian looked a question at me for this over-generous offer, but I ignored it. I would fill the hold with another man's profit if it meant I could take my ship and my men home again. "Or we could lend the strengths of our arms and backs, if you need land cleared, or a barn raised or other such tasks."

But this struck no spark of joy in the visage of our would-be carpenter. I tried again, my tone growing soft and shadowy, like the subject of this speaking – I would offer craft to this crafty man, if it would get my ship back on the water. "Then there are our more surreptitious skills, the which we could offer into your service."

Shluxer seemed intrigued, and I went on. "Perhaps there are goods of some kind, that are wrongfully in the possession of another man: a situation we could easily remedy. Or," and I laid a hand ostentatiously on the butt of my pistol, "perhaps there is a personage whose acquaintance you would like to un-make."

A smile creased the greasy face of my new ally. "Whoa, shit! You guys – you'll cap someone on my say-so?"

I had to blink at the wording, but how many meanings could there be in this conversation? I nodded, slowly so he would understand me. He did, and rubbed his hands together in unmistakable glee.

This is ever the way, it would seem. If you offer a man a generous profit, advancement for himself and his kin in your right hand – and vengeance, no matter how petty, in your left hand, 'tis always the second hand he'll grasp in agreement. The sinister hand.

It was while Shluxer was considering his possible targets and I was pondering the chance that I would regret my offer – sadly a most likely occurrence, but what choice had I? – that I heard a voice call out "Captain!" I turned and stepped quickly toward the Palace, from whence the call came; young Lynch dashed out to meet me.

"Captain – it's the Quartermaster, sir, and the Bosun. And Carter, and Gunner Moran, too. They've gone."

I loosed an oath then that would strike my old granny dead, did she hear it from my lips. "Where have they gone?"

Lynch, who had stopped to admire my swearing, now turned grim once more. "They've gone to the Piggly Wiggly, sir. They've gone to steal grog."

Log #14: Guards and Grog

Captain's Log
Date: 27 June
Location: In a madhouse.
Conditions: As should be expected: mad.

If a man were to ask me what is the experience of captaining a ship, of leading a crew, I would say this: when you are the captain of a ship, everything goes wrong all at once. It is never simply that your vessel is blown into a storm; it is ever that your ship is blown into a storm, when your food stores have turned up rotten, and all your men are drunk on grog poured into empty bellies to quiet the pangs, and the lines have been poorly lashed by fainting fog-headed men, and the steersman collapses in a swoon and heels the boat crosswise to the waves just as the wind tears loose the moorings and leaves the sails flapping and the ship out of control – even as the cry of "Fire!" issues from the galley. That is the life of a ship's captain. But with one difference from my depiction: generally the threats a captain faces are invisible and unknowable before they strike.

Here I had a group of men, three of them my own officers, who saw fit to defy my orders even after they joined their voices in affirmation of my right to command. Four men who were such blithering, vacuous idiots that they apparently did not understand the danger of piling more risk onto the perils we already face, who sought to prod the sleeping animal whose den we had invaded, and whose nature we could not discern: was it, perhaps, merely an aged and toothless dog, who would grumble at our violation of its rest and then turn to sleep once more? Or was it a savage bear with a sore tooth, awakening ravenous from a winter's sleep, which would prove the destruction of us all? In less poetic terms: would a raid on a local establishment spur the far-flung and isolated colonials to flee our wrath, surrendering to our dominant wills if caught? Or would it break the dam and release a flood of heavily-armed soldiers on us? We did not know, and yet those men – my men, my officers, my own *cousin*, men whom I trusted to bear responsibility with probity and wisdom and fortitude – those men chose to take that risk for us all, and prod yon sleeping beast.

While our ship, our greatest weapon and only means of escape, lay mortally wounded on the sand.

And they did this all for grog.

And – most immediate – someone allowed them to go.

I strode through the Palace with Lynch at my heels, to the landward portico. The two men on watch – Shane MacManus and Raymond Fitzpatrick, a man whose loyalty I questioned and another whose witlessness, unfortunately, I did not – took their ease in two of the woven-cloth chairs that had previously stood on the seaward pavilion, but now stood in shaded places somewhat near the front door, and somewhat within reasonable view of any approaching enemies.

Perhaps I misspoke, before; perhaps the essence of captainhood is this: when your subordinates, in everything they do from sleep to eat to work to watch to fight to shit, are incessantly toeing the line of indolence and insubordination, but never quite far enough over it to deserve chastisement. A captain is ever left with two unpalatable choices: berate and punish those who have done very little that is wrong, and be known as a tyrant and martinet, or allow standards to slacken lower and lower until doom is as assured as the captain's reputation for laxity. After all, these men were at their stations, and they were awake and unintoxicated, and they faced the road. Could I really begrudge them a comfortable seat in this tedious duty?

At the moment: a thousand times yes. "AVAST!" I roared as I came through the door and espied their lazy carcasses. "STAND AND REPORT, YE IDLE SWINE!" The two leapt from their chairs with satisfying alacrity, MacManus with a charged musket in his hands and Fitzpatrick sending his chair flying all a-tangle with the vigor of his upright leap. MacManus, seeing no immediate threat but my own humble self, turned and snapped off a crisp salute, knuckles to brow. "Nothin' to report, Captain, sir!" he said, his words brusque and his stare blank. MacManus had served in the Royal Navy and was no stranger to surprise inspections from angry officers. Fitzpatrick shook his head to confirm MacManus's negative reply.

I stepped close, pressing my face within inches of MacManus's. "Where are O'Flaherty and Burke, Shane? Where is Carter? And Moran?"

He blinked and reddened, slightly, though it may have been the heat. "They . . . they left, sir. Half a turn gone, now, fifteen or twenty minutes, I'd say."

I stepped closer, forcing him back on his heels. "And you didn't stop them?"

He frowned. "No, Captain. By what authority would I stop the Quartermaster goin' where he likes, sir?"

"By the authority of your own brain, were it not as shriveled and worm-eaten as his!" I snarled, pointing at the slack-jawed Fitzpatrick.

MacManus's flush deepened. Definitely not the heat. Not the sun's heat, at least. "They claimed to be acting under orders, sir. I had no orders to hold or question or countermand their leavin'. Captain."

Damn it all, he was right. I should have guessed that this was a possibility, and I should have expressly forbidden their departure, or any others'. I can only say in my defense that I had been too preoccupied with the storm and the flapping sails to also fight the galley-fire below – the fire named O'Flaherty. And "grog."

But MacManus was not free of sin, here. I stepped back and stared at him some more, before saying quietly, "Why did I not receive a report of their leaving?"

MacManus paled even faster than he had reddened. "I – I thought you knew, Captain. They said you had ordered them." He trailed off without any word from me. He knew better than that. On a ship, any ship, anything and all things must be reported up the chain of command. Always. All commands, all shouts of warning, even simple declarations of fact, are repeated again and again. Too much depends on men doing the right thing at the right moment, and on the officers knowing the right thing to do and the right moment to do it. If I am told by my Sailing Master that the wind is turning, and I give the order to come about, then the Master repeats it for clarity, and then tells the same to the steersman. The steersman says, "Aye, coming about, sir," and shouts it to the Bosun. The Bosun, who must make the men reorient the sails as we change course, cries out, "Coming about!" And the men, to acknowledge the order and verify that it was the correct order, all shout, "Coming about!" *Then* the ship begins to turn. Not before.

MacManus should have reported the departure. The reason he hadn't was clear to me: he knew I'd have stopped them, and he hadn't wanted them stopped before they accomplished this errand. It was most likely the siren call of the grog which had whelmed his thoughts and suborned him from doing his duty.

I merely waited until he dropped his gaze, and then I began issuing new orders. "We will fortify this door, now. You two will dig a trench and build a breastworks with the earth, to either side of the palace. Take tools from the barn-shed if there be any. And if not, *use your bloody hands*."

I watched them salute and trot off to the barn-shed; I told Lynch off to stand watch for now, and he nodded. Should have had him there in the first place, curse me for a trusting fool.

As I came back through the doorway into the entry hall, I encountered once more another unwelcome complication: our new carpenter, Shluxer. He stood, cowed but trying nonetheless to catch glimpses of the goings-on from where he was, confronted and halted from going any further by a surly and silent Owen McTeigue. I clapped my cousin gratefully on the shoulder, and he nodded and relaxed – but he did not leave.

"I regret, Master Shluxer, that the realization of our partnership must be postponed. I trust that my assurances of your future enrichment will prove sufficient for the nonce, and I would also ask that you endeavor to keep our presence here a secret, moot as the request may be."

"What's going on?" he asked, still craning his neck to see around me and out the front door.

"Some of my men have gone to beard the lion in his den. We must prepare to face the wrath." I turned to McTeigue. "Go find two of the men who brought him here, and have them escort Master Shluxer home. Then –"

Shluxer interrupted me. "They left on foot? Why don't you just go after them?"

I turned to him with raised brow and lowered patience. "Because they left twenty minutes ago. They would reach their destination before we caught them, even at a dead run."

He stared at me for a moment, uncomprehending, I thought – and how amazed I was that he couldn't grasp such a simple problem! Then he said, "Why don't you just take the car?"

Now I had to stare, uncomprehending. "Take the what?"

"The car." He pointed out the door. "What is that, an Accord? It's got balls, for a rice-burner. It could catch them. You got the keys?"

I turned to see where he was pointing: it was the nearer of the two beast-wagons, the one that Juan and Ignacio Lopez had arrived in – the one which we had not shot. I turned back to Shluxer. "That thing could catch them? Before they reached the Piggly-Wiggly?"

He snorted. "Sure. What are they going to do, grow wings and fly? It's a car, dude. That thing could break a hundred, easy."

I stared some more. Surely his language was English, I knew each individual word, but he made no sense to my ears. "Break a hundred what?" I asked him.

He looked at me as if I were the idiot. "M.P.H., dude." And when this clearly offered me no help, he said, "Miles per hour?" as though questioning me, and vastly fatigued for doing so.

It took me a moment, but it started to dawn on me. "That thing," I said, pointing, "that beast out there, could run one hundred miles – that's two days good riding on a strong horse over adequate roads – in only one hour?"

He shrugged, palms up, and raised his eyebrows at me. "Duh. It's a car?"

I merely stared.

His brows lowered. "You really don't know what a car is, do you?"

Slowly I shook my head. I didn't like to confess my ignorance, but a fool's bluff would have been no improvement.

Shluxer's hand darted out and flicked at the wall near him, as through brushing at a fly. Brilliant light burst forth from the ceiling, where shining round objects like enormous pearls hung; we had thought them merely idle decoration, but now they glowed as if they were tiny suns, or great lanterns encased in smooth white glass – but we saw no flame. And from whence had the spark come? McTeigue and I both flinched away, our hands going to weapon hilts in our startlement.

"Jesus Christ," Shluxer swore quietly. He brushed the wall again, and now I noticed a small rectangle with a peg of some kind sticking out of it where his hand touched; he moved the peg so it pointed down, and the light vanished, as quickly as it had come – startling

McTeigue and I anew. Shluxer snapped his fingers, and when I looked at him, he said, "Find the keys. I'll drive."

Log #15: Joyriding

It came to be known that the keys for the beast-wagon lay in the miscellany of odds and ends we had taken from the Dominicans' pockets before locking them in; we identified the correct ring, from among several small rings of tiny-seeming keys, with Shluxer's guidance. Then I must needs ask for volunteers, with myself as first example – though all gods in heaven and earth know that I would rather dive into a whale's mouth from the crow's nest than ride on that thing. But I cannot ask my men to do a thing the which I would not do; if not for honor's sake, then simply because they would refuse to do it, with mine own cowardice standing as example and sufficient justification for their own. But with myself standing tall, and Shluxer smirking at us, soon enough Kelly stepped forward, with only a slight stagger to reveal the source of his courage; and then my good friend Ian took a surer step to join him. Lynch tried to step up, but I ordered the youth back into line. Such heart in a small and youthful chest shamed two more men into taking the step, Lochlan O'Neill and my cousin, Owen McTeigue. I chose O'Neill, as he is a fast friend of Donal Carter and could sway the man to listen to reason; also I trusted McTeigue to stay behind and supervise the fortifications of the Palace should all this go for naught.

Kelly offered to sit on the rear of the wagon, where a footman might ride if it were the carriage it somewhat resembled, but Shluxer refused him and demanded we all crawl inside, after he used the key to open the – doors, I suppose they are, though damned if they don't more resemble a bird's wings, or the fins of a fish.

Perhaps this thing is fashioned from the skeleton of some fantastic beast?

Any road, Shluxer and I were trying to coax Kelly into the sternward bench when there was a crash of glass; on the port side of the beast, Ian O'Gallows was knocking out the last few fragments from the sternward fin-door with the butt of his pistol. I feared for a moment that this attack would anger the beast – and my men stepped back with me, all eyes on O'Gallows – but Shluxer cursed and said he would "roll down the fucking windows." Which made no sense as one cannot roll glass. While we discussed it, however, Kelly found a mount to his liking: he stood on the metal edge below the bench, with one hand grasping the open door-fin-wing, and stabbed his dagger through the – the scalp? The back? The thin metal (or perhaps bone) plate atop the beast, whichever side of the thing one calls it. It gave him a fine hold, and he declared himself ready to weigh anchor. Shluxer yelled and swore again, but I and my men took heart: this further injury once more provoked no response at all from the beast. Perhaps it was not to be feared.

We all took our places, Ian behind Shluxer on the port side and Kelly hanging off the beast's starboard side behind me, with O'Neill white-faced between the two sternward stalwarts. I took the forward bench beside Shluxer, who sat behind a wheel, though I know not how that could steer the beast. He said, "All right, hold on to your butts," (at which saying we all took hold of our pistols) and then applied the key; now we heard the beast roar and growl. Mysteriously, we also heard a blast of music, but Shluxer poked the beast in the mystically-engraved panel facing us, and it stopped. Once Shluxer coaxed Kelly back onto the thing's flank, he having leapt off and drawn his iron at the sound of the thing's roaring, my new navigator plied his hands and feet in an arcane manner, and – we were off!

It was, at first, simply a wonder. Shluxer somehow made the glass window beside me vanish, and then, as we moved farther away from the Glass Palace at a speed faster than a grown man's trot, I could feel the wind, though only from my side. Straight ahead I watched the ground move, the trees coming closer, and yet it seemed unreal – the motion too smooth, and without a direct wind in my face coming from the forward quarter, it felt wrong to me.

Then we reached the road – we had been moving along the track from the Palace, which was lengthy and narrow; this that lay ahead was a smooth-paved road four times the width, at least – and turned to starboard, and suddenly we were moving faster than I have ever moved before on this Earth, faster than a horse at the gallop, faster than ever the fleetest ship raced before the wind and tide. At first I felt near a swoon – a sensation increased, along with my terror, when I saw another beast-wagon apparently aimed directly at us and charging, before it missed us just to our port side, as though we were jousters in the lists. It was followed by another beast-wagon, and another, and another. The road turned to the left, and then the right; the beast-wagon barely slowed, and with each turn, I and my men drifted to the side, like green sailors in their first swell, with cries and murmurs of alarm. It was the most frightful experience of my life, saving only, perhaps, the encounters with Hobbes and the *Sea-Cat*.

Then Ian started laughing.

I looked back at him, incredulous; it was in my mind that he had lost his sanity and was in hysterics. But no, he met my gaze and I saw that he was himself. He had thrust his head out through the porthole in the door-wing where he had broken the glass pane, and the wind of his passing was tearing through his hair and blowing out the collar of his shirt. "Try it, Nate!" he shouted to me, grinning like a child on Christmas morning – though he did flinch away from the oncoming beast-wagons, which trumpeted their strange cries at him, or perhaps at our beast. Shluxer cursed and steered us farther to starboard, giving Ian room away from the jousting wagons. Then I heard a whoop from Kelly on the other side, but his head was above the top of the opening he stood in and could not be seen. I glanced at O'Neill, and saw that he was not amused: his gaze was glassy, his mouth open and slack, his skin pallid and rapidly becoming green; I recalled that O'Neill was one of those who struggled with sea-sickness, and I surmised that the beast-wagon's strange motion was too much for him. It certainly put a flutter in my own gut, though the like didn't affect me at sea, but this thing jerked from side to side far more rapidly than any ship, and the movement forward pressed us back into our seats before the long turns pulled us to the outward side, and it was all very strange. I clapped O'Neill on the knee, and he met my gaze, swallowing painfully, beads of sweat on his brow. "Will ye live?" I asked him.

He started to nod, then closed his eyes and shivered. "Aye."

I turned to Shluxer. "How much longer?" I had to repeat the question, as his attention was fixed on Kelly and Ian; Ian was now seated in the porthole, his entire trunk outside the beast-wagon. He and Kelly were shouting back and forth and in unison, no words, just cries of pure joy.

"WHEEEEE!"

"AYYYIIIEEEEEEE!!"

"YAAAA-HAAAA-HAAAA!"

"Shouldn't that be 'Yo-ho-ho?'" Shluxer muttered.

I said his name again, and he glanced at me.

"Oh, right – uh, how much longer? I dunno – five minutes if they haven't left this road. Maybe less."

I nodded and then clapped O'Neill on the knee again. "Ye'll live, man. If ye have to purge, do it towards Kelly." Then I put my head out the window, as well, to see what all the fuss was about.

The moment I felt the wind on my face, coming from what my eyes and mind told me was the proper direction, rather than blowing from a quarter-turn to the side, then the sensation of strangeness disappeared. My gut subsided its churning, the clench of my jaw eased; suddenly it was as if we were sailing the swiftest ship across calm waters, or riding the fleetest horse with the smoothest gait – I know not how to describe it! Our speed was magnificent, but there was no sense of the motion, none of the up-and-down or back-to-front jerking that accompanied any other means of such speed, whether it be a horse's hoofbeats or a team pulling a wagon or a ship going over waves and swells. I have never felt anything like it. I presume this is what the birds feel when they spread their wings and glide through the air. It was – it was glorious. Soon all three of us, Ian, Kelly, and myself, were crying out with joy as we leaned out of the beast-wagon and waved our hands in the wind.

But then, as I was seated on my own porthole and turned towards Ian to share a grin, Kelly shouted "Captain!" I glanced to him, and he nodded to the starboard bow quarter and shouted, "'Tis them, sir." I turned quickly and spotted my wayward bully boys immediately: there were no other people on this road – reasonable, considering the speed and frequency of beast-wagons on it! These folk must have separate roads for people to walk or ride more ordinary steeds. My men's clothing, too, stood out clearly against the dull green mangroves and other trees to either side of us. They had not yet noticed us as different from any other beast-wagon.

I ducked back into the beast-wagon and marked the target for Shluxer, who muttered, "No shit, Sherlock." I swear, the man speaks an English almost incomprehensible to me. But he turned and stopped, all of a sudden, just as we passed them, bringing us to a dead halt not twenty feet from the four runaways. Remarkable.

Kelly was already off the wagon and facing them, weapons in hands. I opened the portal – after Shluxer pointed out the handle to me – and stood by him; behind his great frame, O'Neill crawled from the beast's guts and heaved up his own. Ian, his face still red and grinning from the wind, leapt to the top of the wagon and struck a stance, fists on hips. He cried, "What ho, me hearties!"

I looked at my men with somewhat less joy. Of the four, Moran looked the most abashed, and would not meet my gaze. Carter simply stood and looked at us with both equanimity and a certain amount of wonder at the means of our arrival; Burke sneered and smirked; and O'Flaherty clenched his jaw with anger. I strode slowly up to them, looking from one face to the next.

"Out for a wee stroll, are we?" I asked sardonically.

"Aye," O'Flaherty spat back. "Out to correct that one's failure," he said, pointing a thumb at O'Gallows. Ian's good humor ended instantly, and he leapt down from the beast-wagon and marched toward O'Flaherty with grim intent, but I waved him back.

"You think the provisions he gathered for us insufficient?"

O'Flaherty, who had been sneering a challenge at Ian, now looked back to me. "Aye, o' course t'were insufficient, man. Ye canna expect a pirate crew to live without spirits. Especially not in the midst of all this madness we go through in this place where you brought us, Captain." He stepped closer. "And don't try to foist it off on me, again. Ye put on a nice bit o' theater for the men, but ye canna have it both ways. If ye be the captain, then the responsibility for our mishaps be yours. And ye knows it."

I nodded, for he was in the right. "Aye, I've made many mistakes, o' course. Any man in command will do the same. What matter, though, is that I must recognize my mistakes, and ensure that more and poorer choices do not worsen our situation beyond repair – as this little excursion of yours would do. What in the name of all the hells were you thinking, Sean?" I shouted, throwing my hands up in exasperation.

Never one to back down, O'Flaherty bellowed right back. "Your man there said t'were no guards! The boys need a bit o' cheer, and we mean to get it for them."

"You daft fool," spake I, with perhaps less diplomacy than the circumstances asked, "I sent Ian off with mere trinkets, and he traded them for a month's provisions. Did ye think we couldn't do the same twice, only this time with rum as the goal? What, do ye not remember the remaining wealth in the Palace we took? – Aye, took under *my* command?"

O'Flaherty laughed, without mirth. "Trade? We're not merchants, Nate. We be *pirates*. We *take* what we want." Carter and Burke both nodded at this, and Moran looked as though he wanted to.

I laughed back. "Pirates, Sean? Ye be pirates?" I stepped up and pressed my chest to his. "Then where be your ship?" I shouted in his face. He stepped back then, but I stepped with him. "You know where. She be on the beach. On her side in the sand, with a great hole blown in her flank. You know – you *all* know," I said, turning to include the other three with a look and a gesture, "you know that I have no compunction against taking what I desire. The world owes me that, as it owes each of you. Aye?" They nodded again, and from behind me, Ian growled, "Aye, it bloody well does."

I turned back to O'Flaherty. I stopped shouting; we needed to remove the spark from this discussion, not throw it into the powder keg. "But we need the ship. We need the *Grace*, Sean – need her in the water and catching the wind. Aye, of course I took note when Ian said there were no guards at the Piggly-Wiggly, but think ye we have no enemies hereabouts? If this be a colony, there will be troops here, somewhere; if it be a sovereign nation, they will have militia. Either way, your little raid would bring them down on us. Now, if we could escape to sea in our fair ship, then I would lead the way, and carry a cask of rum myself! I planned to do just that. But *not –*" and here I shouted once more, as I felt this point deserving of special emphasis: *"NOT UNTIL WE HAVE OUR SHIP BACK!"*

O'Flaherty and I glared at each other in silence. I knew what he wanted: he wanted to name me coward, shame me with my unwillingness to take this risk when such an easy prize beckoned. But he knew that if he said it, I would draw arms to defend my honor – and he would lose against me, with pistol or with blade, and he knew that, too. So we waited, and I watched him swallow the words he wanted to say to me then. They looked bitter.

Then another voice broke into the tableau we had made: "Hey!" We all turned and looked: it was Shluxer, standing with his arms crossed, his face pale and nervous. "If you dudes, you know, want some booze or something, you know, I can get it for you."

I raised one eyebrow and asked what we all wondered: "What is booze?"

He rolled his eyes. "You know, booze. Liquor, beer, whiskey, wine, shit like that." He shrugged. "I can get other shit, too, if you want to get *really* fucked up. But booze, that's easy."

"How much?" O'Flaherty asked, even as I asked, "What risks will there be?" We glared at each other some more.

"As much as you want. No trouble – I got this shit covered, yo."

I looked the question at O'Flaherty, and after a moment, he nodded. I turned back to Shluxer and said, "Yo-ho-ho."

So it went: Ian accompanied Shluxer in the beast-wagon, and the rest of us marched back to the Palace, in silence but for some brief muttering between O'Flaherty and Burke, and Burke and Moran, and then a low conversation between Carter and O'Neill, once O'Neill recovered from his illness – which largely came the moment he found he would not have to mount the wagon once more. I was chagrined to see that Carter did much of the talking, but if I walked closer, they turned to silence until I moved away. Perhaps I should not have brought O'Neill.

I am sure this is not the last trouble these four will cause me, but I have no idea how to prevent them.

The situation is fast becoming dire.

Log #16: Elliot's Beer Run

I can't believe this. I mean, seriously, I just can't fuckin believe this shit.

You know in *A Princess Bride* how Vizzini always says "Inconceivable!" and Inigo finally says "You keep using that word. I do not think it means what you think it means." That's how I feel. This shit here is inconceivable. But just like with Vizzini, who says that about shit that's already happening, which means it's, like, *conceivable,* this shit that I can't believe is happening right now.

I'm on a beer run with a pirate.

I glance in the rearview – which catches me a look at the hole that huge dude Kelly put in the roof with his dagger – and then I stop at a Stop sign. And next to me, this guy Ian – who, no homo, but he's like the best-looking guy I've ever seen, all sparkling blue eyes and curly red-gold hair and tan skin and white teeth (How does a pirate get white teeth? What, did they jack a floss shipment? For that matter, I thought British people all had fucked-up teeth. Whatever: homey's got prom king genes, that's all.) – Ian throws his hands up on the dash to stop himself from flying through the windshield, even though I didn't actually stop hard at all. And he laughs through those shiny white teeth and he's all "She stops like a horse refusing a fence. How do ye keep from flailin' about?" in that Irish accent.

Oh, I have got to go clubbing with this guy. Just being seen with his castoffs would up my game, like, ten levels.

I shrug. "You just get used to it, I guess. I dunno. I had to stop for the sign." Road's clear, so I step on it. The Honda – which is hot, so I'm a little freaked out about driving it around, but it wasn't too bad, I had my shit pretty together, until Kelly just whipped out his dagger and punched it through the roof like it was fucking nothing, and then I thought "What exactly did they do with the guy who owned this car, and all those keys and shit they had? And who owns that house? Fucking beach front with a private cove, that place was like two, three million dollars worth of Florida real estate, easy. So where's the owner? Why did he let a bunch of raggedy-ass thugs dressed up like pirates crash in his crib?" And then I started thinking – maybe they're not just crazy-*looking*. And maybe the people who own the house, and the cars and the keys, maybe they won't be calling the po-po any time soon because they're, like, buried in the backyard or cut up in pieces and sunk in the ocean, like on *Dexter*. Then I started getting a little freaked out like: I'm driving around in a dead dude's car. With the dude who fuckin killed him. Cause that Kelly guy was big, and had no problem stabbing shit, and those four guys we chased down were all thugged up and all – but if any of these guys has ever capped anyone, it's that Damnation guy. When he was pissed off about his boys treatin him like a bitch – man, just looking at him and you know that muthafucka's cold-blooded, like *ice cold*. Him or that crazy fuck with no thumbs. So I'm glad they're out of the car, and I'm just rollin with Pretty-Boy here.

No homo.

Anyway – what was I saying? Oh, right: the Honda's actually got some *cojones*, so it pushes us back in the seats when I hit the gas, and Ian laughs and says "Good Lord of Hosts, this wagon is truly a miracle. It doesna live, and it has na horses nor oxen to pull it. How does it go?"

So I start to tell him – not that I know everything about cars, not a fuckin gearhead or whatever – but you can't tell this guy anything. I'm all "When I step on this pedal –" and he goes "What's a pedal?" So I point to the gas and brake, right, and he comes, like, into my fuckin lap to stare down at them, bending over me like he's about to start polishing my tool. And I'm all "Whoa, back the fuck up, you fag!" and he sits back and says "A lever," but he says it all weird, like, "LEE-ver," and I'm all "A what?" and he goes "A LEE-ver, a pedal's a LEE-ver for your foot." And then I realize what he's saying and I nod and shit, and then I say "So when I step on it, it sends more gas to the engine –"

And he goes "What is gas?"

You can't tell this guy anything.

You shoulda heard how he took traffic lights, when we got stuck at a long red on Kennedy Drive. He fuckin thought there were like, monkeys or something inside it, with lanterns, changing the colored lights. You fuckin try explaining computers and automatic timers and shit – fuck, try explaining electricity. Once you get past "It's lightning," what the fuck do you say next?

Who the fuck are these guys, anyway?

So we get to Casa de Schluchzer, and we're in luck – the parentals are both out. Good, because I do *not* want to explain who my "little friend" is to my mom, and fuck, what if the Depot called here looking for me? Or what if the cops came by? Maybe they think I got kidnapped, I dunno.

Whatever. I leave Ian with the TV, after I show him like three buttons on the remote – and which channel has porn on it – and I go get my shit. First thing is in Dad's office, in the back of his top right desk drawer – it's his "emergency" credit card. Well, Pops, this is a fuckin emergency if I ever saw one. Then I bust a quick shower, cause I'm all stankin from running with that bag on my head and sweatin like a motherfucker when they kidnapped me and shit, and then I go to my room and pack some shit, just the essentials.

And I get my sword. It's a Crusader broadsword, and it cost me over 400 bucks online, and that shit's for real. I feel better knowing I'm armed. Then I stash away a nice little boot-knife I got at a Faire, because it feels even better to be armed when nobody else knows you're armed, am I right? I wish we had a fuckin 9-millimeter, but Mom's anti-gun and Dad's a pussy. Whatever.

I think about leaving them a note, but then I think, *Fuck 'em. Let 'em wonder.* I get Ian and we roll out for the liquor store.

I talk to Ian, and he says they got twenty guys back at their crib – well, no, first he says there's a "score" of 'em, but I'm like "Score? What score? What the fuck's a score? Like a game score?" and *then* he says there's twenty. So I ask what they like to drink, and he says ale and whiskey and grog. And wine for the captain. And I'm all "Aight, what the fuck is grog?" So he says – check this shit – it's rum mixed with water and *fuckin gunpowder*. And I'm all "No *shit?*" and he grins and he's all like "Aye – it gives it a wee kick. Like a beestung mule."

So okay, we go in and get like a case of whiskey and three cases of rum, and I get the guy to bring out three kegs of Coors and a tap, and I ask him to pick out, like, a dozen bottles of wine for the captain. And he asks how I'm paying, and I bust out the credit card and my ID – and for maybe the first time in my life, I'm glad I'm Elliot Schluchzer, Junior.

While I'm paying, Ian loads all that shit in the car, him and the liquor dude heaving the kegs in the back seat, though I have to go out to pop the trunk, instead of trying to explain to him how to do it. Then we roll out and head back.

We drive past Home Depot, and I think about stopping in to tell them I quit – maybe taking a table saw as my severance, like – but I see a cop car in the lot, and I'm thinking they might still be looking for the crazy fuckers who stole a couple hundred bucks' worth of lumber and nothing else. And I'm thinking they might be thinking I was in on it, since I disappeared with them and people around here know I'm into the Ren Faires and pirate festivals and shit. So we drive on by. And I'm thinking I might never be coming back here, if the idea that's bouncing around in my head turns out, and I think about my job, and my car, and my room, and my computers, and my parents, and my whole life – and I think leaving it all behind would suit me just fine. Fuck all of it.

We get back to the crib, and I stop the car at the top of the driveway, where there's a wall all covered with ivy and shit and a bunch of tall trees, mostly palms, and I know there's a rolling metal gate stuck back behind some bushes, and when I reach in and grab it and roll it out, Ian's all shocked and shit that I even knew it was back there. But I'm all, "Homey, no house like this doesn't have a gate on the drive." It just got left open by somebody, probably because it's not automatic – it's an old gate, like from the fifties or something, before they had remotes, and whoever lives here probably didn't want to fuck it up installing a chain drive and sensors and shit. But Ian's all jizzed up and says the captain will be pleased, and I'm like *"Eeeeex-cellent"* like Mr. Burns in my head. My plans are coming together.

We drive up to the crib – and when I see it, really see it, with no bag over my head and my thoughts not all fucked up by what's going on around me, I think, *Yeah, I could live like this.* Even if – no, *better* if they stole it, even capped the guy who lived here and sunk him in the cove tied to a rock and shit. We drive up and Ian gets like the full hero's welcome – and that's before we break out the booze that's got the Honda's back end scraping the ground, the shit's so heavy. Then me and Ian both get three cheers.

And Captain Kane comes out and smiles and slaps us on the back and everything – I hold up for a high-five, but he just looks at me like "What the fuck are you waving at?" and leaves me hanging. But for sure he's happy to see me, and he says so. He thanks me for doing the liquor run, and for driving to catch up with his boys. So I turn to him, and I go like this, talking all slow and raspy and shit: "Some day – and that day may never come – I may call upon you to do a favor for me. Until that day, accept this as a gift." And he looks at me all thoughtful and calculating, and then he nods and says, "Done," and shakes my hand.

And he didn't even know that was from *The Godfather, Part I.* That clinches it.

"So Damn," I say, and throw my arm around his shoulders. "Tell me. What year do you think it is?"

Captain's Log
Date: 27 June, 2011.
Location: 2011.
Conditions: All is lost.

We have traveled through time, he tells me. It's the future, he tells me. He was smiling.

It cannot be true. I must find a reason why Shluxer would lie to me. Then I can kill him and it won't be true.

Three hundred and thirty-three years. All is dust. Everything and everyone we know is dust, now. All – all is lost.

All is lost.

Log #17: Coming Up to Speed

Captain's Log
Date: 29 June ~~1678~~ 2011
Location: ~~Glass Palace~~ Beach House, 10 mi. South of Miami, Florida, United States of America
Conditions: Ship repairs near completion

I don't know how to tell the men.

They have been busy, working steadily – after first celebrating Shluxer's bounty. They emptied a crate of rum that first night, not realizing that Shluxer's rum is more potent than the rum we knew. They were near paralyzed with remorse the following morning. In the afternoon, though, O'Flaherty and Burke got them up and back to work on the *Grace*. They also sent Shluxer for more rum, which he retrieved without difficulty, which made him, once more, the hero in the hearts of my crew.

I will not kill him. I was in my cups myself when I wrote that last entry, having commandeered the whiskey and made a most strenuous and valiant attempt to consume every drop; without mixing it with water, I might add. I spent all of yesterday thus engaged in my cabin, which necessitated this day be spent recovering. At last, I have been able to eat some food, and now I drink but clean water from the Palace's taps. Ah – it is a beach house, not a Palace, avers Shluxer.

I will not kill Shluxer, no. It would not change our situation, I know. He was but the messenger. Too, he has proved most helpful. Not only has he taken up the mantle of ship's carpenter, helping the men to repair the hole in the *Grace's* hull to anyone's satisfaction, and then retrieving for us a great quantity of a white paste he calls caulk, though it bears little resemblance to the tarred rope fibers we have always used to fill the cracks between the planks of the hull – he has also shown us much about this Beach House we have inhabited, and made our daily lives far easier.

I found today that he released our hostages. All but the woman, Flora, the Palace maid. Apparently, at some time on the night of revelry, he struck up a conversation with Ian – and I must note that my dear friend and great ally took responsibility for the ship and crew whilst I was out of my mind with Shluxer's revelations; it was Ian who stayed sober and ensured that watches were kept; we had moved our landward watch post to the gate Shluxer found for us, the which we have reinforced with blockades on the road, and locked in place with hammered wedges and chains. The men stationed there have begun to grow accustomed to the beast-wagons – Shluxer names them "cars" – for they pass by the gate with mind-numbing regularity. But to the point, to the point – too many wonders, too many distractions. Shluxer spoke with Ian, Ian told me later, and mentioned that the owner of the car, the wagon named Honda which we used to retrieve O'Flaherty, would be irate when he saw the damage done to his beast. Ian, laughing, said they could ask the man, as he was locked and under guard along with the other hostages inside the Beach House. Shluxer was most put out by this intelligence, though Ian said he grew calmer when he heard they had been held for no more than a single day, at that point. He asked to be taken to the hostages, which he was; he then told Ian that they must be released immediately, or else the militia assault we have feared would become imminent and inevitable – he called the militia the "police," and also, inexplicably, the Five Oh and the Po-Po. Shluxer has the strangest tongue I have yet known. I despair of mastering it.

Any road, Shluxer and Ian came to my rooms and were repulsed without entry by myself and my fermented companion; they went to O'Flaherty instead, who was nearly as drunk but far more companionable. He granted Shluxer and Ian the authority to handle the situation. Shluxer, in subsequent conversation with the Brothers Lopez, was relieved to hear that they were themselves illegal, and thus unlikely, he claimed, to summon the police, or have said police summoned on their behalf, which seemed his greater worry, since he said we had confiscated their "sellfones." Ian knew not to what Shluxer then referred. Shluxer determined that we should keep their sister as assurance of their continued silence, and then he returned their belongings, saw them into their Honda-wagon, and sent them away.

I want to believe that Shluxer has done us a great service. But I fear that he is gaining a taste for power, power granted him by his knowledge of this world – this time – that is so strange to us. I surmise that he has seldom if ever had authority over others, and like most such men, he revels in his elevation. But as England's Shakespeare put it, "'Tis the bright day that brings forth the adder, and that craves wary walking. Crown him that, and then I grant we put a sting in him, that at his will he may do danger with."

The Bard refers to the crowning of Julius Caesar. I fear I may be cast in the role of Brutus. Which does not end well.

For the nonce, though, we need Shluxer and his knowledge, his power. Using the maid's beast-wagon, he has procured all manner of supplies: fresh tar for the ropes and the hull, spices for O'Grady and a remarkable quantity of salt, the which O'Grady has used to preserve the remaining meat from Ian's trading mission; Shluxer has brought us new provisions, as well, nearly as fine as the goods Ian brought. Though I have not enjoyed all that he brought – those Doritos are vile things, like burnt, flattened goat turds dipped in gunpowder and salt – I must speak well of these Twinkie cakes. Delicious.

When Shluxer learned that we had been drinking the water from the pool on the terrace despite its bitter taste – which he called "cloreen," or some such – he showed us that the fixtures in this dwelling provide limitless fresh water. But to speak truth, as my mother taught me I ever should, to a tongue raised on new rain caught in clay jugs and copper pots, and to the crisp cool drink of mountain springs, the water from within tastes little better than that from the pool. Of course, life on board ship nearly always entails the drinking of stale and sour water; the moment it is stored in casks, it begins to turn, but we needs must drink it anyway. 'Tis at least part of the reason the men prefer grog – though now they are grown mighty fond of the beer Shluxer brought us in metal barrels, this Coors that he insists on referring to as the silver bullet.

What matters most to me is that Shluxer has indeed managed to repair my lovely ship. The hull appears to be even more watertight than when she was new. We will let his caulk dry another day, and then cover it with tar and float the ship once the tide is high. If she doesn't take on water then, we will sail, in three days' time.

Though I do not know where we will go then.

Captain's Log
Date: 1 July 2011
Location: Beach House Cove
Conditions: Improved, at last.

The caulking and tarring is done. The mast is repaired, and the men have begun digging out the sand around the *Grace* to the level of the tide; when the water flows in, it will, with the blessings of fortune, float our ship, and we will once more be men of the sea. I find I am tired of standing on this land. I have been considering a return to Ireland, though I know not what we will find there in this time. I have not consulted with Shluxer on the matter, though if past conversation be any guide, his knowledge of the great nations of Europe is spotty at best. He claims there are no more kings in the world, at least not in any but the darkest and most savage nations; this gave me a cold chill, as it brought to mind Devil Cromwell and his Parliamentarians, and my father. But Shluxer knew nothing at all of Cromwell, or the wars for Charles's throne, or the devastation of Ireland under the New Model Army. It is most odd, what he knows and what he does not.

But however odd the man is, I had best become accustomed to him: he has signed the Articles, and joined the crew of the *Grace of Ireland* as our carpenter. He was sponsored by O'Flaherty and Carter, with whom he has grown most amicable, but his great benefit to our ship and crew would have been enough regardless.

I confess I hold reservations about the man's inclusion in our merry band. When I asked him about the home and family he would leave behind to become a rover – he has mentioned his mother and father before – he shrugged and said, "Fuck them – I want to be a pirate. Yo ho!" He is most fond of that phrase. But it was the first part of that utterance that stuck with me. What loyalty can a man have, if he have none to his own blood?

But perhaps I should ask my father that question.

Captain's Log
Date: 2 July 2011
Location: Beach House Cove

Conditions: The ship is once more on water. Situation on land, alas, has sunk to the depths.

I was right not to trust Shluxer.

This past night, while the men slept on the beach, I came off the *Grace*, where I had been sleeping in my cabin; I find it far more comfortable for its familiarity than even the softest bed in this house. I went inside in search of a cool drink of water. When I entered the kitchen, I heard some noise of struggle; investigating I found the guard outside the prisoner's chamber had been dismissed, and inside, I found Shluxer attempting to defile the maid, Flora. I prevented him, and struck him down; this morning, at dawn, I had him tied to the mast and given twenty lashes. I twice had to order Burke to put his back into it. Burke – the man who wears a devil's grin at the mere thought of applying stripes to a man's back – now he grows reluctant? In truth, I have never heard caterwauling and pleas like those uttered by Shluxer once his pale, scarless skin felt the bite of the lash; he has lived a soft life till now. No more.

O'Flaherty came to me with objection, for my assault on the foul rapist. The stripes he earned, according to our Articles, which prescribe this penalty for any man who attempts to force his attentions on any unwilling woman, and death or marooning for any man who is successful in his vile designs; but those same Articles expressly forbid any member of the crew, and any officer, from striking another. And I had struck Shluxer many times, in my rage. I argued that the defense of our own honor required my actions in order to stop Shluxer, and though O'Flaherty grumbled, he went away.

But he was succeeded by Ian. Who repeated the complaint. Though his reasoning was more pragmatic: in our dire straits, he said we need Shluxer more than we need justice. He felt I should have simply warned the bastard away and doubled the woman's guard, so as to avoid dissension and resentment among the crew, for whom Shluxer has gained a most favorable hue of approval – and whose crime, generally speaking, is frequently shrugged at indifferently by my men, despite the penalty I had had included in the Articles. I am afraid Ian and I both became intemperate in our discussion of this matter, until at last I ejected him from my cabin and locked myself in, to keep this log and to brood on our circumstance. And aye, to keep from laying eyes on that slug Shluxer, lest I open his belly for the gulls.

I cannot face the crew. I cannot lie to them, and I cannot speak to them without addressing our situation; I know the talk amongst them is of little else but where we are, and where we must go. I hope once we put out to sea, I will gain the courage and the strength to tell them the truth; I know if I do not, then Shluxer will, and he will say it – poorly. Until then, I have given my orders, and I will stay in my cabin while they are carried out. I have entrusted the maid's safety to Lynch and McTeigue until we depart, as they see the situation my way, I know – indeed, Lynch was so enraged he demanded Shluxer's throat be cut for his crime, but I ordered him to let the blood spilled by the lash suffice. After all, I did prevent Shluxer from achieving his intent. Lynch was not satisfied, but he agreed and swore to abide by my wishes.

We must get to sea. All will be well when we are on the waves once more.

Log #18: Betrayal

Captain's Log
Date: July 4, 2011
Location: Miami, Florida
Conditions: Back-stabbed. Marooned. Stranded. Heart-torn.

I was nine years old when my heart first broke. 'Twas after I rode King Henry, the bull that I had been charged with keeping (along with keeping all our other animals) during my mother's three-week absence in Dublin. When my mother finally returned and walked into Uncle Seamus's house, where I lay with my leg broken and a thousand imagined torments piled up in my mind, a thousand possible punishments she could lay upon me for my crime – which seemed unforgivable, then, and only slightly less so now, when I understand how she felt – my tongue seemed to dry up in my mouth, my throat swelling shut with fear even as my eyes stood wide as church doors. I stared at her face, looking for a sign of how my doom would fall. I saw anger, there, and bitter disappointment – but most of all, I saw betrayal. She had trusted me, her only son, to care for her home and livestock in her absence; and not only had I failed, but I myself had been the instrument of her home's destruction with my blind, foolish mischief. When I saw how deeply that betrayal of her trust had wounded her, I began to weep. I turned away, unable to look at her any more. I longed for her to kill me and end it all.

She came to my side where I lay on a bench, swaddled in blankets. She exposed my broken leg and examined the splint and the set of the injury; she felt my brow, turned my face to her and looked at my eyes, opened my mouth and examined my tongue. Then, without having spoken a word, she turned away and walked out. In the next room I heard her say, "We'll leave before dawn. Put him in the wagon in the morning."

Needless to say, this did not assuage my fears, nor my guilt. She couldn't even stand to talk to me, not even to yell and rage and curse my stupidity. And we would be leaving? Where would we go? Was this the first stage of my own punishment? Dawn – because I faced execution like a common criminal? Was the instrument of my chastisement so prodigious, so awful, that we had to travel to reach it?

Was it a dungeon?

A torture chamber?

Would she have me thrown in the ocean, or abandoned on a mountaintop for wild animals to rend and tear and devour?

I tried to ask my uncle Seamus when he brought me supper, but he shook his head and refused to speak to me, surely forbidden to do so on my mother's word. Only my exhaustion from hours of worry put me to sleep that night; I still woke when it was the deepest dark, and picked up the thread of my fretting without hesitation.

Within an hour, still before the dawn's light reddened the sky, my cousin Patrick, Seamus's eldest son, who had escorted my mother on her journey to Dublin, brought me in a bowl of morning porridge. When I had eaten and stumbled through my morning wash, Patrick came and lifted me in his arms, carrying me out to the wagon. He set me in the back, propping my leg on a bundle and cushioning my back with blankets. When he saw I was secure, he went back into the house. He hadn't spoken a word.

That was the first part of my punishment. Cousin Patrick drove the team and my mother sat beside him, and they spoke to each other only in voices too low for me to hear. They did not say a single word to me, not for the entire week we traveled. If I said I was hungry or thirsty, Patrick would stop the wagon and bring me bread or a leather bottle of water; if I claimed to feel sick or in pain, my mother would come to check on me, examine my leg, touch my face, check my eyes and tongue as before. Sometimes she would give me a sprig of herbs to chew, or dissolve somewhat in my water and have me drink it; sometimes she would simply return to the wagon's seat and Patrick would drive on. Her gaze was indifferent when she looked at me, no more caring than if she were checking a dog for worms. She didn't even look angry any more.

I began to fear that I had lost her. That we were on our way to the place where she would abandon me: perhaps placing me into a monastery, or giving me over to an apprenticeship, or selling me into a workhouse. I stopped complaining of pain or hunger, and drew into myself, becoming little more than a shell surrounding my fear and sorrow.

And then one morning, after a brief breakfast, my mother and Patrick washed and dressed me in my best clothing – still only a wool tunic and trousers, but they were finely made and clean. They put me in the wagon and off we went, still in silence, my fear growing still more intense by the minute, though before I would have sworn that it could not be greater. But this was it. We were here. My doom had arrived.

Imagine my surprise, then, when we turned off the road at the gate of a fine manor house, just visible behind a screen of elms and sycamores. A man in armor, holding a pike, challenged us at the gate, his eyes hard and suspicious, though his speech was polite enough.

My mother told him, "Tell Lord Blackwell that Maeve of Drogheda requests an audience. And she has brought her son."

The guard blinked and stepped back when my mother named Drogheda. I was confused; we lived in Belclare, clear across Ireland from Drogheda. What was going on? Where were we? Who was this Blackwell? The guard opened the gate for us, instructed Patrick to halt the wagon just inside, and then strode quickly to the door of the manor house and vanished within.

My mother stepped down from the wagon's seat and came back to me. She helped me down, stood me up straight and brushed off the road dust and bits of hay from the wagon bed. Then she stood, tall and proud with her fists on her hips and her chin high, and looked me over. I tried to stand as well as she, my broken leg splinted well enough to take my weight, and I lifted my chin, despite my fear that that she was about to inform me that she was handing me over into the service of some English lord, that she would never see me again and was happier for it, seeing as I was such a dangerous and disobedient child. I held back the pleas for mercy, the oaths of love and of the eternal perfection of my future obedience to her every whim, if only – if only she would take me home with her. The tears I could not stop.

She spoke at last – for the first time in nearly a month, speaking directly to me – and her voice was hard and proud. "Though we call you Nate, your name is Damnation. Damnation Kane. The Kane is from me, my family name, and a good Irish name it is, even if the

English cannot spell it properly. You are *my son,* blood of my blood, flesh of my flesh."

She paused then, and her gaze moved to the manor house that loomed before us, built of cold white stone, like ice and snow, without a flower bed or a statue or a single scrap of decoration to lend charm to its cold facade – as I was about to learn, the house was the perfect reflection of its owner. Then my mother said, "It is time you met the man who gave you your other name, and the other half of your blood. Your father."

My father? My mother had never told me of my father. I think she had never spoken those words in my life. Whenever I asked her, she left the room. If I asked anyone else, no matter who it was, the reaction was ever the same: the face closed up, and turned sad. The eyes pitied me, and then looked for my mother, wherever she was. I learned to stop asking.

But now, at this moment when I had begun to doubt my mother, the one strong pillar that I did have in my life, which had always held me up despite the apparent non-existence of a father, and in this place, this manor house which, for all its stark exterior, still it was all finished stone and dark, rich wood, and large enough to house my entire village – here and now I was to meet the man who made me, whose blood ran in my veins. And – what? Did Mam plan to leave me here with him?

Did I want her to?

I could feel my body begin to shake, the fear in me being replaced by – anticipation. Hope. I did not want to leave my mother, but all of my life I had longed for a father, for the *right* father, a strong and upright and just man, a man I could take pride in claiming as my own, even as he claimed me as his. Immediately I began to spin a tale in my mind whereby he could have remained out of my life until this point and still been an honorable man: he was wealthy, obviously, and a lord, so perhaps theirs had been a forbidden love. Perhaps my mother had hidden me away, and never told my father of my existence; perhaps he was wed already when they had made me, and in her deep love for him, she had left rather than destroy him with her shame. Perhaps on her recent trip, she had found that he was now a widower, or in some other way free to love her – to love *me.*

The door opened. My heart seemed to stop – but it was only the guard. He came back across the lawn – which, though it could have supported two or three good milch cows, was clearly trimmed by hand, the blades all perfectly uniform in length – and beckoned peremptorily to my mother. "Come. Bring the boy. Leave your man with the beasts."

I saw my mother's jaw clench and her knuckles turn white. I glared at the guard, prepared myself to kick him in the shins for angering my mother, noting carefully where his armored greaves ended, just above his ankle. But then I hesitated. This man was my father's man. Surely I had to defend him, as well? Didn't we share allegiance? And what had he said to upset her? Was she as nervous as I, to see my father, to realize or end the hope that their love could be rekindled? Was she upset that she had to present me to my father in such a situation, when I had broken her heart with my betrayal of her trust? Was it – it couldn't be because of *Patrick*, who had to stay out here with the horses? It couldn't be: Patrick looked palpably relieved to be excused from going into the house, and I wasn't sure I didn't envy him.

But no. This was my father's house. *My father* was inside. Of course I wanted to meet him, to see his home, his belongings, his manner of living. Didn't I?

I had little choice, of course. The guard turned to lead us in, and my mother grabbed my arm in an iron grip and hauled me limping along at a rapid pace. I could no longer make sense of my emotions: they were too many, and too mixed.

At the door the guard turned us over to a serving man. Tall and thin, old but not in his dotage, the man wore a crisp black suit with a white cravat, a powdered wig, and a deeply contemptuous frown. He gave us a long appraisal, his lip curling more with every moment, my mother's flush deepening with every lip-curl as her grip on my arm tightened into pain. Clearly this man was not familiar with my mother's pride, or her temper. Any moment, I thought, she will swing me around her head and beat this man to death with my body as her club.

The man said, "This way. Do not touch anything." Then he turned and led us down a long hall, the walls of which were as blank and white and clean as the outside of the house, the only color coming from the sconces set on the walls, where pine torches burned with a red, popping flame, the plaster above them seared black with soot. With its high, vaulted ceilings and the doors we passed, doors of dark oak bound with iron straps, this place looked to me like the most sinister and frightening church one could imagine.

Who was my father, that he lived in this place?

The serving man knocked at a door, and then swung it open. He blocked the doorway with his body, snapped his heels together and said, "The strumpet is here, milord. With the boy."

I glanced at my mother, sure the swinging and clubbing would now commence. But I was shocked to see that all the color had fled her face, leaving her as pale as snow. She looked – scared.

The serving man nodded and stepped aside. Mockingly, he bowed us into the room, but my mother nodded at him just as if she were royalty, and with her head high and her jaw firm – though her face was still pale – she swept me into my father's presence.

The first thing I saw was the wall before us, behind him: the windows were covered with heavy drapes, blocking the light, casting the room into darkness despite the early hour and the bright sun outside. Other than the windows, the entire length and height of the wall was covered with books, shelves and shelves of books and piles of unbound pages. I had never seen so many books in my life – I hadn't thought so many could exist in one place. Those books buoyed up my spirits: my father was the richest man I had ever known! Perhaps all of the lean times, the ragged and mended clothing and the nights when we had to drink and dance and laugh because we had no food to fill our bellies – perhaps those days were all over for us now. I looked around at the other walls: this room was not blank and empty, as the rest of the house had seemed. Other than a cross large enough to hang me on – which, while something that my pagan mother wouldn't have in our own home, was certainly nothing new to me in Catholic Ireland, though I did wonder why it wasn't a proper crucifix with the figure of Christ suffering upon it – the walls were covered with battle-trophies. Broken shields, dull and rust-flecked swords and axes, wooden clubs and steel maces with dark stains on them still (perhaps that wasn't rust dotting the sword blades, after all) bows and arrows, flintlock pistols and older wheel-lock muskets, all hung below a row of torn and muddied flags and pennants which lined the walls just under the ceiling's beams.

My spirits took another step up. My father was a warrior! And a great one! Could it be that I would actually have something to be proud of, someone I could brag about to the other boys, when I had heretofore had nothing but sullen silence and fists to answer their teasing with? Oh, I could not wait to tell Angus about this! Him and his father, the best wrestler in our tiny village – pah!

He stood up from behind his desk, and my gaze snapped to him then. My father. And the moment I looked at him, I know I could not brag to the other boys about this man.

Because my father was English.

I recognized the bluff jaw, the stocky physique of a man well-fed on beef and mutton and ham for all of his life. I knew the Puritan's coat, unrelieved black wool, worn even in his own study in his own home, even on a warm summer morning. I recognized the blond hair turning gray, the sallow cheeks, and the pale eyes, the color of smoke in a winter sky. And I knew that look of utter contempt, the look every Englishman wears when he sees an Irish face.

In later days, thinking back on that moment, I decided it might have been the worst part of my first encounter with my father, that when he looked at me, his expression changed not at all. He didn't see a son, neither a source of pride nor of shame, neither heir nor by-blow. He looked at me, and all he saw was: *Irish*.

He came around the desk, which was massive and plain like everything else in this house, including the master himself. He stood in front of me and measured and weighed every inch and ounce of me with his eyes. At first I looked carefully, searching for my features in his: perhaps the ears? Something of the chin? But I could not meet his cold, hard gaze, and finally I turned to contemplation of his boots. They were large, heavy, and plain.

"He looks Irish," were the first words I heard my father say in my presence.

"He *is* Irish," my mother responded. My father snorted.

"What name does he use?" he asked.

"Nate," I spoke up. "Everyone calls me Nate." I raised my eyes to look at him when I spoke, as I had been taught.

It wasn't a particularly hard blow; more what one would use to swat a fly, perhaps a wasp. Something unpleasant that one would want to smash. But still, it knocked me back, mainly from surprise; I had never been struck before, not by the back of a man's hand.

That was the first time my father touched me.

"Children are seen and not heard," he said to me – or at least in my general direction, as he did not lower his gaze to meet mine.

116

"His name is Kane," my mother said, her voice quivering but controlled, her pale face now highlighted by two bright spots of red burning high on her cheeks.

He nodded. "Good. He will never use the name Blackwell, nor FitzBlackwell. I will not acknowledge him, not even as my bastard. Is that clear?"

"Yes," my mother said.

When he struck her, it was no harder than when he had struck me; my mother didn't even rock back, though she turned her face away. I was looking at his face when he hit her, and it did not change, not a hair, not a wrinkle. It was as if a man were correcting a dog, or giving a plowhorse instructions to turn, or stop. There was no anger there, no outrage, not even any pleasure.

By the gods, there was anger on *my* face, then, as I charged him, yelling wordlessly, my small fists flailing. This time he struck me harder, knocking me sprawling on my back, the taste of blood in my mouth. My mother's arm swung back, her mouth opened – and then she stopped herself, shaking with the effort. Her teeth bit into her bottom lip hard enough to draw a thin line of blood. She started to kneel down to me, and then stopped herself again, and turned away with her head bowed.

My father looked at me dispassionately with those eyes of ice and smoke. "He has spirit. Good." He looked at my mother again. "But the both of you are far too pert. Like all your cursed heathen race. When you address me, particularly when you acknowledge my commands, you will say, 'Yes, my lord' or 'Yes, Lord Captain.' Is that clear?"

"Yes, my lord," my mother said, her voice as cold as his gaze.

He turned back to me, running one hand over his chin; I could see now that his hands were criss-crossed with scars, the fingers gnarled from old breaks, his wrists as thick as my legs. This man had spent his life using those hands to do violence. Had it always been against women and children as well as men?

"Of course you did not come here hoping that I would accept him as my get. Does he need a place? I will find a workhouse that will take him. Or better, a ship that will transport him to the Indies. The Lord Protector needs men on the sugar plantations there. He is large enough to cut cane, I judge."

My mother took a deep, heaving breath, and turned back to face him, once more outwardly calm. "No. My lord. I only wished him to meet his father, my lord. To learn of his heritage."

He snorted again. "Looking at him now, I think there may be some question regarding that connection to myself. I find it difficult to credit that your insipid Irish blood would so overwhelm my own that no trace of me would be visible in the mongrel thus spawned." He met her gaze. "You were virgin when I took you, but afterwards? Surely a woman of your charms would have no trouble finding an Irish peasant to rut with. If you were quick enough, you could have whelped at the appropriate time to claim a greater sire for your brat."

My mother smiled, though there was no humor in it. "Whether you believe it or not, my lord, there were no others. Not then, and not since." She looked at me then, and nodded to the man who stood before us. "Lord Blackwell is your father, Nate. His blood is in your veins."

I got to my feet, struggling with my splinted leg; both of them stood and watched without offering to help. I went to her, taking her hand in mine. I was too afraid, too angry to speak, but I wanted to beg her to take me home, not to leave me with this man, not to give me away to a workhouse or a plantation in the Indies. I said nothing, but I looked at her with tears in my eyes. She nodded. She squeezed my hand.

She curtsied to my father, and said, "I thank you for your time, my lord. I assure you, you will never need see us again." We turned away and started to leave.

"You should marry, woman," he said. My mother stopped, but did not turn back. "Your boy needs training. Even an Irishman could teach you both some better manners. Your beauty has not faded, nor your figure." He strode to the cross on the wall, running his fingers along it idly.

My mother turned, and speaking to my father's back, she said, "Somehow, Irishmen are reluctant to wed a woman raped by an Englishman, and with a half-English child because of it." She squeezed my hand, and when I met her gaze, I could see a love more fierce than I could have imagined, stronger than any adversity – stronger than any shame could ever be. "I have given up hope of marriage, then, rather than give up my son." She leaned close and put her hand on my cheek, bruised where he had struck me. She whispered, "You are *my son. Mine.*" I nodded, and she kissed my head. She straightened and took a deep breath. "Come, Nate," she said to me.

Lord Blackwell said, "You call him Nate. Is it Nathaniel, then?"

My mother stopped and spoke over her shoulder. "No, my lord. When he was born and I presented him to you, you told me then that he was your damnation, and mine." She met his gaze then. "I named him as you commanded.

"His name is Damnation Kane."

***

I have been shot, stabbed, beaten, burned, and near-drowned. I have suffered insult, injury, heartache, shame, sorrow, and unquenched rage. But that day, when my father struck me down and gave me reason to hate every drop of English blood in my veins – which was, in truth, the reason my mother had brought me there, to show me and give me warning of what lurked in my blood, in the parts of me that came from my father and which she feared had begun to show themselves in my act of wanton, selfish destruction – what I felt then was the deepest agony of my life.

Until I woke in the Glass Palace this yesterday, stuffed into the wardrobe in my adopted chamber there, my head pounding from the blows rained on me and my vision blurred from the drugs fed to me. Until I staggered downstairs and out to the terrace to find that my ship, and my mutinous crew, had left without me.

I am marooned.

Log #19: Mutiny

Captain's Log
Date: 4 July 2011
Location: Miami, Florida
Conditions: Betrayed, bereft, abandoned. Determined nonetheless.

It has required much of the past two days to unknot the tangles in my memory, to see through the snarled skeins and remember: who betrayed me, and how. (It has not helped that this day, apparently one of violent celebration – perhaps a tyrant has been overthrown? – I am continuously awakened and disturbed by explosions. Child's toys, I am told, that explode in smoke and noise more than flame. Had I my ship, I would show them a proper booming: the roar of a full broadside. *That* for the Em-eighty, ha! Without the *Grace*, I have no desire to celebrate.) I have spent the time striving most earnestly, and I believe I have remembered it all, or nearly so.

The time I have not been casting back inside my aching skull has only served to dizzy me more. By a most remarkable turn of events – led by a most remarkable woman – I abide no longer in the Glass Palace. I am lodged in a smaller, more human and far more comfortable domicile, the which lies in South Miami, according to my most generous hostess, Flora Lopez. The maid of the Glass Palace, my erstwhile hostage, and would-be victim of the foul Shluxer's lust.

This is what I remember: the *Grace* had been made ready, and I had given orders that we would sail with the morning tide. I bided in my cabin aboard, as I had been for the hours and days following Shluxer's flogging – though I cannot now recall much of that span, nor how I occupied it; all is blurred and befogged.

It was O'Grady's suggestion. I remember that. But does that make him a conspirator? Or was he led, a mere puppet? Fah! It matters not. Clearly they are all mutinied, every man jack of them, the faithless bastards.

O'Grady came to me and said he had prepared a special feast, a farewell to the Palace we were abandoning. He told me it were best served ashore, in the Palace itself, with the plate and crystal and cutlery found there in their native setting, as it were. He told me, too, that my officers wished a proper dinner, with the Captain at the head of his table, all the gentlemen of the ship to break bread together. Grateful for the opportunity to smooth the feathers ruffled by the Shluxer affair – and pleased by the apparent abandonment of the usual course that required all of the ship's crew to eat together as equals, a policy to which I generally do not object, but occasionally one does tire of sailors' manners at table – I agreed, and we dined well. Indeed, 'twas a most cheerful company, with a sumptuous repast and a vast quantity of wine.

I assume it was in the wine, whatever foul concoction they poisoned me with. I tasted nothing untoward, but many of the vintages here are uncommon strange to my ancient Irish tongue. I will say that I suspected nothing, saw no hint in their behavior that they planned this blackguardery. Shluxer was sullen, as one would expect given his tender back and wounded pride; the others, O'Flaherty, Burke, Moran, Ian O'Gallows, were all joyed at the ship's recovery and our departure anon. Vaughn was his usual distracted self, responding to direct queries with direct answers, all in seriousness fitting to a churchman – frequently therefore becoming the butt of many crude jokes made at his expense but without his disapproval; I swear that man lacks the tiniest morsel of humor – but elsewise silent and contemplative.

The dizziness came on me suddenly, and I presumed it was but the wine and the food as my cup did runneth over. I excused myself and rose, and staggered, to much laughter. I remember catching myself on the table and upsetting dishes. I might have wondered why the wine so affected me, an Irish sailor – what potable on this green Earth could make such a man as I stumble? With whiskey in my blood and the sea in my legs, how could I lose equilibrium? – but I do not recall it, and if I did, I was too addled to make aught of the issue. Then – was it O'Flaherty? Or Ian? One or both gave me a shoulder, suggested the upstairs Palace rooms rather than my cabin aboard, as recommended by proximity and my extremely shakeous pins. I do not recall agreeing, nor arguing; I do not recall staggering, nor walking upright and manful, nor being carried like a babe to my bed.

No: I recall coming to myself in monstrous befuddlement, my vision blurred, my head spinning like a ship's wheel as it comes about in a headwind, my belly churning like a storm surging o'er the rocky shore – face-down on my bed while someone bound my hands together behind my back. When I protested, muzzily, I was hauled upright – and I promptly vomited on at least one of my captors. There were curses, and perhaps some laughter, though that might be my memory's failing; then one of them – presumably he who had received my offering of lightly-used provender – struck me a mighty blow, and all went dark. Then after a time of no time, I woke sprawled on the floor, my shoulders aching mightily from my bonds, my ankles trussed as well, and men's boots around my head, their voices murmuring over me. I may have groaned, I may have moved; whatever the cause, they fell on me, striking me again and again. There were many hands that struck me, and I have a village-worth of bruises to show for it; but I could not look up from the rug under my nose, and I cannot recall any specific voice – save one.

Shluxer.

They put me in the closet, bound hand and foot, and put a bag over my head; I do distinctly remember Shluxer striking me then, for I recall his grunt of effort and words of encouragement from another voice, which said the name Shluxer. The raper gave me a series of weakish blows that nonetheless accomplished a fair piece of work, bleeding and bruising my face and head quite satisfactorily. I fell and was kicked; my ribs are sprung from it even now. My consciousness was lost then.

I awoke to daylight peeking under the door. After a goodly time spent praying for death to end my suffering, and many fruitless attempts to free my limbs – though the bag on my head, loose and untethered, came away easily enough – I managed to put my benumbed fingers on the blade that is ever in my boot, and was soon freed, though still terrible sick and dizzied, weak and battered. I burst forth from the closet in spite of my maladies, intent on rushing any guard left without, but there was none. I collapsed to the floor, spent by the effort, and the time again goes blank.

It was not long before I awoke once more, as I was lying in bright sun, yet my skin remained largely chilled. I managed to regain my feet, and with the walls as my guide and necessary support, I made it down the stairs and out onto the terrace. I looked out upon that beauteous little cove, with its white sand and its bright blue sea, the gentle curve of the spit, like a mother's arm gathering her children to her bosom, the gentle strength of the tall, supple trees – and I cursed the sight, cursed it for its one lack.

My ship – my *Grace* – was gone.

I must have collapsed, then, still weak from poison and beating and betrayal. The next thing I recall was the blessed relief of a damp cloth daubing gently at my face, cleaning away the sticky blood, though not, alas, the pain. I opened my eyes, and when my vision cleared, I beheld Flora, the maid of the Palace, kneeling beside me with a cloth and an admixture of terror and pity on her gentle face.

After a moment of confusticated thoughts, which ended with the relieved awareness that she was unarmed and likely to remain so, I closed my eyes again and said, "Thank you."

In a shaking voice, she asked, "They – they are gone, see? The others?"

I tried to nod, but the motion spun my head like a child's top. "Aye, they be gone, sure as sure can be. And not apt to return to this place, curse them all to the blackest pits."

She returned to cleansing my wounds, now with a surer touch. I opened my eyes again, and saw that the terror had largely left her features; she flashed a brief smile at me when she met my gaze.

Unable to do otherwise, I surrendered myself to her ministrations, and in a short time my wounds were cleaned, daubed with a strange-smelling salve from within the Palace, and plastered over with odd, sticky, flesh-colored patches; whatever mysteries these things held, still I felt much improved. I begged her for a glass of water, which she gave me, retrieving another for herself. I toasted her, and she tapped my glass with her own, a faint smile again on her features.

She said, "You no can stay."

I sighed and turned my face away from her. I had no wish to consider any exigencies but one: my ship was stolen from me. I had no wish to consider any proposition save one: to regain my lovely *Grace*. All else came to ashes and dust beside that.

The lady pressed me. "You no stay. Missus, she come home, today. You no can stay! She call pole-ees." This broke through my despondency and rage, reaching the practicality in me. I had no wish to confront the Enchantress, nor to explain to her the damage we had done to her home and grounds, her servants – and especially her larder, and her cellar, fast emptied by a score of hungry pirates.

But my newfound and unexpected helpmeet had still more kind succor to offer me. "You come, my house. Yes?"

I looked at her, her bedraggled state, unwashed these past days of her captivity; at her kind smile, despite the haunted look lingering in her eyes. And, gratefully, I nodded my acquiescence.

Thus do I find myself the guest – albeit not an entirely welcome one, as Flora does not dwell here alone, and her good mother and her brothers, the same Juan and Ignacio I had as my guests priorwise, do not look kindly on my tenancy here – of my former captive, whom my former ally and present Nemesis, the cursed black-hearted Shluxer, did attempt to defile. For nigh on two days I have slept on a pallet in a sort of store shed they call a "garradge," I have recovered from my hurts, steadied my spinning brain-case, and with the kind gift of paper and a sort of charcoal wand named a "pen-sill" from mine hosts, I have writ down my memories of betrayal, both old and new, familiar ache and newfound sharpness. Should I recover the *Grace* – Nay, *when* I recover the *Grace* – I will place this with the rest of my log. It is still a Captain's log, by damn, even if my ship be far from me; still and always she is mine, to the death.

One more matter should be noted: yesterday, while I largely and profoundly slept, I did awaken once to the sound of raised voices near to the walls of my garradge. I waited until the shouting stopped, hand on my knife as small but welcome defense, for though I knew not the words – 'twas the Spanisher's tongue, I feel – I could hear the menace and violence in the voices. When it was over, and I had heard the departure of a deep-growling beast-wagon, I groaned myself to my feet and, feeling a great thirst, staggered into the galley for water; into the house entered the brothers Lopez, who checked on seeing me, and then shook their heads and went back to muttering in their own speech, though they cast glances both suspicious and irate at me the while. I know not what troubles them, but I have no doubt as to my part in their misery. Nor would any who know me doubt that I shall remove my thorny self from their hide, just as quickly as I can; I have no wish to be a burden on anyone, neither on friend nor foe. I have imposed on this family enough, and more than enough.

I must find my own way, to my proper place once more.

Log #20: To Arms

Captain's Log
Date: 5th of July, 2011
Location: Miami, Florida. The home of the Family Lopez.
Conditions: Marooned, but regaining my land legs.

I awoke in my garradge feeling much improved of body, this morn. I emerged to greet mine hosts, and found that Maid Flora's brother Alejandro, a lad of only ten summers and the youngest child of Mistress Clara Lopez, was the sole Lopez yet returned from the Elysian fields of slumber. Alejandro was enraptured by the images on their magic window. This was much like the magic window which Vaughn had shown me at the Palace, before that thrice-damned sanctimonious hypocritical poisoner O'Grady had smashed it, only this window was smaller; I sat down beside him to attempt to learn what I could from this ever-mysterious oracle. The lad quite sensibly was stretched prostrate across a thin rug on the tiled floor; the reclining couches in this house, like those at the Palace, are utterly absurd in their sybaritic decadence; I find them too comfortable for comfort. I think no one but a hedonistic nobleman of old Rome – nothing less than a new Caligula, a Nero – would need a seat so laughably soft. Why have a bench that does not support you, but rather swallows you into its pillowed embrace? I must note that if these sorts of engulfing pillow-thrones are commonplace, methinks the people of this time will prove easy pickings for a rough and ready pirate crew. One could storm and loot an entire house before the inhabitants even managed to raise themselves out of the depths of their chairs.

Though young Alejandro had sense in his choice of place, I soon found the magic window's images far too lunatic and manic to observe. I tried asking the boy – who speaks a better English than his siblings or mother, and so has frequently served a turn as translator in my time here – for explanations, but beyond the knowledge that this was some depiction of a story (or perhaps a hero?) named Dragon Ball Zee, I was more frequently instructed to be quiet so as not to interrupt the beguiling madness behind the window. It soon made my head ache and swim at once, as though I had drained the foul dregs of a cask of new whiskey, and I excused myself to perform my morning ablutions.

This has not ceased to amaze me. Maid Flora kindly instructed me in the use of the washing-room (Ell Ban-yo, I believe is the Spanish), and I have learned from observation that these people bathe daily. The boy Alejandro, indeed, bathes even more frequently, being impelled to do so by Mistress Lopez whensoe'er the boy returns enmuddied by his games. This washing-room has the same incredible water-spouts as did the Palace; I cannot fathom where such a wealth of clean water is stored in this modest home. It has not rained since I arrived here, and I saw no aqueducts, and yet the well has not run dry, nor have the Lopezes evinced the slightest worry that it will do so. I have taken my lesson from them, and have made use of this unending water to clean my tarry hide as I have not done in months, a task that a single rinsing cannot accomplish. Maid Flora was kind enough to launder my togs, as well, offering me the underclothes of either Juan or Ignacio to cover my nakedness in the meantime – I did not ask which, owing to the intimacy of the clothing in question. I was forced to remain cloistered in the garradge for the sake of propriety; the thinness of the shirt and britches would have made any public appearance quite indecent. I was most gladdened to return to my proper clothing.

When I was finished cleansing my carcass, which was now returning to its former state of pinkness, I found that Maid Flora and Mistress Lopez had arisen and made a fine meal to break our fast; I made my best effort to be glad company to my kind hosts – especially as I have observed that their menfolk seem generally sullen at meals; Juan and Ignacio are habitually silent, or else spend the time at table staring at the magic window, observing the same strange ritual I saw with Vaughn, involving several men in colored smallclothes kicking and chasing a child's ball across a grassy meadow. They named it foot-ball, which seems to me a childishly simple name – though it is a childish game, as well, so small wonder. This morning, neither brother was even present: Juan had not returned from his employment, and Ignacio had not risen from bed.

Allow me the indulgence of paying my hosts yet another compliment, in regards to the table they set, which is ever generous as well as sublimely sumptuous to the palate; so accustomed am I to sailor's fare, salted and boiled and peppered meat and biscuit, with hunger as the only spice, that I fear I make quite the glutton of myself, though these ladies seem gladdened by my visible and audible appreciation. Once we were sated, Maid Flora prepared to leave for the Palace. Her brother Juan, who has employment at some sort of tavern, owned by one MacDonald, returned then, his master requiring his services in the dark hours of the night – which makes me wonder at the sort of base, lawless establishment this MacDonald runs, that he serves his customers when decent folk are a-bed (and, too, if I might find a decent mug of grog and a comely wench there for my own self; Juan seems to think not). Juan's return roused Ignacio, and the ensuing conversation, held in Spanish, with the pertinent elements translated for me by Maid Flora, resulted in Ignacio and Mistress Lopez extending an invitation to myself to go to market with them, had I any need to make a purchase.

I had great need, though at first I could not communicate it. Apart from my boot knife, its blade a mere handspan in length, I have been left utterly defenseless by those black-hearted scoundrels who stole my ship. The Lopez family nodded at the word *pistola*, though Juan and Ignacio exchanged a dark look when I spake it – but I could not bring them to understand either "sword" or "blade," "rapier" nor "cutlass," nor any other word I could manage. Finally I took up a cooking knife – a blade of goodly heft, I must say, though of course it has no fighting balance – and pantomimed a duel. The Spanish word is *espada*, it seems. More conversation followed, resulting in a question, delicately proffered, regarding any available funds; I showed them my ring, gold with a cabochon ruby inset, and they seemed relieved.

We departed in their wagon-beast and soon arrived at a shop where the proprietor bought and sold goods of every stripe and kind imaginable. Upon entry, I was dazzled by the display: there were ladies' parasols and gentlemen's canes, coats and hats and boots, jewelry and paintings, magic windows, musical instruments, and a thousand things I could not fathom. At Mistress Lopez's urging, I offered the man my ruby ring; he gazed at it through some arcane eyepiece, and then he said, "Fifty bucks." Before I could express my confusion – was he offering me fifty male deer in exchange for a single gemstone? How had he gathered so many? And what would I with such a prodigious herd? – Mistress Lopez exploded into violent Spanish, with much shouting and gesticulating, which the merchant returned in kind. I gathered, when I realized Mistress Lopez indicated a display of finger rings, which generally had smaller stones than mine or none at all, each ring sporting a small slip of paper reading 50 and 100 and 200 and 350 and the like, that the man's first offer was offensively low. At the end of the haranguing, the man counted out five pieces of green-tinted paper, all numbered 100 and bearing a portrait of a distinguished gentleman with spectacles and white hair, and Mistress Lopez nodded in satisfaction and gestured that I should retrieve the paper and surrender my ring. I was still confused by the term "bucks," as there were no deer represented nor named on the paper; as they seem to be named "dollars," I will call them such here. I was not offended by his attempt to gain my ring at a tenth its worth; rather I felt some kinship. A proper pirate he would have made, I wot.

At Ignacio's urging, I asked the man for a *pistola*, such apparently being within his purview. He walked me to another display, behind metal bars and a pane of fine, flawlessly clear glass, where there were a dozen or more weapons much like the strange one we had taken from the man MacManus shot at the Palace. Even as I hold one now, I am confused by the configuration, and the lack of a proper wooden stock, but the greatest puzzle of the weapons to me is their size! Like a child's playthings, they are! And all without ramrod or lock of any kind, flint or wheel or even match. I asked about the largest, a piece of black iron still half the size of a proper *pistola*. The man looked askance at me, scratching at his large and bearded chin, and then asked, "You got a license?" My bewilderment answered his question, because he then asked, "You got any more cash?" On my returning precisely the same response again – namely a confused silence – he snorted and said, "You can't afford that one."

I was alerted by Mistress Lopez's action, and I peered at the paper affixed to my choice. "It says 500, there. Is it not the same as these?" I waved my dollars at the man.

He narrowed his eyes. "What the hell else would it be? It ain't goddamn pesos. But I gotta sell you a license, too, and that'll cost ya 200 on top of the gun."

That put the majority of the weapons here out of my reach. I considered haggling – or releasing the wrath of Mistress Lopez once more, who still looked daggers at the merchant, though he avoided her gaze most assiduously – but as I could not fathom this talk of licenses, I decided to take him at his word.

Thus I indicated a *pistola* which was labeled 200, and he gladly sold me that. I asked for the license he spoke of, but he gave me a look so laden with sardonic contempt that I at last grasped the nature of this "license" – that it was a bribe. There must be some law controlling the sale and ownership of weapons, here. Cromwell had done the same to my beloved Ireland, as the damned English had done to our Scotch cousins, too. I wondered if there were some vile tyrant with this land in his iron fist – though if that were the case, it seemed terribly foolhardy of this man to display forbidden weapons to all and sundry.

This world is a terrible confusion to me.

Any road, I returned four of the five green dollar-papers, and the merchant gave me the *pistola*. I hefted it – satisfyingly solid, albeit small – and then asked the man, "How does it work?"

Apparently I am a terrible confusion to this world, also.

We left the shop as unarmed as we came, for the merchant did not sell powder and shot – what he called Amm-owe – and thus I had naught but a boot knife and a small oddly-shaped club.

The company journeyed on to a place that brought me great comfort, owing to the familiarity of the sights, the sounds, the very air redolent of pasties and meat pies, sugared snacks and fruit, and ale, and mead, and wine – this, *this* was a proper market. Stalls in rows filled a great open square, with a multitude of voices raised: in negotiations, both friendly and pointed; in the joy of discovery, and in sorrow over broken dreams – as the price is revealed beyond the wanter's means, as the customer walks away with hands empty and purse un-lightened. Merchants spread goods on blankets, across tables and chests or strung on lines between poles; some under tents and some under the open sky. Clothing sold beside fresh food beside tools beside objects I could not hope to identify, beside boots and sandals that would not have looked amiss at home, three centuries ago and thousands of miles away.

This was, bespoke a sign at the entrance, the South Miami Flea Market. I did ask why the market was named for pestiferous vermin, but could not make myself understood to my companions.

Ignacio quickly guided me to a large stall that sold goods to hunters: mock waterfowl, apparently for use as lures; bows and arrows of a sort I had not seen; game bags and boots, coats and hats, all in a shockingly ugly sort of mottled green-brown cloth that looked filthy and mud-caked even when clearly never worn. I presented my new small, odd club to the merchant and asked for amm-owe; the man looked, nodded, and said, "Thirty-eight." He rummaged through some crates behind his table and presented me with a small square box; he lifted the fitted lid and showed me an array of small brass trinkets. When I did not react at all, he asked for my *pistola*, which I gave him; he opened it smoothly, pulled the brass trinkets from their rack – they are round and oblong, somewhat like smooth thimbles, or perhaps replicas of a large animal's teeth – and placed them into holes in the *pistola*. They fit perfectly, as he showed me, and when I nodded, he put them back in the rack, gave me back my empty weapon, and traded me my last 100-dollar paper for the box of amm-owe and four new sheets of paper numbered 50, 10, 10, and 5. At my request he repeated the opening and loading of the *pistola* twice more until I saw the way of it.

We meandered through the rows, the sights and sounds easing knots in my viscera I had not known were there; there is a dis-ease in being in such a strange place as this land, that may not be immediately apparent even in one's self, but which, when it be even slightly ameliorated by familiar surroundings, is replaced with a relief and a bliss that makes one nigh giddy. So a spring came back in my step, and before long, I found myself whistling and laughing aloud, as Mistress Lopez poked and frowned her way through goods and sundries, taking very little and leaving a string of sour-faced merchants in her wake.

Partway along our third row, we came across what I sought – or so I at first believed. It was a merchant – a prosperous one, with tent and cloth-covered table – who sold weapons, the kind of weapons I knew and longed for: blades. For the first time, when I espied the black scabbards and gleaming naked steel, I hastened forward alone, leaving my companions well behind me. The merchant was engrossed in conversation with a thin spotty-faced youth, and so I strode directly to the table of goods and clapped hands on the first likely-looking weapon: a rapier of moderate length with a simple guard.

To my disappointment. I did not even need to draw it from its sheath to know that it was a piece of work so shoddy as to hardly deserve the name "sword." The steel was far too light, the blade clearly virgin and too dull to cut my fingertip, and the hilt rattled, so poorly was it affixed to the tang. A slip of paper attached to the hilt with string read "Captain Jack Sparrow: $125." I dropped the sorry thing, pitying this Captain Sparrow had he ever possessed such a miserable blade, and took up another, this a sort of broadsword with a hand-and-a-half hilt – useful for heavy work.

But this was even worse. The grip was a leather slick to the touch even without the blood and sweat that soon enough coat one's hands in any combat. I bared the blade to find that its maker had apparently never even heard of a whetstone, so dull was its edge, and there was no balance at all; it was no surprise that this one also showed not a nick, not a scratch, no evidence of use. This one bore a tag reading, "Aragorn: $180." I made a noise of disgust and threw this miserable metal stick down on the table, where it rattled against the first.

"Hey! Careful with those!" the merchant called out.

"Why?" I retorted. "They seem entirely harmless." He turned back to his companion, though he kept his gaze on me. Perhaps one of these odd-hilted pieces, which seem the favored and popular style here: a long, two-hand hilt, cloth-wrapped, with a round guard merely the size of a large coin – smaller than a man's fist on the hilt, which, one would think, would entirely defeat the point of a guard. I took one up, bared the blade – single edged and slightly curved, like a saber, but straighter than any saber I had seen, and with a triangular tip – and examined it. I was surprised to see that this had something of an edge, but – the *steel*. As an experiment, I laid the flat of the blade across one raised knee, and pressed, almost delicately.

The blade snapped.

"Hey!" the merchant – the blackguard – shouted again, now leaving his conversation to accost me, but I denied him the chance.

"How dare you, sir!" I shouted, and rammed the inch of broken blade affixed to the hilt into the table before me with force sufficient to bite into the wood. "How dare you sell weapons that would kill the wielder ere he ever had a chance to defend himself 'gainst his foe!" I took the blade in hand and snapped it again, with not more force than the first time; I dropped the pieces of – it could not be genuine steel; was it tin? Perhaps painted wood? – on the ground and thrust my extended finger into his chest, surely doing more injury than I could have done with a similar thrust of one of his blades. "I have seen shoddy workmanship before, sir, but this is beyond the pale! Is there no craft in these at all? Were they manufactured by trained dogs, sir? Are these toys for children, perhaps?" I punctuated my words with ever-stronger thrusts of my finger-rapier, first halting his froward motion and then forcing him back. "Or do you perhaps have an arrangement with a band of rogues, highwaymen who set upon your customers at your signal, assured that the man will be defenseless howsoever he believes otherwise?"

The blackguard, cowed by my righteous fury, blinked, and held up his hands placatingly. "No, no, they – they're just for display. They're replicas. You know? Lord of the rings? Pirates of the Caribbean?" This last phrase gave him pause, as he took in my piratical appearance, frilled shirt and vest and sash over loose pantaloons gathered into my high boots.

I scoffed at him. "A pirate would be gladder of a marlinspike or a belaying pin in fist rather than one of these. For myself, I would rather have my empty hand," and here I lunged forward again and slapped him across the cheek with that same empty hand. And then I bid him good day, took up the arm of Mistress Lopez, who had approached the hurly-burly when she heard me shouting, and marched off with my dignity, but still no blade.

I found it at last among a jumble of swag – clearly the emptied contents of a traveling trunk or sea-chest – which included clothing, a bit of jewelry, a leather belt, some books and pens and paper and the like. The scabbard was beaten and scarred, as a scabbard should be, and the blade was as well, but these were the scars of use. This was a proper saber, the blade perhaps two feet in length – a mounted man's weapon, made for slashing rather than thrusting, yet capable of both, and light enough to parry well, while heavy enough to block a cutlass-slash. As I admired the blade, which had a serviceable hilt and a proper balance just beyond the guard, the merchant told me of its provenance. It had come from Cuba, he said, from the revolution; he told me it had belonged to a man allied with someone named Shay, a rebel against the tyrant who had ruled that land. The rebels had taken it from a wealthy landowner, vassal to the tyrant and oppressor of the people; the man had had it engraved to show its new ownership and purpose – the merchant indicated the words, still visible despite age and wear: on one side of the blade it read "Sangre," on the other, "Muerte," and on the hilt, "Libertad." Blood, death, and – the third word needed no translation. I had my sword. The man asked 150 dollars, but gladly took my remaining 75 and one of the gold coins I carried in my boot, having plucked them from the lining of my vest earlier for this purpose. We shook hands, and I thrust the sheath through my sash: once again, I felt whole.

And none too soon, it chanced, for at that very moment, a voice called out "Ignacio! Hey, Nacho!" We three looked back the way we had come, and saw four young swaggerers approaching, all wearing something blue, a shirt or headscarf or shoes dyed the color, all with the grins of hunting cats who find a nest with helpless chicks inside. The one in the lead spoke again. "Hey, man – we was just coming to see you, *puto*." I recognized the voice as the one shouting outside my garradge, the day Juan and Ignacio had been so exercised, and at that moment, I recognized the blue headscarf: it was the same color as the one worn by the man MacManus had killed, blood spilled on my orders, at the Glass Palace a week or more ago.

These were his friends. And they were looking to spill blood, too. Ours.

Log #21: A Heated Discussion

In the heat of the moment, my mind racing but still not keeping pace with events, I chose caution as my watchword: though I suspected the ruffian's voice was the one I had heard that day outside the garradge, and I was even more suspicious of the colored headscarves that resembled the cloth worn by the man killed by us at the Glass Palace, I was not positive these men here and now were enemies, and so I did not act precipitously – though I lost the element of surprise, therefore. I believed I could gain it back, but first I needs must wait and watch.

They approached Ignacio – which was all to the good, as it allowed me to draw Mistress Lopez well off to the side and out of harm's way. While their captain spoke, I noted one crewman craning his neck, keeping a weather eye out for enemies or allies of their intended victim, while two more fanned out around Ignacio, though none came too close. I saw that the watchman had a hand under his shirt, at his belt, and I marked him as armed, though with blade or *pistola*, I knew not.

The captain spoke in a thick patois, which I render here as well as my poor ears and poorer memory allow. "Orralay, we didn' 'speck t' see you out here, vattow. Where's your brother at? He here? We was just talkin' 'bout hittin' him up at Micky Dee's, maybe, you know, catch him on break, you know? But this is cool – we can talk to *you* now, instead." He glanced at his mate, who shook his head to indicate no intruding sails on the horizon – perhaps owing to the unusual magnificence of my finery, they apparently failed to notice me, or didn't connect me to Ignacio; the latter was a welcome advantage, the former an offense I could not let stand – and the captain grinned and stepped in closer, lowering his voice (Howbeit, since he needs must speak over the market crowd, I could still make out the lion's share of his speech.) to say: "'S funny who you run into when you go out, verdad? Hey, you didn't run into 'Lito, did you? No? Haven't seen him anywhere?" Ignacio had not moved nor reacted to them apart from backing water a step or two as they approached; he surely wished to keep his mother out of the fray, and could not retreat without leaving her behind – so was willing to submit to a likely drubbing so that she might be safe. A good son.

One who should not fight alone.

The captain here dropped his facade of amicability, his features turning to a mask of rage on the instant as he reached out and twisted Ignacio's shirt in his rough grip, saying, "Lessee if we can help you remember, *puto*."

I recognized this as my signal flag. I pushed Mistress Lopez firmly behind a rack of wide-brimmed straw hats, holding up a hand to tell her to bide there, and then I stepped out, the sheathed sword held low in my left hand, wishing I had taken the opportunity to charge my new *pistola*, but glad I had more than an odd club to face four strongarms. I spoke loudly, saying: "He has not seen your shipmate. Nor will he. Nor will you, this side of Hell." I came to stand close behind Ignacio's left shoulder, facing the captain, whose face was now slipping from rage into bewilderment. Surreptitiously, I put my right hand close by Ignacio's belt. I smiled at the captain and then spake: "I sent him there myself when I shot him."

Befuddlement turned to black rage, and the captain loosed his grip on Ignacio – which action I had awaited. Quickly I seized the good son's belt and flung him sprawling behind me; in the same motion I lunged forward with the sword in my left and planted the hilt in the captain's belly, blowing out his wind. As the captain stumbled back, I drew my new blade with my right and flung the empty sheath at the left-most foe; it did no harm, of course, but no man can help but flinch when somewhat comes a-flying at his eyes, and that gave me some treasured seconds with only two foes.

A long lunge with now-bared steel took one through the upper arm; he howled and fell back.

The last one was he who had a weapon at his belt; he was slow to react, but now he pulled up his shirt to reveal a large and bright-gleaming *pistola* – one I much admired, if I may be so bold with another man's implements. A quick step with the left and a downward slash at the uttermost of my reach, and the tip of my blade parted his belt and knocked loose the weapon ere he could draw it. His over-loose pantaloons, now untethered, slid down to tangle around his thighs as his weapon clattered to the ground.

This put me in vulnerable position, extended over my left leg with my back to the wounded man. But it did serve to put my empty left hand near my boot, wherein lay my trusty knife, and also near the captain, whose right hand closed on the *pistola* in his belt – though he did not draw it, rather choosing to step forward and within my reach.

One would think these people had never fought before. I suspect, in fact, that a foe who returns fire on these mongrels is indeed unusual; I assume, also, that the captain did not want to draw and fire in such a crowd, but instead sought to close and club me down with gun in fist.

Instead he got a boot-knife thrust through the back of his hand. He gasped, loosed his pistol, raised his hand to stare at his wound – and I regained my balance, rose up and planted my swinging foot into his nether region. I tell you, these Spaniards may seem swarthy, but they are white men, nonetheless – for that man's face turned as ashy pale as any Irishman in midwinter.

The last man, he who had dodged my scabbard, now came forward with bared steel of his own, a dagger clutched in his grip and descending towards me. But the motion was too large for a short blade and close range, and I stepped back so he cut only air. I brought the sword around, reversed, and laid the dull back edge across his temple, stunning him; I finished with the hilt on his crown, which laid him out.

I spun about, expecting an assault from the first man I wounded. But lo and behold, he was well-occupied with a dread and implacable foe: the swinging arms, flashing feet, and shrill screechery of Mistress Lopez. The man backed away, arms up to defend his face, and stumbled over a pile of goods, which sent him a-sprawl. Ignacio caught his mother, who was moving forward, fire-eyed and eager for the *coup de grace*; though it was a struggle, he managed to draw her back to safety.

I turned to survey the field, and saw that the rearmost rogue, he of the cleft pantaloons, was down on one knee, his britches clutched in a fist as the other hand stretched out for his fallen *pistola*. For myself, I would have let the tatters fall; though I quail at revealing all that lies below the waterline, most particularly in a sunny market with women and children all about, still the loose cloth was obviously hampering his balance and movement, and I would fain be naked and alive rather than a clothed corpse.

Which fate to avoid for myself, I leapt forward and stomped down on his questing fingers. The bones crunched like empty sea-shells under my boot. The man roared and choked and spluttered until I lifted my knee into his outthrust chin, flinging him back into the darkness of unconsciousness. I bent and retrieved his *pistola* into my left hand; thus securely armed, I stepped back to survey my opponents.

Their fortitude in battle fails to impress. I have seen swaddling babes who dealt better with their hurts than these dogs.

I took a moment to consider my course. Of course these rogues, and any more of their bloody-minded mates, would place responsibility for my actions on the Lopezes following this day's events; I had hoped that my admission of responsibility for the dead man would shift their sights to me, but Mistress Lopez's intervention, howsoever kind and timely and stout-hearted, had surely linked us as allies if not shipmates.

What could I do to counteract that impression?

"*Lopez!* Blast your dog's heart, thou gutless milksop, come where I can see you 'fore I blast ye to hell – ye or your haggard witch of a mother, aye."

Though startled, and clearly deeply confused, Ignacio stepped forward, pale and shaking, his eyes darting from one wounded rogue to another. "Bring me my scabbard, ye mawkish dastard," I spat. I pointed imperiously with my blade while I kept the pistol and my eyes hove tight to the captain, who clutched at his nethers with one hand while he tried not to look at his knife-thrust hand, holding the shaking appendage far and away out to his side, blood a-drip, like a man averting his gaze from somewhat sacred – or profane.

Ignacio retrieved the sheath – and then stood unmoving, staring dumb as a statue at me. "Bring it here – put it through my sash." He came, albeit slowly; his hesitation and apparent unconcern for the severity of our circumstances began to raise true impatience in me. These men, though wounded, were none of them incapacitated; they could rally at any time. And who knew how many more of these scalawags or their allies might come across this picturesque tableau we set? Our immediate departure was called for, yet I needs must tell this boy to bring the scabbard to me. And now – "On the other side, ye dolt!" I clouted him on the shoulder with my hilt, though it would have appeared to mine audience that I had sorely boxed his ear. Not that I wasn't thus tempted.

I nodded when he had it where I wanted, and then told him to clear out and hold back his harridan of a mother (I took comfort in the sure knowledge that the stout-hearted Mistress Lopez, for whom I had and have great regard, could not understand my words.) I hurried him on his way with a boot to the stern that was of course more powder than shot. When he was clear, I bent down over the captain, who would not look at me nor at his trembling hand. I moved around so I could keep a watch on the others over his shoulder, and then I cleaned my blade on his sleeve. "I see you white-livered curs know no more of fighting than your friend did – nor no more of spirit than that ragbrained fool I sought to make my servant. I see I will need to abandon him and his brood, and find another berth to claim. 'Tis just as well – the sister wriggles pleasantly enough, but she will not stop weeping. It wears on a man."

He turned to look at me then, his eyes still creased with pain and the skin of his face turned now to a greyish pallor, but anger blazed into his gaze and colored spots rose on his cheeks. I grinned at him. "But look on the happy side!" I sheathed my sword and laid the pistol's barrel against his temple, smiling all the while. "When I've weighed anchor, you and these other toothless rats need not fear you will cross my path again." Here I stopped smiling. "'Twould be a preferable fate for you, methinks." I drew back the *pistola* and smiled wide once more. "Here – let me help you with that." I grabbed the hilt of my boot knife and tore it from his wound, perhaps somewhat unkindly. He cried out and cradled his stabbed paw, arching his back and laying out flat on the ground; I quickly wiped and sheathed the blade and snatched the *pistola* still tucked in his belt.

I stood, now carrying a proper weight of iron. The rogues were bled dry of fight, and so I bid them a fond farewell and gathered the Lopezes to me with a curse and a vile threat, and we made off.

Upon returning to House Lopez, I asked Ignacio to waken his brother so we could have parlay. I explained the reasons for my ungallantry, saying that I hoped to convince the rogues – whom Ignacio called the Latin lions, though I think Latin kittens might be more *apropos* – that I was a black-hearted villain who had taken the innocent Lopez family hostage, and they had not revealed my presence previously for fear I would wreak a dread vengeance on their innocent loved ones. As much as possible, that impression had been made today; now we needs must turn these Latins' attention away from bloodlust by giving them something to mollify their rage – their rather righteous rage, truth be told. And so far as I knew, there was only one thing we could offer that they desired.

Juan spoke to Maid Flora using these strange Verizon praying-stones; I cannot comprehend how they can cast a voice over more miles than a man could see on a clear day at sea, and the Lopezes could not explain it to me, trying words like 'lectrissity and sattalights before throwing up their hands in surrender, but howsoever it works, Juan summoned his sister to home many hours before she would be expected. 'Twas good, as speed was of the essence; I had no doubt that the Latins, once they had licked their wounds, would come here to find us, and we must be elsewhere when they do.

A terse Spanish conversation followed Maid Flora's arrival, with many apparent curses and more than a few bitter, fear-sickened looks cast my way. I could not complain: my presence in their lives, begun by my action when I led my men into the Glass Palace, had brought them little but misery. Even my good deeds, saving Maid Flora and now Ignacio and his mother, were only made necessary because of me, because of my allies and my enemies.

Once this is finished, I must leave this place. I must not rely on the kindness and forbearance of others who have no reason to look kindly on my presence in their lives, and I must not force the peril of association with me on these innocents. I must have my *Grace*. I need mine own good home.

Within an hour's time, Mistress Lopez was dispatched with young Alejandro to a friend's house across town and out of harm's way, and myself with Juan, Ignacio, and Flora departed in a pair of beast-wagons for the Glass Palace. With shovels.

We had a corpse to retrieve.

Log #22: Taking a Dip in the Ocean of Time

Captain's Log
Date: 7th of July in the year 2011
Location: The Glass Palace
Conditions: At heart's ease, but with blood high and passion enkindled.

Since last I was able to keep this log, while waiting for Maid Flora to return home for our parlay and then in the minutes before we departed for the disinterment, there have been developments. Now I find myself once more at the Glass Palace in the Matheson Preserve, and now I am in the employ of the Enchantress, Lady Elizabeth Cohn.

And I am at war.

The recent course of events began with our quest to recover the mortal remains of one Manuelito Nieves, known as 'Lito to his fellow Latin Lions. 'Struth, it did seem like a fine stratagem at the time, howsoever gruesome it was.

There is truly something unnatural in digging up a corpse, even if one has the finest intentions. In my nineteenth year, back in the Ireland of my birth, my cousin Conor O'Malley was taken by the damned English and hanged as a cattle thief. He was guilty, of course, but only of the crime of being Irish and hungry. Any action which follows from that may be forgiven, but will surely not be if 'tis English mercy one seeks. The English threw his body into a shallow and unconsecrated grave outside the infernal prison where stood the gallows, and so his brothers Steven and Brian, along with myself, must needs creep under the watchful eyes of the English bastards standing watch on the walls of the keep, to bring Conor to a proper kirkyard for a burial that would grant him rest, rather than the everlasting torment granted him by the English, may all the curses ever cursed light on their black souls. But when we began to dig, even though our hearts pounded with fear and excitement for the thought of the English nearby and the blood that could be spilled if we moved too quickly or too loud, the overwhelming feeling when the shovel bit into the earth was one of wrongness. I wanted to apologize to Conor, and to the earth that held him, and to all the ghosts and spirits and gods that roam the aether all around us, even though I knew our intentions were just. I knew, and Steven and Brian knew as well, that this – this was a thing that one simply does not do.

And here we went, the Lopez brothers and sister and I, to do it once more, and the same feelings all came along for the cruise. Though discomfited by our purpose, I was somewhat gladdened to be returning this man 'Lito to his shipmates. He was a rogue who died honorably and was treated honorably by his foes, with words of prayer spoken over his interment; but nonetheless, a man should never be placed in the earth by any but his kith and kin. Even rogues have mothers, and should feel the tears shed over them by such, instead of gruff words spake by reluctant tongues. Enough that we took his life: we should not steal his fare-wells.

Maid Flora assured us that the Enchantress was away from her Palace; she was, it seemed, a lawyer, and thus frequently in distant cities to attend to the needs of her clients. At first I was somewhat aspraddle that a woman could be in such a profession, but then I bethought myself of my own mother and her strength of spirit and of mind, how she has led the clan ably for all of my life; then I recalled a lawyer's need for deception and artifice, and how that is not foreign nor even difficult for most women, and I understood. I was not for a moment surprised that this world, so strange and complicated and absent of any reason or sense, would have a wealth of opportunities for lawyers, nor that the resultant lucre could purchase a Palace. We paused outside the Palace's gate while Flora proceeded in to confirm the Enchantress's absence, and then we three, Juan, Ignacio, and myself, brought their beast-wagon as close to the spot as possible. They revealed a small cargo-hold in the rear, lined with a strange shiny cloth – it looked to me like sailcloth, though it was a blue bright enough to shame the sky, and had that strange wet-seeming sheen that I have observed to be most popular and beloved amongst these people (Truly it brings one to wondering: have they never heard the wisdom that not all that glitters is gold? Do they care nothing at all for aught that lies beneath the surface? Sure and their possessions would say: *Nay*.). Juan called it a tarp, and said it was made of "plasstick." Any road, 'twould serve to enwrap the carcass – though we had shrouded the man when we planted him, to be sure.

I think I need not record at length the details of that gruesome and horrific chore. Suffice to say that we removed him from the embrace of Mother Earth, that we assured ourselves that he was still recognizable, and was not so rotted as to make the looker incapable of gazing on his features – 'twas I who pulled back the shroud to confirm this, while Juan looked away and Ignacio retched in the bushes – and then we placed him in the beast-wagon's hold, wrapped in the tarp to prevent corruption from marring the wagon-hold. Then Juan and Ignacio were off to deliver their grisly burden unto the only inhabitants of this Earth who would want it.

Maid Flora made an honorable attempt – limited, as ever, by her insufficient command of my tongue and my even greater incompetence in hers – to offer me lodging in the Lopez home for another night, but I would not hear of it. This endeavor may have been doomed from the start, and myself inextricably linked with this humble family in the reddish eyes of the Lions – indeed I did fear that to be the case, though I placed responsibility not on any misstep or poor stratagem of ours, but rather on the notable dearth of either perceptiveness, or the reason and sense which nature gave a hedgehog, on the part of our adversaries; but if our attempts were to prove futile, still I would not be so foolhardy as to give the cads a single target encompassing myself and five innocents. I refused her kind offer, though I did allow myself to be cajoled into surrendering my finery for laundering in her capable hands, my best alternative to this being wearing shirt and vest and breeches and boots while bathing in the cove. These items were in certain need of unfilthing, owing to the soileous nature of my activity this day, a perspiratious fight in hot sun and an unearthing of a rotting corpse and its consequent enearthing of mine own carcass. She offered the Palace's bathing facilities, as well, but I told her I preferred the infinite clean water of the ocean rather than stewing in a tub full of my own filthy skin. I accepted a robe and loose drawers for the nonce, being assured of the return of my finery within an hour's time.

Thus did I find myself swimming naked across the blue water of the Palace cove and back, across and back, glorying in the salty taste and pure smell of that water, scrubbing myself with handfuls of white sand and sluicing clean liquid over me to wash away the stench of combat and corruption. 'Twas relaxing to such a degree that I would swear the water in this cove had wafted here, driven by current and wind and tide, straight from Ireland, solely for my benefit. When this fancy struck me, granting a laugh and a smile, 'twas followed shortly by another cogitation: this water could even have come to me from my native *time* – for was not the ocean now the very same ocean then? Was not the earth that held it and the wind that drove it – were these not the same, then and now? Perhaps this breath of air, that splash of water – perhaps they began when I did, and have circled the world entire an hundred times, only to waft here, to me, and be the balm I most need. My heart was much eased by this thought. My people I have left far behind me: only bones and dust mouldering in the Earth remains outside of my heart and memories; my country, my struggles, and my enemies are all lost to time's changing course. My home, my possessions, all that which I coveted and longed for, the world over – all this is passed, now, passed and past.

But this good Earth, this clear water, this soft wind and bright sun, the lovely glimmering of stars and moon in the sable velvet night – those all remain to me, all familiar, all mine, as much as ever they were. My Ireland is gone, but the Earth is still my home, and I am welcome here.

My bath and pleasing ponderations done, I was glad to accept my finery and a hearty plate of food and drink from my kind friend Maid Flora – once I had covered my nakedness with the borrowed robe, to be sure. I made much first of the snowy whiteness of my shirt, the pure crimson of my vest and the deep black of my pantaloons, all as bright as new cloth and without a hint of mark or stain. They smelled of flowers, too, which was an additional kindness; one thing I will say of this time and place, it is strangely perfumed: the stench of the beast-wagons is as noxious as any bilge or city sewer I have encountered, yet the people and their clothing are almost miraculous in their clean, lovely aroma, without whiff of sweat or the stink of sickness anywhere. I could not be quite as complimentary of the food, though it was a satiating repast, to be sure; still, I could not understand why she did not simply give me a proper hunk of bread, slice of meat, and lump of cheese, rather than assembling them all together into this thing she called a sanwitch (Perhaps San Huiche? Her accent makes a literate rendering most difficult.), combined with a piece of green leaf I had rather she fed to a cow or pig and then given me the cow or pig, and some sauce she called moose-tard which I would fain have removed, except it covered the strange taste of the bread, which was rather off-putting. She did give me a bottle of ale to wash it down, which was most welcome. When I had finished, I bade her back to her maid's duties, though she assured me laughingly that her day was most often idle, as the Enchantress was rarely at home and even more rarely demanding of any especial service; Flora was most complimentary to her kind mistress, and grateful for her employment here. Once she had left, I took the time to clean my boots, polishing them with the tail of my borrowed robe, before I returned to my proper attire.

Then I moved out to the end of the strand, to the redoubt constructed by that capable traitor Moran – a refuge as yet undiscovered by the Enchantress, it would seem and was surely to be hoped – and lay down for some rest. The clean sea breeze and warm sun, both contradicting and complementing one another, made for a most wondrous atmosphere, made only finer by the shade cast by the dense greenery. I slept for some hours, my head pillowed on the robe, and woke most refreshed. Maid Flora had supplied me with a small bottle of clean water, made of some strange clear material far more flexible than glass, which I drained and put aside, intending to refill it from the Enchantress's terrace pond, once darkness came to cover my movements.

For I had determined that, for the nonce, this was to be my berth. I could ask for no better bed than the sand and soft pillow-robe, no better blanket than my own clean and flower-scented finery, no better security than all-concealing forest and the ocean on three sides, no better safety for my new friends than my own disappearance to this place unbeknownst to the Lions, and our hopes placed on our plans to sever our ties. With the kind Flora to give me sustenance, and the loving embrace of constant and eternal Nature to give me peace, I was as happy as I could be, thrown out of my time and off of my ship.

Rested, refreshed, and revitalized, I had to see to my last necessity then: my armament. I had a honing-stone in my pocket, and I gave my boot-knife a brief polishing to return its fine edge, and then I turned to my new sword, the aptly-inscribed Blood, Death, and Liberty – apt for in shedding the first, it had prevented the second and preserved the third, at least for now. The fine white sand brought a proper color back to the slightly tarnished steel; I would remember to beg oil from Maid Flora to protect the blade's surface properly. Then I carefully and meticulously honed the edge to a razor's sharpness.

My blades thus seen to, I turned to the greater puzzle: my guns. I was now in possession of three pistols, my own recent purchase and two taken as spoils of battle. The pair of looted weapons were similar to each other, but unlike mine own: mine had a round wheel-piece, set side-to and pierced with six holes that held shot, if that's what the amm-owe I had purchased was intended to be, yet I could not find where the powder and wadding were to be placed around that shot. But as an experiment, I placed six of my new-purchased brass-ended shot-thimbles into the holes, closed the pistol and then pulled the trigger, aiming idly at the bole of a tree – and I was rewarded by a sharp report and a hole appearing where I had aimed. In amazement, I opened the weapon again and found a mark on one of the brass thimbles, as if someone had taken hammer and awl to it; upon removing it, I found that the thimble was now hollow and empty, the interior blackened and smelling of spent powder; the round tip was gone, presumably now residing in the tree.

I realized that the amm-owe thimbles are cartridges, not unlike canister shot for ship's cannons. They hold the ball in place, and contain the powder, as well. The spark is made with a sharp strike of metal on metal, much like a flintlock but even simpler. Most amazing is that the weapon seems able, owing to these cartridges and the wheel mechanism, to fire six shots without reloading. Six shots! I was stunned and amazed.

And ready to find those mutinous blackguards who stole my ship and give them what-for.

The pistols looted from the rogues in the market were much like that we had taken from their dead shipmate. That weapon had proven most mysterious to us, with its trigger that would not pull and its unfamiliar shape and mechanisms, until Kelly, who had had its keeping, had thought to ask Shluxer about its use. Shluxer had called it a Nine-mill O'meeter, and had showed us how the small lever which, when pressed, revealed a minute red dot; this was called a Safety, and would lock or unlock the trigger and firing mechanism. He showed us how to remove the box of shot from the handle, what he called   "bullits –" I had not been watching his demonstration carefully enough to identify them as being akin to my amm-owe shot-thimbles, though I recognized them now, in examining my looted *pistolas* – and how to handle and fire it. We had scoffed at the thing then, with its quiet sound and the weak recoil of its firing, almost without fire or smoke compared to a proper powder-and-shot *pistola*, but Shluxer assured us it was sufficient unto its purpose. I presumed these two would be as well, and I made a place in my sash for all three of my shooting irons.

The sun was setting, then. I returned to the Palace and refilled my bottle; Maid Flora appeared, having seen me from within, and at my request brought me a proper loaf of bread (the which was still largely tasteless and strange, as if uncooked but rather allowed simply to stale to some hardness above that of dough and below that of proper bread) and a lump of cheese, three good pickles and a bottle of ale. I assured her my needs were well-met and I would not disturb the Enchantress, who was due to return soon, and then I bade her good-night and returned to my redoubt. I supped, dipping bare feet in the cool blue water and watching the waves ripple to me and away again, the eternal heartbeat of the ocean, writ small on this shore and large on another where waves crash against rocks with the roar of thunder, but always present, never-ceasing. What need have we of God? If thou seekest something infinite and eternal, and spellbinding and breathtaking in its glory, its generosity and power, its boundless gifts of life and the pure hell of its rage – look no further than the ocean.

I watched the water until it was no more than reflected starlight sparkling on a field of black, and then I lay down once more and slept well. I dreamed of home.

***

I was shaken out of my sleep, and sprang up, bared blade in hand, before I recognized Maid Flora in the gray light of early morn. Tears streaked her cheeks and fear hollowed her eyes, so I did not need to wait for her broken English to explain why she had come for me. Still, once I calmed her slightly, I learned somewhat.

Our plan had not worked. Juan and Ignacio had suffered the wrath of the Lions, and had been beaten savagely. A kind neighbor had gathered them from the street and brought them home, where they lay even now, delirious and in great pain and risk of death. Flora feared the Lions would return again, seeking my humble self.

But I would seek them out first. And they would learn that Hell itself hath no fury so black as that of an Irishman.

And no Irishman wreaks vengeance half so terrible as doth Damnation Kane.

Log #23: To Safety. To War.

Maid Flora and I rode her beast-wagon back to the House of Lopez – now become the Infirmary of Lopez. The moment we arrived, she dashed within to check on her brothers; I followed more slowly to allow them some time as an uninterrupted family. I walked the perimeter of the house, seeking any enemy, any watchful eye that might be seeking me – that might have used those men as bait to draw me out, those men who were beaten but, strangely, not killed, not dropped in a river or a marsh to be seen no more outside of Hades; no, these men had been left alive in the street, and I could not but think this was done to a purpose. For the moment, I saw nothing – but I would need to take steps to ensure that the only traps sprung from here onward would be those I set.

I went within and found young Alejandro standing guard bravely, a wooden club in his hands and a look of grim determination on his face which almost, but not entirely, hid the terror in his eyes. I nodded to him, and he squared his shoulders, stood straighter, nodded back to me. "Be steadfast," I said, and barely bit back the "lad" that wanted to follow these words trippingly from my tongue; but this would not have improved his confidence. I went on: "Your family needs you to protect them, now. Keep a weather eye and a ready shout, should ye see aught of the foe. Aye?"

He nodded, a bit of color returning to his face. It does wonders for a young man when he is treated as if the "man" matters more than the "young." I was glad to see him move purposefully to the front window, where his eyes and shout might do more good than would the club in his small hands. Ye gods, the thing was half his height – what sort of combat weapon was that? A bludgeon should rarely be more than a belaying pin in length, else it is too slow and unwieldy to make good use. I noted the words "Louisville Slugger" on the smooth, polished wood, but it meant nothing to me. I moved past him and along the corridor to the sickroom.

Both men were asleep, and obviously should remain so. Were that not true, I fear the profanity I would have uttered upon seeing their wounds would have shamed the sun behind the clouds, chased the moon out of the sky, and brought a blush to every tender, innocent cheek for miles around. In silence, but with those terrible curses ringing in my head, I swore on my mother, my ship, and my own honor to avenge every hurt on these two innocent men.

Then I must leave that sorry sight before my anger overflowed and whelmed my sense. I have never sat easily when an innocent is harmed. What man could? But the cruelty and savagery exercised on these two men – these two *faultless, guiltless* men – was not only beyond what I might perchance accept done to a child-beating English rapist, but far worse, 'twas all done because of *me*. 'Twas done to them because those filthy mongrels could not reach me. Those wounds: they are *my* wounds.

I suppose I made some sound in my retreat, or perhaps his injuries kept him from resting easy, but Ignacio stirred then and woke. I confess I would fain have slunk away, too craven to face his accusing eyes, but as I could not bear to increase my shame, I stepped to the side of the low bed and knelt, gently taking up his hand in mine. When his gaze cleared as his mind rose from the realm of sleep, he recognized me. "It didn't work," he said, and I could not but smile – though keeping that smile longer than an instant was impossible as I looked on his eye swollen shut and split at the brow, on his nose bent to the side, on the broken teeth barely visible past his torn and bloody lips.

"Nay, it did not. My fault, lad. I overestimated them, thinking them human." I tried to chuckle as if this were witticism rather than barren truth, but not much more than a wheeze emerged from my tightened throat. Still, Ignacio smiled at the corners of his mouth, and squeezed my hand.

"They didn't – we didn't have a chance," he said, the words slurred by his accent and injuries so I could barely comprehend – but damn me if I would ask him to repeat himself. "We got there, and showed them the – 'Lito, and Juan started to say we were sorry. But Agro hit him and he fell, and then he kicked him in the head – and then the others got me. And I try to say, 'I'm sorry, I didn't do it,' I try to say, 'Please –' But they no listen. Then I no can talk or do nothing. They kick me until it all go black." He pulled his hand away from mine, turned his face to the window beside him and away from me.

"Do you remember the faces? Any of the ones who kicked you?" For the bloody rage which I felt building in me would best be unleashed on those who shattered this boy's teeth. Fortunately, he nodded.

"Two of them at the market yesterday – the tall one and the one Mama hit."

"I remember them," I told him.

Then his gaze went flat. "*Si* – and they remember you. Now they will find you and kill you, and then they will kill all of us, too, so we no talk to *la policia*." (I had learned in my time here that *la policia* were a sort of civil guard who sought out and apprehended malefactors. I had also learned – with absolutely no surprise – that these men could not be trusted, that they could be bribed, or swayed by their own loves or hatreds, and that they sometimes did more harm to innocents than to the rogues they hunted.)

I stood then and settled my weapons in my sash. "No, my friend. They will not kill any of us. And they will not need to find me." I leaned down and placed a hand – gently – on his shoulder. He turned to look at me with his good eye.

"I will find them."

***

When I emerged, I sought out Mistress Lopez and Maid Flora for a council of war. The first task must be to move this poor family past the horizon and out of the range of my enemies, for the span of time whilst I am working to destroy them all. This was, therefore, the first point of contention: Maid Flora did not want her brothers moved, and Mistress Lopez would not surrender a foot of ground to such scalawags. I did manage to convince them that great danger awaited both of the brothers here and now – far greater than the danger of moving them. My assurance that I would swiftly distract the Lions' cretinous, half-formed thoughts from the House of Lopez was sufficient to overcome Mistress Lopez. A happy chance, as I could not assure her that I would protect her home, nor that no harm would come to it once they left; I thought it highly likely that the Lions, seeking me, would burn this place to the ground.

But no harm would come to the family: on that I was determined. We came to the knowledge that another city to the north, one Orr Land-oh, had friends the family could visit, as well as a place called Dizz Knee Whirled which Alejandro would gladly see. The inevitable monetary objections were quickly overcome when I pressed the eleven remaining gold coins from the seam of my vest on Mistress Lopez, accepting no argument nor polite refusal. These refusals fell away when I told them to seek a surgeon for the two brothers; this use of my money seemed fitting to them – as indeed it was, as was the conversion of any excess into funds for the maintenance of these kind folk.

The only concern that remained was Maid Flora's position at the Glass Palace, which she would not surrender and was most loath to abandon. But we arrived at a solution for that, as well.

I straightened my new shirt and dusted off my new breeches, as we stood at the door, waiting for our knock to be answered. Maid Flora smiled anxiously at me and patted a stray hair into place. The door opened, and there stood the Enchantress herself.

Maid Flora explained, as clearly as she was able, that she would need to leave her post for at least one sevenday, perhaps two, in order to nurse her sick brothers. She offered an alternate servant in her place: myself, whom she introduced as Daniel Kane.

The Enchantress eyed me most suspiciously. "You're supposed to be my maid?"

I made a passable leg, knuckling my brow in manner I hoped fitting. "Milady, I would not ask you to open your home to a man without scrap of introduction or recommendation. I would never ask you to trust a stranger to care for your environs and property without any knowledge of his fitness for the task. I ask only that you continue to trust in the good heart and wise discernment of your servant Flora, who verily doth recommend myself and my skills to you – and that you trust, as well, your own natural womanly intuition, which surely tells you that I mean your kind person naught but comfort and joy, as I most sincerely do." I crafted my winningest smile for her, then.

She did look askance at me when I bowed: then when I spoke was she taken aback. At the last, she began to smile. When I finished with the matching expression on my own physiognomy, I hoped it was not too bold of me to presume my place at the Palace was assured.

It was not. The Enchantress looked me over from stem to stern, and then said, "Well, you'll certainly be decorative to have around the house, won't you?"

Thus did I become a domestic.

We returned to the House of Lopez, and Maid Flora joined her mother in preparing for their journey to Orr Land-Oh – which preparations gave the appearance of twin typhoons, two waterspouts circling through the house, sucking up and belching out clothing and necessaries and ephemera in staggering quantities and with much sound and fury. I, in the meantime, asked for and received the assistance of young Alejandro. I faced one more impediment: though the Lions' den, a ramshackle house and garradge which the rogues claimed for their base of operations, stood near the House of Lopez, the Glass Palace was some ten miles away – too far to walk back and forth while in pursuit of justice. But I would never master the beast-wagon in time, nor did I wish to make the attempt. Fortunately, there was another solution: a thing called a "bike," a staggeringly uncomfortable seat and a strange handle atop a pair of wagon wheels, which one moves forward with a sort of walking motion on two levers called "petals," though they resemble flowers not at all. Over the course of that afternoon, Alejandro taught me to ride it; I found that my experiences riding horses, combined with my years of keeping myself upright aboard ships in stormy and wanton seas, made it fairly simple to master the balance needed to keep the bike upright. Moving my feet on the petals but not actually walking was far more difficult, but I persevered, and found success.

I asked for and received detailed instructions for locating the den of the rapscallions from Ignacio, and then I bid the Lopezes a fond and heartfelt farewell, and sent them off. Then I mounted the bike I had the loan of from Ignacio, and set off to work.

The Lions' den itself was simplicity to identify: it was the shabbiest, most dilapidated house on an otherwise tidy and ship-shape little road. I secured the bike nearby with chain and a most ingenious little lock-and-key provided by Ignacio, and then I walked the streets all around the den, observing the movement of the local villagers, the paths by which one could approach the den, both openly and surreptitiously, the local tavern and shops where the Lions surely procured their necessaries. Then I returned and found myself a sheltered place from which I could observe the house and those coming and going.

Their time was spent largely in the garradge and on a sort of open porch appended to the front of the house. The entire time I watched, which comprised several hours, I could hear a strange rhythmic chanting over a drumbeat and an assortment of weird and eldritch noises, shrieks and whistles and thrums, and others I could not begin to name. I never saw the ones doing the chanting, so I had to presume that there were people inside the house performing weird incantations or rituals; though strangely, no one seemed to react or even acknowledge the noise other than occasionally bobbing their heads up and down with the drums, perhaps agreeing with or approving what they heard. As for the words, they were all Greek to me. The garradge and the paved area before it was glutted with beast-wagons and various associated equippage; they had the maw of one beast propped open and several of them spent much time with their heads thrust deep inside the gullet. I wondered if they were feeding it, or killing it? I know not.

Several of them took their ease on the porch for the entire afternoon and evening; they talked and laughed and drank and smoked, and shouted at each other and at the passersby. I did note that several passersby approached the men seated on the porch, talked to them briefly and then made some kind of quick exchange, but I could not see what was given nor received. The visitors always left quickly, after. I know not the meaning but I wonder of the possibilities regarding my intentions.

Once dusk fell, they began to depart, mostly in groups in the various beast-wagons drawn up by the garradge. The house did not empty, and the lights that shone through the windows implied that it would not – some number of Lions must abide there, and the others gather round during their idle days.

And then, near the end of the evening, a happy chance: one of my known and sworn enemies, the tall ruffian from the donnybrook at the market – that same one whose pantaloons I had untethered, and whom Ignacio had identified as one of his tormentors – departed on foot and in my direction. I drew back and watched him pass, and then I set off in pursuit, keeping my distance.

He headed toward the row of shops I had observed in my explorations, perhaps meaning to visit the tavern close by; and in the dark alley behind the shops, I saw my chance. I sped my pace, approaching closer – and then, only a few paces from where I meant to strike, the rogue heard my step and turned. His eyes widened in recognition even as I leapt forward, hands outthrust to grapple and choke him. He leapt back from me, hands reaching to his belt for his *pistola* – and he stumbled over a pile of refuse on the ground, trash brought down by trash. I was on him before he recovered, and struck once, twice, thrice, once into the hollow under his right arm to stop him using his weapon on me, and then to the throat and last to the temple, which incapacitated him.

I took his *pistola* – 'Struth, these dogs do grant a veritable armory unto me! – and dragged and shoved him, groaning and coughing, into the deeper darkness of the alley, where none would disturb us. I found there a large metal box, on wheels, which reeked of filth; apparently a receptacle for rubbish and kitchen leavings. I observed that it had short metal poles, like spars, outthrust from the uppermost corners on one side – and that these were very nearly the same distance, one from the other, as my foe's widespread hands.

Splendid.

I introduced his brow to the metal box – twice, as the first meeting did not make a sufficient impression – and then drew my boot knife. I removed the rogue's shirt by means of the blade, and cut the cloth into two long pieces. Then I tied his wrists to the two poles, with his face pressed against his new and odiferous acquaintance, and his bare back presented to me.

How I wished then for a cat-o-nine-tails, or even a tarred rope end, or cane, but alas, I had naught of the kind; not even my sword, which I had left with my servant's clothes in a sea-bag borrowed from the Lopezes and now concealed in the shrubbery outside their house. The flat of the blade would have sufficed, though I would not want to sully my new-polished blade with this cur's flesh.

Fortune provided, however, and I observed a number of wooden platforms stacked on the ground, perhaps something meant to display goods at market, though they were rough-made and dirty. They might be used as on a ship, where we place bags of flour and salt and the like on raised wooden platforms to ensure that seawater does not ruin the dry goods. Any road, they were constructed of a wooden framework to which were nailed wooden laths – and those would do just fine. I broke one free and swung it through the air to get its feel.

My man began to regain his wits, then, and some amount of spluttering and cursing and threats emerged – the last rather laughable, considering our relative circumstances. He was still too stunned to test his bonds, though I would trust my knots against his outstretched arms for as long as I needed him held; still, 'twas time to be getting on. I took a moment to remove his headscarf, from which I fashioned a gag against his impending cries.

Then I pronounced his sentence. "For every mark you left, with your coward's boots, on Ignacio Lopez, you will bleed. And another stripe for every mark your cursed mates left on Juan Lopez, too. We will set the number of lashes, then, at one hundred."

He grunted in surprise when I began.

He was screaming against the gag when I had to replace my lath, which broke after thirty.

He was unconscious before sixty.

He received the full number, nevertheless.

I left him there tied to the metal box with his back awash in blood, for his mates to find. I retrieved the bike, and then my seabag, and then I rode to the Glass Palace. I crept beyond the darkened house to the strand and my redoubt, where I have kindled a small fire on the seaward side, eaten the bread and cheese from House Lopez that I had in my bag, and now I complete this log. Now to bed: and I shall sleep well.

Log #24: Clean and Clear

Captain's Log
Date: 8th of July, 2011
Location: Redoubt at the Glass Palace
Conditions: Exhausted with hard work, but successful.
Methinks things are clearer, now.

The Enchantress . . . is a pig.

I did not believe this position would be difficult; how much disorder could one person make? Especially one high-born woman? Now I know better.

The woman arises each morning, swims in her pond in smallclothes that would be indecent even under proper dress, and then, following her toilet (which includes still further bathing, as though she must wash off the first bath), scatters raiment like a bird shedding feathers in spring: clothing which I, as her maid, am expected to retrieve, launder, and stow in its proper berth in her closet. Though once that closet has been but briefly explored, it becomes instantaneously apparent why she is so indifferent to her attire as to cast it on the floor: she has more apparel than my entire village could wear, back home. And this material, strewn across the floor of the closet, and her chamber, and her bed, and the soft chairs in her chamber, and any other surface that can hold an article of dress, is not part of her attire for various occasions or functions, no: she considers it and discards it before she chooses her splendifery for the day. The apparel has not even been worn! Her maid, of course, is required to replace each piece in its proper place, neatly folded or rolled or hung or stretched, as the item warrants. It is more difficult, and time consuming, than stowing cargo in an undersized hold and lashing it tight for stormy seas.

Then there is the kitchen. Now, I am a pirate and an Irishman, and I have seen ship's galleys that resemble the aftermath of a raging fire, sparked by a thunderstorm flooding rain, onto a battlefield churned muddy by boots and blood. But the Enchantress doth lay waste to that hearth to a degree unmatched by a score of filthy seamen. Egg shells and fruit peels, puddles of water and juice, crockery and glass containers and sliver utensils – 'tis a wasteland, a ruination, a shipwreck on a rocky shore. Which I then must clean.

Two hours spent arranging women's fripperies, another lost to hot water and rags, to crockery and kitchen scraps – I wish often for a good kitchen hound to dispose of the excess food bits properly – and then I can attend to the floors.

I have never been so happy to see a broom as I was on my first day in this role. I could not find it, at first, though Maid Flora had identified for me the antechamber where the implements of maidery were to be found; the broom, however, did not abide there, but rather stood in a corner of the large barn-shed, which I now know to be a garradge. Why did I search high and low for the broom, one might ask? Because at first I made the attempt with – the vacume. A machine risen straight from Hell, fashioned no doubt in the infernal forges of the iron city of Dis, forges sparked by the Devil's infinite fiery hatred and fueled by the suffering souls of the damned; and that which they make there takes into itself every evil thought, every miserable suffering breath that wafts across its surface. That is the wellspring of that thrice-damned monster.

Maid Flora had instructed me to use the vacume to sweep the floors before mopping, and had shown me the beast in its den, which was the closet stocked with maid's tools. She had pantomimed its use and pointed to me the lever that brought it awake, once it had been tethered – by something that may be a leash and may be a tail or similar appendage, I know not – to a certain hole in the wall, round with two thin vertical slots into which fit a pair of metal pieces on the appendage-lcash. I did not understand how the thing was to remove dirt, but I had nodded that I understood her instructions, at least. And when the time came, I followed them: I moved its round, squat body out of the closet, uncoiled the leash and slotted it into the wall, and then I pressed the awakening lever, marked "ON."

And then the beast *roared*. I was so startled I leapt back, striking the body with my foot and casting it away from me; the thick trunk-like appendage which one held when making use of the beast flipped about – and then it sought its prey. I know not if that thing be the bastard child of the Asiatic monster called an Oliphaunt, or if it be some strange hybrid of serpent and badger, but whatever it is, it is a predator, and it is *hungry*. It leapt and cavorted across the room, the end of its trunk-appendage roaring, a terrible inhalation drawing sundry bits into its maw where they were swallowed whole – a piece of paper and a pair of coins that had fallen when I leapt back and dashed them from the counter with my groping hand, and the cap for a jar of soap which I had opened in the closet, placing the cap in my pocket, from whence it now fell and was swallowed.

Then it came for *me*. I dodged to the side and kicked the body, hoping to stun or damage it, or perhaps, with luck, strike the awakening lever and put it back to sleep – though I confess I was too terrified to know what I was doing; that roar! *That terrible roar!* – but the action merely whipped the trunk-mouth around toward me again. It struck at my leg and attached itself, leech-like; its roar instantly grew more shrill, the keening of a hunting beast with its victim in its grasp. I shouted and struck at the trunk with my hands, but could not dislodge it, so strong was its grip on me. I could feel it pulling at my flesh through the cloth of my pantaloons, and I feared becoming envenomed and paralyzed and devoured at leisure, drawn slowly into that terrible, tiny maw. I grabbed at the body, lifted it over my head, and threw it across the great room with a shouted curse – and detached its tether from the wall, which killed the beast, or stunned it. Taking no chances, I drew my wheel-gun, which I have kept in my pocket at all times against an ambuscade by the Lions, and placed that monster in my sights. When it did not move, I used the handle of a mop held in my left hand to shove it before me into an empty closet in the room where we had imprisoned the Lopezes during our earliest acquaintance, my gun trained on its body the entire time lest it come awake once more and strike. In that closet, I swear, that horrid beastie will stay. I am well-satisfied with a proper broom. Even though that immobile rug makes it most difficult to sweep properly in the parlor. Who glues a rug to the floor, so that no one can sweep underneath? The Enchantress is most peculiar to me, and no less so is her abode.

It required all the hours remaining in the day to finish the floors, but I saw the job done properly: I holystoned the tile with fine white sand I brought in from the cove, and a scrub brush and bucket from the maid's closet. Then I let it dry while I attempted to sweep the glued-rug rooms, which did not garner good results; and then I swept out the sand and swabbed the deck as Maid Flora had instructed me, using the sweet-smelling soap from the closet, even though its scent nearly overpowered me. Then the same treatment for the terrace, and I was feeling as though all was properly ship-shape and myself back in command – until the Enchantress came home.

"Daniel, did you hear?" she asked me as she strode quickly in her strange, precariously high-heeled shoes and her raiment that a Dublin whore would blush to wear.

"No, milady," I replied, my eyes firmly fixed to the far wall, high above anything improper that might cross before my gaze, anything uncovered, anything round and firm, anything tanned by the sun.

"Huh – I thought Flora would have texted you, too. Her house got shot up in a drive-by! Can you believe that?"

I could not understand it, and thus could not believe it – but I understood the operative words: *Flora. House. Shot.* "Was anyone hurt, milady?"

"I don't think so – Flora didn't say so, anyway. She said the neighbors called her and said a couple of gangbanger cars came by last night and just pulled up in front and unloaded. There's a lot of damage. I asked her if she called the police or anything, but she said no – but of course undocumented workers don't usually call the cops, do they? She said it was all right, that I shouldn't worry about the house, that they'd take care of anything when they came back. She just said I should talk to you about it. Do you know Flora's family? Are you going to check on the house for them?"

I nodded, after a moment spent unclenching my jaw, which had tautened with rage. "Yes, milady. I know her family, and her home, well.

"I will take care of it."

***

The bike took me to the vicinity of House Lopez, and then I chained it and proceeded cautiously on foot. From thirty paces away I could see an hundred holes blasted in the wooden walls of the home, and broken glass in all the windows; I could also see the head of a man on watch in a beast-wagon just beyond the Lopez property line, his gaze roving the street most haphazardly, the loud rhythmic chanting I remembered from the Lions' den emerging from the wagon, though again, I could see no musicians nor ritualizers. I shook my head: the man on watch was using neither his ears nor his eyes to advantage; any proper bosun would have had that man on his knees with a scrub brush, if not lashed to the mast and bleeding from his back, if he kept a watch that slipshod at sea – assuming his incompetence and imbecility did not have the vessel smashed on unseen rocks, that is.

I had taken the liberty of borrowing a length of slender but strong rope from the Enchantress's garradge – I had noted it when seeking a broom, and a sailor never passes up good cordage – and as night fell and I observed the man's miserable habits, I plotted my strategy. I did not know the man on watch, but he was without doubt one of my foes – a suspicion easily confirmed by the shirt he wore, a bright blue color much the same hue as the headscarves I had seen before – and I knew the man had most likely pulled a trigger and blown a hole in the home of my friends. In their *home*. Where dwelt their mother, and the boy Alejandro. Had he known the family Lopez was far gone when he aimed, when he fired? I doubted it.

I would ask him.

I crept up behind his beast-wagon, my wheel-gun in my hand, and around to the side opposite his post. Then I lay on one shoulder, my legs under me so I could move with rapidity if he did so, and, reaching under the belly of the beast, I aimed and fired a shot at the house. This brought a most satisfying response from the man, who cried out like a small child startled awake by nightmare and then leapt and stumbled out of his wagon, cursing and brandishing a *pistola* of his own. He had heard the shot strike the house, had heard the blast somewhere close, but he knew not where – and in his confusion, he simply ran to the house and stood staring, dumbly. It was child's play to come up from behind and lay him out with a blow to the back of his head. A glance up and down the street showed that we two were alone; I took up his *pistola*, dealt him a blow or two with my heel – for the honor of Lopez – and then trussed his arms and legs. I dragged him to the small meadow behind House Lopez, where we might converse unseen by people on the street, hidden as the meadow was behind a wooden fence. I left him under a tree, and then opened the heavy garradge door to gain entry to the house and gather the other materials I required. Then I prepared him and waited for him to awaken so we could begin.

He woke soon after, and when he did, I hauled away on the rope which I had tied to his thumbs; he was soon standing on his toes, his eyes wide, his head shaking – any shouts silenced as I had bound his mouth shut, at least for the nonce. I tied off the rope on the fence, and then I aimed my wheel-gun at his left eye, and waited there until his entire body was shaking and the beads of sweat ran down his face. He tried to let his weight back down onto his heels, and learned what it meant to be strung up by one's thumbs – and then he raised up onto his toes once more, to save his thumbs from being pulled from the socket, or off entirely. This same fate had maimed my traitorous former bosun, Ned Burke, when the tribe of maroons he had been preying upon after escaping into the jungle of Hispaniola from his indenture had captured him and strung him up by his thumbs, leaving him hanging until, after days, he had – fallen down.

I put the barrel of the pistol into the hollow of my man's throat. "Do not shout," I said quietly. He nodded. I removed his gag.

"Please, man," he began, but a thrust of the gun barrel into his throat stopped the words there.

"Did you fire at that house?" I asked, pointing.

I saw the lie begin in his eyes, but he saw me recognize it, and he swallowed it untold. He nodded instead.

I laughed, darkly. "So have I. Only their cowardly surrender kept me from putting a shot into the brothers themselves, when first they came against me." I turned the smile into a snarl, and pressed close, bruising his throat with the pistol. "You insult me when you presume that these dirt-faced peasants are my allies. My – *friends*. How dare you think that this, this *filthy scum* could be the bait in a trap for me. For *me!*" A blow to his nose with the pistol's butt set the claret flowing down, and surprised him enough to fall back off of his toes – stretching his thumbs agonizingly, though as of yet his hands stayed whole. He opened his mouth to scream, and I shoved the pistol into it.

"Be. *Silent*." I ordered him. He followed orders. When he recovered his balance and eased the pressure on his thumbs, I removed the pistol's barrel and asked him my questions.

"How many of you are there?"

"Nine – eighteen. Eighteen since Francisco got fucked up in that alley."

"And your leader – is it Agro?"

"Yeah. Man, let me down, man – shit!"

"Agro is the one I stabbed in the hand at the market, yes?"

"Yeah, man, he fucking pissed at you, essay." (Perhaps the last word was the letters S.A., but that holds no clearer meaning for me.)

"Do you know who I am?"

"Naw, man, we call you the Sparrow, after Johnny Depp, you know? Fuck, this fuckin' *hurts*, essay!"

I grabbed his chin, pressed the barrel of the gun against his broken nose, which brought a shudder and a groan. "My name is Damnation Kane. Remember it. Tell the others.

"And watch your step." I lowered my aim and fired into the ground. The shot struck his *pistola*, and scattered sparks, which ignited the circle of rum-soaked rags with gunpowder sprinkled o'er (gunpowder gathered from the cartridges that had been in the gun) that lay under the tree's limb from which his rope descended. I pulled on his rope until his feet lifted free of the ground, and he swung directly over the flames, which tickled at his toes and his heels, even up to his ankles, but no higher. I tied it off there, and then dealt him a mighty blow to the belly, setting him swinging like a pendulum and silencing his cries for a time. I left him there and walked to the street and his beast-wagon. I splashed it with the remainder of the rum, and fired one more shot, my pistol laid flat on the puddle of liquor, which ignited and began to burn merrily.

I went back to the bike and rode to my redoubt at the Palace, confident that my message would be received. I would be alert for the response, whatever it may be.

Log #25: Lady of Mercy

Captain's Log
Date: 11th of July, 2011.
Location: Alone in a place that mystifies me.
Conditions: Have suffered from some small injuries; but far worse, from despair.

I find I have underestimated these people somewhat.

The Lions did their level best to lure me into complacency, simply by doing nothing at all that was of any import. I have watched them for the past two days, after my last capture and chastisement of one of their crewmates, and prior to this day's events, and they never once perceived me, never detected my malignant presence so close to their home. As far as I could discern their actions, they also never sought me out: did not speak to those who might have seen or spoken to me, did not endeavor to uncover my whereabouts, and happily but most inanely, they did not wind and follow my clearest trail – clearest still despite all my efforts to confound it – my connection to the Lopezes. I presumed these Lions were made kittenish by fear, and thus I grew o'erconfident myself.

Then, this day, as I rode my steed (I find the local word "bike" too grating on tongue and on paper, so it will be my steed henceforth in this record.) toward the Lions' den, I was utterly startled to hear the sudden growl of a beast-wagon, accompanied by a shout. Now, I am surrounded by beast-wagons whensoe'er I make my way along the roads and byways of this place, and so here, too, I grow complacent, inured to the beast-wagons' stench and the cacophony of their incessant growling and gurrumbling as my steed carries me along the edge of the road beside them, often close enough to touch.

But this growl was louder: hungrier. *Angrier*. As was the shout, which comprised an epithet so foul, and so insulting to my noble and beloved mother, that even my sailor's tongue dries up at the thought of repeating or recording it. When I heard these noises, I cast a glance back over my left shoulder – but it was too late.

The Lions had found me, or had followed me, perhaps. Even as I recognized them behind the glass eye of their beast-wagon, the monster struck me, struck my steed's wheel, and cast me into a most ungainly flight. I landed, all a-sprawl, atop another beast-wagon, one of a line sleeping by the side of the road; I struck my head and crumpled, stunned, to the ground.

I had sailed all the way across and fallen on the far side of the beast-wagons – which may have saved my life, for the Lions came about and bore down on me once more, while my wits were still addled; I shudder to think what would have become of me had they been able to strike me anew with yon growling metal behemoth. Even without that, I was in danger enough: they drew arms and blasted a broadside at me as they drew abreast the beast-wagon I had struck and behind which I crouched, struggling to rise to hands and knees with head twirling and limbs as weak as a newborn babe's, with blood pouring down from a wound on my brow and blinding my right eye.

Had I thought the growl of the beast-wagon loud? Or ominous? It was as nothing to the wave of thunder that split the air as the Lions opened fire. 'Twas louder than an entire firing line of a score of British soldiers, and the shots went on far longer than I could expect, three and five and ten and fifteen seconds without cease, without pause to reload, seconds that each seemed an hour. The lead poured into the beast-wagons between me and the Lions, shattering windows and holing the metal flanks; but they did not penetrate to me. The plastered stone wall on the other side, perhaps the back wall of a row of shops as it was unpierced by window or door, rang with ricochets as holes appeared and shards of stone flew as though goblins swung pickaxes, digging for gold with supernatural vigor and avarice. The shards struck me, gashing my cheek and my right hand; this fresh pain awoke me sufficiently to crouch and cover my much-abused head. I tried to reach for the pistol in my pocket – for I wore my maid's clothes in the name of camouflage on the streets of Miami – but I could not control my limbs well enough to do so; my arm felt encased in hardened pitch, weighted with lead.

Though it seemed forever, 'twas not, and finally the Lions' wagon growled and squealed as they spurred it for home. I could do no more than rise to hands and knees and then collapse, eyes shut against the spinning of my dizzied head, my back against the beast-wagon that had shielded me from certain death. I patted its metal flank and gasped out a grateful thanks to its sturdy protection.

Thus, when the voice spoke to me, I thought at first that the beast was responding. I opened my eyes, felt my stomach lurch as the world turned topsy-turvy once more, and closed them again – but not before I had spotted the very human person who knelt before me, and who had spoken – though I realized then that I had not made sense out of said speech.

"I must beg your pardon, but I fear your words lost to my befuddled ears. Wouldst speak again, I pray?" While speaking thus – and stumbling slightly over my words – I had managed to open one eye, the left, and force the spinning world to stand still enough for me to make out the person who addressed me, though my stomach heaved like a boat crossing a ship's wake.

It was a woman, I saw – though her hair confused me at first; 'twas as short as a man's – with a kindly face, concern in her eyes as she looked at me through the spectacles I had but rarely seen in Ireland but frequently here. I could not discern her age: her hair was grey tending to white, but she had all her teeth, and her skin, though wrinkled, was smoother still than any other white-haired woman I have ever seen. She wore a loose frock, open from neck to waist, with a thin blouse beneath, both in jarringly bright colors; I was surprised to see she wore short britches that left her legs bare, and I averted my eyes for propriety's sake.

My speech had made her smile – 'twas a fine smile, one that lit her whole face (and the gaps 'tween her front teeth bespoke a lusty and adventurous spirit, a most popular and sought-after feature in a lass back home in the Ireland of yore) – and now she repeated herself more slowly. "I asked if you needed an ambulance, but if you can talk like that, you might not." Her smile faded to deep solicitousness once more. "You're bleeding pretty bad, though. Why don't you just stay right there and relax until the police come. *Whoa!*"

This last word came as her mention of police – *la policia* – brought me to alert and I began to stand upright. But quicker than my dizzied head and shaking limbs could heave me upright, her hands caught me at shoulder and knee, and with surprising strength for such a small woman – she would have stood no higher than my shoulder, had we been both standing – she pushed me back down to the ground.

"Don't move," she said, in a voice accustomed to command. "You hit your head, you're bleeding and you probably have a concussion. You might have been shot, too, and not feel it. The police are already on their way. You need to stay still until they come, and then if we need to, we can call an ambulance or they can take you to the emergency room."

"No *policia*," I said, panting as my head spun anew from my exertions. "I have no wish to make their acquaintance. I am hale and whole, I assure you – their cannonade struck the beast-wagon, not me. My injuries are from my fall alone." I managed to raise my bleeding right hand and place it atop hers, which was still on my left shoulder. "Please, my lady – if you will but help me to my feet, I will take my steed – my bike – and depart in peace, I assure you. I have a safe place to recover my wits and tend my wounds."

She looked at me for a few long moments – nay, she looked into me, and through me; rarely have I seen such a piercing gaze, such a wise and perceptive mien, and I began to think her a druid as of old – and then she rose to her feet. "Tell you what," she said, her voice showing a pleasant rasp. "If you can get up by yourself, I'll take care of the rest. That sound fair?" She crossed her arms calmly over her middle and waited.

It only took me three tries, and then I was standing. Out of breath and panting like a blown horse, to be sure, but I had not allowed myself time to rest in between attempts, as I felt the imminent arrival of *la policia*, and I most assuredly did not want to make their acquaintance. As I understood their usual role, they would choose a side to take: the Lions', which would not bode well for me; or mine, which would likely rob me of my vengeance. So I rose to my feet and stood, listing slightly to one side as my knee throbbed and my head spun. But I met the small woman's gaze, and raised an eyebrow, daring her.

She laughed – a splendid laugh, one with that good rasp that spoke of long, rich life, full of many laughs before, as well as shouts and songs and tall mugs of ale and glasses of whiskey – and shook her head. "All right, tough guy, let's go." She turned to lead the way, but I stumbled as I made to follow her; she caught me, and served as my balance until I caught my own once more. "Come on. Around the corner, there's a little cafe we can sit in and stop your bleeding." She wrapped one thin, strong arm around my waist and held me up as I made my dizzy, halting, humbled way to the place she described.

It was like an open-air tavern, a most pleasant place with tall shrubs in pots and bright paint on the walls, many tables with tiled tops in bright colors and silver edges, the chairs silver as well, with cushioned seats of red-dyed leather. My kind helpmeet steered me through the tight spaces between tables to a larger, rectangular table set against the wall in the back of the tavern, with two long benches instead of individual chairs. She let me fall into one of the benches, and then grabbed a square of white – was it paper? It did not feel like cloth – from a black-and-silver box on the table top, and pressed it against my head. "You O'Kay?" she asked. Why was she asking about my clan? I was not of the O'Kays, but I had heard of them, I thought. Perhaps not – there are many clans, and my head had now begun to throb instead of spinning. "Are you all right?" she asked slower, and at this I nodded, slowly.

"I am as well as can be, my lady, I assure you."

"Hold this," she said. She took my hand from the table top and placed it on the paper square, now wet with blood, pressed against my brow. "Order some coffee. I'll be right back." She went out, pausing to speak briefly to the barmaid, who nodded and came back to the table.

"Your friend says you fell, and you need a minute to sit down. Are you O'Kay? Is there anything I can get you?"

Why did all of these people want to know my clan? "I am well, and my thanks to you for your kindness. I wish to have coffee, if I might." After a moment, likely spent staring at the blood on my head and hands, she walked away, to return in a few moments with a small cup full of dark, steaming liquid. I took a sip, as I was parched from my ride and exertions, and found it hot and bitter and distasteful. The Lopezes drank this stuff by the gallon in the morning, but I found I could not stomach it. Still, I had not the strength to ask for ale or tea, and so I bit back my tongue's protests and drained the cup. It heartened me, somewhat, though coming back to myself made me more aware of the pain in my head, my hands, my leg. I put my elbow on the table top and lay my head in my hands, holding the paper on my wound and taking a moment to rest.

The moment did not last long. "Come on, Irish – we gotta go." I looked up and saw my helpmeet coming quickly toward me. Her mien was focused, but not panicked: thus I stood as quickly and smoothly as I could, but did not draw the wheel-gun in my pocket. She withdrew a piece of green paper, the local money, from her britches, and tossed it on the table, and then beckoned me out of the tavern. Once back on the street, we turned away from the direction of my crash, and walked as swiftly as my aching head and limping leg allowed.

"Whither go we, my lady?"

"That's a good question," she said, scanning the street ahead, turning back to check behind us and then speeding our pace slightly. "The cops will be here any minute, and people are talking about you as someone involved. Apparently the people around here know the gang, they're local – "

"Aye, they are – the Latin Lions, they style themselves. They den not far from here."

She looked squarely at me. "So you know them, then. This wasn't an accident, I assume? They were after you?"

I started to nod, but my head was aching rather fiercely, so I spoke instead. "Aye, we have had a difference of opinion these past few weeks, the Lions and I."

She stopped dead, and drew me back into the mouth of an alley. She turned to face me; I did the same. "All right. So here's the thing. You need to convince me, right now, first that I should help you, rather than turn you over to the police, and second that if I do help you, it won't put me in any danger."

I drew myself upright and made as deep a bow as I could – not deep enough to do proper respect to a kind and gentle lady, but deep enough to show my intent. "I thank thee, my lady, for the assistance you have already provided. I will trouble you no further." I turned on my heel to walk away – and my damned leg collapsed under me. Once more, I was caught and held upright, like a babe in arms or a doddering bloody drunkard, by a woman who weighed half as much as I.

She helped me upright and then shook her head. "You need help, Irish. Decide if you want it from me or the cops. And if it's me, convince me."

She was right. I took the wheel-gun from my pocket and presented it to her, hilt-first. After a moment she took it, opened the wheel, and examined the six shot-thimbles inside. Then she nodded, closed it and tucked it into her belt at the small of her back. "All right. You didn't shoot, so I'll accept that you were just the victim of a drive-by. Do you have any more weapons, or shall I begin to feel safe around you?"

I made another shallow bow. "My lady, I am now entirely at your mercy. My name is Damnation Kane."

She smiled and shook her head. "Nice to meet you, Damnation. I'm LaDonna Joy."

I raised one brow. "LaDonna? Is that not Spanisher for The Lady?"

She shrugged, raising one hand, palm up. "Close enough. Do your friends call you Damnation?"

"Nay, my lady. They call me Nate."

She nodded. "I like that much better. All right, Nate, come this way – my hotel's down the block. We can get you fixed up." She turned to go, after scanning the street once more for danger and checking the pistol in her belt, and I followed, comfortable in the merciful hands of the Lady of Joy.

We won our way to her rooms without further incident; she sent me into the washroom to clean my wounds, and went out to gather medical supplies. Then I was placed in a chair while she stood, not much taller than I was while seated, and cleaned my wounds, declaring the head wound not so serious, after all. She applied first a clear, scentless ointment and then bandages to my hurts, and I must confess they felt markedly better for her kind ministrations. Then she brought us food – a strange round bread she called bagels, with thin slices of a fish called locks and a thick butter-like spread she said was creamed cheese – all of it most delicious. I told her something of my history, though I was vague as to my origins and how I had arrived here, saying merely that I was a sailor and had been stranded on strange shores by my crew, who had betrayed me. I told her the tale of the Lopezes and the Lions, saying merely that I had incurred the blackguards' wrath and then pledged to avenge their assaults on my person and the innocent family I had befriended and endangered. She told me she was a teacher, which interested me when I asked after her students and she told me she worked in a public school; apparently these people send *all* of their children to school for twelve years– twelve years! What could there possibly be to learn in that time that could not be better learned in an apprenticeship, or better still, at sea, the place that best teaches a man how to live? She was on a vaycayshin, she said, a concept I did not quite understand – but I was more mystified still when she told me she lived in a place called Orrigun, that was better than *three thousand miles* away. I tried not to show how dubious I was at this – surely the New World is not so large! That would make the equivalent of all Europe! – but she laughed at me, knowing I did not believe her, sure nonetheless that she need not convince me to win my friendship and trust. After all of her kindness, she could have told me she lived on the moon and flew down to the Earth to gather these bagels once a month, and I would have nodded and wished her a fine trip back into the sky. We pirates, and even more we men who must live under savage and contemptible oppressors, do understand the importance of withholding the truth of one's origins and vulnerabilities; we know a lie told to protect is no sin at all.

After an hour in this pleasant company, seated in this remarkably cool room with this fine companion, I felt much relieved, and begged her leave to return to retrieve my steed. "Oh, I moved it. It's in the alley next to the cafe, behind a dumpster. If nobody's stolen it by now."

I thanked her again. "If they have, I feel sure I have the strength now to walk to my lodgings. I will impose upon your kind hospitality no further. My great thanks, again, for all of your help, dear lady. Please, if you ever have need of my assistance, do not hesitate to send word: the Lopezes will most likely be able to get me a message; ask for Flora Lopez on Nightingale Street."

She nodded, and patted my shoulder. "Thanks, Nate. And thanks for the conversation – it was getting a little lonely, without somebody to talk to. That's the only problem with taking vaycayshin by yourself. I'll actually be glad to go home again, even if I will miss all this warm sunshine. Well, maybe the rain will have stopped by now – though I won't hold my breath. Look me up if you ever get to Orrigun. Little town on the Columbia called Saint Helens, north of Portland. Find the high school, and you'll find me."

I gave her a proper bow, which she returned – along with my wheel gun, which I took with a nod of thanks – and then I took my leave of my newfound friend.

I found my steed, unmolested behind the wheeled metal box – a dumpster, she had called it; very odd words, these people have – and though it was somewhat bent and wobbly, slatting like a sail in a contrary wind, I made it back to the Glass Palace. The Enchantress was gone, apparently for the evening, as the sun was setting, and so I took advantage of her absence by resting myself on her reclining bench, helping myself to a bottle of wine from her galley; I lit the magic window to keep myself entertained, pressing knobs on the wand until I came across the scene Alejandro Lopez had called "news." It spoke of the weather, of the strange activity the local men pursued, running about in their undergarments, which was for some reason called "sports" though I saw little in it that would amuse anyone over the age of five – and then something appeared called "Breaking News."

What I saw then ruined my peace and joy entirely.

Log #26: Letter from the Gallows

(Translated from Gaelic)

Date Unknown: The 9th Day after the Cursed Mutiny. A Letter to my Captain and the Man I once called Friend, and would give my Right Hand to call such again: Damnation Kane, EVER AND ALWAYS Master of the *Grace of Ireland*.

Captain.

I do beg ye not to misapprehend the apparent Coolness of my Address. 'Tis not because I love ye any the less than when I called ye Nate, and thought of ye as my Brother. But I ha' failed ye so utterly that I cannot speak ye familiar until I ha' redeemed myself. I may ne'er do so. I will not ask Forgiveness, for how could any Man of true Heart and hot Blood forgive Betrayal so base as ye ha' suffered? Na'theless, I do, 'pon my knees, offer to ye my humblest and deepest Apologies and Regrets. When ye did set me Mate, an honor that warms my Soul e'en now, in the black depths of my despair, ye gave me the task of preserving your command, your fine Ship, above all else. And now I do fear she will be lost.

Curse me, ye will ne'er forgive me. Curse me to the end of days. And curse that gut-worm Shlocksir thrice again. Ye ha' ne'er failed as Captain, sir, but perhaps that once, when ye allowed that Spawn of Corruption into our company, whate'er our need may ha' been. Aye and perhaps one other time, when ye let those pestilent mongrels O'Flaherty and Burke take Authority that ye should ha' kept. Well I know that the men did give ye little Choice. But blast me, Captain, better ye had taken on whole new Crew than keep those two aboard with Daggers e'er pointed at your Heart, and Lust for your Ship in theirs.

But whate'er missteps our twisted and malignant Fate has pushed ye into, ye ne'er lost our Ship. Nay, that sin be mine, and the fault lies in me that landed those poxy fools on the poop deck in your place.

'Twas Shlocksir's plan, Captain, tho I know O'Flaherty and Burke and Carter all pressed for a Sea Battle. The land-grabs we ha' done e'er since stealing your *Grace* ha' brought a fine heap o' paper, and little else besides, pleasing no one but our ferret-eyed whore's son of a Carpenter. Too, the loss of the boat means we can no longer anchor the *Grace* and reach the shore at our Leisure, and that too pushed us into this ill-fated Folly.

We did try to take a Ship, this day. A Ship bearing passengers, as Shlocksir avowed that our sweet *Grace* could not threaten the cargo vessels that sail these Seas, so large as those Ships be. But Shlocksir told us of the Ships of the wealthiest merchants, Ships he called yots, if that were his word aright. These yots sailed Unarmed and Unsuspecting of Attack, and we could hail the yotsmen as if in Friendship, or perhaps as tho we were in Distress, and we should find Riches aboard.

We made South-South-West for a day, headed for the Keys, as Shlocksir named them, islands where the yots made passage to and fro. We sighted a Fine Specimen, a Ship twice the *Grace* from stem to stern, with three decks, white as snow and with Music and Good Cheer pouring out to our ears e'en a half mile distant. Shlocksir called it a "party boat," a "day-tripper," and said we could handle it with ease, may the Devil gnaw at his greedy heart.

Shlocksir ordered us to come alongside and board her. Why that bag of rancid suet fancies himself capable or deserving of Command, I ha' not an Idea. And less why O'Flaherty and Burke allow it. But they do, for Shlocksir is e'er shouting commands, e'er the wrong ones, and they ne'er gainsay him but when the Ship should sink if they held their tongues, as when he ordered us to come to Port when he meant Starboard, and there were rocks to Port. Yet all other orders we follow, in our Folly and to our Doom. We did so now, tho he railed at the slowness of our approach for some Minutes, until Burke took him aside roughly and pointed out the direction of the Wind, which was against us, but apparently past the understanding of a calf-brained lubber such as this.

But he was not the only calf-brained lubber, it seemed, as the Captain of the yot did nothing to stem our approach, nor to escape. He came to the rail and bespoke us through some Magickal Device that made his Voice Boom like Storm Waves crashing ashore. All vile Shlocksir spake in return was that we be Pirates looking for a Good Time, and bearing Grog. He did ask for permission to come aboard, and had me and Sweeney smile and wave. Certain 'tis that we two looked less Forbidding than Burke or Kelly. And that, it seemed, were enough, as we were able to come alongside and make Fast to their rail.

Then we climbed aboard, and the time for smiling was done. We went Armed, secured the Men, there being but ten aboard and eight Women, one lass in uniform, which did Mystify us, but Shlocksir claims 'tis the way of things here. Tho I know not why we do continue to take his word, the Mendacious Idiot. They did not believe our Menace until Carter, who has been almost continually drunk these past nine days, shot the Mate, killing him on the spot, his Blood pooling on the deck making a most Persuasive Argument. The Captain then, too late, did raise a Shout, but Burke beat him unconscious and then heaved him o'erboard. All was silent but for Tears after that.

We searched the Ship, finding little enough of value. Some Spirits, some Victuals, a fair quantity o' Jewelry on the passengers, some strange objects Shlocksir claimed valuable, naming them selfowns and laptops. Nothing worth the Hanging we surely now have waiting for us ashore. We trussed up the remaining passengers and crew and made to Depart. But then Shlocksir said that we should take Hostages.

I did see his eye fall on the comeliest female passengers, both wearing little more than skin, both Young and Shapely. I knew he did not mean to keep them as Hostages. I saw other men, Burke, and Carter, and perhaps more, grin at Shlocksir's idea. I did speak against it, Loud and strong, aye. I named Shlocksir a Vile Rapist.

His response? Naught but a grin and the words, "No, man, I'm a pirate."

I moved to Strike him then, but he drew his Pistol on me. I had no Doubt he would use it. I might ha' charged anyway, for I could ha' had him o'er the rail e'en as he Killed me, and then he would drown and save the Women, but I could not abandon the *Grace*. And so, to my Shame, I backed down, and let Shlocksir and Burke haul those poor screaming lasses aboard our ship, our ship blessed by your own Sainted Mother and baptized in your Blood.

Ah, God, what have I done?

I could not, Captain. I could not let them get away with this, not this. As we were departing and preparing to cut loose from the yot, I did loosen the bonds of one of the Crewmen. I did Whisper to him that we would likely head East, as Shlocksir had mentioned afore, aiming for Bermuda or a similar Port of Call.

I gave him our Ship, Captain. I know that, even as we sail away filled with good Cheer at our Success, the forces of Just Retribution are descending on us. I know that the Magick of this day, of this place, can surely find us wheresoe'er we go, can surely outrun and outgun us. Shlocksir has said this many a time, making much of our ability to Surprise as our Greatest Asset, and our ability to sneak away and vanish in the vasty Ocean.

But now they know where we are. They will find us. They will likely destroy us, and your Ship with us.

I am sorry, Nate. So very sorry. I will await your Forgiveness, or your Vengeance, when I am in Hell, my corpse dangling from a Gibbet.

I be standing Guard o'er the Hostages. Kelly is with me, and sober, for a Wonder. We are agreed that Blood will spill afore we allow Innocents to be despoiled on our Blessed Ship. Kelly rests now, and I write so that I may stay awake. It has been two days, and hard days, since I did sleep; ten days since I did sleep well.

With each Sunset I do gain another day's doubts. Every night, I lay in my bunk, for I be demoted from Mate, o' course, and broken down to a sailor's berth, and as I lay I do cast back o'er the last day, the last two or three or ten days. Did I do all that I might? Did I choose aright, this day? These last ten nights, the Question that consumes my Mind is this: did I do what I could to bring back the *Grace*? To bring her back to her Owner and Captain, to bring her back to the course she was meant to sail?

I cannot think how we could ha' done differently.

That first day we thought ye in your Cabin. I swear that to be God's Own Truth. I remember drinking too much Wine and falling asleep at table the night afore; Master Vaughn feels sure we were Drugged, as he also fell unconscious in his cups tho he had but one or two glasses of Wine, and for myself, I ha' not lost my Wits to the

175

Drink since I was a wee lad. In the morning, my head pounding like the Devil's Dancing Hoofsteps, I asked after ye, and O'Flaherty said ye were sleeping off the Wine and should not be disturbed. He did say we should make way, tho, so as not to lose the Tide; he said that 'twould be a fine Surprise for ye to wake and see the *Grace* far out to Sea already.

I suppose it was, at that.

Ye ha' been in the habit o' staying in your Cabin of late, and my head Ached so that I could not but wish I was Asleep, myself. Surely I could not, did not think straight, else I would have, *I should have!*, checked to see ye for myself. But I did not, to my Shame, both as Mate and Friend. Instead I did take Command in your Absence from the poop deck, and got us out to Sea and running well.

'Twas then, Four Bells through the Midmorning Watch, that the Truth was Revealed. O'Flaherty put Carter on the wheel and called all Hands on Deck. Then he told us that ye had been relieved o' your Command. He told us that ye had not only Beaten and Whipped a man Unjustly, and tho Shlocksir be unfamiliar to the men, his crime is not mysterious to their thoughts, and so they fear his Fate for themselves, as I did try to tell ye then, Curse me, but also he did say that ye had Lied to us. Ye had withheld Vital Information, because ye did not Trust us to take it like Men, and, he said, ye likely had some Villainous Plot in mind, perhaps to Betray us and take on new crew, men more to your Way o' Thinking. I stood to Defend ye and your decisions as Captain, but was Silenced by what O'Flaherty said next. We ha' traveled through Time, he said. Three Hundred Years, he said, and more. All that we did know then, all is now dust and ashes, and Relicks in a Museum.

We were so stunned by this that we did not object when O'Flaherty took Command, naming Moran as Mate, Burke to Gunner, Carter as the Bosun and Shlocksir as Navigator. He told us his intentions: we would find our way back to our own Time, but first we had to do what ye, in your Cowardice and Broken-minded Befuddlement, Forgive me for repeating his words, what ye had failed to do. We must take Advantage of this strange Miracle which Providence had cast in our way. For we do be the only Pirates in these Seas, the only Pirates in Two Hundred Years! He said the people here do be soft and trusting as Lambs. He did not even need to look at Shlocksir to make his point, for we all knew that he was right. He said we did not even need to Pluck this ripened Fruit that hung all around us; all we need do is open our mouths and let the rich Juices run down our Gullets 'til our Bellies be filled. Then we would find our way Home, and live like Kings.

'Twas a masterful job, Captain. He scattered our wits with his Revelation, like a grenado cast into our midst, and then in one stroke, he blamed ye for the Devastation he had wrought and also gave us a Way out of it, one which appealed to our Greed as well as offering a chance to not feel the Terror of being 300 years Lost.

Ye should ha' told us, Nate. Tho the result be not deserved, still ye should ha' told us. It went poorly when I asked after ye. The men shouted me down and named ye Traitor to the Company for keeping such a Secret. When Moran stood and did swear that ye lived and were unharmed, that he would ne'er spill the Blood of his own Cousin, the men were well satisfied, and agreed on the spot to follow O'Flaherty as Captain o' our *Grace*.

There were Three, tho, who came to me later and did express deep Misgivings about your loss and O'Flaherty's gain. We met again, often, o'er the next few days, as our Misgivings grew under O'Flaherty's Command and Shlocksir's guidance. When we saw the heading they intended for us to follow, we decided to take Action.

'Twas miserable, Captain. The only one excited was Shlocksir, who sweated and capered about so you'd think him a young Horse, new-broken and ridden hard and let to Pasture. The crew did Question the Value in such a simple and unambitious Assault, for we put four men in the boat and rowed ashore at Night, and robbed a Store, something named Seven-Eleven. We took their paper money and some small supplies, and Naught else. Aye, 'twas easy and free o' Risk, but where were the great Rewards promised us? That were the grumbles.

Tho I admit: those Potato Chips are entirely Delicious.

The next night, to Silence those grumblings, our Target was a Grog Shop. Along with more paper, of which Shlocksir seems inordinately fond, we captured crates of Liquor, and had a fine proper Drunkening. The next night we waited until later, and then took a Tavern, just after it closed, using Kelly to burst the door in. We took a grand lot o' paper that night, aye, and more Rum to keep the crew jolly.

We saw then, myself and my three Companions in Misery, that this would be our Fate: we would run up and down the Coastline, Robbing local shopkeeps o' paper and Potato chips and Grog. Shlocksir would be happy with his piles o' green scraps, O'Flaherty with his usurped Command; Burke would surely find opportunities to Exercise his Cruelty (He has already flogged two men, and Savagely), and the men would merely stay drunk, and Complacent Thereby.

We four could not Stomack this. What Pride was there, what Glory, in Midnight raids on unarmed townsfolk? We are Pirates, by God, Gentlemen of Fortune! And Irishmen, too! Half of us joined this crew because we did know that Damnation Kane would give us the chance to spill English Blood, and to Fight, in some small way, for our Country against her Oppressors. Who were we fighting now, Seven-Eleven? We found it less than satisfying.

But the men were Drunk. And the Course we followed was, if nothing else, Supremely Easy. We made out to Sea at night, fished and lazed during the Day, then sailed to shore after Nightfall, cruising until we spotted a Target, when we would anchor and send out the boat, with Shlocksir, Burke, and two men to row. Why would the crew Rebel against that?

We needed our Leader, the Man who could wake up their Blood and give them Purpose again. We needed ye, Captain.

So finally, we four decided to steal the boat, and make our Way back to ye. I agreed to stay aboard the *Grace*, to watch out for Her so Well as I could. Three Nights ago we had our Chance, when O'Flaherty found a quiet cove to anchor in after our petty theft, and Declared we would spend the Night at rest, without a watch, so that all could Celebrate the ease of our Success. They did get Masterfully Drunk, and we did Steal their Boat.

When they did find the boat gone, and with it their Ability to make these easy raids on townsfolk, our Leaders did rant and rail. At last, then, they decided to make an Assault on a Ship.

And here we are.

Now my three Compatriots, young Lynch, your cousin Owen McTeigue, and Master Vaughn, are gone with the boat, and I know not what has become of them. And I squat in the companionway outside the Mate's Cabin belowdecks, and listen to the Wailings and Whimpers of two Terrified and Innocent Women who are prisoned where once I made my berth. I hope it will not come to Blows if they come for the Women, for Kelly and I will stand Honorably, but we will Not Win, and I hate that Blood may be spilled on our lovely Ship. And I hope that the local Navymen will find us, but will not sink us, for I Dread most of all if these Serpents in the shape of men be allowed to Pillage and Plunder at their will. If they earn some ill Repute for their Beastly deeds and Savage treatment of Innocents, then what show of force, what sort of Ship, what manner of destructive Magick incomprehensible and Terrible to us will be brought to bear? We must not risk that. This cruise must be Stopped now.

God Almighty, let the Risks I take be for the best for my Ship, my Captain, and my Friends. I Beg of Thee.

Ian O'Gallows, Mate of the *Grace of Ireland*

Log #27: Vanity and Vengeance

Captain's Log
Date: 14 July 2011
Location: Redoubt at the Glass Palace
Conditions: Victorious! And no longer alone!

Mine enemies are SCATTERED, my companions RETURNED – this night is a BLOODY DAMNED GOOD NIGHT! The BEST since we left Ireland, auld Ireland, alas. I believe I will have another drink. Ah! Sweet nectar, staff of life, blood of Erin renewed! Ha ha haaaaa!

Captain's Log
Date: 15 July 2011
Location: Redoubt
Conditions: No longer drunk. All else continues as before.

Yesterday did not dawn presaging victory. I had at last eased my limp, and was all but recovered from my smashing by the Lions' beast-wagon; while recovering, I had plotted a new course from Palace to den, and had discovered the means of my vengeance, and the tool to end the threat of the Lions entirely. But I had no hope of accomplishing my goal, and so the speedy recovery of my corporeal health – aided, no doubt, by the kind ministrations of My Lady of Joy – gave way only to a deep spiritual malaise, as I rose and gazed at the sun dawning bright and clear over the ocean, rising on another day when my vengeance and justice, both, would again be frustrated ere sun's set.

The seed of my plan began humbly, even inauspiciously. The Enchantress – who saw my several hurts, surely, but said nothing at all, did not ask after my welfare nor express sympathy (Though I admit I would not have been pleased to have a comely woman such as she commenting on my weakness or defeat. But she could have

180

excused me from my maidish duties, blast the luck.) – had requested that I clean a locale she termed, quite without irony, her "vanity." This, as it obtains, is a table and chair set hard by her bathing-room, equipped with a massive mirror and the brightest lights I have ever seen outside of the sun itself, and covered, from table's edge to table's edge, with an alchemist's wildest and fondest imaginings. Or perhaps 'twould be his worst nightmare: it was nearly mine. Bottle after bottle on top of bottle beside jar behind phial before box between piles, of perfumes and powders and paints and – only the Devil knows what else. I could not fathom where the Enchantress applies these concoctions to her loveliness; I have observed some small difference in her appearance, though solely due to the Enchantress's penchant for swimming. I would have thought I could see her as her true self in the early morn, but by the time I arrive for my maidery, she is already adorned for the day – surprising, that, as I come somewhat early and she is rich, which led me to believe she would stay abed; but nay, every morning, my arrival at the door is greeted by a perfumed and painted Enchantress, looking as lovely as a flower at dawn and smiling a welcome. 'Tis only after the greeting and some polite conversation that I descend to the status of servant once more, and am quickly forgotten. But even that painted face was but little different from the natural physiognomy I was wont to observe after her exercise in her terrace pool; surely there was no call for the sheer quantity and variety of materiel she possessed, and apparently utilized, as all of the containers were stained and smudged, often with caps and lids loose or misapplied, and all of it covered with a fine powder in various light hues; damn me if I could spot a tenth of it anywhere on her lovely face, though in truth I did not make a frequent and minute inspection of such. And the tools! The brushes and combs, the pincers, the calipers, the razors, the trowels God's mercy, but I would not find such equippage unusual in the possession of a surgeon – nay, nor even a torturer in the employ of the dread Inquisition. There was one silver device that, I swear, looked to be intended for prying open eyelids in order to remove the ball itself, or perhaps merely to stab it with one of the sharpened instruments that abounded there.

I am so sublimely relieved that I am not a woman.

Any road, this vanity and its witches' brews were my task, and I set to it: I removed and cleaned, with cloth and water, every bottle and jar, and polished every implement I could, setting them all aside so I could swab the table itself, once cleared of its mighty burden. But there were some articles, and, as I discovered, some areas of the tabletop, that were stained and marred with splatters and spills which a wet cloth simply could not remove. The Enchantress had already departed, leaving me on my own with this conundrum. I considered the soaps and tinctures in the maid's closet, but I did not believe they were equal to this task – and as the table was of fine, polished wood, I did not want to holystone it clean for fear of damaging its surface. I had already been taken to task for marring the gleam of the galley tabletops in just this fashion, though as they were granite, and my abrasive merely fine sand, I think 'twas the fact of the Enchantress witnessing me at this task rather than any permanent harm I did which brought me this chastisement. How do the people of this time bring such surfaces clean if they do not abrade them properly? Filth must be scoured away!

Ha: a good lesson for the confrontation with the Lions, as well, not so?

So I went in search of turpentine. Among the elixirs and salves on the vanity I had found several which resembled paint, and I knew that turpentine acted as a solvent for such. I presumed it would not be stored in the house, if such were kept here at all, for the sake of its powerful odor, and so I investigated the garradge. I did indeed find a metal jar – most odd; like a box with a round spout in the top, and a lid that screwed on over it – with a clear liquid inside, most pungent, and the words "Paint Thinner" on the jar-box. This finally proved most efficacious on the vanity, though the resultant stench required that I leave all of the Palace windows open for the day, and still earned a light rebuke from the Enchantress, who claimed it gave her the head-ache. Though I must boast she was most pleased and impressed with her vanity; perhaps she is not alone in that sin, though I think my own pleasure in a job well done, no matter how seeming trivial, be not wrong. I am only glad she did not notice the stains made in places by the paint thinner on the wood of the table; but then, I had covered them carefully with the myriad jars.

But in the course of examining the various containers in the garradge, opening each and peering within at its contents, inhaling any vapors exuded, I found another liquid, with a similarly pungent smell – though this one was far more sweet – in a red box with the words "Caution – Flammable" on the side. Intrigued, I poured a small amount, no more than a sip, from the large jar-box into an empty glass from the galley; then I used the Enchantress's magic fire-cabinet (Have I not recorded this ere now? The Enchantress, most strangely in my mind, prepares her own meals rather than employ a cook – though she does leave all of the washing-up for me, of course. She makes use of a device in her galley which, when a knob is turned, summons a clean blue flame from nowhere, like a fairy light, under a black iron guard which she calls a "burner." I have been using this to light a candle, taken from a box of clean white tapers marked Emergency Candles in the maid closet, and then using that candle to light my fire in the Redoubt. A wonderful convenience.) to light my candle, and, placing the glass of sweet liquid on the terrace, I touched the flame to it.

And it burned. Oh, how it burned! Indeed, the heat was so intense, and lasted so long, that when the flame was finally exhausted, I lifted the glass and was burned by its touch; a second attempt shielded by a cleaning rag was more successful, but when I brought the glass to the galley water tap in order to cool it, the rush of water touched the glass with a hiss, and then cracked it so deeply that it fell into shards at my wondering touch.

Thus did I find my weapon against the Lions. As for my approach, which must be changed now that the Lions have discovered my route and my means of travel, as well as my vulnerability atop my steed, I had asked the Enchantress the day before if she could descry a path from her home to the Lopezes' village some miles to the north-west; I told her the press of cars (the local term for the beast-wagons, and a most peculiar one) was too great, and I sought a quieter, less-traveled road. She amazed me when she went to her own beast-wagon and returned with a map – a map such as I have never seen before, of such infinitesimal detail and mathematic precision that it makes every chart and log-book I have seen or made look like a child's scribblings. I should not wonder to hear that these people never get lost, if they have maps such as this – though, of course, that may be the Enchantress's particular boon, like her private cove and Palace and the like.

So now I had a way of once more reaching the Lions' den undetected – it took only an hour's exploration with map and steed to find a road well-suited to my task; my leg made it a painful hour indeed, but this merely served to whet my appetite for vengeance – and a way to wreak havoc on it once there. Yet had I no hope: for I could not destroy the Lions alone.

Then the miracle happened.

Around mid-day, as I emerged from the Palace onto the terrace by the cove, taking a moment's ease after swabbing the floors, I heard – a signal whistle. A sailor's whistle, that is, which is three notes, low, high, and low again, with the middle note held longest. My eyes, half-closed with a comfortable lethargy in the warm air, snapped open, and my jaw dropped. I stepped out to the sand, looking to the forested strand from whence I believed the whistle had come – and what should I spy but the most-welcome figure of Balthazar Lynch, a wide grin on his thin face, as he stepped from the greenery, waving with the vigor of a young child whose father has returned home. "Ahoy, Captain!" he cried out, a greeting I returned with equal vigor and joy. A joy which was doubled, and then trebled, when the flora behind him parted to disclose first my good friend Llewellyn Vaughn, and then my cousin, Owen McTeigue, over whom I had fretted much, as I feared either his loyalty or his life lost to the mutiny, and neither could I well abide.

A joyful reunion had we then. I fed them well from the Palace's stores, and gave them each a chance to bathe – something they had not done in the fortnight since my ship was stolen from me, cleanliness being neither near nor dear to those faithless swine who stole my ship. They told me the tale I had largely expected, though I had never known if it would be confirmed for me: that the mutineers had put the *Grace* out to sea after telling the crew that I slept in my cabin, much the worse for wine – and Vaughn agreed that he and I, and Ian O'Gallows, had been drugged by a conspiracy made up of the other men at that last dinner: O'Flaherty and Burke, O'Grady, Shluxer, and Hugh Moran – the last I declare to be my cousin no more, as I disown the traitorous serpent – and Donal Carter, as well. The three prodigals were quick to assure me that my friend Ian remains loyal, and stayed with the *Grace* to try to ensure her safety; I said a brief prayer then for the safe voyage of both good ship and good man, a prayer I have oft repeated, and do so again now. They told me of the petty thefts that marked the height of ambition of that verminous carpenter, and of their own theft of the boat and subsequent journey back, using a chart made by Ian ere they left the

Grace; they had sailed with the boat's small mast for three days before reaching the cove and quickly finding evidence of my habitation in the Redoubt, which gave them reason to wait and watch – a course amply and quickly rewarded when they sighted me on the terrace not two turns of the glass later.

They did swear their loyalty to me as captain of the *Grace* most vociferously and eloquently, and offered me their good right arms in whatever course I plotted for them – even the pacifistic Vaughn, clearly angered by the loss of the ship he loved too, to such small-hearted pilfering to line the pockets of blackguards with chaff no more valuable than their own tarnished souls.

I ordered that first they must rest for the remainder of the day, and recover from their difficult journey.

Then we had some Lions to beard in their den.

Once I had my loyal shipmates, the doing of the deed was largely simplicity. I distributed to them the *pistolas* I had collected, keeping my wheel-gun for my own use, and then we set out after sun's set, walking by my newfound and less-traveled road. Two hours' journey found us near the Lions' den, and close to the hour of their usual dispersal, leaving perhaps a half-dozen within the house. I set Lynch and McTeigue to watch the exits fore and aft, leaving Vaughn to watch the street, alert for *la policia*. Then I crept about the house, splashing it with the sweet fire-juice from the Enchantress's garradge. After I painted the foundations thusly, I gathered my men to the front, the only portion I had not imbued with the liquid, and then I used flint and steel to strike a spark and set the flame. It caught, and spread, and soon roared hungrily, belching smoke as it devoured the dilapidated wooden dwelling. I would have been content to cook them all within, but soon a ragged shout was raised and Lions came stumbling out the front door.

And there we shot them all down. Six men, felled in barely twenty seconds as they gathered in a knot before the house, and we four rose from the darkness at my signal like avenging angels, and opened fire. We approached once they had all fallen, and I saw that one was still breathing – 'twas Agro, the leader and instigator of all of this. I aimed at him, and waited until he saw me in the light of his burning home, and knew me. Then I shot him dead.

We departed quickly, to the sound of a banshee wail that I knew, from young Alejandro Lopez's magic window, signaled the approach of *la policia*.

Thus was justice served.

Now: to win back my ship.

Log #28: Tantalized

Captain's Log
Date: 16 July 2011
Location: 50 mi. south of Glass Palace, camped on sand-beach
Conditions: Joyed to return to the sea, though my ship is uncommonly shrunk. Weather is glorious for sailing, if rather hot for breathing.

We have come a fair distance along the coast today, thirty miles in my estimation. The boat sails well, for a ship's boat. The prevailing winds are largely against us, but I have three stout, lusty companions and four oars, and we make headway even against the wind. We are determined, aye, *fixed* on our goal.

Our leave-taking was rapid, even somewhat abrupt, but 'twas better so. I spoke to the Enchantress in the morning, before she could depart for her day of law-warping; I asked her for assistance in sending a message to Maid Flora. She looked at me most peculiarly, and then stepped to a smooth white gewgaw, an object I had oft polished, but had never recognized as having a useful function – but lo! She lifted a raised, rectangular block, which revealed several bumps on its underside, numbered one to nine and naught, some others bearing symbols and strange words: Mute and Talk, and Ready-all (No, I think perhaps that was Redial, a word I am unfamiliar with.). The Enchantress pressed several of the bumps with her thumb, and then held the object to her ear; then it was that I understood: this tackle-block was akin to the tellafone, like the Verizons my friends the Lopezes carry. Indeed, in mere seconds, the Enchantress was exchanging greetings, and then she handed the tellafone to me, and I found myself speaking to and hearing the words of Maid Flora, though she were far, far away at that very moment.

I will remember, now, that tellafones come in various guises, shapes and colors; the key is the numerals in that strange pattern: three across, three down, and the naught below 8.

I told Maid Flora that her family could return safely, though I had to apologize profusely for the damage done to their home; I assured her that all the villains responsible were now utterly destroyed, and her family's injuries all well avenged. She expressed gratitude most becomingly, which I demurred, of course. Then we said our goodbyes and her voice vanished from the tellafone, which I returned to its mistress, who set it back in place atop the smooth white box-piece. She said, "So Flora's coming back? Then you're leaving?"

"Aye, milady. My task here is complete, and Maid Flora's family is again safe, and hale. I must sail on."

She made a pretty pout. "Too bad. I was getting to like having a handsome houseboy. I was going to get you a nice Chippendale outfit for a uniform, so I could sexually harass you all day."

Though I comprehended little of that, I did grasp her main thrust. I stepped close, seized her in my arms, and kissed her passionately. When I took my lips from her soft, sweet mouth, she sighed most prettily, and said, "Oh, my." I kissed her brow and said, "I must go, milady. But I am not glad of it."

I strode out of the room, then, to mount my steed, which I meant to return to House Lopez ere we departed. The Enchantress – a name most apt, aye, in more ways than I knew! – came running out after, calling my name. I stopped and turned to her, and she took my hand and filled it with the paper money of this time. "Here," she said, "You earned it. And this." And then she gifted me with one last, sweet kiss, one I will carry with me fondly.

I returned the steed to its owners, and placed a letter of thanks and farewell on their doorstep, and then I walked back to the Glass Palace (Now that the Enchantress was gone for the day, I had no fear of being seen and questioned crossing her demesne), to the Redoubt, where I found my men ready to depart. I exchanged my maid's clothes for my proper finery, heaving a comfortable sigh of relief as I armed myself anew, with sword and wheel-gun firmly in my sash where they belonged. I did keep the servant's togs as a useful disguise. And with water casks filled from the magic tap and some last few bottles of wine gathered from the galley, we bid the Glass

Palace a very fond farewell. It was our first refuge here, and served us all a great kindness; we owed it a debt of gratitude.

We found a secluded beach to make camp that first night, and leaving McTeigue and Lynch to set a fire and watch the boat, Vaughn and I made our way to a 7-11 shop we had spotted a mile or so northwards. There we exchanged some of my maid-money for victuals – I must say, maids are quite well-paid in this place! I seem to have earned a 50-paper every day I worked at the Palace, and only half of those days did I work a proper servant's watch, from near dawn to near dusk; those same twelve hours in Ireland would have earned me a crust of bread, a bowl of milk, and a soft kick out the door! But perhaps I was given a gift, rather than wages – and perhaps it was not by maidish prowess that I earned it. Any road, while culling out our foodstuffs, Vaughn found a rack of broadsheets, several of which featured prominently a remarkable etching of the *Grace of Ireland*, and portraits of O'Flaherty and Shluxer – whose name is spelled "Schluchzer," it seems, though for this record I intend to continue use of my own spelling, for simplicity's sake. Vaughn gathered them up and added them to the purchase. As the clerk evaluated our goods and named me a price – which he would not dicker over, not even a cent! – Vaughn scanned one of the broadsheets and spoke most excitedly to me: the pamphlet reported a location for my ship! I told him we must seek out a proper map if we could locate a cartographer – at which point the clerk pointed and said "Maps over there, dude." (The last word is unfamiliar, but I have rendered it here as similar to "duke," which title it did resemble in sound. I thus take it as compliment.)

Apparently 'tis not only the Enchantress and her wealthy peers who can acquire such wonderful maps as she showed me; they are for sale at the local shop, and for far less than the cost of a meal. (Though I must then question the price of their food, for surely a bag of those potato chips, no matter how delicious, isn't as valuable as the assurance that one never need be lost and wander aimlessly to one's doom, as has been known to happen on the moors and in the deep forests of home.) Any road, Vaughn and I pounced like hungry dogs on the rack of maps the clerk indicated, and took one of each thus offered us. We made our way back to camp with our booty – in strange bags, made of stuff so thin and strong it resembles spider-silk, but which the clerk, when asked, named "plass-tick" – and there we ate, and read, and plotted our course on our new maps.

This day was spent making headway on that same course. We should reach our destination on the morrow.

Captain's Log
Date: 17 July 2011
Location: Treasure Harbor, Islamorada
Conditions: Frustrated. Trapped like Tantalus.

Like Tantalus indeed: standing in a stream of cool water, beneath an apple tree heavy with fruit, starving and thirsting both; this was that Greek tyrant's curse in Hades. When he reached up for the fruit, the bough would withdraw, and the water below would rise; he would then crouch down to drink, and the water would recede, and the branch then come lower to tempt him with its bounty – hence the word "tantalize." I feel it now, though I think I have not sinned so sorely that this be my just reward.

Not a mile to the south-west of our camp, the *Grace of Ireland* sits at anchor. Perhaps two miles to the north-east, my men may all be found, both the good and the bad, the penitent and the insubordinate. Yet so close as they be, neither crew nor ship are within my grasp.

My ship is at the Islamorada Coast Guard Station. By land, she is guarded by locked gates, high fences, and armed men; by sea she is even more unreachable, as a constant stream of beast-ships come and go all day long, all grey steel, with cannons and swivel-guns visibly mounted in the bow; not a sail among them, but all moving as quickly and easily, and loudly, as do the beast-wagons on land; and every one manned by generous crews of proper military sailors, alert and disciplined. This coast be well-guarded, indeed. And so too is my ship.

I did not intend to steal her. On the journey down, Vaughn pointed out that, her reputation as a corsair notwithstanding, the *Grace* is my ship, bought and paid for, with my name on the bill of ownership as well as the logs and charts. He argued that I could simply claim that my ship was stolen from me – as indeed it was – and with three stout men (and the Lopezes, should the word of four Irishmen insuffice) to swear to my identity and the veracity of my claim, I might just be able to take back my ship with a smile and a handshake. Thus, upon our arrival at this tiny island south of the mainland of Florida, we beached the boat and left Lynch, as the youngest and least credible witness, to guard, and then Vaughn, McTeigue and I went forth to press my claim.

Our first gauntlet was the thick-skulled cretin at the gate – thick-skulled he must have been, for surely that rock atop his shoulders was not full of brains. He could not understand my accent, first, though my brogue is negligible – gods, some of my men speak Gaelic as much as English. Never in all of my travels have I failed to make myself understood with the King's English, until now, and I vow the fault was not with my tongue. When I had slowed and emphasized my words sufficiently – approximately what I would think a drunken Ourang-Outang would require for comprehension – for the dolt to comprehend me, then the man could not grasp my name. When I shortened it to Nate, and this abbreviated moniker sunk through that ponderous browbone, then he could not understand my mission and purpose for requesting entry.

Thank the gods, Vaughn was there to stop me drawing steel and running him through! And thank all the saints and devils as well that I did not need to treat with that imbecile after I had won entry to the station, or even Vaughn could not have restrained me.

But 'twas all for naught, even so. My name on the logbook and ship's papers, and my intimate and minute knowledge of my ship, did not serve to establish my ownership of her; according to Lieutenant Danziger, the stolid, middle-aged officer with whom I parlayed, I must have a "registration." Even my identity was called into question, and indeed our word was not good enough – though the man was clear that he did not name us liars, and I believed him; the Lieutenant was a man of morals and sober intelligence, unlike his buffoon of a watchman. He called it "red tape," and when that mystified us, he explained it was a colloquialism for rules and regulations and laws, Byzantine in their complex convolutions, but inviolate nonetheless. Apparently I must have a birth certificate – though I would think my birth could be stipulated without witnesses, since here I am – a social security card, and a drivers license or some other – I believe he called it foe-toe-aye-dee; perhaps this means "identification," another term he bandied about in our fruitless negotiation. As I do not understand what these things even are, I know I cannot procure them.

I must wait for another path to my ship to appear.

Stymied in that direction, I asked Danziger where the men were who had stolen my ship from me, and was directed to the Monroe County Sheriff's Office on Plantation Key, to the north-east. We reported our failure back to Lynch, and then McTeigue and I made the trek on foot – all of these islands are connected by a series of bridges the likes of which we have never seen, nor even imagined, stretching for miles across the ocean itself. How could anyone sink piers so deep? Not even the Romans, nor the druids of old could have matched this feat, and I do not believe these people even notice this wonder. The Lieutenant simply instructed us to follow the road, neglecting to mention that said road crossed a mile or more of deep blue sea.

We reached our destination and were greeted by another guard at the front gate, though in this case he sat behind a large table inside the building's entrance – though the edifice resembles a strong fortress, such miserable laxity in security means it would not withstand the rudest assault, if the enemy may simply walk in through the doors, to be confronted by a single clerk scribbling on papers behind a table.

I will remember this if we decide to take this place by force. The initial approach will not be difficult.

This uniformed functionary directed McTeigue and I to the detention block, on the building's third floor. This was a tighter ship: three men in a locked and inaccessible chamber watched over the antechamber at the top of the stairs, with no cover anywhere that was out of their sight, as the chamber had immense glass windows on two sides; their *pistolas* were prominent on their belts, and the only way past them and to the prisoners was blocked by a steel portcullis.

This is where the challenge would be, but still: 'tis only glass, and only three men. I presume the key to the portcullis would be found behind that glass, and might be taken from a corpse, if there be no cooperation.

McTeigue and I entered the antechamber, which had benches along the walls, one of them occupied by an elder couple, most fretful in their demeanor – perhaps they knew one slated for execution soon. McTeigue and I approached the glass and hailed the men within loudly; they nodded, and one spoke into a black metal wand, which magically transported his voice to us as though he were in the room and standing at our shoulders.

"Can I help you?"

"Aye, gratefully. We are here to see the men taken by the Coast Guard – the crew of the *Grace of Ireland*, if you please."

The man nodded. "Have a seat." He turned away from us and spoke to the other two. I looked at McTeigue, who shrugged, and we moved to the nearest bench and sat.

"Excuse me – did you say you're here about the pirate ship? The men on the ship, I mean?"

I was addressed by the older man. He and the lady – likely his wife, by their clasped hands – looked on me somewhat strangely, though I wore my maid's uniform this day, and McTeigue wore simple sailor's clothes, canvas pants and a brown homespun shirt. I could not have known them, of course, but still they appeared somewhat familiar.

"Aye," I said, and extended my hand. "I am Damnation Kane, the rightful owner of that ship, which was stolen from me by those dastardly rogues."

The man clasped my hand. "Elliott Shluxer."

Log #29: Innocent

Needless to say I was taken aback. Peering closely, I could see some of the vile Shluxer's features in these two: presumably the mother and father of that raping, thieving, mutinous rogue. Ere I could speak again, the man confirmed my presumption: "Elliott Shluxer is our son. Do you know him? Have you seen him? Is he all right?"

I pulled back my hand – which took some force, as he had clasped me tightly, with the strength of a parent's desperation – and I began galloping through my mind for somewhat to say; for these people were innocent, whatever their despicable son had done, and did not deserve to share in his opprobrium; which, alas, was the entirety of what I could think at this moment. Then I was saved.

"Shluxer! Come to the window, please. Shluxer." It was the guard in the glass box, and as he spoke, Master Shluxer turned away from me instantly, and he and Goodwife Shluxer hurried to the window. The guard informed them that the younger (viler) Shluxer would come to the barred door, and they could speak to him through it, but they had to stand back out of reach. A guard emerged from the glass box and led the couple to a spot some six feet from the portcullis, and then nodded to the two guards remaining in the box. I beckoned to McTeigue, and we quickly withdrew to the top of the stairwell, out of sight but still within hearing.

I have not the stomach to record precisely all that that mewling, white-livered cur vomited out to his parents. He cried his innocence, of course, and begged them to believe and succor him. I took his pleas for their credulity as clear sign that he lied with every breath he took and with every venomous syllable which hissed out between his serpent's lips; an honest man trusts in the truth, and takes his reputation, the knowledge of his character, as his only witness. But clearly the dog's parents doted on him, and took him largely at his word. Not entire: there was some question as to how he had fallen in with – are they my crew, still? Mine enough, aye – with my crew, as he had apparently vanished without trace from his place of employment, and the prevailing opinion had been that he had simply run off, a child trying to escape responsibility, as Shluxer was apparently wont to do, intelligence which did not surprise me at all. And then – what was unknown to me previously – it came out that he had stolen from them! From his own mother and father, from his blood, taken property and money from their home! I spat in disgust, hearing this new evidence of Shluxer's corruption.

But the weak-hearted blackguard cried most piteously, and told his doting, gullible parents that he had been kidnapped and pressed into service, that he had been whipped by the ship's master for his unwillingness to do their – our – evil bidding. McTeigue had to restrain me at these slandcrous accusations, though thankfully Shluxer did not name me; in retrospect, I presume he wanted to lay the whole blame at the feet of his own erstwhile companions, rather than cast fault at some apparition the authorities knew not, hight Damnation Kane. I mastered myself quickly enough, aided by the disgust I felt at this mongrel's bootlicking, at his puling, his lies, his cowardly attempts to escape all culpability for his actions; disgust which quickly subsumed my rage. To be insulted by this dog – why, that were no dishonor, at all.

Soon enough their time was finished, and Shluxer's cries and pleas grew quiet – slowly, as he kept up his carping, like the lowing of a hungry calf mixed with the whimpers of a spoiled lapdog, even as they dragged him away to his cell. His parents called out assurances, saying they would engage a lawyer for him – at which I felt some relief; there was to be a trial, then, with lawyers and perhaps a judge, even a jury? Excellent: perhaps that gave us some time – and calling out something about bail, a term I knew only as it referred to removing water from a leaking boat. But the Shluxer elders said they would "bail him out;" was this metaphor? They would save the sinking ship of his fate? I knew not, and I determined to enquire.

The Shluxers did not look at us nor speak as they hurried past, the woman huddled miserably in her husband's arms, with tears streaming down her cheeks. Ah, such power, such purity in a mother's love! Alas, that such goodness should be so wasted. Once they had departed, McTeigue and I returned to the antechamber and were hailed by the guards in the glass box presently.

"Who do you want to see?" the man asked through his metal wand, which seemed to carry sound like a speaking tube.

"Ian O'Gallows," I answered promptly. I longed to demand Shluxer's return, so I could slap his fat cheek and force him to recant his lies; I longed even more profoundly to summon O'Flaherty, so I could avenge myself on he who began my undoing; but I knew I would not be able to lay hands on either rogue, not with guards and portcullis between us. My next greatest desire was for the truth – and to confirm the hope that my good friend had not, in fact, betrayed me.

"Have a seat. We'll bring him to the door. Did you hear the procedure?"

"Aye – two paces back and no contact."

He nodded. "It'll be a minute."

It was somewhat extraordinary to stand there, McTeigue at my side and the guard flanking us, and watch as Ian was brought along the corridor beyond the portcullis; I watched his expression turn from confusion – who would be calling for him? – to astonishment when he recognized me, to deep sorrow when he knew that he would now have to face his crimes. He came to the portcullis with head bent, and then slowly raised it and met my gaze.

"Captain," he said, acknowledging me. Then he waited.

I gave him time to think, knowing that silence and a man's own conscience are often the only tools needed to elicit a confession. But he neither spoke nor lowered his gaze, though I held his eyes with my own for a good minute or more. Perhaps his conscience did not weigh him down, after all – but he had shown sorrow on the sight of me; what of that?

At last I spoke. "Stand you in mutiny, O'Gallows? Or are you loyal, still?" I spat the last words, as if dubious of that remote possibility, though I had the word of Lynch and Vaughn and McTeigue that Ian was and had always been true to me.

His eyes flashed fire, and he drew himself up proudly. "I have never wavered in my loyalty, Captain. You, and God above, be my only masters, sir, from now 'til I do rest in Neptune's cold bosom." Then he slumped again, and his gaze at last fell to the floor. "But I have failed ye, Captain. Failed ye and failed in my duty to the good ship we both love."

I looked him over from head to toe. I believed him, in his protestations of loyalty; but I agreed with him in his estimations of his performance. I crossed my arms and said, "I will hear your explanation."

He took a deep breath, clasped the portcullis with both hands, and then told his tale.

He began to describe their crime, the addlepated assault on what Vaughn's broadsheets had called a yacht, a pleasure boat on a pleasure cruise with her wealthy owners and their guests; I cut him off, as I had known of this already from those same broadsheets, which described the boarding, murder, robbery, and the stealing away of two innocent lasses, surely bound for Shluxer's foul lusts, and perhaps some others' evil attentions, as well. I hurried him on to the capture of my ship, and made clear I wanted to know of her condition, and how he had protected my *Grace* from those who would do her harm.

He turned first to the guard. "There is a letter in my effects, which was intended for this man, and is so addressed over its seal. Can he have this from thee?"

The guard considered. "I'll ask." He knocked on the door to the glass cube, which was opened; he relayed O'Gallows's request within, and was answered. He nodded and stepped back out, and then addressed me. "You can read it here, but you'll have to put it back in evidence after you're done. Do you want it?" I glanced at Ian, who nodded, and then I assented. The guard signaled one within the cube, who stepped out to take his place watching McTeigue and I, and then the first guard departed down the stairs.

Ian drew in a deep breath. "All right. The letter will tell ye of all I have to say on the mutiny and the attack on the yacht." He drew himself to attention, and then he reported.

"We were heading east, a few points north of due, in clear weather, making five knots with current but little wind. 'Twas just after dawn, and I had the watch with Desmond on the wheel. I looked to our stern, and I – I saw the ship. No sail, but it bore down on us like a falcon stooping on a rabbit, and as it drew nearer, I could make out the swivel guns on the bow, so I knew who it was, aye." He looked me in the eye and said, "I did not raise the alarm. I knew they might fire on us, without warning, perhaps, but I did desire that they take the ship, and I sought to give her to them." He shook his head slowly. "I'll not apologize for it, sir. I hoped they'd keep the ship whole if we did not fight, and I deemed it better if she be in their hands, than in ours."

I bit my tongue. I disagreed with him, for I could have taken my ship back with some ease, I thought, if my men still crewed her, if I could remind them of their former loyalty, and put the question to them as to which captain they had flourished under; but now she was out of my reach more surely than before, and only the mercy of the gods kept her afloat, rather than holed and sunk in the pursuit. But I only nodded, and motioned for him to go on.

"But fortune failed me, and O'Flaherty rose then. As he came out of his cabin, he did look astern, and spied our pursuer. Aye, one could hear it, by then, too, and perhaps this is what roused him at that poor moment. He did raise the alarm, and the men leapt to stations. A great, booming voice blasted to us across the waves, ordering us to surrender without resistance. But O'Flaherty ordered us to come about and fire the starboard cannons into their bow. Desmond began to spin the wheel, and the men jumped to the shrouds – and then they did open fire on us, aye."

He shook his head, ran his hand through his hair. "I have never heard nor seen the like. It sounded something like thunder, with storm-waves crashing on rocks below. It sounded like an avalanche of iron, if such a thing could be. And we took fire as if a thousand swivel guns were aimed at us, rather than the one. It chopped up the sails and the shrouds, and we lost the wind. Then it paused and a single rifle shot rang out, and Desmond fell, wounded – a miracle of marksmanship, to hit a man on one moving ship from another with a single aimed shot – and then the thunder roared again, and the wheel just – *disappeared*, in a hail of splinters." He showed a gash in his forearm, now partly healed. "I dove to the main deck, but a splinter caught me in the air. 'Tis a wonder that Desmond survived." He looked me in the eye again. "It confirmed for me that I had chosen aright. We could not have resisted that assault. Perhaps our cannon could have disabled them, but as that ship was solid steel, I think not – but damn me if they couldn't ha' sunk us without breathing hard.

"They came up to our stern, and raked the sails once more with that thunder-gun. They grappled and boarded, their booming voice calling again for our surrender. O'Flaherty and Burke had mustered the crew on the deck and were shouting at us to fight to the death. But just as the men of the steel ship began to leap aboard, I struck.

"I grabbed a hold of the chain on Burke's wrist and clubbed him with my sword hilt. I swung him, half-stunned, into O'Flaherty, felling them both. Carter spun about with a snarl, but I flung my sword and fouled his aim before he could fire at me; then I was on him, and laid him out with my fists, the slack-brained lout. The men knew not how to respond, to take my side or O'Flaherty's. I heard a shout and spun about to see Kelly, who had been below guarding the two lasses; he had come above and was just finishing off O'Grady, who had leveled his aim at me and was now off to a pleasant nap with something of a lump on his skull. The men turned to look at Kelly, then back at me, and by then the steel ship's crew had all of us in their sights."

He sighed and dropped his gaze, wrapping his hands around the bars of the portcullis. "'Twas then, and I'm right sorry to bring ye the news, Captain – aye, and you, too, Owen – but your cousin, Hugh Moran, did draw and aim with a shout. They – they cut him down. I ha' ne'er seen the like: every man had a thunder-gun, and 'twas not as if Hugh were shot, but rather like he *exploded*, like a grenado, blood spraying from a hundred wounds in seconds. He be dead, Captain."

I nodded. "Were any others hurt?"

"No, sir. The rest of them surrendered, following my lead, and Kelly's – aye, and Shluxer's, that milk-hearted coward, though he was crying and begging for mercy when he threw his weapons down. *Our* men kept their pride, even in defeat, sir.

"They manacled us and put us below. They towed the *Grace* back with us, and docked her at their fortress. I think – I hope – she be there still. They ha' taken Desmond to a surgeon, and put the rest of us in these cells." He spread his hands. "And here we be."

I nodded. The guard returned then with Ian's letter, which I read on the spot. I looked Ian over, and then closed my eyes and took as deep a breath as lungs could hold. Then I let it out, and pronounced my judgment.

"Ye have not failed in your duty to the ship. You protected her as well as you could, and I have no doubt she still rides on the water instead of resting below it because of you." He straightened with every word, as if heavy weight fell from his broad shoulders. But I raised a hand. "But you *have* failed *me*, O'Gallows. For you put my ship out of my reach, and though you did not steal her, still you could not bring her back to me, nor remind my men of their loyalty to *me* and not to O'Flaherty." He hung his head, nodding once as he acknowledged the truth of what I said.

I turned to McTeigue. "Come, we are done here." I nodded to the guard. "We are done. Put him back in his cell. He can think on his actions there." And without looking back at my friend, I strode out.

Of course it was but posturing. I knew it unfair, even absurd, to hold O'Gallows responsible for the way I had lost my ship. If I should not blame those who took her – and aye, I blamed them – the only other fault must be mine own. I kept secrets from my men, and thus lost their trust, and then I let those bastards trick me and steal from me. But absurd or not, I could not but feel a deep, burning anger at all those who lost me my ship – of which Ian was one. Thus, my childish tantrum.

I will get him out, aye. I will get them all out. With a lawyer and this bail of which the Shluxers spoke, if possible. But if not that, then I will use force. Mutinous or not, they are my crew, my countrymen, the only others of my time in this peculiar world, and I will have them back by my side.

Though I do not know how.

Log #30: Bondsman and Countryman

Captain's Log
Date: 17th of July, 2011
Location: Treasure Harbor
Conditions: Storm, high chop.

We intended to travel today in pursuit of the bondsman, but weather prevents. We know not if this be a storm, or weather familiar to these seas but strange to us, but the waves are the height of a man even here in this small bay where we camp, and the sky is bruised iron above. So we stay encamped, this day. We take the opportunity to practice with the *pistolas*, to mend tears in clothing, to sharpen blades and make small repairs to the boat and her single sail. Perhaps the sky will clear and the seas calm tomorrow. If not, the men will abide where they are another day, or more.

Captain's Log
Date: 19th of July, 2011
Location: Treasure Harbor, Islamorada
Conditions: Poor

I do not mean that our situation has worsened; rather, it has largely improved. But it has become apparent that we desperately lack the funds to do what is needful; hence we are now poor men, in the simplest sense of the word.

Upon leaving the prisoner's level of the keep, McTeigue and I returned to the man of the watch at the front door. We inquired of him for advice as regards the hiring of lawyers, and the meaning of "bail" as it relates to these incarcerated men rather than to a leaking boat. He did look at us most strangely, of course (I believe I should include this as a caveat whensoever I speak to a native of this time at any length or penetration: "This will cause you to look at me quite strangely, but..."), but he did answer. As to the meaning of bail that pertains here, he informed us that such was a monetary bond used to ensure a prisoner's future cooperation if paroled; this struck me as a most civilized, and prudent, manner of behaving with accused men, allowing them the dignity of freedom on the strength of their honor, while also buttressing that honor – which, after all, is passing weak in many and many a man – with the strength of their avarice. I have always known that what a man will not do for honor, he will do for gold. The watchman elaborated by saying that the greater the crime, the greater the risk that the prisoner would violate his parole, the higher the price of the bond. This, too, is most reasonable, though it puts us in something of a pinch, owing to the number of bonds we must provide for, the severity of the crimes, and perhaps the somewhat less prodigious honor of those same men, the relative fragility of their sworn word.

He pointed out a large board made of some extravagantly soft wood, with placards and broadsheets and pamphlets affixed thereto, and advised me to look there for both a lawyer and a bail "bondsman," apparently one who would lend the money for bail at sometimes usurious rates. Examining these, I found a mystifying array of these bondmen, and a plethora of lawyers, every one of them offering fast help and cheap rates – but not a one professing great learning, nor knowledge, nor expertise. No, I am incorrect: some of the lawyers admitted to several years of experience, which, one supposes, is equivalent to expertise. But even those thus qualified featured the seemingly magical words "Fast" and "Cheap" far more prominently than aught else.

What sort of a place is this, where people value time and money more than ability or virtue? Especially in this instance, when the commodity to be treated this way is no less than one's liberty. Why would a man seeking succor in the face of blind, heartless justice turn to one whose heart beats with the clink of coin on coin, or whose veins run not with blood, but with the hourglass's sand? Is this world naught but a market, with all the people crying their wares from birth to death? Are we men, or pins on a hawker's tray?

Beggar them all, with their Fast and Cheap: I looked for a placard pledging the one quality I have learned to seek out before any other, and treasure most dearly in a man: loyalty.

I found none of it.

There were a number of pamphlets, as well, which offered proper money in exchange for jewelry and valuables; I took some note of these moneychangers and merchants, as one presumes they who display their wares before criminals in this gaolhouse would be ready to consort and conduct business with men who lack honest reputations – or, perchance, who lack proper proof of ownership of the goods to be sold. It is always in a pirate's interest to know where to find men of this type. It is a pirate's blessing that there are always men of this type to be found.

McTeigue solved the conundrum of the cornucopia of bondsmen for hire when he found one who, though his pamphlet cried out "Fast" and "Cheap," those were emphasized less than were "Trustworthy" and "Honest." That was our man: Honest Avery. We took his pamphlet and returned to camp, to report to Lynch and Vaughn, and to use Vaughn's maps to find the place of business of this bondman, this Jonas Avery. By the time we had done so, the march of time had brought the close of day and the unfurling of a deep velvet sky of purple and black, sparked with silver stars uncountable, every one a glory and a joy to behold. We sent a prayer to these stars, and whatever gods do look down on us from those skies, to keep and protect our friends who were locked in iron cages, and to guide our future steps to find their freedom, and keep our own.

And aye, I sent another prayer winging above, or perhaps below. For there is something e'en more inexorable than the turning of the stars through the sky, or the sands slipping through the glass. We never know how many turns of the glass, and of the stars, we have before us; we know not how many days will rise between now and the end; nor if those days will seem too many or too few. But this we many know: any who cross Damnation Kane may hear, if they but listen, the iron hooves of Vengeance bearing down, bearing down on them, and that dread charge – it comes soon.

Two days later, delayed by the storm, we made an early start in the boat, as Bondsman Avery does business on the mainland. It did not take us long to reach the shore, and there we beached the boat and covered it with limbs cut from the tall, spindly trees that stand and wave all along this coastline; the shorter of these trees have fronds as wide and stiff as a windmill's sails, in easy reach of a blade in hand, and these made excellent camouflage. We walked from the beach to a road, which we then found on the map, and made good time from there.

But alas: our journey was very nearly for naught, as we discovered once we arrived at Honest Avery's shop – a small, dank, space, where Bondsman Avery labored within a pile of paper that might smother a man, with but one other to assist him, and that a woman; it seemed the only aspect that the man cherished in these offices was the sign outside, which proclaimed "Honest Avery Bail Bonds" in glowing red letters three foot high. This did certainly attract one's attention, but what good is it to bring in custom without any decent room to entertain or hold discourse? Fah – I am no tradesman, and know not their secrets. We did speak with the Bondsman in that inhospitable room, and soon he understood what we sought; he was a man of some substance, though without cleanliness. He picked up his tellafone, which was black, grimed and cracked, and covered with far too many bumps and tiny glowing red spots, like the eyes of miniscule imps; he pressed many of the bumps, which seemed to irk some of the imps – for their eyes blinked – and chased some others away. He spoke then, haltingly, in rapid bursts broken by pauses both brief and lengthy, occasionally interrupted for the pressing of more bumps and more angry imp-eyes. At one point he began to speak to us, with the tellafone still pressed to his ear, and then turned his eyes downward and spoke into the handpiece again. I found this at first confusing and then, strangely, impolite, like a man wooing a lass at a tavern, but who pinches the barmaid's bottom in passing before returning to the girl on his knee.

But at last the Bondsman found what he sought – and after observing the road he traveled to reach that destination, I was both relieved that we had found a man who could make his way through this convoluted labyrinth of words for us, and despaired by the knowledge that, should we ever find ourselves sailing with our own wind, without a pilot to guide us, we will be lost – and then he listened at length to the tiny squeaking that was just audible to us from his tellafone handpiece. He wrote some words and numbers down, and then blotted them out with strokes of his pen; then he thanked the squeak and put down the tellafone, slowly. Whereupon he gave us our sad news: my men were charged with armed robbery and kidnapping, and for those serious crimes, there was no bail. They could not be freed without trial.

Howbeit, as I have intimated, the morning was not fruitless; for even as we four looked at one another, entirely lost and rudderless, Bondsman Avery hauled us back on course. "What you guise need," he said – I know not why he used the word, unless he knew somehow that I was not in my usual finery – "What you guise need is a lawyer. D'you know one?" We demurred, of course, and then the Bondsman, who was a kindly-faced fellow with far more jowls than hair, smiled broadly and said, "I know just the one. Let me call him and see if he's free."

He was indeed, and within two hours we were seated at a table in a quiet tavern, discussing the matter of our imprisoned brethren with one James McNally, Esquire – a man whose suitability as our guide through the arcane halls of law was made clear from his first words, which revealed an accent that warmed our hearts. At last, on these strange shores, we had found a fellow Irishman!

Master McNally felt as full a comfort in our presence, as when he heard my brogue – after a blinking pause at my name, the which I have been accustomed to all of my life – he smiled grandly and said, "Ah, ye boys are from the Old Country, are ye?"

I nodded slowly. "Aye, from the Old Country, in truth. God's truth, that is, sir. God's truth."

We shook hands, Master McNally hesitating not for an instant at taking the rough hand of McTeigue or the young one of Lynch – 'tis the sign of a good man, that, the sign of a decent man – and then sat and shared a fine repast with us while we spoke of our situation. Master McNally listened and asked questions – many of which we did not know the answers to, and some we could not even understand the question itself – and wrote down our useful responses in a small logbook he produced from a pocket in his coat, a book which I much coveted, I confess, as this log I keep grows both ponderously long and also truly precious to me. And by the end of our parlay, and our luncheon, Master McNally had – well, less bad news than Bondsman Avery, any road.

"I think I can help you," he told us. "I can certainly try to help your friends through the process. Though they have probably been assigned public defenders by now, perhaps they'll trust me more, once they know I have been engaged by you. Are you sure they would not have told the police anything at all? None of them?"

We exchanged a glance. "Are you certain that *la policia* would not have tortured answers out of them?"

He blinked several times and then shook his head. "Sorry," he said. "Hearing you say 'torture' and '*la policia*' in an Irish accent put me in mind of a band, an Irish band – the Pogues, d'you know them? P-O-G-U-E-S, that is?" We shook our heads, and he discarded the issue with a wave of his hand. "Doesn't matter. I am sure the police will not torture your men, not beyond keeping them in a small room for several hours and asking questions all the while. Not under any circumstances."

My heart eased to hear it. I believed these people to be civilized – perhaps even too much so, in some ways – but the English were civilized too, and the English did not use torture; except on Irish prisoners, of course. "Then aye, I am sure they will say nothing, not a word, not a sign. Even admitting your name is sometimes enough for a conviction, back – where we come from."

"Shluxer," Lynch murmured to me. "Aye," I said, nodding. "Elliot Shluxer might talk. Probably will talk. And he will blame the others, for all of it."

Master McNally nodded. "That's where they've gotten the charges from, then. But if the men haven't confirmed or denied anything, then I can speak with them first about what they should or should not say, and maybe we can cut this off before it really starts." He replaced his logbook in his pocket and withdrew a tiny wallet, well-worn; from this he took several green money-papers, which he placed on the table. "Now, lunch is on me, and happy I am to pay for men of Erin – but there is the matter of a retainer for my services. Let me give you a number, and we'll see if we can go ahead from here."

He named a figure. I bit my tongue, and nodded. "Aye, that'll do."

It would not: it was ten – fifteen times over again what I had in my purse. But this was the lawyer we needed, the only one I would engage; I believed we could trust him, and that is more precious than gold or green paper.

We shook hands on it, and then he raised one finger. "But one thing I will require as payment. For now, I know what I need to know to speak to your men, and to the sheriff. But before this goes to the end, wherever that may be, I will need your whole story. I need to know why twenty-some Irishmen were sailing a tall ship through

Floridian waters, and why you have no definite address, and look and sound like the pirates your men are accused of being, only three hundred years out of date. If I earn your trust, will you give me that tale?"

I thought. I nodded. We shook again. He went off with purpose in his step, to see to our men.

I turned and looked at my three companions, and said, "We are poor."

It took some hours of parlay, of conversation and wrangling, cajoling and argument, but at last we had a plan. Vaughn left to purchase more broadsheets and guard the boat, and I took Lynch and McTeigue in search of a market. This took some time to accomplish, and the sun was halfway to the horizon before we found a local man who could direct us to that we sought, largely, it seemed, because the people of this time name it a "flea market," for reasons I cannot fathom, and when I asked passers-by for a market, they inevitably shrugged or pointed to a shop which sold foodstuffs. Then another hour passed before we arrived at the "flea market," and our time was growing short.

But fortune was with us, and we quickly found a woman selling clothing of the type and, more vitally, the hue we sought. Soon we were all clad in what we have come to call our highwaymen guises.

That was the spring of it: Lynch mentioned, as we discussed how we could achieve our goal without suffering consequences even more dire than those awaiting our shipmates, that highwaymen covered their faces with scarves and hats pulled down low o'er their brows; and some of the boldest had been known to commit their thefts, travel to the nearest inn, and there have conversation, even drink, with those whom they had robbed mere minutes before. Then as we discussed where we might procure such hats and scarves, so that we too might escape recognition and subsequent infamy, it came to me: how we should dress and where we might find the necessary articles. Now, all was prepared, all was in readiness.

That night, after the sun had set, a small corner market, occupied only by the Oriental proprietor at the time, was robbed of all of their money-paper, both that kept in a drawer and that held in a strongbox (the which was not locked! It swung open with the mere twist of a handle!) and some of their food, particularly their potato chips. Said money-paper proving insufficient, a grog shop was next – and aye, they lost some few bottles along with the paper. None were hurt, both clerks being most cooperative with their heavily armed assailants.

The culprits? A trio of men, all wearing cloth caps, scarves over their mouths and noses, and tartan shirts. They said nothing but a gruff demand for money, and ran away into the night once the paper had been surrendered and some small plunder collected. Based on the blue color of the shirts, and the scarves over the men's faces, one might think these three were members of the Latin Lions.

Now we are no longer poor.

Log #31: Seeking Grace

My ship is gone! Gods damn them, did they sell her? Sink her? Was she turned merchant, or guardship? No – surely not, not in these waters, not these people, who have their bloody ugly iron ships with their thunderous flatulence, that deafening growling cough like an ox with consumption –

Christ and Saint Patrick, Lugh and Goibniu, Manannan Mac Lir and aye, Morrigan, ye hag, I beg you all: bring me back my *Grace*. Bring me back my Lady, my – mother.

Captain's Log
Date: 20 July I forget the cursed year
Location: Treasure Harbor, but no bloody treasure here, is there?
Condition: Somewhat endrunkened, but fires blaze within undamped. We are on the course!

We know where she is. The *Grace*, I mean, the last piece of home, she that carried us here and will protect us now if only we can find our way back to her. Oh, alas that she has gone! Damn them all – curse the sailormen of Florida and their Coast Guard, damn the storm for its wind. And blast those black-souled, bloody-eyed shite-mouthed bastards who took my ship from me at the first: a curse and a pox and all the furies of Hell descend on those God-rotted, devil-fucking mutinee

Damn, I broke my pen. Perhaps a curse on the drink, too – it be strong rum they have here. Well: just the necessecerariess – just the facks. The *facts*.

Yesterday when the sun rose we broke our fast, and went to Master McNally's offices. When he arrived, we gave him the money-paper, and he thanked us and excused himself to get to his task. He gave me a small card with a telephone number on it (and the proper writing of the word, too, hah). We left and took the boat back to

Islamorada, to Treasure Harbor again. Then I walked to the fortress of the Coast Guard, because I wanted to look at my *Grace*, my beloved, beautiful, perfect, wondrous –

She was gone. I tried to ask the guard, but he would not tell me, the damned imbecile. I looked for Lieutenant – whose name I misrememember – but no, he's gone, I can't see him, I can leave him a message with my telephone number but I don't bloody have one, do I, ye sodding lump, and where's my blessed ship?! Couldn't find out. Got physically thrown out of the fortress, banned from returning, as if I want to. Wanted to draw and fire right then, challenge them to a duel, they don't even wear swords I could cut them down with an eye shut and a hand tied to a foot, like I saw that man, that one man – a Gypsy, that's who it was, aye! Gypsy did that to all comers back home, when Uncle Seamus took me to town. Home. Gods, will I truly never see it again? Never? But Mam – she's alive, back then, alive. I can't lose her. She's all – she's all I have, all my family, only one.

Can't lose her again here. Can't lose her now.

Right: they threw me out, I did not kill them. I came back here and talked to my men. We made a plan, a good one. These are sailors, yes? Then there must be taverns nearby where they drink, and mollyhouses for the whores. So we found a tavern, already had a sailor in it while the sun was high and hot – Christ, it's hot here. Already drinking at noon – he must be Irish, ha-*haaaa!* – and we waited.

That night, this night, some bloody night, the sailors came in, we sat with them and bought them drinks, said we were sailors, too, from Ireland, o' course. Got them drunk – took a while, and I barely had my wits left for matching them, and Lynch, he passed out, poor little puppy. Though we had to buy his whiskey for him and give it on the sly, for the barkeep said he was too young to drink – what in the name of Lucifer and Saint Patrick is that? If he can hold the mug, he can drink the drink, ye bastards! And Balthazar Lynch may be young, but he be twicet the man as that tub of guts behind his bar, with his smug stupid face of his. But we got them to talk, McTeigue and me, about the ship, about my *Grace* – said we heard gossip about sailing ship, and that she had sunk, broke my heart to say it, aye, but they shook their heads *No* and all was well again.

Three – two? days ago, there was a storm. Bloody cack-fisted baboons could not handle the *Grace's* lines and sails proper, and the wind broke the mast, he said, but we think only a spar. Probably the one Shluxer made, that daft cur, all he touches turns to shite, why not my ship, too? So they gave her away – no borrowed, they borrowed – no, *lent* her to a man, a man who cares for ships, a scholar of the seas, can't think of his name, but they told me where to find him, where to find my *Grace*.

Then McTeigue and me, we beat them to a bloody damned pulp. Ha.

Came back here, made McTeigue carry Lynch. He wanted to shave Lynch's belly and, y'know, farther down, to pay the boy for falling to drink and needing to be carried, but I wouldn't let him. Lynch's a good man, good lad, shouldn't be manhandled by drunk Irishmen. So McTeigue asleep and snoring, with Lynch in his arms, after he apologized to the sleeping boy, and embraced him, and fell asleep thus. He be a maudlin drunk, aye.

Done with this log now. Going to sleep.

Captain's Log
Date: 21st of July, 2011
Location: Treasure Harbor, Islamorada.
Conditions: At least my head is done aching.

When morning came, this day, none of the three of us were capable of greeting her. The sun was well overhead before McTeigue and I could stir our bruised bodies and pounding heads, and though Lynch had risen earlier, he was still green and vomitous, sitting in the shade with his back to the ocean, for the motion of the water made him sick to watch it.

Though I did not recall it, I had apparently waked Vaughn when we returned from the tavern last night, and despite larding my report with many furious drunken ramblings, still I managed to relay to him what we had learned of the fate of the *Grace*. And good Llewellyn, my true friend, he left this morning, ventured forth to find her, trusting to the luck of the Irish to keep we three drink-addled sots safe, e'en in our stupor.

And find her he did. As I wrote last night in this log – though much of my script is illegible, and the rest is as maudlin and pathetic as I accused McTeigue of – the storm that passed four days ago, now, did some damage to the ship, for she was never properly battened down after her capture, and the men of this Coast Guard know not the handling of a proper masted ship, as they ken only their great grumbling iron monsters. So the *Grace* was buffeted about, and Lieutenant Danziger brought in a man he knew, an expert in ships of the *Grace's* form, what men here and now call tall ships for the height of the masts, to look her over. This man, whose name we got as Napier, though in truth it is Navarre, Claude Navarre, is the master of a house of ship's lore called a museum, Vaughn says. Vaughn seems much enamored of the place, and of the man; I think my educated friend has grown tired of the poor conversation we simple sailors can offer him.

We knew the location from the sailors in the tavern, and Vaughn was able to sort our description – addled twice, I am sure, in the hearing and in the retelling by the drink that soaked both our ears and our tongues – and he found it, this museum, and Navarre, and my beloved *Grace*. He made his way to Navarre's presence, professing great interest in the ship which he could see anchored in a small but well-guarded harbor beside the museum, which held several other ships – some passing strange, Vaughn told me on his return – but I had ears only for news of the one. Vaughn, with an educated man's tongue and manners, even if three centuries out of date, was able to inquire of Navarre about the *Grace* and how she came to reside there. Navarre had convinced Danziger that no one could, or would wish to, steal this tall ship, not in this age of single-masted pleasure boats, and yachts and guardships without a foot of canvas anywhere about them. Therefore the best place for the ship was somewhere she could be cared for properly, and also studied, with security being but a minor concern: at this museum place, where the scholars learn the lore of the sea and the vessels and men who sail it. Danziger agreed, and while we were on the mainland engaging Master McNally and collecting his retainer, the Coast Guard towed my ship to this museum and anchored her there, with locked chains attaching her to the dock and stopping access from the land, with two Coast Guard sailors standing watch on shore.

Vaughn has convinced me that Navarre is correct. For the nonce, until I have a crew once more that can sail her, the *Grace* is truly best left where she is. The museum's harbor is better protected than that of the fortress, as there are trees to act as windbreaks against any future storm, and Navarre and his fellow sea scholars know how to rig her properly; Vaughn reports that she has now been battened down as well as we could have done it ourselves.

What is more, Vaughn has told me that he wishes to leave our company, and remain in proximity to the ship, and perhaps eventually in the employ of this place of learning and this Navarre, who has apparently become Vaughn's friend already. Well, there is sense there: Master Navarre studies men who sailed the seas in the past, and Vaughn is one such, as well as being erudite himself. I am sure they will get on famously. And as McTeigue and Lynch and I have work to do to find the cost of Master McNally's services, and it is such work as Vaughn should prefer to avoid and I prefer to separate from him both for his sake and the work's, I have agreed that Vaughn will split from us and find lodging on Marathon Key, where this museum is, and my beloved *Grace*. Vaughn's eyes verily sparkled when he mentioned the library he found within those walls; I believe he will do little but read, eat, sleep, and converse with Master Navarre, for as long as he may. I wish him well of it.

As for we three, we will seek other lodging as well. As the *Grace* be not here on Islamorada, there is little reason for us to remain. There is also reason for us to go: I do not wish to encounter our two informants, since this log has confirmed my drink-addled and fog-bound memory which says that we and they raised a proper donnybrook in the tavern once we had that knowledge we sought. And withal a tavern brawl is but a tavern brawl, no matter what land or age you be in, still I know that the light of day and the pain of bruised faces can change willing participants into aggrieved victims. Too, in any conflict or fractious negotiation, I know well that we, the outsiders, would soon find that all the rest had closed ranks against us, and we would bear the full brunt of whatever censure might result.

And I shudder to think what would occur if they found our highwaymen guises. I have no wish to see that gaol from the inside.

But first I must see my *Grace*. On the morrow, Vaughn will take us to the museum, and no guard shall stop me from walking her decks once more. Then we will depart, for calmer waters and broader horizons, for a place more familiar, and therefore both safer and more to our advantage in the search for and capture of funds. We return to the Redoubt.

Log #32: Muse and Rave

Captain's Log
Date: 22nd of July, 2011
Location: Marathon Key
Conditions: The *Grace* is well, and apart from my longing to sail her once again, so too am I.

We departed Treasure Harbor and Islamorada this morn at dawn, and sailed the boat to Plantation Key, four miles to the north-east. Vaughn and I disembarked at the first pier we found, and ordered McTeigue and Lynch to sail about until they found a decent site for a camp, then claim it and send one or the other to the museum to find myself and Llewellyn. They made off to the east as Vaughn and I walked by the dwelling to which the small pier belonged; we made no particular effort at stealth, and yet we remained undiscovered. It amazes me how slack these people are in keeping a watch; they are as sightless as falcons in hoods. Or perhaps frightened tortoises is more *apropos*, since they often do not come out of their shell-houses.

Once we were to the road, Vaughn's maps quickly led the way to the Museum of Nautical History, where, before we went in and introduced ourselves to the master of the house, Vaughn led me down a path of white stones to the harbor, where I clapped eyes once more on my ship.

She looked well. A touch battered and bruised, my poor lass, but no worse than when we sailed here to these shores dragging the *Sea-Cat* behind. Her rail was broken and a terrible long gouge marred her smooth side above the waterline; this was likely where the Coast Guard had boarded her. The broken mast rumored to me by the drunken sailors was indeed Shluxer's spar, as I had surmised and hoped; a simple enough repair, and one that could be taken on after she sails once more under my command. To say true, I will be glad when there is no part of my ship that bears the taint of Shluxer; I resolved then to tear out and replace the boards he had shaped and

214

placed for us, as well. I was only glad it was not my cabin which had kenneled that mongrel; I could stand to sleep where O'Flaherty had been, for while I would never forgive him his betrayal, at least he was an Irishman, and one of my own time; and a mutineer is not so very far from a pirate, if we be judged by our actions. Had Shluxer's foul carcass begrimed my cabin, I would have been forced to burn all the furniture, and even then the stench might have clung to the walls and the floor, and ne'er come out but at night, when it would creep into my nostrils and make me dream corruptions, visions of his vile physiognomy and noxious deeds.

McNally told us that murderers face death if found guilty in court. I pray that Shluxer will swing.

Vaughn and I could not approach the *Grace*, as the pier she was anchored by stood barricaded and guarded by two sailors of the Coast Guard – fortunately not those I knew from the tavern nor my visits to their fortress on Islamorada, so I remained unrecognized. I might have fought my way past these two: I had my wheel-gun in my pocket, and their alertness was no keener than that of the house-dwellers on the shore, though in these two that same lack was less forgivable. But to what purpose should I fight? I could not sail the *Grace*, not with only Vaughn to help me; and even if I could, such an act would make it impossible to help my men, as I would most likely be joining them soon after in the gaol. These be no waters for a pirate, not with the iron ships of the Coast Guard and their telephones and magic windows and thunder-guns.

I will be glad to return home. Christ, to tell the truth I will dance a jig for a year. I will light candles in church and slaughter a bullock in the fairy-ring near Mam's house, and sing praises to any other god or devil who might have aided me in this: my fondest wish. Fond, indeed.

Do you hear me, oh ye gods? Grant me this boon, and I will repay. I, Damnation Kane, swear it. I swear it.

After filling my eyes with sight of my *Grace*, Vaughn and I returned to the museum door and entered; he led the way to another door, discreetly tucked away to one side, which read *Offices*; we went through this and were greeted by a comely lass seated at a table, who smiled and asked if she could help us. As this was Vaughn's terrain, he took the tiller, then, making our introductions and proper courtesies to the maiden – who seemed somewhat bewildered when

Vaughn asked, quite politely, after her parents and the place of her birth. But we won a bright smile again when Vaughn asked her to tell the Director that Llewellyn Vaughn had returned with a companion eager to make the acquaintance of Monsieur Navarre. She rose and departed with this message, soon returning with the man himself.

The morning which followed is something of a haze to my memory. Navarre, a Moor or African of late middle years and a most noble bearing, hails from a land called Haiti, a large island to the south; he and Vaughn spoke French to one another often, though only after I assured them that I took no offense. I did not, in truth, for even when they spoke English, the conversation traveled a path I could not follow: all scholar's lore and the truth found in the pages of a book. I do not belittle this; the people of Ireland have ever cherished wisdom and the prodigious strength of the written word; this is why I keep this log, that I may someday offer my own experiences as knowledge that will serve to help others, to warn them or inspire them; and I am able to keep it thanks to my own schooling in letters, which was not brief nor simple. But my life since boyhood has been spent on ships, not in libraries, and my proclivities do draw my hand to sword-hilt and ship's wheel more than to pen and paper, these pages notwithstanding.

But I could see that Navarre and Vaughn are already fast friends, as both grew animated as they spoke, and even after a mere two days' acquaintance, they laugh at one another's jests, and kissed one another's cheeks in farewell. I am gladdened that Vaughn has found a kindred soul; I at least have my crew, who are my countrymen and my kin, and like-minded to myself; Vaughn is the sole Welshman in our company, as well as the only scholar, and now that we are three hundred years from home, his loneliness must be sharp indeed.

For myself, Vaughn introduced me to Navarre, who shook my hand; the man believes I am something called a "reenactor," and rather than inquire what this is, I merely agreed, as it seemed to explain both my finery and manner, as well as the strangeness of my *Grace* in these waters. In talking about the *Grace*, I found my common ground with Navarre, for he finds her nearly as wondrous and beauteous as do I. He inquired if she was a replica, and at Vaughn's wink, I agreed that she was; when asked then from what land and time, I told him the truth: she was put into the water in 1671 in County Cork. He smiled and nodded, so I presume this was a proper response.

The man won my friendship when he offered to take me aboard. I had to contain my eagerness as we approached – and my disdain as the guards admitted us without challenge merely because Navarre nodded; though 'tis true, these people do not live in a conquered land, nor suffer the depredations of sea raiders as Ireland has done for nigh a thousand years – but once we climbed aboard, I worried not at all, as Vaughn drew Navarre into an animated conversation, and left me the run of my ship.

She is well. And I am well once more, now that I have laid hands on her timbers and felt her beneath my feet. I still find a smile on my face and in my heart, even now.

I did slip into my cabin to check for despoiling, but no harm had come to my effects. O'Flaherty apparently had not found my secret cache, where I keep my most precious things, including my private logbook; I left that where it was, but I put into my pocket the gold chain my mother gave me when I first commanded the *Grace*, and my spyglass, which I have wished for many times in these past weeks away from my ship. I returned quickly to the deck, where Navarre and Vaughn had not missed me; we completed our tour, thanked Navarre profusely, and then parted ways. We found Lynch waiting for us by the road, and he brought us to the camp where McTeigue was roasting fish for our luncheon. In all, a fine, fine morning.

Captain's Log
Date: 23rd of July
Location: Key Largo
Conditions: Waiting for dawn's light so we may sail easier to the Redoubt. Wind and waves light, sailing is pleasant.

Lord, what fools these Floridians be!

We spent the afternoon discussing our course. Now that I have touched my ship and met her caretaker – a man worthy of trust, at least in this matter of my *Grace* – we would depart, Lynch and McTeigue and I, and Vaughn would seek lodging here on Plantation Key. But before we would leave these waters, we wished to make one more strike, giving Vaughn a stake for food and a roof, and leaving the local authorities seeking fruitlessly for three blue-clad highwaymen hereabouts. But Islamorada is awash in Coast Guard sailors, and Plantation Key similarly inundated with sheriff's men from the gaol; neither struck us as fertile waters for casting our net. So we determined to sail for the mainland and seek our victims there, or perhaps in Key Largo, the long island we must sail past to reach Florida's eastern coast.

But then our victims came to us.

It started well before the sun struck Earth at close of day, and so we decided to delay our departure and observe these peculiar happenings.

First came three men with a large white beast-wagon, taller than a standing man. They drove it onto the sand at the far end of the cove where we were camped, where a cliffside rose above the shore, creating a space enclosed on two sides of a triangle. Then they placed wooden posts in the ground and used rope to close in the third side, leaving but one easy entrance – although 'twas a most flimsy barrier. From their beast-wagon then they hauled out three silver barrels, which they set in large tubs filled with ice – which would have seemed a miracle to me, on these hot shores, but a month ago, before I had lived in the Glass Palace and eaten from the Enchantress's magical cold-cabinet.

Then from that same beast-wagon, whose hatch doors they left propped wide open, began to emerge the most god-cursed ear-stabbing cacophony I have heard in my life. It had something of a rhythm, but no sound-minded person could have identified it as music. Until I saw with my own eyes people arrive and begin to dance.

And by Lucifer, how these people danced! We Irish have always known the joy of dancing, and known it for a good thing, unlike those Puritan fanatics of Cromwell – but none of us ever saw dancing like *this*. Christ almighty, 'twas jarring enough to see what they wore: these were young women, *lovely* young women, in less clothing than a swaddling babe! And the way they gyrated and writhed and spun, and pressed themselves, rump and thigh and belly and breast, against the loins of the men, clad only in smallclothes, as well – well, it was quite the show. I was very glad for my spyglass, though I kept needing to fight McTeigue for it. It all made me remember how long it has been since I have had a woman – aye, three centuries it has been; no wonder I am so filled with lust! But if the way these lasses dress and dance be any indication, it should not be hard to find a maid happy to roll in the clover, and it should be quite a ride indeed!

Damn me, but I have got off the course. Aye, though the dancing whores – I mean, *lasses* – and the infernal gut-twisting music were fascinating, even more so was this: as people arrived, they were met at the gap in the rope by two of the men from the noise-wagon, who collected a sheaf of money-papers from each person, handed them a bright red cup, and waved them past the barrier. As the sun began to set, they drew together a large bonfire, and when the sun touched the ocean in the west, a score or so arrived and joined the bacchanal, swelling their numbers to at least a hundred. McTeigue and Lynch and I exchanged grins and nods and then made our plans to take advantage of this bounty placed on our very doorstep.

I approached the men at the gap in the line, with McTeigue to my left, twenty paces away, and Lynch to my right, midway between myself and the ocean. I smiled and nodded as the two men – barely more than lads, they were – looked up at my approach. I beckoned them close, as though I wished to speak quietly under the thunder of their horrid music, and when they brought their heads near mine, I presented to them my wheel-gun, and the sword I had kept concealed behind my back. They were entirely unarmed, and proved most willing to be led; soon I had emptied their pockets of a most impressive packet of money-papers and sent one of them up the beach to where Vaughn kept watch on the road, and the other, with my sword at his back, walked with me to the noise-wagon, which he at last, blessedly, silenced.

It was the easiest raid I have ever had. Meek as rabbits, these people were; not a weapon among them. Not one. Most had no money – certainly the lasses had nowhere to keep it – but those who did had much, and gave gladly, once they saw my compatriots and their own hopelessly trapped and exposed position. One fellow was more reluctant than most, and when I saw the thick wad of folded money-papers he produced from his pockets, I understood why he hesitated to surrender it; but when I passed over the strange packet of tiny pills, held in what I believe was more of this plass-tick I have seen before, he seemed most relieved and less grieved by the loss of his money. Though he was saddened once again when I demanded his jewelry, a pair of gold chains as thick as my thumb, three gemmed rings and a pair of diamond ear-bobs. Still he gave them up without a struggle.

We bade them all lie on their bellies, eyes shut and hands on head, and then we four raced for our boat and were off to sea before the first of them moved – perhaps because we fired shots over their heads as we departed, which arrested all motion for some time.

What a haul! Some 5000 in money-paper, plus gems and gold from some of the lasses and the wealthy pill-man, and not a scrap of trouble nor of searching and seeking for a target. Perhaps there is room here to be a pirate, after all.

Log #33: Pain Shop

Captain's Log
Date: 25th of July, 2011
Location: Redoubt at the Glass Palace
Conditions: Complicated.

A man might wonder, were he to come across my tale at a bookseller's someday – gods, do they still have booksellers? – or hear my exploits recounted in a tavern over mugs of ale: whyever did I become a pirate? I may flatter myself that I am a man of parts, of some good education, of courage and determination: what turned me into a rover of the infinite seas?

There are many reasons, as there are with any single moment in a man's life: as when one comes to a crossroads and must needs take one fateful and decisive step, there were innumerable steps before, and every one a necessary predecessor to the one moment we isolate and ask, "Why that step?" But there are indeed some steps, some causes, that I can identify as weighty in the scales of my life's measuring.

Any man who turns pirate must love the sea, and I do. The wind and waves, the graceful motion of a ship that can turn in any direction, course to any horizon and beyond, that freedom and beauty, the bright sky above and dark depths below: they wait behind my eyes when I sleep, and they bring me out to greet the morn again. Too, a gentleman of fortune like myself must have some love of gold, an appreciation for the finer things in life, or joy wrought simply from the clink and shine itself; and aye, I have a touch of that curse of Midas. Though for myself, as for some of my crew – Ian O'Gallows be one such, and young Balthazar Lynch – it is more than love of gold: we have a thirst for adventure, and our true reward is glory, a name which echoes and resounds through the ages and strikes fear, or admiration, or – well, something. But this, too, is a kind of greed.

Ere a man joins this Brotherhood of the Coast, he must have a reason in his heart to do violence, to spill blood and still breath.

Llewellyn Vaughn lacks this, which is why he sails with us but is not of us. Some, like Ned Burke, are cruel, and relish the infliction of pain on those weaker than themselves; some, like Kelly or MacManus, have a gift for mayhem such that it clears away all other paths in life: they would march as soldiers did they not sail as pirates. Many of us, including myself, have a burning anger in us, a desire for revenge that drives us to draw sword and pull trigger – or a temper hot enough and quick enough to make a man an enemy with but one irksome encounter. Aye, I have that, in truth.

But the one quality that every man jack of us carries, that every corsair shares, is this: impatience. A man who loves the sea can always find a place on it that suits him, if he but takes the time to cast about for a good berth on a good ship. Gold can be earned thus too: many a man's fortunes have come from simple trading and transport across the waves. And any score that needs settling can be done over the course of years and lifetimes without danger; or even better, it can be forgotten.

But damn me, I cannot wait. I have no gift for it. And so, 'tis a pirate's life for me.

And because I be a pirate, and have a lust for gold, and for adventure, and a hand ready to become a fist when my blood is high, and because I cannot bide my time, I have made our lives – passing convoluted. Alas, 'tis my nature.

When we sailed from Key Largo with the dawn, we sailed without Llewellyn Vaughn. I confess that in the excitement of the raid on the people of the noise-wagon, I had forgotten that Vaughn was not to accompany us, and he, caught up in the brouhaha as well, did not think to mention it. But it was well: Vaughn was eager to travel on foot along the roads and byways of this place, to cross the bridges that somehow traverse the ocean itself between these southern islands, these Keys; he said it would give him an opportunity to observe more of this world where we find ourselves. We gave him fair share of the booty, some thousand dollars, as these money-papers name themselves, for his keep, and fond farewell wishes and friends' embraces. Then we three pirates sailed for the Redoubt, which we struck a few hours before night fell. 'Twas a fine homecoming of sorts; my spyglass gave us a clear view of Maid Flora and her mistress the Enchantress, at their ease in the Palace; these familiar faces, these familiar surroundings where I write this – they put smiles on our faces.

But then, this morning, the reason for my meditations on piracy and my own nature arrived. I took my men creeping to the road before dawn brought Maid Flora, and we made our way to town. I sought to sell the jewelry we had captured, and thought of the shop where I had traded my ruby ring for a wheel-gun and a license for same, and my first money-papers.

I could not at first recall the course to reach it; I had traveled it before in the back of the Lopez beast-wagon, and it amazes how different the landscape looks on foot. But I found it, as much by chance as by recall, and about midday we crossed the threshold of Morty's Pawn Shop. There were customers within, and as we sought privacy for our transactions, we passed the time in looking over the stock and the prices, affixed to each piece in ink on a slip of white paper tied with string. I saw chains similar to those we had from the pill-man, with *200-* tied to them, even *275-*, and a pair of earbobs priced at twice that with diamonds less fine than those in my pocket. I grew eager thinking of the profit we stood to make here.

Aye, a lust for gold, indeed. A pirate I be.

When the shop had cleared but for the three of us and the corpulent fellow behind the cases filled with goods for sale, I hailed him pleasantly, asking if he recalled our prior encounter and exchanges; he gave me naught but a cool stare, at first, but then admitted some small acquaintance with my rather unforgettable self. I produced our booty with a showman's flourish, and laid it all out on the glass counter top, for his appraisal, and praise, I expected.

I did not get what I expected.

Morty – for this was the shopowner himself – snorted a derisive laugh, poking at the booty with one grimy finger. "What's all this crap?" he sneered.

I knew not the term he used, but I could not mistake his tone. Still, I assumed it was merely a haggler's opening ploy, however insulting it sounded. "We wish to offer these fine pieces to you, to enrich your stock in exchange for enriching our purses."

He looked the three of us over, again with an insulting and contemptuous air about him. I began to feel my temper, that piratical anger of which I spoke, rise behind my eyes.

"Your mother get tired of standing on the corner?" he asked, his lip curled and one brow raised sardonically.

I took this to mean that he thought my family owned a market stall, or perhaps simply stood on corners hawking our wares; I presumed he insulted me by implying that at my age, I still found employment only with my mother, incapable of finding my own trade, and I swallowed my pride again. I forced a smile on my face, over the protestations of my lips. "Nay, my good man, we traded for these." Aye – the jewels in exchange for a lowered pistol, a blade sheathed unblooded – a fair price for some shiny baubles, not so? "What will you offer us for them?"

He snorted, and poked at the chains, flicking the diamonds with his fingertip. "Twenty bucks."

I remembered the bucks from my first visit here, but surely he could not mean a mere twenty dollar-papers? "Twenty dollars? For which?"

"For all of it, ya dumb mick," he barked, and then sat back and laced his fingers over his belly.

I took a deep breath, and the ire subsided slightly. For a moment. Somewhat like the trough before the great wave crashes over the rail. "Come, my good sir: you have similar goods on display and costing better than a thousand dollars, all told; surely you will profit from these, as well? Profit enough to offer a fair price for them?"

He shook his head. "You want a fair price? Show me the receipt. Show me the insurance valuation. Hell, show me the gift card that says, 'Happy Birthday, enjoy your gangster pimp bling.'" He leaned forward, thrusting a finger at me like a fat, stubby rapier. "But you can't. Because that shit there is hot. It's stolen. So a fair price for you is whatever the fuck I say it is. You get me now, shit-for-brains?" He sat back once more, shrugging his shoulders with his hands spread wide. "Twenty bucks. Or shove that stuff back up your ass."

Now the wave crested, and I could not hide my anger. I placed my hand on the wheel-gun in my pocket, an unmistakable signal of intent, but did not draw. "I will take an apology from you, sir. Only after that will I and my companions depart." I waited.

He snorted a laugh again. "Go fuck your drunk mother, mick."

The moment that word "mother" left his vile worm-lips, I reached across the counter and seized hold of his shirt, intending to drag him bodily to my side of the display cases. But with a shout, he fell off of his stool, his weight tearing away my grasp. He landed heavily on his knees, and bent forward, scrambling under the counter, presumably for a weapon to defend himself.

We didn't give him the chance. Lynch snatched up a heavy gold filigreed box, the sort of thing a lady keeps her jewels in, and flung it at the cur, opening a gash in his forehead and knocking him back on his heels; he clapped both hands to his head with a cry, giving up his attempt to arm himself. McTeigue vaulted the counter and seized the man's right wrist, which he twisted while dealing him a kick to the right leg that sent him a-sprawl, all his weight falling on his badly-angled arm in McTeigue's grip, eliciting a high, womanish shriek of pain.

"Lynch, the door!" I shouted, and the lad slipped past me to the shop's entrance, which he pressed his back against, and, drawing his *pistola*, he scanned the street over his shoulders, keeping a watch. I leaned over the counter and grabbed the man's bent arm from McTeigue. "Get him up," I ordered, and McTeigue hauled on the man's belt.

He came up swinging, his left arm flailing about and smacking McTeigue weakly on the shoulder and chin. My cousin responded with a sharp, hard blow to the man's kidney, which turned the pig a pale green and left him whimpering in pain. I hauled up on his arm then, pulling him forward into my fist, which turned his Hebrew nose into an Irish one – flat and bent and bleeding. I pressed his face onto the counter and leaned on the back of his neck as he spluttered and coughed out blood, and McTeigue took hold of his left arm and put it on the counter as well, looking to me then for orders.

"Look for the key to the door. Rummage his pockets." As McTeigue did so, a look of distaste on his face at having to reach into the fat man's pants, I ordered Lynch to turn the sign on the door so that it read "Closed" rather than "Open." McTeigue found a ring of keys, which he tossed to Lynch, who quickly found the right one and bolted the door, barring any interruptions.

I had McTeigue right the bastard's stool, and then place that massive posterior onto it. Then he and Lynch ransacked the shop while I kept the shite-pile's ugly face pressed to the glass and gave him a lesson in humility. He struggled mightily as soon as I drew my boot knife, and I was forced to have McTeigue hold his head still while I carved my mother's name into his scalp. Fah: I didn't carve deep, only deep enough to let blood flow, and I did it under his greasy hair, so he need not be disfigured at all – but perhaps he would remember my mother's name, and the reason why he should not say such things about that sainted woman. He flailed at me with both hands until I put his right hand on the glass pane beside the one that held his head, and then struck a sharp blow to the back of his hand, shattering the glass and slashing his skin in several places; after that he held still but for the whimpering. It would have been vociferous cries for help, had we not gagged him with a wad of cloth from his wares.

Lynch collected the pistols and jewelry on display, and found the man's money-drawer, adding its contents to the impressive pile of dollars McTeigue had drawn from his pockets. But it was when Lynch stepped through a curtained doorway to the storehouses in the back of the shop that he came across a locked metal chest, bolted to the floor, with a keyhole in the front; that was when I realized that this might be a more profitable day than I ever expected. But experimentation quickly showed that none of the keys on the ring fit this metal chest. A simple query as to the proper key's whereabouts elicited only a spat curse, mixed with blood from the broken nose.

So we must needs ask more vigorously.

Lynch found a coil of bright-blue rope with some sundry goods, and tied the cur's wrists behind his waist, his fingers interlaced and shoulders twisted back. Then, with the aid of a strong hook in the ceiling in the back portion of the shop, we introduced Master Morty to the *strappado*, the favorite torture of the Inquisition and the cause of many a confession: the rope binding his wrists was brought up to the hook and through, and then McTeigue and I hauled the prisoner upwards until his feet left the floor, all of his weight pulling his shoulder blades back and his arms nearly out of their sockets – especially as much weight as this slovenly mongrel carried. 'Tis nearly the equal of the rack, and far simpler to carry out; had he not told me the location of the key then, we could have pulled down on his legs to pull his arms out of joint entirely, or slashed at his feet with a thin metal rod, or perhaps set a fire under him as I had done to the Latin Lion at the House of Lopez. But the first lift of his body was enough, and soon we had the key and opened the chest to find treasure within: stacks of money-paper in bound bundles, totaling more than thirty thousands of dollars.

But the avaricious joy of our success soon gave way to chagrin. Though the black-tongued rogue had denigrated my honor and that of my blessed mother, he had made me a most eloquent and sincere apology for same, and so I considered the matter ended. Thus I could not justly kill him. But left alive, he would soon have brought *la policia* down on our necks, and we should find ourselves in gaol for this and other crimes.

This, then, is the price of that impatience I have told is the hallmark and signet of piracy. Were I a patient man, I would have walked out of the shop when he insulted me, and planned my vengeance carefully and properly, so that nothing would set *la policia* on my trail. Or I would not have come here at all, preferring to sell my wares in the marketplace – earning perhaps even more money than this man would have given me in fair trade (Though not so much as we have taken from him now – there do be rewards with the pirate's life, aye.). But I would not wait to sell, and I would not wait for satisfaction. Now I have possession of a man whom I would not kill, and I cannot allow to go free.

We took the only option available: we kept him. We waited until nightfall, and then we left the locked shop by its back door, with the fat shopkeep bound and gagged and stumbling between McTeigue and I, as Lynch led us along back alleys and dark streets to the Redoubt, at last. Here we will hold him hostage until I think of a way to solve this conundrum to our advantage.

Aye, a pirate I be. Impatient, intemperate, lacking foresight.

But wealthy.

Log #34: Free Men, Bound Men

Captain's Log
Date: 26th of July in the Year 2011
Location: The Redoubt, for the nonce
Conditions: We make ready to sail for Plantation Key.
Wind and weather fair and calm.

Huzzah! My men are freed.

Or will be soon.

This morning, after my spyglass told me the Enchantress had left for the day, I hied myself to the Glass Palace and renewed my acquaintance with Maid Flora; a most amiable reunion it was, indeed. After I had heard the news of the Family Lopez – Juan had lost his place at Squire McDonald's tavern, but he and Ignacio both had found employ as gardeners – and had given a vague recounting of my own exploits, one which glossed over or expunged the assorted violences and robberies and the like, I introduced the Maid to my companions (with whom, of course, she was familiar, having been held captive by them and the rest of my men for many days, but she had never been properly introduced, which I did now out of respect for her kind and unexpected assistance after the mutiny) and begged use of the washroom and telephone. These kindnesses being extended, I cleansed myself thoroughly and then made contact with Master McNally, who tendered his most welcome report: lacking evidence of direct involvement in any wrongdoing, the charges were being dropped against the bulk of my crew. Burke, Carter, and O'Flaherty, the instigators and actors of the most heinous crimes (for Burke and Carter had committed the two murders aboard the yacht, and O'Flaherty had spoken for the crew there), and of course the vile Shluxer, thief, kidnapper, and would-be rapist, would remain in the gaol awaiting their time before a magistrate. I saw this as further welcome intelligence, though not as a surprise, as I had instructed McNally not to intercede on behalf of these four, the cause of my overthrow and theft of my ship. The only troubling news from McNally was that my first mate and friend, Ian O'Gallows, and Kelly, who had stood by his side against the mutineers at the last, were to be charged and tried, Ian for participating in the raid on the yacht, Kelly for breaking in doors and aiding Shluxer and Burke with the robberies ashore. These last, McNally told me they had on viddy-oh; it took some time before I understood that this was a way of saying they had seen Kelly's face on their magic windows.

But as for the rest, as soon as Master McNally got through with what he termed "red tape," they are to be released, free men. Most likely it will be on the morrow. And so we have readied the boat, and rolled our hostage in a large sheet of blue plass-tick which I discovered in the Palace's garradge, with his arms and legs bound by cords, so that Morty the Shopkeep now resembles a mere bundle of goods at our feet. Now we will set sail for the gaol and our glad reunion.

Gods send that it be so.

Captain's Log
Date: 28th of July
Location: Plantation Key
Conditions: I have my crew. I but lack my ship.

There was gladness indeed when my men came out of that gaol and stood once more in the bright sunlight, blinking and grinning. We had sailed through the day and night, and with a favorable wind had arrived in time to stand waiting to greet them into the free air. But in truth, my expression was not one of pure delight – though when I saw their joy at being free turn to chagrin and remorse when they saw me, when their eyes dropped to their feet and they doffed their caps and stood round-shouldered, like guilty boys before a stern father, my heart was lifted. Perhaps their loyalty is not wholly lost, I thought then.

I approached closely and stood face-to-face with each man, lingering longest over those who should be most ashamed at their dishonor, namely mine own kin, my cousins and clansmen Liam Finlay and Malachy Rearden. I saved another glare for Abram O'Grady, whom I still suspected of complicity in the conspiracy, for the drugged food that had laid me low when they stole my ship had been prepared by O'Grady's hands. Not a one of them met my eyes, a wise choice for them all. But I only said, "Let us leave this place and its watching eyes," and led the whole shuffling, downcast troupe to the beach where we had landed, on the south side of Plantation Key – the same beach where we had raided the noise-wagon – and where Lynch and McTeigue had laid out the makings of a fine feast, bread and cheese and meat and ale in good quantity, along with several bags of those delicious potato chips, purchased from a nearby shop called a grocery.

The walk had done the men good, as they had been locked away out of the fresh air for many days and unable to stretch their legs properly, and they raised a cheer when they saw their welcome. But I gathered them round, first, and spoke, to this effect.

"All right, lads, you're free, now, thanks to the efforts of Master McNally – returned to a proper Irishman's state, aye, for such as we are not meant to be held in irons. And as your friend and countryman, I mean to offer you all a proper celebration of this happy event, and break bread and empty a mug with you all." They raised a fine cheer at this, though the tone of my next words sobered them again.

"But be warned: I am your friend, aye, and your countryman – 'tis why I engaged Master McNally on your account, for I could not stand to see you all behind bars and at the mercy of the courts of these lands, which may indeed have stretched every one of your necks for your crimes had I not done this – but I am no longer your captain. You are not now my crew. I cannot be your captain, you see, because I do not have my ship: it was lost to me when *you mutinied.*" I threw the last words at them like a blade, like the crack of a whip, and they flinched back from them, and from the fire in my gaze. As I expected, one of them stepped forward to protest that they never had turned on me – 'twas MacManus, who has ever had more steel in him than most men – but I shouted him down. "Aye, Shane, ye *did, all* of ye. I know ye were not the ones who poisoned me; I know exactly who was behind *that* foul and cowardly attack –" here I stopped my pacing and stared directly at O'Grady, who paled and shook his head, but said nothing – "but I also know that ye *all* were told that I lived, and had been marooned on these strange shores. *And ye left me there!* Ye took my ship and sailed on, under other men, under *mutineers* and *betrayers* and *poisoners!* Ye followed that mongrel Shluxer, *and ye did it as free men!*"

I paused and allowed that to hang in their ears for a moment, as it had weighed down my heart for weeks now. Then I lowered my voice and made my confession. "I know that you all doubted me, and I know why. Because I brought you – here. I lost our way. And then, when I discovered the truth of where we are, of what has happened to us, I did not tell you. I did not trust you all to hear the truth. That was my sin – and I believe I have paid for it. And perhaps, in these last weeks in that prison, you have all paid for your sins, come right with the gods and your own consciences. I would expect so.

"But you have not paid *me*. You are not right with *me.*"

I raised my voice again, my words ringing out as I spoke now of the future. "I hereby swear that I will never again keep anything from you, or from any man, that you have a right to know. I have seen what secrets may do. I mean to regain my ship, and I mean to find a way back home, to our proper world and time. I do not know how this will be accomplished, but I intend to make the first step: the *Grace* will sail for Ireland." A buzz of whispers raced through them then, and I looked each man in the eye when it had subsided – and I saw hope there. I went on.

"Because I brought you here, I will take you back with me, if I can. But for now, you have berths only as passengers, not as crew. I mean to recruit new crewmen from among the locals here to help me sail home, and to have a share in whatever profits there may be from this voyage." There was another murmur at that, this one louder and more grumptious. I raised a hand, and it silenced. "Unless," I said, and paused again. "Unless you can prove your loyalty to me. Unless you can accept me as captain, as master and commander and sole authority over this ship and its crew, and convince me of your sincerity. Know now that this quartermaster foolishness is over – over and *done*, and I will *never* hear of it again. I will never allow another man even a *sliver* of authority over my ship. I have learned that lesson, oh yes.

"But know as well that I will be open and honest with you, and will listen to your advice when you have it to give, and will follow it when it be wise."

One last pause to let it sink into them, and then I said, "Think on it. Think on what you wish to do, if you would sail my ship with me, or go as cargo – and if you would join me, how you will win my trust once more. Till then, let us eat."

We fell on that feast then, and filled our bellies and our hearts, with food and ale and glad shouts and songs and dancing, and many a cup was raised and drained in my honor and Master McNally's as well. I sent Lynch to find a telephone and invite that worthy to our feast, but when he accomplished this task, McNally refused, with regrets, claiming he was too occupied with O'Gallows and Ó Duibhdabhoireann, whose continued incarceration frustrated him mightily and made him even more determined to free them. Lynch bore back Master McNally's request for parlay with myself on the morrow, which I agreed to, and will go to attend in an hour or so.

But first I must recount the events that greeted me this dawn.

I was roused, gently, by Lynch; though I had drunk my fair share of ale the night before, I had not had more than my fair share, and so had no regrets nor any difficulty in waking this morn at Lynch's quiet hail. When I met his gaze, I saw that he was smiling, his eyes bright and shining. "The men wish to see you, Captain. They are waiting at the water's edge." I rose quickly and followed him, rubbing sleep from my eyes and combing my hair with my fingers as I went.

Until I saw the men. Then I stopped in my tracks.

They knelt, every one of them, in a line behind McTeigue – and Lynch hurried to a spot directly behind my cousin and fell to his knees as well. McTeigue held my sword, unsheathed and gleaming in the dawn's pearly light. I approached and stood before him, and he offered me the hilt, keeping his fingers on the blade. When I took it, he pressed his left forearm onto the edge and drew blood. Then he spoke these words clearly:

"By my blood, my freedom, and my life, I swear my loyal service to Captain Damnation Kane, for as long as he will have it. And if I break this oath, may this sword take my blood, my freedom, and my life."

He released the blade and bowed his head. I said proudly, "I accept your service, Owen McTeigue, and I thank you." I tapped the blade on his shoulder, and my cousin rose with a smile and took my hand gladly, before taking his place on my right, facing the line of kneeling men. I stepped forward to where Balthazar Lynch reached out his hands for the blade, and soon young Lynch stood at my left shoulder, a thin cut on his left wrist and a proud gleam in his eye.

The next man was Shane MacManus. He slashed open his left palm, and his right, presenting the wounds to me as he swore his loyal service to me. I paused and considered them, and then I nodded, tapped him on the shoulder to accept his oath, and bade him rise.

And so it went: the deeper the shame the man felt, the deeper the cut he gave himself on my blade. I accepted their own estimations of their guilt and their penitence, and their oaths to serve me, bound by my sword and their blood. Until I got to O'Grady, who knelt awkwardly with his wooden leg, at the end of the line. I had heard the night before that the guards in the gaol had taken his wooden leg from him, leaving him to hop around his cell, offering him a beggar's crutch when he was brought out for meals. I knew this shame was penance enough for following along with the mutiny – but what of the poison, and the plot?

O'Grady took my sword in his hands and placed it against his cheek, under his one good eye. Slowly and deliberately, he cut himself three times, until the blood ran down his neck and dripped off his chin to the sand below. Then he pressed the edge against his own throat, and lowered his hands.

"I swear my service to thee, sir, and my undying loyalty, whether thou want it or no. I swear to thee, on my soul's salvation, that I did not poison thee, or O'Gallows or Vaughn, and I did not know those bastards did so. I swear I thought thee to be in thy cups, as they told me that thou and the others had been drinking before dinner." He swallowed roughly, the motion moving the cold steel against his throat. I saw a tear roll down his cheek, mixing with his blood. He closed his good eye. "I wait your judgment, sir."

I bade him rise, and join the others. I had suspected O'Grady was innocent of my poisoning, as the man has not a deceptive bone in his body, and because the drug they used was likely one from this time, as I had never heard of a potion with those effects from my own age, and this pointed the finger at Shluxer, not at any of my men. Still, 'twas better to be sure, and now that I had heard and seen his sincerity, I was.

I turned and faced my men, with their blood on my sword. I pulled open my shirt, and with the tip of the blade, I cut my breast over my heart, and added my blood to theirs. Then I swore my own oath.

"I swear, by my blood, my freedom, and my life, that I will treat you honorably and lead you as wisely as I can, for as long as you choose to sail with me. I hereby set all of you free, to choose your own course, whether it follow mine or not. And I swear that, as I brought you here, I will bring you home, or die in the attempt."

I raised my blade to the sky and cried out "To Ireland!" And every man there echoed me.

"TO IRELAND!"

I have my crew once more.

Log #35: The Gallows Log

(Translated from Gaelic)
Ian O'Gallows
19th of July

When first I was put in this place, I feared I would ne'er see the Sun, nor breathe Free Air again. I feared I would ha' my Neck stretched ere a Week had passed. In Truth I was somewhat stunned that the Cap'n o' the Coast Guard Ship what took us did not Hang every man Jack of us from the yardarm, and send us with our Ship to Davy Jones, with a Curse to chase us down to Hell. Sure and he had evidence enow to know our Crimes and our Guilt.

Now that I ha' been here three Days, I fear only that Tiresome Hours, without any employment, amusement, or e'en Punishment, will pile up so high they do Smother me. So, to avoid this Fate, I ha' requested paper and pen from my captors, so that I may follow the lead o' me Cap'n, Damnation Kane, who doth keep the Log faithfully.

So here be me Log.

They did capture us on July the 15th, four Days past. They made it back to shore in mere two or three Hours, with us all Manacled and sitting on the stern deck o' that thundering steel Hell-Ship. That Devil's boat made thirty, forty knots, without sail nor oar. At *least* that many! Methinks I did not need to do what I did, and give them the *Grace's* heading. Sure and they could ha' found us as easy as they took us, as easy as they brought us back.

They kept us from talking on the Ship, tho speeches were made with the Eyes. If O'Flaherty could ha' killed me with his Glare, I would ha' been spared these empty Days in this Cell, aye. Burke, as well. Tho the opposite do be true, too: if my Hands had been free, them two Mutineers would lie flat wi' Wrung Necks and Black Tongues by now. Aye, and perhaps a puling pissbucket of a rapist, as well, tho that tub o' maggoty fishguts Shlocksir be barely worth the effort to Strangle. But he be worth it, na'theless. He cried, the suety fop, like a bairn without his mam's teat to fill his Mouth. Fair made me sick.

We made the Keys ere Night fell, and they put us into three cells at the Fortress. And they took off the Manacles, and left us unguarded. Ha! The minute the Door shut behind the guard, I took hold o' that damned O'Flaherty and Flung him into the bars, Head-first. He reeled back, stunned and Bleeding, but he be an Irishman, and he put up a Fight, aye. But tho he be the stronger, I be Younger and Faster. And Smarter and *Prettier*, while we be talking on it, ha ha! Burke he would ha' come to his man's aid, but he were in another Cell, as was Carter, who might ha' done the same. Burke roared at me, laying on the Curses like mortar on a wall, until Kelly, me good mate Kelly, took it in his mind that Burke should be hushed, and then he made it so, wi' but three good Blows of those cannonballs he calls Fists. Burke be paid back for what he did to Kelly back in Ireland, when Burke took the Bosun's Whistle from Kelly.

O'Flaherty took a bit more convincing, but soon enow he was down for a wee Nap, too, and sleeping like a Babe, aye. I could ha' Strangled him then, but I had cooled a mite. Too, I felt that killing a man while in gaol and about to be tried for my Life would be somewhat Rash. I but gave him a Kick in the Teeth to remember me by. Then I spoke wi' the men.

"Listen, all o' ye," I said. "I don't give a Fig for who ye would ha' for Cap'n o' this crew, or if ye think ye be a crew at all. *I* say we be the men o' the *Grace o' Ireland,* and o' the blood o' Old Erin herself. We be the Wolves o' the Irish seas, sons o' Lugh and Cormac, Cuchulain and Fionn MacCumhaill. Aye?" They growled and grumbled an *Aye* to that. Then I lowered my voice and looked every man in the Eye. "Men o' Ireland ha' nothing to say to the men o' the law. Not to the gaolers, not to the judges, not to the Headsman, if it come to that. Nothing but our Names, that they may remember us, and a Curse for them to Choke on. Be we agreed?"

And they agreed, every Man. Then the guards came in, saw O'Flaherty and Burke Unconscious on the floors, and asked after the events leading to such a State. And the men, they did me Proud. Not a Damned Word did they give those bastards. Naught but a Hard Stare and a few mouthfuls o' spit cast to the floor at their feet. Good men, they are. All but Shlocksir, o' course. He opened his gob and drew breath to squeak like the Bilge Rat he be. But Arthur Gallagher, old Lark, as we call him for his Singing, Lark threw a punch, quick as a

Fox, into Shlocksir's ballocks, and knocked the traitorous air right out o' him, without the guards bein' any the wiser.

In an English prison, they'd ha' every man of us flogged for fighting. Here they mere posted a man outside our cells to watch us. The Men grew confident at that, for sure and we'd all expected the flogging; and the air eased somewhat. We stayed silent for an hour or more, glaring at the guard. Then Lark started singing. Soon enough we'd all joined in, and we Sang down the Moon and up the Sun.

Then they came for us. Manacled, led into a great Beast of a wagon, like a Tinker's House on wheels, but with two long benches the only furniture in it. Half the Men in one wagon, half in another just like the first, and they drove us to another Gaol. This'n be larger, but with smaller cells. The Cell where I lay now and write these words be three paces by four, with two bunks stacked on one Wall. I share with Lochlan O'Neill, him the men call Salty for the White in his Hair and Whiskers and his Thirty Years before the Mast, which ha' pickled and tanned his hide with Sun and Sea air. Salty be a fine bunkmate, aye, quiet and thankfully free o' stench. Sure and these bitty cells might weigh on many a man, but for tars like us, who would sleep Six Men in Hammocks in this same space when the Ship be full o' cargo and the Weather bad abovedecks, this be a fine Cabin for two.

Naturally I figured that once we met the local Inquisition, they'd drag us out o' these Fine Quarters and lock us in the Dankest Pit they had. These cells must be the reward they hold out for waggling your Tongue, I thought. That and the Food, which is better than what I've eaten on most voyages once the fresh grub be gone. Yet they ha' not taken these luxuries away. Not yet.

They do not Torture, either. Or they be Right Slow in getting to it. That first full day, they came for each o' us, Three at a Time, tho they put one man into one room, sitting at table with two Men dressed like Merchants, with open coats and neck-scarves, clean white shirts and shoes which shone. They asked us Questions for an hour or two. And that's all: they but asked. They did not even Strike us. Not even Salty, tho he told us later in the galley (Aye, the gaol has a galley, where all the prisoners sit and eat together.) that he had Cursed them till his Tongue was Raw. But nothing, naught but Question after Question. Soon I found I could simply ignore them as they blathered on at me. Made me feel quite like a Married Man, ha ha.

Nay: my Difficult Hour came when I had to face my Cap'n, my friend and the Man I had Failed, when I gave his ship to these men with their soft hearts and their Thunder-Guns. Cap'n Kane came the second day we were in the small cells. The guards summoned me out and brought me to the main Portcullis, at the end o' the corridor lined by our Cells, and there, two paces from the bars, stood my Cap'n, his Brow Thundrous and his Eyes flashing Lightning.

I made my Report, and he responded as a Cap'n should. Enough said o' that. I am right glad that he be wise enow to see where fault truly lies, for while I ha' surely Sinned, I be no Cursed Mutineer. I ha' failed. But I did not *betray*.

Then, yesterday, a Man came to us, starting with myself, and said he be our Lawyer, name of McNally. He said he were engaged by Cap'n Kane. He bore Proof, a note in the Cap'n's Hand which instructed us to listen to this man's advice, and I did so. McNally heard the whole tale from my Lips, tho he knew much of it from the Cap'n, including my own Hand in our capture and in protecting the Virtue of our hostages from the yot. Instead o' callin' me Traitor for giving up the *Grace*, McNally told me this was a Good Thing, that my actions were – Laudable, I think he said. He complimented us too on not speaking to the law in our Questioning sessions, which earned a laugh from me. "Does anyone?" I asked him. "Why? For fear of their foul breath?"

But now McNally says I need to talk to them, and tell them everything. He says the law needs a Sacrifice, a Patsy, he called it. Someone to point the Finger of Justice at and proclaim *There be the guilty one!* A Trophy for the wall, that's all it is. But McNally says we must give them this. And what's more, he says that the Cap'n has Ordered it so, has Ordered us to talk to these bastards, these – they're not English, but they might as well be for the way they treat us. Not Cruel, no, but like we be Beneath them, like dirt, or spittle under their Bootheel which must be Scraped Off and Washed Away. As tho we be Filth to be cleansed, instead of Men. Aye, they be English, in truth. They be *West* English, that's what they be.

And I am to confess to these West English? To the law? Aye, Nate Ordered it, I believe McNally's word on that. I see the Cap'n's reasons, too. If we talk, it be O'Flaherty and Burke, Carter and Shlocksir wi' the Noose about their Necks. Them what led, and them who did the Killing. And for their Mutiny against my Cap'n and friend, they should do the Devil's Dance at the end of a Rope, aye, for certain sure, and I'd watch 'em and Smile, for what they done.

But he wants me to talk to the *law*. He wants me to cooperate, and turn on my fellow pirates. Aye, it be an Order, but we're not on Ship. And Curse me for it, but Cap'n's been wrong afore – ne'er should ha' hired on that Shlocksir, ne'er should ha' Whipped him just for trying on that girl. Turned the Men against him, and Look at us now.

I don't know what to do.

20th of July

McNally came back again today. He told me the men be Waiting on me to Talk. All except for Shlocksir. That whoreson be Singing Hymns from the choir loft, all about his Innocence and all our Evil Ways, how we Forced him to do it all against his Will. Figures that even in saving his own greasy Skin, he comes out a Coward and a Weakling.

McNally told me too that the West English all but Promised that if we Tell the Tale, and if it be True, then we'd go Free. He says they don't believe Shlocksir, for the witnesses from the land-grabs and the yot tell a Tale somewhat Different from the one that poxy bastard be Spinning. A tale what our Story will line with Right Fine, methinks. McNally's not sure about me, nor Kelly. I was on the yot, with a Cutlass, and Kelly Broke in doors for the land-grabs. We may have to stay in here. Tho he Swears we will not Swing for what we done, even if they hold us to our Crimes.

After he left, I had other visitors. The two lasses we took off the yot, who Kelly and me stood Guard over. They came to – to thank us. For protecting them. Christ.

I'll talk. There be Good Men in this crew, in this gaol, and they shouldn't be here. Perhaps I can talk them out of here, even if I can't find my own way to Freedom.

26th of July

No need to write in this of late. I been busy Reciting my lessons for the West English, and I don't want to recount that tale. Damn me, but they want to hear the Same Story over and over and over, like wee bairns at bedtime. "Tell us again, Uncle Ian, about the yot. Tell us the one about when the Coast Guard caught ye." My Tongue be tired of it.

But it Worked. The men'll be released today, all but Kelly and me, and the four bastards who be our scapegoats, our Sacrificial Lambs. Tho really, they be more Weasels and Mongrels. Our Sacrificial mongrel-weasels. They be staying here.

McNally says, and the West English agree, that if Kelly and me agree to stand in Court and Testify against the four mongrel-weasels, we'll be set Free, too. We'll plead Guilty to Theft and the like, and leave wi' Time served and parole that would keep us here in Florida. West England, says I, whate'er flowery Name they write on the Map.

Be it too much? To stand before a magistrate, point my Finger, put the Noose on them myself? I sailed with those men, whate'er they done. Carter was a good Man, too, a Good Tar, and Burke ha' fought many a Battle for us. O'Flaherty, too, standing Side by Side with me with lead flying and steel singing. Can I do that to them? Can I Kill them with the law?

27th of July

Aye, I can. Hurts to write. With the men gone and Kelly elsewhere, Burke and O'Flaherty caught me in the Galley and tried to beat me to Death. Did a fair Job of it, too. And all the while Cursing me for opening my Gob to the law.

Damn them anyway, I be no coward. If I clap shut now, they'll think they beat a Fear into me. I'll not have that.

I'll tell myself we're on Ship. They be Mutineers, and I be the first Mate. I'd be the one to tie the Knot on their Necks and cast them off the yardarm, asea. So aye, I'll do it here, too. For my Cap'n, and my – is it Honor? Is it? Do I have any of that? Will I still, after I do this, after I help the English to kill Irishmen?

I know not. I know nothing. It all hurts.

Log #36: Filling in the Holes

Captain's Log
Date: 31st of July in the year 2011
Location: Plantation Key
Conditions: Hopeful.

Two good men were released from their bondage, today: Ceallachan
Ó Duibhdabhoireann and my friend and first mate, Ian O'Gallows.
We met them at the gaol when they came into their first sunlight of
the last fortnight, we having been alerted to the happy occasion by its
architect, Master McNally. As they emerged, we gave them three
rousing cheers, a proper welcome for heroes. Aye, heroes: they saved
my crew from descending to the vile depths of Shluxer's lusts, and
then spared these men, and my ship, from destruction at the hands of
the Coast Guard. Heroes they are, and so I named them – and then I
named Ian to his former post as First Mate of the *Grace*, and Kelly to
Bosun in place of Burke, which met with a roar of approval. I have
also named my good cousin Owen McTeigue to Gunner, replacing
Hugh Moran, who met his doom and found justice for his crimes.

After we returned to our camp, and the welcome feast which
O'Grady had prepared, Ian and Kelly soon heard of the events
occurring in their absence, including the oaths sworn on this beach, on
my sword. They instantly clamored for the chance to swear their own
oaths, which I happily granted and accepted their sworn word to serve
me and my ship. I swore to them, as well, so that now I bear a cross
on my breast to remind me of my duty to my men.

I have all of my crew, now. All that remain worthy of trust, any
road. All that I need to do is what must be done: to get us home.

Captain's Log
Date: 1st August 2011
Location: Plantation Key
Conditions: Busy

Vaughn has managed to gain us access to the *Grace!* That silver-tongued devil, who knew he had it in him?

But indeed, Monsieur Navarre has come to see that we, the captain and crew of the *Grace of Ireland,* were best suited to see to her repairs and proper maintenance: to replace her yardarm, patch the many holes and tears in her canvas caused by the thunder-guns of the Coast Guard (In truth we could not patch it, and were forced to make new sails; Monsieur Navarre was able to find us new canvas, which the men sewed under Salty O'Neill's supervision. The old sail I had stowed for future use; we can cut it down or use it for scraps. Foolish, perhaps, to save it; but it came with us from home.), as well as splice new line to replace the cordage similarly destroyed, and craft a new rail and wheel. Yes, and repair the gouge in her flank – aye, my fine lass needs a fair bit of doctoring. We have no carpenter, but seeing how well the last replacement carpenter worked for us, I think we will muddle through on our own. Monsieur Navarre and his fellow scholars may prove able assistants in this, and they are certainly eager to serve.

I have paid McNally for services rendered, and promised him a cruise on the *Grace* in respect of his kind friendship to us. Some 25,000 dollars remain in our treasury.

Captain's Log
Date: 2nd August
Location: By the Nautical Museum of Monsieur Navarre, and close to the *Grace*.
Conditions: The repairs proceed rapidly. But one thorn remains.

I am unsure how to resolve the issue of our hostage. Morty has proved a simple enough matter thus far: we simply dug a thieves' hole on the beach, shadowed by the cliff and bordered by the surf, and placed him in it, covered over with palm fronds – this, it obtains, is the name of the tall slender tree, the palm. A man or two to guard, armed with the very *pistolas* we took from that foul-mouthed rogue, and some small food and water tossed in, generally the scraps from the crew's meals. And there it is: a kept man.

But he lives in town, and runs a shop. He must be missed. How long until someone finds his way into the pawn shop and discovers it ransacked, with the proprietor's blood on the glass countertop? Are they looking for him even now?

The easy solution – simply to fill in the hole, with or without a pistol-shot first – calls out to me. Its song sounds sweeter by the day.

Captain's Log
Date: The Third of August, in the year 2011
Location: 30 mi. South by south-west of Plantation Key, in open water
Conditions: She sails!

There are a myriad of sights in this world to make a man feel small. The sight of a tree standing proud and strong and two hundred feet tall: crouch under it – for even at a man's full height, one is crouching under that enormity – and know that it grew when your father's father's father was but a babe, and back before that, and that it will live on, and grow taller still after you are dust – and you will feel small. Stand beside a mountain, or under a cliff; swim in a river's current, or cower beneath a storm's sky-tearing fury, and you will know how insignificant is this thing we call a man. The glory of God's creation? Perhaps, and perhaps not. Withal, just a man.

Too, there are a thousand means for a man to feel like a giant, to grow prodigious and glorious. Cut down that great tree, hew it and shape it into a house or a church, a fortress or a ship, or a bridge; then stand on what you have wrought – ah, then is a man grown tall. Climb the mountain, scale the cliff, bridge the river – or swim up the current, thews and sinews straining, challenging the mighty rushing water – and laugh at the storm raging without while you sit comfortable and warm and dry by your hearth, under your strong roof: then you feel a match for the world, then you feel deserving of God's special attentions. Nature makes us small – but by conquering it, we grow large again.

This is never more true than now, for I sit at a table in my cabin aboard my ship, the *Grace of Ireland*: a masterwork of wood and nails, canvas and rope, held on course, no matter how the wind blows or the currents press, by the minds and muscles of men! And yet, what are we but ants on a cork, adrift in that endless expanse of water, a landscape immeasurable, inconceivable in its whole, its breadth, its depths that may hold wonders and terrors undreamt of? Even now, in this time that is my own distant future, men do not truly know what lies beneath the waves. I have asked Monsieur Navarre, and though men have now ways of seeing deeper than my own people ever could, still they cannot see all. If I traveled forward – Gods forbid! – another three centuries, or six, or more, I do not believe men would know the sea as well as we know the land. Beneath the waves is not our world, and we are not welcome there, below, in the cold silence.

So am I small, for being one speck on this world of the ocean? Or am I large, for sailing across it, for making use of it, turning its incalculable might to my advantage? Who is mightier, the steed or the man atop it?

I know not. I know this: here, on my ship on this mighty ocean, I am alive.

We have taken Master McNally and Monsieur Navarre aboard and set out on a brief pleasure cruise: thus do we pay our debts to these good men. They are well-satisfied with the arrangement: Master McNally has spent much of this past day at the ship's bow, feeling the wind and the spray in his face, his eyes roving the boundless horizon and a smile creasing from ear to ear. For some strange reason, he has a penchant for standing on the rail and shouting, "I'm the king of the world!" Well, it is his first time aboard a proper sailing ship, and the speed and power, the freedom and the grace – 'tis a glory to behold.

Monsieur Navarre has not stopped asking questions. He is fascinated by every step we take, every line we pull, every knot, every shout, every chantey – not one aspect of a ship's sailing or the men who crew her is beneath his notice, or free from his probing mind. I now know how an animal feels when it is captured and examined by a natural scientist, like Vaughn: we are the curiosity that drives Monsieur Navarre. Still, he seems most entertained, to judge by the sparkle in his eye and the spring in his step.

I do not doubt that my own eye and step have the same joy and light. I am where I belong, aboard my ship with my crew, and what's more, I am at last free of O'Flaherty, and of the noisome Burke, ever lurking about and leering, the black-hearted bastard. There are no Englishmen aboard the *Grace*. My heart is full.

Captain's Log

244

Date: 4th of August
Location: 60 mi. due East of last position.
Conditions: Weather remains ideal, ship is hale,
companions are stout-hearted, amiable, and true.

Master McNally made an intriguing suggestion last night at dinner, the which we ate on the deck under the velvet sky. He paid the ship and crew – and the captain, as well – the very kindest and most eloquent of compliments, which dazzled me so that I find I cannot recall a single moment of it, and would not try to re-create his words with my own humble pen. But the thrust was that this cruise has been one of the great joys of his life. Then, after he raised a glass and we all gave a huzzah to honor him and his words, he sat and told me that I should consider this as an occupation for my ship.

"You could build cabins in the hold – maybe take out the guns on the middle deck and build them there, or use that as a dining area – a galley, right? Because the gun ports could let in light and air. I'm telling you, people would pay hundreds, maybe even thousands, for a nice, quiet, intimate cruise on a beauty of a ship like the *Grace*. With the way pirates have gotten popular lately, thanks to Johnny Dep and the Caribbean Muveys –" (I did not slow him to ask for clarification of these strange names, but have simply rendered here his words as he spoke them, to be understood perhaps another day.) "– you fellows could really draw the crowds in. I could get you all set up with a business license, handle the paperwork and whatnot; it could just – well – *sail!* All the way to the *moon* and back!"

His excitement was infectious – and the idea is sound. If the people here feel as he does, if they spend their lives – as they seem to do, from what I have seen – locked inside houses, trapped in enclosed beast-wagons, surrounded always by noise and stink of their metal constructions and their glassed windows, rarely breathing the free air, then a proper cruise on a proper ship would indeed be a joy, a fine way to spend a day or three, and worth remuneration.

Perhaps this place and time need not be so hostile to us. Perhaps we could – stay.

Captain's Log
Date: 5th of August

Location: Plantation Key, at our camp on the beach.
Conditions: Complications arise.

On our return from the joyful cruise, we were welcomed by news somewhat less rapturous. I had left MacManus and Sweeney behind to watch Morty in his thieves' hole, but they instead watched a bottle of rum vanish down their gullets. Morty very nearly escaped – prevented only by his own clumsiness, for he fell back into the hole as he was climbing out, and injured his leg; he cried out and roused the somnolent MacManus, who found the wherewithal to aim a *pistola* in Morty's general direction and halt his rambunctiousness. The vile-mannered shopkeep had stripped his own clothing off, used it as a flail, weighted with sand in the pockets, and knocked the palm fronds down into his hole. Then he used these to fashion a ladder of sorts, stout enough to propel him up the sloped sides of the pit. A fine plan, had his weight not smashed through his improvisation at the critical moment.

MacManus and Sweeney have had their five lashes for drinking and sleeping on watch, but the problem remains. Thus, this night we will take Morty out in the boat, bring him to a sandbar or small deserted island somewhere in the Keys, and maroon him.

I should shoot him. Somehow, I cannot. This will have to suffice.

Log #37: Time to Go

Captain's Log
Date: 7th August 2011
Location: Maritime Museum, Plantation Key
Conditions: Peaceful and calm

Today, all is well with the world.

The men have doffed caps and shirts – they would have removed their shoes as well, but like all sailors in warm climes, most wear none – and are lounging, idle and at peace, some on the sand, some in the surf. O'Grady is below in the galley, mixing a new grog concoction, essaying an experiment with the spirits of this age and place. He hopes to improve on the old mixture, which is ale, water, rum, and a touch of gunpowder; it is effective, but neither pleasing to the palate nor soothing to the gullet. Vaughn, of course, is inside the museum, ensconced within Monsieur Navarre's books – assuming he is not ensconced in Monsieur Navarre's arms. I am glad that Llewellyn has found a kindred spirit here, as there were none among the crew. I have feared that he might face harassment; sailors, I have learned, are either fire or ice, never a temperate middle ground: some are welcoming of all peoples and creeds and those who walk other paths through this life, and others are cantankerous and contentious with all but their closest mates, and will often turn on them, too, given the slightest provocation. I cannot say whether all of my men would be welcoming of a man like Vaughn if he did not hide his desires, as he ever has, until now. But then, it is possible that Vaughn will not rejoin the crew when we sail from here. I do not know what would call him home with a sweeter voice than that which sings to him now.

Of course, it is possible we will not make it home. I do not know where our course might lead, once we reach Ireland; I know not how it led here. I recall the strange storm, the light, the shaking, the surge of the water and the burst of shrieking just before we came to these shores; was that when it happened? If it was, how do I find those same conditions? And will it send us back, or – somewhere, or somewhen, else?

I find myself thinking of something which Monsieur Navarre brought to my attention as we were cruising through the Keys and he had loosed the hounds of his curiosity. On the stern of this ship there are runes painted; Monsieur Navarre had noted them during his initial inspection of the *Grace* after the Coast Guard brought her to him, and he inquired of me as to the language and meaning of the script. I told him that my dear mother, who has great knowledge of the old ways, had performed a rite when my ship was new, blessing the *Grace* and asking the gods to protect the ship and her captain and crew. The runes are ancient Druidic writing, and read – if memory serves – "Name of my Name, Blood of my Blood. Blood of the Earth, Breath of the Earth, Flesh of the Earth, Spirit of the Earth, carry my Blood and my Name, and shield my Blood and my Name, safe through all time." The bit about the blood and the name is for my great-great-grandmother, Gráinne Ní Mháille, called Grace O'Malley, for whom my ship is named and from whom I claim all of my abilities as captain and sailor – and aye, as a pirate, as she were one of the greatest who ever sailed the seas and raided the damned English. All that blather about the Earth, that is the usual Druidic folderol – I confess I kept very little of what Mam taught me of her faith.

But it is the last part which strikes me. "Through all time." It seems a strange phrase – especially since we have indeed come through time.

Then there is Monsieur Navarre's second question about the runes, which regarded the paint Mam used to apply them. Monsieur Navarre said that it showed some luminescence at night, especially by moonlight, but that he had scraped a small portion to examine carefully, and it appeared to be, or contain, blood. He asked what might make up this strange stuff, but I know not. 'Tis Druid's stuff, that's all. They were, and are, over-fond of both blood and moonlight. I recall bleeding as a part of the ritual, but I did not know what Mam painted with my blood on my ship, nor have I the first inkling as to why it may glow.

Mam – what did you put on my *Grace?*

I think I will go put the men to work. I have purchased a great swath of canvas and a spool of good rope, and I want spare sails made and the cordage stowed properly against any future need.

Later

We weigh anchor. *Now.* Vaughn overheard Navarre on the telephone, reporting that our ship and crew were all present and accounted for. Vaughn said Navarre exclaimed "They left him on an island?" and asked, "Which of them will be charged?"

Morty has been found. They come for us. We go now.

Last watch. 7th August.

We are twenty miles away and sailing well. We are not pursued; if we are sought, they do not know our position. I do not know how long it will take them to find us, with their magic windows and telephones, or to catch us with their iron beast-ships and thunder-guns. I do not know if they will seek to capture us, or merely sink us. We did not kill the Coast Guard men who stood watch over the ship, so as not to incur further wrath; a blow to the head and ropes and gags, that is all.

Vaughn is despondent. I am sure now that he did mean to stay, in this time and place and with Monsieur Claude Navarre. My sins have harmed my friend. It stabs at me.

We did not have opportunity to take on supplies for a voyage across the wide ocean, so we will make a landing and revisit the place we know, rather than hope to find that which we need by dumb luck – the risks are less in the familiar place, despite the difficulties.

To market, to market, to rob a fat pig . . .

Captain's Log
Date: 8th August
Location: 15 mi. off shore, bearing North-East
Conditions: Fine sailing, ship well-stocked, men in good spirits.

We landed yesternight at the Glass Palace, anchored in the cove and made shore by boat. Though we had but very little time, as we wish to avoid discovery and pursuit, I felt I must pay my respects to the lady of the house, and so I crept in upon the sleeping Enchantress (Praying that this old title is as misapplied as I believe, for if it is not, I will no doubt be transformed into swine along with my men for this, as this Circe will have less mercy for her Odysseus, methinks) and wakened her with a kiss – and then had her chamber door guarded, so she could not alert the Coast Guard nor *la policia*. She is not pleased with me. But I remain unswined.

I took nearly the whole crew with me, as we must transport goods and supplies back to the ship. We were not an unobtrusive group, fifteen pirates creeping along the side of the road with pistols and rifles and swords – but the night cloaked us well. We had to make our way on foot – curse these people for abandoning horses for these bloody beast-wagons! – but we could trot, most of the way, and the road was familiar and so required no consideration as to route even in the dark, so we made good time.

We reached the Piggly Wiggly with the dawn.

I let Ian take the lead, as the man has held something of an ill wish for the master of the market since his first visit here, when he was all but named drunkard and thief. Ian bore a wide grin when he thrust a *pistola* in the same man's face and inquired if the good sir remembered him. He did.

We got quickly to work, then. There were but half a dozen people in the place, four of them women, and so two guards sufficed, with another man crouched by the entrance should other shop-goers or clerks arrive. The rest of us dove into the treasure trove, the endless bounty, the horn o' plenty that was the Piggly Wiggly. Food and wine, ale and spirits, even tools and implements – sewing needles and soap, string and a large rack of very convenient gunny sacks, printed with the name Piggly Wiggly and with handles attached. We took it all. Every man of us filled one of those wheeled metal carts, with hams and beans, beef and pork and fowl and even fish, lemons and limes, oranges and apples, flour and rice, salt and pepper, oats and cheese. And wine. And ale. And rum – a generous plenty of rum. We were joyed when O'Neill found a shelf filled with tobacco, tubes of rolled leaf as the Indian savages of legend smoked as well as the strange thin white tubes that O'Flaherty discovered when we first came here, and even some proper pouches – we filled four of the gunny sacks with the stuff, and a few of the men capered with glee at our haul.

We pressed all of the people into the back storerooms and bound and gagged them there. Then, not a turn of the glass after we arrived, we were leaving, making off into the dawn's rosy light with a caravan of metal carts piled high with goods. 'Twas a fine raid, aye, 'struth.

I was somewhat anxious that we would be noted and pursued on our way back, slowed as we were by the booty, and made even more noticeable as well; but these folk do not keep farmer's hours. No more than a dozen beast-wagons passed us on the road to the Glass Palace and the cove where our ship awaited us. Though we garnered a number of strange glances, no one stopped to question us.

We returned and loaded the ship. I refrained from stealing one last kiss from the now-enraged Enchantress, instead calling her guard away from her door in silence; she would soon enough realize herself to be alone and free in the house, but by then we would be gone. And indeed, we were.

This place, this time – it is the greatest temptation the pirate in me has ever known. They are so docile! So complacent and innocent, so unprepared for the invasion of armed ruffians; and so willing to give over all of value that they possess at the first threat of violence to their persons. Or else, as with Morty, so brash and arrogant that they believe themselves invincible, which makes it ever so simple to prove, as with Morty, that they are but men, and their tools and the wonders of this age do not keep them safe, not from us. We could have our way with these people, carve a swath along this coast like a scythe through a wheatfield; we would be rich. We would be legendary.

But there is a hidden danger here, far greater than any British man o' war, than any bounty luring privateers to our wake. Though this land be rich, it is the richness of a bee's nest: full of golden sweetness, but swarming with a thousand stings that might do anything from annoy a man to strike him dead. The coast Guard, *la policia*, the courts, the beast-wagons, steel ships, thunderguns and *pistolas* – the danger of capture or outright destruction is staggering. We would never survive, if we turned pirate in this place. That is the trap.

Nay: we must leave. We do not belong here. We must be in a place that we understand, where the risks and the rewards are familiar, and can be weighed properly, one against the other, and a happy balance struck. We must go home.

Captain's Log, August 9th

We have made 166 miles thus far, though our course is somewhat skimble-skamble; we sail north, then east, then north; we see the line of the coast off the port side, and turn away from it, but we use the land as our guide and so do not drift too far away, tacking and turning our way home. Thus far, still no pursuit.

Captain's Log, August 10th

We have decided to sail away from the land. We have a good wind moving us north-east, which way we mean to go, and Ian and McTeigue have convinced me that we can find resupply anywhere we make land in Europe, either with the money-papers we possess or as we took from the Piggly Wiggly. It stands to reason that if one land in this time is as we found Florida, settled and well-populated, somnolent and ripe for the plucking, but with a sharp sting waiting when roused, then other lands to the east would be similar. So as long as we are quick to strike and quick to withdraw, we should be able to have our way.

Thus we bear out for the open ocean, and Ireland. Home.

Log #38: The End of the Voyage

The night is dark, clouded, and in the darkness there is little more than silence. Through the silence, something moves; it is large, and solid, and would bring notice if there were any nearby to sense its passage who were not already a part of it. It does not break the silence, but it bends it: an occasional creak of wood and rope, now and then a pop as a corner of canvas flaps with a capricious breath of wind; sometimes a man coughs.

Then in the distance, like the opening of a sleeping eye, dawn begins. The growing light shows first the waves, like wrinkles in the blue-green skin of the world. Then the white sails appear, as if they catch and gather in the light the same way they do the wind, filling with the sun's first gentle rays. As the light grows, the silent presence becomes a ship that rides over and breaks through the waves, now, as the breeze rises and sends the drifting water against the ship's smooth hull, as if the dawn had woken the very air, the great ocean itself.

When the sun's edge breaks the horizon, off the starboard bow, the man standing at the wheel squints and looks away. His eyes flash over the sails, which are buckling and heaving: the dawn has brought a new wind from a new quarter of the sky. The ship begins to slow, and its graceful motion becomes choppy – where it was a great owl, gliding through the still, dark air, now it is a jackrabbit, jouncing, jolting across the ground. The man's eyes flick to the ladder that leads down to the next lower deck, and his lips thin. He begins to turn the wheel, then shakes his head and stills his hands. He coughs – louder than he needs to, likely.

A door opens on that lower deck, and a man steps out. He is tall: he must duck to pass through the door, and then he stands with broad shoulders and a straight back. Black hair blows on the wind, and blue-green eyes, the same color as the water below, squint in the sunlight which dazzles the ocean waves. His gaze goes to the sails, and he frowns; he crosses to the ladder and climbs rapidly to the top deck, where the man stands at the wheel, a relieved look on his face as the tall man appears. The tall man says, "Change course with the wind, Salty – three points north."

"Three points north, aye, Captain," the man at the wheel says, satisfaction in his voice. Even as he speaks, he is already turning the wheel to the left, and the ship shifts with a creak and a groan, and then slides into place like a lock into its groove, the sails snapping taut once more, the waves now rolling under the ship instead of crashing across it. The ship picks up speed and again glides like a bird in flight. The Captain claps the man at the wheel on the shoulder, and then stretches and yawns. He walks the ship, inspecting everything he can see and touch, now frowning, now nodding.

More men emerge as the dawn light strengthens and paints the sky bright pink and yellow and blue; the Captain hails some and orders them to the lines, to adjust ropes that have stretched and slipped, knots that have loosened in the night. Puffs of smoke begin to emerge from a small pipe, as the stove in the galley below heats up for breakfast. The man at the wheel is relieved; he hands over control of the ship with a comment on the new heading, and then he turns an hourglass set into the side of the wheel's post just as the sand runs out. He stretches, shaking and flexing his fingers, which are scarred and gnarled though still strong, and then goes below, to the galley and food.

The Captain, having looked over the whole of his domain, now stands at the starboard rail, the bright sun warm on his face and the ocean breeze cool. He looks out at the water, the sky, the line of the horizon. Then he frowns. His body turns, his shoulders squaring, and his head leans forward as his eyes narrow. From a pouch at his belt he removes a brass tube, which he holds up to one eye.

In the lens he sees a scrap of white.

He watches it, moving only with the roll of the ship over the waves, for several minutes. He exchanges greetings with men who pass by on their tasks, several going to or coming from the head at the bow of the ship; some lowering buckets on ropes into the water, bringing them up full and splashing water across the deck, others re-coiling ropes that have shifted in the night or polishing salt spray off of metal surfaces.

The Captain lowers the glass. His expression is troubled. He begins to turn away, and then stops and looks back at the tiny white scrap, which has grown somewhat larger, more definite. He glances at the men, then the scrap. Then his features firm, smoothing slightly: a decision is made. He raises his voice. "All hands on deck!" he calls, his tone strong but not urgent.

The call is repeated below, and within minutes, the yawning, bleary-eyed man who had been behind the wheel is the last to emerge. The crew have seen the Captain standing at the rail, and they gather around him. The Captain looks them over, nods, and then turns and points. "Look there," he says. "Lynch – get above. Take the glass." He holds the brass tube out to a slender youth, who takes it and tucks it behind the wide leather belt about his middle. The youth jogs to a rope ladder and scrambles up, into the rigging above.

The other men line the rail and squint into the bright morning air. "'At's a sail, sure," one says, and the others nod and mutter.

"There be some sailin' ships in these waters, bain't there?" asks a thin man with delicate features.

"Aye," the Captain says. "But not with square sails. Lynch!"

The youth has reached the top cross-bar of the main mast, and now sits astride it and puts the glass to his eye, holding the mast with his other hand. He finds the white object on the horizon and frowns at it, his brows lowering as he strains to see it clearly, struggling to keep the object in view despite the motion of the ship, greatly exaggerated here, forty feet above the deck. Then he pales.

Below, another man, hard-eyed and bearded, mutters, "We be th' only ship wi' square sails – th' only one for a hunnerd years. That'n can't be such." Another man nods, but he is frowning as he does so.

Then the bearded man's eyes widen. "Oh, Christ in Heaven, *no –*"

The young man on the mast interrupts and anticipates him. "Captain!" he shouts, his voice breaking high and shrill. "It's the *Sea-Cat!*"

There is a brief moment of utter, shocked silence, and then a groan goes through the men. The Captain looks up and shouts, "Are ye sure? At this distance?"

"I stared at that bastard for two months, Captain," the youth retorts. "Aye, I'm sure. It's him. I can see the Scourged Lady on the bow."

"And he's closing on us," one of the men on deck mutters. Indeed, the scrap of white has become a spot, now visible to all, and obviously square. The mutters rise, and feet begin shifting, hands clenching into fists around the hilts of swords and the butts of pistols.

The Captain wheels on them, his eyes bright, his expression determined, fearless. He speaks in a calm voice, just above quiet. "All right. He's three, four miles off, still, and we're running slow. O'Grady – go below and finish the breakfast, then douse the cookfire. We'll need to eat well, so double rations. Desmond – can ye take the wheel? I need Ian on the lines."

A man rubs at his shoulder, shrugging his right arm, testing it against pain. "Aye, Captain. I think 'tis healed enough."

The Captain nods, then raises his voice. "All right! Raise all topsails! All canvas up! Desmond, go eat now, then on the wheel – follow the wind, wheresoever it goes, aye? We'll sort out our course later. For now – speed! McTeigue, with me. Go, ye sea-dogs! Hoist the sails!"

Men burst into action. Three scramble up the rope ladder to join Lynch above, where they stretch themselves out along the top yardarms, poles no thicker than a tree branch, their legs curled about to hold them up as they yank at knotted ropes. The knots loose, and sails unfurl; the men slide down the masts to the lower crossbars, and, grabbing at ropes attached to the corners of the flapping sails, tie them quickly to the crossbars. The sails fill, and the ship accelerates. The mast-climbers return to the deck, where a conversation has been rattling quickly back and forth between the Captain and McTeigue, with much pointing of fingers and shaking of heads. The Captain finally curses and says, "Load them all anyway." He shouts for his glass, which the descended Lynch jumps to put into his hand before going below to gobble oat porridge and sliced ham, with a cup of ale to fortify himself.

The Captain moves to the aft rail on the highest deck, where the wheel is, and looks out at the square sail on the horizon. He puts one eye to the spyglass, points the glass at the ship, and then stands there, unmoving but for the rocking of the ship beneath him, for half a glass – fifteen minutes. Behind him his men are finishing their barely-warmed food and are readying weapons, loading guns, sharpening blades, arming the ship's cannons – twenty-four in total, twelve on each side, split evenly between two decks.

The Captain lowers his glass with a curse, rubbing at his watering eyes. "He's still gaining on us," he mutters. He strikes the rail with the heel of his hand. "Gods *damn* ye, Hobbes, ye son of the Devil's whores." He turns and looks at the sails above him, which are bellied full of wind; the man Desmond is on the wheel, now, a hunk of ham in one fist, and he has lined the ship up perfectly with the wind. "McTeigue! O'Gallows! To me!" the Captain roars.

McTeigue leaves the men loading the cannons, and O'Gallows, a tall, square-jawed fellow with golden blonde hair and sparkling blue eyes, ceases his harangue of two sailors who had apparently tied a poor knot in a line, and joins McTeigue and the Captain on the poop deck.

"He's faster," the Captain says. "We cannot run this time."

O'Gallows curses and looks back at the ship, which has indeed grown larger, the shape of her sails, her dark hull, a lighter smudge of a figurehead at the bow, all clear now against the blue sky. "If we turn now, he'll match us," he says. "We can't trade broadsides with the *Sea-Cat*. She has more iron."

"We can't fight man-to-man," McTeigue says. "We don't have enough men."

"We need to cross her bow as she's coming," O'Gallows replies. "She's got no fore-chasers. We can give her our broadside and then turn and run. If we hole her at the water, or break her mast, we'll be faster, then."

"But he'll turn when we turn, and then it's broadsides for all – or else he'll follow close and grapple to our after rail, and board us," McTeigue says.

Suddenly, the Captain, who has been hunched over with his thumbs tucked into his sash, straightens and grins. "Not if we turn fast enough," he says. "Go bring me the torn sail and some line, and two men to help ye," he orders O'Gallows, who moves off with a puzzled frown. The captain turns to McTeigue, after glancing at the sails, and then over his shoulder at the pursuing ship. "Right – starboard side first. Stagger the broadside – fire three above and three below, then shift the crews and fire the other three. Then have them cross to the port side and be ready to do the same again."

McTeigue is wide-eyed, mouth agape. "Nate, how, by Lucifer, are we to fire both sides at the same target? Christ's bones, how will we manage to fire the one?"

The Captain slaps him on the shoulder. "Don't worry, cousin. The *Grace* will wheel and dance like a falcon in flight, I promise ye. Now go – ready the guns! Starboard first!"

As McTeigue races off, the Captain shouts. "Kelly! We'll be needing the sharpshooters – ready the rifles at the mainmast!" A large, one-eyed man nods and goes below, to the armory beneath the main deck. Just as he disappears, O'Gallows struggles up the steep staircase – almost a ladder – on the opposite side of the deck, with a large coil of rope draped over his shoulders. Behind him come two men lugging a long roll of canvas. They go towards the poop deck, and the Captain comes down to meet them on the main deck. He explains their orders, pointing and miming with his hands; O'Gallows's puzzled frown turns into a mischievous grin, and he and the other two draw knives and begin cutting slits in the canvas, threading the rope through and tying knots.

The Captain returns to the aft rail and watches as the pursuing ship grows, men now visible aboard her. As he watches, the grin slides off of his face, and his eyes grow first worried, then determined. He makes a fist, and pounds it down on the rail, once, twice, three times. He strides away, barking orders as he goes.

***

She is close, now. She has clearly been battered and then repaired – there are lighter-colored boards, new wood not yet stained the dark gray of ocean-going vessels, in her hull, and her mainmast is taller, now, and raked, tilted back towards the rear of the ship; the mainmast is also gaff-rigged, now, which it was not before – perhaps that is what has gained her more speed. They had been evenly matched in their last encounter, when the *Sea-Cat* had chased the *Grace* across the Atlantic – and, apparently, across three centuries, as well – but now the English ship is the faster of the two. She still has no cannon in her bow, but she is near enough that her men have begun firing muskets, hoping for a lucky hit; at this range, from moving ship to moving ship, there is no other kind of hit but a lucky one. The man on the *Grace's* wheel hunches his shoulders and ducks his head, nonetheless.

The Captain is standing beside the wheel, looking back over Desmond's shoulder at the *Sea-Cat*. He does not duck. To his left and below, at the starboard rail of the main deck, O'Gallows and his two helpers crouch, waiting, an ungainly bundle of canvas and rope in their sweating hands. The *Sea-Cat* is not visible from where they are, and so their gazes are locked on their captain's back, and the left arm he will use to signal them when the time is right.

"What in the nine hells is he waiting for?" O'Gallows grumbles, trying to crane his head out to the side far enough to catch a glimpse of the other ship. He cannot – lucky, perhaps, as this would make him a target for musket fire – and he returns to his crouching and staring. "If they get too close, they'll bloody well ram us and board even as we fire." His gaze flicks to the two other men, who are exchanging worried frowns at these words, and O'Gallows falls silent and waits. Near them crouch six more men, including McTeigue and the young Lynch, by three large cannons. They, too, wait, and stare at the captain's back.

The Captain waits for – something. His eyes rove the forward rail of his enemy, seeking something, or someone, among the line of men firing and reloading muskets. Then, at last, he shakes his head and raises his hand, as his gaze flicks between his ship and the Sea-Cat, gauging a distance that has nearly become too close. But then he smiles. A man steps up to the rail of the *Sea-Cat*, a tall man, pale and gaunt, with white-blonde hair and deep-set eyes; from a distance, he has the appearance of a skull.

"Hello, Hobbes, you sodding bastard," the Captain whispers. He raises his arm higher, and waves. The gaunt man lays a finger along his hat, nodding so slightly it is nearly imperceptible – then he draws his thumb across his throat in an unmistakable gesture. The skull grins. The Captain smiles in return. "Choke on this," he mutters. Then he drops his arm and shouts, *"NOW!"*

O'Gallows and his two men throw the tangle of canvas and rope over the rail, and then run to the lines securing the ship's mainsail, which is gaff-rigged like the *Sea-Cat's* – tied at top and bottom to a long pole that juts out to the side, rather then sitting fixed to the mainmast like the bar of a cross; this means the mainsail can be moved to catch the wind as the ship turns. The tangle hits the water and sinks, though ropes trailing from it are still tied to the ship. As the tangle is dragged through the water, it opens into something like a parachute, the corners of the square canvas gathered together and tied to the ship: a sea-anchor. Instantly, the ship begins to slow, and turn, as the sea-anchor swings wide and drags. Desmond spins the wheel, O'Gallows swivels the gaffed mainsail – and the *Grace* turns, as swift and graceful as a falcon, and presents her broadside to the bow of the oncoming *Sea-Cat*.

"FIRE!" yells McTeigue, and almost as one, six cannons explode in red flames and black smoke. The three above are four-pounders, loaded with chain shot – a pair of cannonballs attached by a stout length of chain, which spin like a *bola* when fired – and are aimed high, at the masts and sails of the pursuing ship; the three below are eight-pounders firing round cannonballs aimed at the waterline of the enemy ship, intended to sink her. The chain shot strikes true, and the foretopsail is torn in half, spilling the wind and losing a fraction of the Sea-Cat's speed, but the heavier guns are aimed too low, and the round shot splashes into the ocean.

"Raise your aim, curse you!" McTeigue shrieks as he and his men scramble to the next three guns, their movements mimicked below.

"Ian! Now!" roars the Captain, and then he draws from his sash a pistol – a revolver – and fires several shots at the men who have been shooting at him. Now *they* duck.

O'Gallows leaves his companions holding the mainsail's lines and leaps to the rail, where the sea-anchor is attached to the capstan for the starboard anchor – and where an axe lies ready. He snatches up the blade, swings it over his head, and with a single blow shears through the two-inch-thick rope that holds the sea-anchor in place.

At the same moment, the six remaining cannons fire. This time, all six hit, but again, the heavier cannons miss their mark, striking the ship's hull well above the waterline, punching holes in the wood but doing no real harm. The chain-shot tears at the main foresail but does not destroy it.

The moment the cannons fire, Desmond spins the wheel back to the left, and with a groan, the ship begins to turn. The two men on the mainsail lines struggle to reorient the gaff to match the new heading – running with the wind again, straight away from the pursuing *Sea-Cat*. But they slip, their curses turning to cries of pain and warning; O'Gallows drops the axe and leaps to them; he catches at the rope sliding through their hands, and together, they get the mainsail under control. The rough hemp rope is now marked with blood.

"Ian!" shouts McTeigue. "Take the port guns here! I'm going below to aim for those blind fools!" He races to the ladder and disappears. The gunners move to the port side, which at the moment faces nothing but empty sea, and prepare to fire the cannons.

O'Gallows turns his head to respond to McTeigue, but he has already gone below. He curses. "Captain! I've the gaff and McTeigue's below – ye must fire the guns!" He braces his back as a gust of wind catches at the mainsail, and his companions curse at the pain, but none of them lets go of the line.

The Captain curses and looks down at the sea. The sea-anchor, cut loose from the ship's starboard rail, has sunk lower and swung under the ship – and now it comes taut on the *second* line, run around the stern of the *Grace* and tied to the anchor capstan on the port side. With a groan and a shudder, the ship begins a second rapid turn, now to the port side. The Captain nods and then leaps the eight feet down from the poop deck to the main deck, where he grabs a slow match – a length of fuse, smoldering at one end – from Lynch and crouches by the touch-hole of a four-pounder. "McTeigue! On your mark!" he roars.

"Aye!" McTeigue calls from below.

This time, the *Sea-Cat* is not caught unaware; the pursuing ship begins to fall off, turning away from the wheeling *Grace* – presenting the larger ship's port side, rather than her bow; a larger target, but a target that can also fire back.

The *Grace* turns, Desmond straining against the wheel, his face white with pain, O'Gallows and his two men straining against the mainsail lines, every other man straining eyes and ears, waiting for the order to fire to echo out from the lower deck, waiting for the target to come into view. As she does – and she is a large target now: the sea-anchor has slowed the *Grace* appreciably, and the *Sea-Cat* has closed rapidly even while taking fire – they can see that her side will be to them. "Prepare to fire!" the Captain shouts. "To fire stations after the broadside!" There is a chorus of *Ayes* in response.

Then they wait.

The ropes creak. The men grunt. The waves splash. The ships turn, and turn, and turn, and then – "FIRE!"

Six cannons blast from the *Grace*. The chain shot rips through the shrouds, cutting several lines and tangling others; the Sea-Cat's sails sag and flap. And – at last! – two eight-pound cannonballs, each four inches in diameter, strike the hull just at the waterline and crash through, followed by the frothing sea. A cheer begins and is cut off as the Captain roars "PREPARE TO FIRE AGAIN!" and moves to the next set of cannons. Now is the dangerous time, when the *Sea-Cat's* cannons – she carries eighteen on a side, and enough men to fire all, reload and fire again – may blast away, smashing the sails, the mast, the hull, the guns, and the men of the *Grace*, crashing through flesh and metal and bone, striking deadly flying splinters from the wooden hull wherever the cannonballs strike.

But she does not fire.

From below, McTeigue again yells "FIRE!" and six cannons blast. The chain shot does little harm, flying mainly between the masts; another round shot punches a third hole in the hull at the waterline.

"FIRE STATIONS!" the Captain bawls. The men below run to the pumps; above they drop buckets into the sea and raise them on ropes, ready to douse flames; canvas sheets are lowered and soaked, ready to smother sparks, as well. O'Gallows and his two helpers tie the mainsail's lines to cleats, all three flexing their shaking, bloody hands with hisses of pain. "Sharpshooters to the mast!" the Captain calls as he strides to the ladder up to the poop deck. "Ian – cut it loose!"

O'Gallows's axe strikes again, and the sea-anchor slowly floats to the surface and falls behind. The Captain takes a moment to watch it sink, raising a hand in salute. Lynch and two older men move to the mainmast where they untie long rifles from a rack; they tie pouches of ammunition to their belts. Then one crouches at the rail, and the other two climb the masts, Lynch at the foremast and the other man on the mainmast; they straddle the yardarms and raise the rifles, taking aim at the *Sea-Cat*.

Now fire comes from the *Sea-Cat* – but it is musket fire, not the cannons. Their sharpshooters are in place, as well, and far more numerous. Lead balls whine and crack against the *Grace*, and the men duck and curse, but stay at their stations. McTeigue begins to reload the cannons, but it is a slow and laborious process, especially for one man working alone. But he continues, undaunted.

Now the *Grace's* sharpshooters begin to return fire – and it is immediately clear that something is different. The crack of the guns is sharper, flatter, and with almost no smoke; then after each shot, they move a brass lever up, back, forward and down – and they fire again. The man at the rail does not even move a lever, simply aiming and pulling the trigger, again and again, firing without reloading. Their accuracy, too, is far greater, and men on the *Sea-Cat* cry out and fall, one after another.

But the *Sea-Cat*, after the apparent mistake of turning broadside and then failing to fire any cannon, has already begun turning to follow, and now she is aimed straight for the *Grace* once more, and drawing closer by the second despite the damage she has absorbed, her momentum carrying her as the smaller ship slowly begins to pick up her lost speed. Not soon enough: for the *Sea-Cat* comes within pistol range, and then she turns slightly, presenting her left fore-quarter to the starboard and stern of the *Grace*.

The Captain, standing on the poop deck, locks gazes with his opposite number, who is now close enough that the whites of his eyes are visible. With a start, the Captain realizes there is another man, standing in the shadow of the Sea-Cat's commander: he is dark-skinned, African or West Indian, and his head is shaved clean; he wears a strange robe and a brimless cloth cap. This other man is smiling, and the evil in his expression is enough to make the *Grace's* captain shiver, even from this distance. The Captain looks away.

Just then, at a shouted command that is audible even on the *Grace*, so close are the two ships, a dozen men stand from behind the *Sea-Cat's* rail, where they had been concealed from the sight of the *Grace's* three sharpshooters. These men hold guns, but they are not rifles, nor muskets, nor even pistols.

They are thunder-guns.

They open fire.

A hail of lead crashes into the *Grace*. The two sharpshooters in the rigging are struck almost instantly; Lynch drops with a thud and a cry to the deck, and the other man slumps into the mast, dead before he falls from his perch. The men on fire stations at the starboard rail are struck, as well – how could they not be? – and one falls into the water and is gone in an instant. O'Gallows is struck, a bullet creasing his hip and spinning him about; he falls with a snarl and a curse, clutching at his injury. The third sharpshooter, the hard-eyed, bearded man at the rail, is hit when a bullet passes through the wooden partition concealing him, hitting him in the leg; splinters fly and slash his cheek and hands. He drops his rifle with a grunt, falling onto his back on the deck.

The Captain, seeing his men brought down so quickly, draws a second pistol from his sash and leaps to the starboard rail of the poop deck, firing with both hands, yelling curses at the top of his lungs, curses that cannot be heard through the thunder of the *Sea-Cat's* gunmen.

One of the men on the *Sea-Cat* is struck, then a second; two others shift aim and fire at this new threat.

The Captain is struck, twice, and is knocked back. He falls from the poop deck and crashes onto the main deck.

All goes black.

Ship's Log
Llewellyn Vaughn, Ship's Surgeon, recording.

We have escaped from the Englishman Captain Nicholas Hobbes and his *Sea-Cat*. That ship was slowed by our cannonade, taking on water and her sails and rigging damaged. They fell quickly behind after they fell off the line to fire on us.

Captain Kane lives, though he has not yet regained consciousness. I have bound his wounds, but he has lost some blood, perhaps one and one-half pints, judging by his pallor. A bullet remains in his right shoulder, perhaps lodged against the scapula, from the entry wound. The shot to his left arm passed through the wrist and away. Francis Murphy and Seamus O'Finnegan are lost, Murphy killed in the shrouds, O'Finnegan over the rail. Lynch, MacManus, O'Gallows, and Sweeney were all wounded; I have removed a bullet from MacManus's left quadriceps. I believe it was slowed by passing through the ship's bulwark, and did little harm, but it may have splintered. He will have to be watched carefully. O'Gallows and Sweeney suffered minor flesh wounds, which I have sewn. Lynch is more grievously hurt, the bullet passing through his left side. I hope it did not strike the kidney. He fell to the deck and broke his arm, as well; he lost consciousness when I set the bone. He has lost blood as well, and his slighter figure leaves him little to spare.

The ship is undamaged. McTeigue has the command, while O'Gallows rests and recovers – he has torn nearly all of the flesh off of his hands, attempting to hold the mainsail as the ship turned, and Fitzpatrick and Doyle with him – and steers us for the nearest land, which is the coast of the same America we left behind. We have come some hundreds of miles north, but without the captain and after the confusion of the battle, we know not where we are, nor where we will strike land. I only pray it will be close to civilization, and we may perhaps find a surgeon who can save the lives of our wounded crewmen. They are beyond my help, now.

I pray, as well, that the *Sea-Cat* will not find us again.

One last observation: I believe I have discovered the means by which Captain Hobbes was able to follow us across the Atlantic through the darkest night despite any subterfuge attempted by our wily and devious Captain. After Captain Kane fell, and I had performed my duty, I met with McTeigue on the poop deck to give my report of our casualties. I happened, in my exhaustion, to lean on the aft rail, and I noticed a silvery light shining, though it was night, and there was no moon in the sky. Leaning out further, I discerned runes, old Celtic pagan script, painted on the stern of the ship. They were glowing, brighter than a lantern, with a silver light. I cannot read the Druids' tongue, but I believe one of the runes represents the word for *blood*.

The *Grace of Ireland* is Captain Kane's ship. His blood was spilled on the deck this day – and as I recall, the same occurred during our first encounter with Hobbes, in Ireland of yore. And again, the night we fought the *Sea-Cat* a second time and were hurled, by time's tempest, into the Year of our Lord 2011.

I do not know an explanation which I can rationally accept. But three instances – hypothetical, not confirmed observationally but for this last – that makes a pattern.

I will discuss this with the Captain, if he survives. If we all survive.

Recorded this night, the 8th of August, 2011
Aboard the *Grace of Ireland*
Bound for unknown shores

Afterword

The Adventures of Damnation Kane is the only thing I've ever written that started with a name.

Not entirely; I knew that I wanted to write something about a pirate, and after I knew that, I knew I wanted to write something about a pirate taken from his or her native time and brought to ours. But after those broad strokes, before I decided that I wanted to make the pirate Irish, or that I wanted to mostly avoid the classic pirates of the Golden Age of Piracy in the Caribbean, or had any idea of where the story would go, the next thing I thought of was – his name.

The desire to write about pirates came mostly from the *Pirates of the Caribbean* movies, which is why there are so many references to them in this story; the inspiration for time traveling fantasy came from the *Outlander* series by Diana Gabaldon, one of the finest pieces of fantasy writing that I know. Damnation's name was inspired largely by the pirate fiction of one Jeffery Farnol, a British-American romance author from the first half of the 20th century, whom I discovered after my fascination with the POTC movies, and the International Talk Like a Pirate Day popularized by Dave Barry, got me a copy of George Choundas's indispensable book *The Pirate Primer*. His Primer is an amazing piece of work. Choundas watched every pirate movie and read every pirate book he could get his hands on, and then catalogued every piece of pirate speech he heard or saw. While I was reading through it, I realized that half of the very best instances of pirate speech all came from this one author, this Farnol guy. So I got myself a reprinted copy of one of his books, *Black Bartlemy's Treasure*, and then – I was lost. It was a pirate's life for me, at least as a writer.

There's a lot to love in Farnol's books, but the very best thing for me was the names of his characters, his pirates. Farnol apparently took the Puritan tradition of naming children after virtues (Charity, Faith, Increase, et cetera) and turned it on its head: he has pirates named Resolution Day, and Abnegation Mings. This struck me like a bolt of lightning, and I knew I wanted to do the same thing with my pirate. And then – I still remember, it was in the shower – it just came to me. Damnation. Damnation Kane. Was his last name from Solomon Kane, Robert E. Howard's Puritan warrior? From Cain and Abel? I don't know: I've never read the Howard stories, though I have been aware of them; and I'm not much of a Bible-reader. Wherever my subconscious got it, it just fit too perfectly to be anything else.

Thinking about the Puritan connection for similar names brought me Damnation's parentage: because what Puritan would name his child Damnation? One who did not want that child, who was threatened by it. An exploration of only vaguely familiar British history got me Cromwell and the massacre at Drogheda, and then I had my time frame. Everything else followed from that. The one last piece, the name of Damnation's ship and his family history of piracy, came from Morgan Llewellyn's wonderful historical novel *Grania*, about Grace O'Malley, the Pirate Queen of Ireland. And so here we are.

This book was originally written as a weekly serial; I hope that the logbook format isn't too choppy for a smooth reading of the complete story. I started the serial blog in 2013, while I was living and teaching high school English in Oregon; it's entirely possible that the placement of the main action in sunny Florida was a reaction to the dismal weather in the Pacific Northwest. The Lady of Joy is a real person, a good friend and retired teacher; the depiction is as true to life as I could make it, and the Lady herself finds it very flattering, I'm glad to say. Nobody else in the book is based on anything other than my imagination. I kept the blog going, adding a new chapter every week, for more than a year; I had to let it lapse around then because my wife and I relocated from Oregon to Arizona, where we now have too much sun. But I hated having given up on Damnation's story before it was finished, and I also thought that the story was strong enough to live as more than a blog. I did try to interest one local Arizona publisher who specialized in maritime fiction, but it didn't work out; I decided then that it was time for me to move into self-publishing.

I sincerely hope that you have enjoyed reading this story. If you have, please make sure you have the entire volume; it is published both as a single paperback book, and as a quartet of short e-books. I am still posting the continuing adventures of Damnation: currently I am about halfway through the second volume, and all of the chapters are online and can be found through my website, theodenhumphrey.com. When the second volume is complete, I will collect it, as well, and publish it just like this one.

It's been a long road and a lot of work to make this book happen: but there's nothing I'd rather be doing than this. And if there is one person who reads these words after purchasing and enjoying my book (Or borrowing and enjoying the book – really just reading and enjoying is the point), then I am satisfied. I am blessed. I am complete. Thank you for making that happen. Thank you so much.

Please come check out my website, theodenhumphrey.com, and I hope you keep reading the Adventures of Damnation Kane.

Theoden Humphrey
Tucson, Arizona
April 2018